PENGUIN BOOKS

A Question of Guilt

Having worked as a police officer and head of investigations before becoming a full-time writer, Jørn Lier Horst has established himself as one of the most successful authors to come out of Scandinavia. His books have sold over two million copies in his native Norway alone and he's published in twenty-six languages.

By the same author

The Katharina Code
The Cabin
The Inner Darkness

A Question of Guilt

JØRN LIER HORST

Translated by Anne Bruce

PENGUIN BOOKS

PENGUIN BOOKS

UK | USA | Canada | Ireland | Australia
India | New Zealand | South Africa

Penguin Books is part of the Penguin Random House group of companies
whose addresses can be found at global.penguinrandomhouse.com

First published in the UK by Michael Joseph, 2021
This edition published by Penguin Books, 2022

001

Copyright © Jørn Lier Horst, 2021
English translation copyright © Anne Bruce, 2021

The moral right of the author has been asserted

Typeset by Jouve (UK), Milton Keynes
Printed and bound in Great Britain by Clays Ltd, Elcograf S.p.A.

The authorized representative in the EEA is Penguin Random House Ireland,
Morrison Chambers, 32 Nassau Street, Dublin D02 YH68

A CIP catalogue record for this book is available from the British Library

ISBN: 978-1-405-94165-5

www.greenpenguin.co.uk

MIX
Paper from
responsible sources
FSC
www.fsc.org   FSC® C018179

Penguin Random House is committed to a
sustainable future for our business, our readers
and our planet. This book is made from Forest
Stewardship Council® certified paper.

I

A fly landed on the rim of his water glass. Swatting it away, Wisting sat down in the shade of the parasol. After drinking half the water, he checked the total number of steps on his phone app – almost four thousand, and it was not yet noon. Most of them had registered as he walked back and forth across the grass with the lawnmower. His aim was to walk ten thousand steps every day during his holidays, but the daily average was down below eight.

Some years before Ingrid died, they had each received a step counter for Christmas from their son, Thomas. For the first few days he and Ingrid had competed to see who walked most. Eventually, however, the step counters were left lying in a drawer. But he always had his phone with him.

Squinting at the screen, he opened his browser. The latest news was of Agnete Roll, who had disappeared the same day Wisting had gone on holiday, though she had not been reported missing until two days later. The first articles to appear had described the search for her, but with each subsequent update the story had looked less and less like an ordinary disappearance. It had begun to resemble something different, something Wisting had witnessed before.

Now the leader of the search party no longer explained which areas had been fine-combed. The case had stepped up a gear and acting head of the Criminal Investigation Department Nils Hammer was the spokesperson.

The press coverage actually contained nothing new.

Agnete Roll, thirty-two years old, had been in town with her husband when an argument sparked and she had left for home before him. Half an hour later, he told his friends he was heading home too. According to the online newspaper, the missing woman had last been seen when she left the pub in Stavern town centre just before midnight. That had been four days ago.

Each time Wisting picked up his tablet, he expected one of two things to have happened: that Agnete Roll's body had been found, or that her husband had been arrested and charged. But so far this had not been the case.

He put down his iPad and took another gulp from the glass. Stretching out his legs, he leaned his head back and watched as a seagull wheeled above him.

He still thought there was something special about a physical newspaper, but nowadays it was too long to wait until the next day for a news update. Especially if something was unfolding. He liked having access to the latest news, whenever and wherever he wanted. Besides, it was reassuring to know that he had mastered the latest technology and new methods of acquiring knowledge and information.

He was unaccustomed to following a potential murder case from the sidelines without playing an active part in the investigation. From the facts he had gleaned from the media, a great deal jarred. Agnete Roll's husband was not named, but Wisting had found him on social media. Erik Roll, who was one year older and worked in a local IT company, had waited nearly forty-eight hours to report her missing.

Missing-person cases were always difficult, but he had already worked out how he would organize the investigation.

The approach had to be both wide-ranging and in-depth. Wide-ranging in order to cover everything, and in-depth in order to focus on whatever stood out and might point the investigation in a particular direction.

He knew that Hammer and the others would be knuckling down and that Erik Roll would be a person of interest.

The iPad on the table allowed him to log in to the police computer system and read the case documents, but he had consciously refrained from doing that. Being on the outside was something he would soon have to get used to, as before too long he would be getting ready to retire.

All the same he felt curiosity tugging at him. The key to missing-person cases was almost always to be found in words and incidents from the days before someone went missing.

A sudden noise made him open his eyes wide. The lid of the mailbox slammed shut out in the street on the other side of the house.

He remained seated until he heard the postman drive on. Only then did he get to his feet, walk through the house and exit on the opposite side. A smoky-grey cat, lying in the shade beside the garage, leapt up and darted out into the street, disappearing into a neighbour's garden.

Wisting cast a glance down towards his daughter's house. He had promised to take in her post, and she had now been away from home for five days.

Approaching his mailbox, he removed the contents: a collection of advertising leaflets but also one letter, a white envelope with his name and address written in neat capital letters. He turned it over, but no sender's details were marked on it.

Line's box contained nothing but the same junk mail.

He dropped it all straight into the recycling bin and made his way home, curious about the letter he had received.

Only rarely did he receive letters these days, at least of this kind. He hardly ever received bills either, as most of them were paid by direct debit. The black handwriting on the envelope was unusual and almost looked professionally printed. The 'W's in William and Wisting were virtually identical and made him think that this must be some kind of personally addressed advertising material, while the 'i's were slightly different and gave the impression that it really was handwritten.

Taking a sharp knife from the kitchen drawer, he sliced the envelope open and removed the contents: a plain sheet of paper that had been folded twice. It looked as if it had been crumpled up and then smoothed out again. In the middle of the sheet there was only a series of numbers: 12-1569/99.

These numbers were written in a similar style to the address on the envelope. Precise and painstaking, stiff and straight.

He hovered in the kitchen with the paper in his hand, aware of what he was looking at, but baffled nonetheless.

It was a case number, labelled in the way cases had been organized when he began in the police. These days, new criminal cases were allocated eight-digit reference numbers, but in the past the case number was designated in such a fashion that it was possible to decipher it. The last segment, after the slash, was the year, 1999. The two initial numbers indicated which police district the case belonged to, with 12 signifying the former police station in Porsgrunn. 1569 was the actual case number, a sequential number given to new cases in chronological order.

He laid the paper down on the kitchen table and stood gazing at it.

Police district 12 also encompassed the local station in Bamble, a neighbouring district, but Wisting had never worked there. In size it was similar to his home district, with around fifty thousand inhabitants. They had approximately the same number of criminal cases per year, around three thousand. Case 1569 should therefore be a case from the summer of 1999.

This was so long ago that the case had probably been deleted from the electronic records. He would not be able to find it in any computer system, but the files should still be held in an archive somewhere.

He tried to cast his mind back, wondering if there had been any special events in the summer of 1999, but could not think of anything. Line and Thomas had turned sixteen in the June of that year and were about to start upper high school that autumn. He could not recall having gone on any summer holidays. Line had had a summer job at an ice-cream kiosk in Stavern, or had that been the following year? He did remember that Thomas had been working at the marina.

He left the letter and headed out on to the terrace again, where he sat down with his iPad to look up the year 1999. By then major newspapers already had their own web pages but it was difficult to retrieve individual coverage. However, there were Internet pages listing the most significant milestones of each year. The notorious triple murder at Orderud Farm in Akershus took place on 23 May. In Russia, Boris Yeltsin's government resigned and fifteen thousand lost their lives in a Turkish earthquake. There had been local council elections in Norway and Bill Clinton had paid a visit to Oslo.

Having conducted a search for Porsgrunn combined with the year number, he ended up with an incomprehensible list of results. Some of these were police matters, but there was nothing at all that made sense.

Case 1569 had not necessarily received media coverage, but the anonymous sender must have a particular reason for sending him that number. It must be a case to which he had some kind of connection.

Or not.

As a detective, he had received any number of anonymous letters, normally lengthy, full of conspiratorial thoughts and disconnected allegations. Some were directed at him personally and concerned cases on which he had worked, while others had simply found their way to him in his capacity as a criminal investigator.

Moving inside again, he studied the unusual formation of the individual letters. A black felt-tip pen must have been used. The strokes were approximately one millimetre in breadth. There was a stamp on the envelope, which had been postmarked the previous day, but that failed to reveal where the letter had been posted.

It felt intrusive to receive such a letter in his mailbox at home. No threat seemed to be involved, but it was unpleasant all the same. Disquieting, as if it contained a warning of more to come.

Opening a kitchen drawer, he took out a roll of plastic freezer bags, tore off two and used a fork to prod the letter into one bag, the envelope into the other.

This entire business had begun to irritate him. It was not something he could ignore. He felt compelled to track down the case.

There was no longer a police station in Porsgrunn, but

if he were lucky the case may have been included in the boxes moved to the new police headquarters in Skien. He might then be able to get an answer as early as today. In the worst-case scenario, if the case files had ended up in the national archives, it could take a few days.

He rang Bjørg Karin in the records office. A civilian employee, her work was nevertheless one of the most important elements in the force's daily operations. She had been employed in the police longer than he had, was familiar with all its labyrinths and was his go-to person when he needed to decide where to turn within the system. In all likelihood, she would know who to phone to request a search in the archives of a neighbouring district.

He omitted mention of the anonymous letter and simply said that his enquiry had to do with an old case in an adjacent district.

'Can you requisition it for me?'

Bjørg Karin asked no questions. 'I'll phone Eli,' she answered. 'And then it'll be here by the time you come back.'

Wisting assumed Eli worked in a similar post to Bjørg Karin.

'I'd really like to have it sent over as soon as possible,' he said.

'I see,' Bjørg Karin replied, though it did not sound as if she genuinely did. 'We get the internal mail tomorrow around noon.'

'That would be fine.'

They were about to round off the conversation.

'One more thing,' Wisting said, glancing again at the letter. 'Can you ask Eli to check what kind of case it is and let me know?'

He understood from Bjørg Karin's response that she

found it strange for him to be asking to have such an unknown quantity sent over, but she made no comment and merely promised to comply with his request.

Wisting moved out on to the terrace again and sat down to read the online newspapers. Half an hour later, Bjørg Karin called back.

'I've spoken to Eli,' she said, holding back a little: 'Could this have to do with a murder case?'

'I expect so,' Wisting replied. 'I only have a case number.'

'She's sending it over,' Bjørg Karin continued. 'It'll arrive here around lunchtime tomorrow.'

'Excellent,' Wisting said.

Getting to his feet, he walked to the railings and gazed across the town spread out below him.

'Who was murdered?' he asked.

'Tone Vaterland,' Bjørg Karin told him.

The name meant nothing to him. He repeated it to himself but it held no associations.

'Then I'll see you tomorrow?' Bjørg Karin asked. 'You'll drop into the office?'

'See you then,' Wisting confirmed.

2

Tone Vaterland hopped on her bike. The pedal scraped the chain guard each time she pushed down and it began to rattle when she picked up speed. It had been like that since she fell in a ditch last autumn. The front brake didn't work the way it should either, but that didn't matter so much. Soon she would have no need for it. She would turn eighteen in six weeks' time and would take her driving test at the beginning of September and inherit her mother's car.

She had no choice but to cycle along the E18 main road. This was the third year of her having a summer job at the snack bar at Norheimsletta. In the first year, either her father or mother had driven her to and from her workplace. Usually her mother. This year they were on holiday further north and she was on her own at home for four whole weeks.

It was only a matter of a couple of kilometres along the busy highway. On warm days like this she was in the habit of stopping at Stokkevann lake for an evening swim to wash the stink of the deep-fat fryer from her hair and put on clean clothes. That was the worst aspect of the job, the smell of frying smoke and cooking oil that permeated everything. She kept a bag with a change of clothes outside beside her bike to avoid the smell clinging to it. Apart from that it was a decent job. She was well paid and there wasn't too much to do but enough to make the time pass quickly.

Most of the people who stopped were on holiday, on the move, but there were also a few regular customers. One or two of them were disgusting, coming out with smutty remarks that she had learned to ignore. And then there was Moped-Rolf, who never spoke a word, with the exception of *number eight and cola*. Number eight was his selection from the menu, a beef burger with a half-litre drink on the side. He always used the loo, both before and after he ate, sometimes spending as long as a quarter of an hour in there. But it had been a few days now since she had seen him.

Between the trees on her right she could see the glitter of water.

Turning off the highway on to what remained of the old road, she dropped her bike where the path began.

There were no other bikes and she couldn't hear any sounds from the shore. She would probably have the place to herself.

She slung her bag over her shoulder and ran the last stretch along the path down to the landmark U-shaped rock. A number of wet patches on the stone told her it had not been long since someone else had been there.

She looked around. Almost all the way across on the other side of the water there was someone in a canoe, but that was all.

Pulling the Bamble Snack Shack's purple shirt over her head, she kicked off her shoes and shrugged off her jeans.

Two nights ago, she had swum naked.

She looked around again, wondering whether she should try that again. The canoeist was paddling in the opposite direction and there was no one on the path. All that could be heard was the distant hum of traffic on the E18.

She took her towel and placed it down at the water's

edge beside her shampoo bottle to make it easy to grab them both. Then she quickly undressed, hiding her underwear beneath the bag, and prepared to dive.

She felt so free and stood still for a brief moment, revelling in that feeling. Soon to be eighteen years old and alone at home for the entire summer. Earning her own money. But that wasn't all. She had finally broken up with Danny too.

Taking another small step closer to the edge, she stretched her arms out in the air and joined her hands above her head. Then she bobbed up and down before launching herself, gliding several metres underwater with her eyes closed and breaking the surface effortlessly.

The water was even warmer today than yesterday evening. Her long hair clung to her face and she pushed it away with one hand as she peered up at the shore. Still no sign of anyone else.

She swam a few strokes on her back before twisting round and moving on with a steady breaststroke – raising and dropping her face above and below the water line, finding her rhythm.

She had work tomorrow as well, but after that she would have two consecutive days off. She and Maria were going to take the bus to Langesund. Maybe they would get in to the Tordenskiold Disco since Maria knew one of the bouncers.

Twenty metres from land, she turned and swam back. Once she had found her footing, she staggered across the stony lakebed towards the shampoo bottle.

A few birds flew off from a tree by the path, but apart from that everything was still completely silent.

Filling her palm with shampoo, she let the bottle float on the water as she massaged the suds into her hair. Then, crouching, she used the shampoo to wash the rest of her body while she kept an eye on the path. Afterwards, she swam a few strokes out from shore, ducking under and rinsing before quickly drying off and throwing on her clothes.

She was just in time, because she could hear someone approach along the path.

3

Wisting woke as usual just before 4 a.m. After swinging his feet out of bed, he stood up and padded, half asleep, to the bathroom. He refrained from switching on the light to make it easier for him to fall asleep again once he had answered the call of nature.

His sleepy thoughts turned to the case from 1999. It had nagged at him for the rest of the day, making it difficult for him to drop off, and was still churning around in his head.

Case 12-1569/99.

There was very little on the Internet but from what he had read it appeared to be an open-and-shut case. A man had been arrested after only three days and had subsequently been sentenced to seventeen years' imprisonment.

The thin, weak flow of urine splashed into the water at the bottom of the bowl.

What preoccupied him most was the letter. Obviously someone was keen to draw his attention to the old case and that person had succeeded. He just couldn't fathom why.

As he finished off, he realized he would not be able to fall asleep again for a while so he moved into the kitchen and filled a glass with water.

The envelope and letter still lay on the worktop. He lifted the bag containing the letter and held it up to the light at the sink. He had worked on cases where the impression of what had been written was left on the next

13

sheet in the same pad. This had helped unmask the sender, but there was nothing of that sort here.

Laying aside the letter, he fired up his iPad and checked the online newspapers as he drained the glass of water, but there were no updates of any interest. The most important news to impart in the course of the night, according to *VG*, was a new report on eating habits. Nevertheless, he stood staring at the bright screen. Suddenly an idea struck him, a possibility he was keen to test out before he went back to bed.

He carried the iPad and the bags containing the letter and envelope into the study. He kept envelopes in one of the drawers and various pens and pencils in another. Choosing a black marker pen, he placed the iPad inside a large envelope. The screen shone through the paper, allowing him to read the headline, and he used the pen to copy it. *Consumption of meat must be halved.*

When he removed the iPad from the envelope, the message remained, in what closely resembled printed lettering.

This was what the sender could have done, used a computer screen as a light board to achieve handwriting with no special characteristics.

Leaving the results of his experiment on the desk, he returned to the bedroom. The window was open a crack and he pushed the curtain aside to peer out. A swarm of insects circled the light from the streetlamp above the mailbox stand.

It would not stop at one, he thought. There would be more letters.

4

This was the third time she had tried to call, but there was no answer now either.

Oda Vaterland put down the receiver. Her disquiet had grown into anxiety, a niggling sense that something was wrong.

Tone had been alone at home for almost three weeks, but they had talked on the phone every single day. The arrangement was that Tone should ring when she got home in the evening, but she had failed to do so last night.

This had happened once before, when she had been at Maria's house watching a video. She had arrived home late and was reluctant to phone and wake them. But then she had made the call the very next morning. The phone was in the hallway, right outside her bedroom. No matter how tired she was, she would hear it ring.

Oda turned to face her husband. He had been the one to suggest they travel up to Beisfjord by themselves and leave Tone at home.

'She's not answering,' she said. 'I wonder if I should call Maria.' Arne nodded as he munched on a slice of bread.

Maria's mother answered. Oda explained the situation and Maria came on the line.

'Have you spoken to Tone?' Oda asked.

'Not since yesterday. She's on the evening shift this week.'

The clock on the wall behind Arne showed almost half past eleven. Her daughter should be at work in two and a half hours.

'I can't get hold of her, you see,' she said.

'I can tell her you phoned when I see her.'

Oda hesitated. 'Do you think she could be at Danny's?' she asked.

The reply came without hesitation: 'No. They've split up.'

That was good to hear. She had never liked Danny Momrak, and she was pleased that his relationship with her daughter was over. At the same time, she felt a stab beneath her chest. The only logical thought left in her head was that Tone might have been with him.

'Do you know if she's met someone else?' she asked.

'Nothing serious,' the girl replied. 'Not that I know of, at least.'

'Well, thanks anyway.' She ended the call. By now, Arne had got to his feet.

'Do you think I should phone Danny?' she asked him, but then an alternative idea crossed her mind: 'I can ring Erna and Torfinn.'

Arne nodded. Erna and Torfinn were their neighbours, pensioners who had babysat Tone when she was little. Oda knew their number off by heart.

Torfinn picked up. 'Is something wrong?' he enquired. 'You're not coming home until the middle of next week, surely?'

'That's right,' Oda answered, uncertain now of how to proceed. 'I was just wondering if there might be something wrong with the phone,' was what she decided on. 'Tone's not answering. Maybe the receiver's not been replaced properly.'

'I see,' grunted the man. 'I can go round.'

'You know where the key is?' Oda asked. 'In case she doesn't open the door.'

It was stashed under the carport roof. In previous summers when Tone had gone north with them, Erna and Torfinn had looked after the house, taking in the post and watering the plants.

'What's your number up there?' Torfinn asked. 'And I'll call you back.'

She struggled to remember the numbers in the correct order. Arne helped her get it right before she hung up.

They waited in silence. Oda cleared the table as Arne stood by the window scraping paint off his fingers, waiting to head outside and continue the work. The house in Beisfjord was his childhood home. They had talked about selling it, but nothing had come of that. Perhaps mostly because there were not so many interested buyers.

Ten minutes passed. The ringing of the phone made her stomach lurch.

It was Torfinn. 'There's nothing wrong with the phone,' he said.

'Was Tone at home?' Oda asked.

'No,' he replied.

Arne had turned around and now stood with his back to the window. 'Ask about the bike,' he said.

'Is her bike there?' Oda asked. 'She usually leaves it right outside the door.'

'It's not there,' Torfinn told her.

'When did you see her last?'

Torfinn cleared his throat. 'I'll have to ask Erna.'

She heard the two of them discuss this and arrive at the conclusion that Erna had seen Tone two days earlier.

'That was on Saturday,' he relayed to her. 'But we'll keep a lookout for her. I can ask her to call you when she turns up.'

Oda thanked them and rounded off the conversation. She managed to keep her voice calm, but despair was making her hand shake. After fumbling to replace the receiver, she was left standing with a feeling of helplessness. The distance was so great. They had taken two days to drive up here. Even without an overnight stop, it would take more than twenty-four hours to reach home.

'Have you got the number for the snack bar?' Arne asked. 'Maybe she's changed shift with someone.'

That was a possibility, of course, and would explain such a lot. Tone could have had an early night yesterday and got up early this morning.

Her fingers struggled to find the right page in the address book. When she found the number, she handed the book to Arne. 'You call,' she said.

Arne picked up the phone and dialled. Once he had introduced himself, he asked for Tone. The answer was brief.

'I see,' Arne said. 'But she was at work yesterday evening?'

Oda understood the direction the conversation was taking. She pulled out a chair and sat down.

'Phone Danny,' she said when Arne had rung off. 'It might be . . .' She saw his reluctance.

'Do you have the number?' he asked.

She read it out to him. The phone rang for a long time.

Danny lived at his mother's house. His parents had never been married and had separated immediately after Danny was born. He was one year older than Tone, and they had made a handsome couple, but he was no good for her. After junior high school, he had spent two years learning

18

his trade as a mechanic, sometimes working at his uncle's workshop, but not on a permanent basis. She had heard stories of parties and fights. There was also some talk of hash, and she knew that Danny had been caught stealing at the retail centre. It had not happened while she was at work there, but all the same it had been uncomfortable the first time Tone had brought her boyfriend home. Although he had behaved politely, it had been difficult to sustain a conversation with him.

'Is Danny at home?' she heard Arne ask. A minimal response followed, presumably from his mother. Oda gained the impression that the son was in bed fast asleep.

'We can't get hold of Tone,' Arne continued.

There was a short response at the other end.

'I know that,' Arne replied. 'I just wondered if he might know something all the same.'

Oda stood up again and came closer. 'She's gone to ask him,' Arne explained.

Danny's mother returned to the phone almost straight away. Oda was standing near enough to hear what she said.

'He hasn't seen her since before the weekend,' was the reply. 'Sorry,' followed by a click as the receiver was put down.

'She sometimes goes for a swim,' Oda said, 'on her way home from work. On her own.'

The thought had been there for a long time, like smouldering embers.

'Maybe something has happened,' she went on. 'An accident of some kind.'

'We'll wait until two o'clock,' Arne said. 'If she doesn't turn up at work, then we'll call the police.'

5

The post had not arrived by the time Wisting left home and he also checked Line's mailbox just to be sure.

He drove the short distance down to Stavern, through the small town and into Larvik. On the way he encountered two fire engines responding to a call-out, first a fully crewed outfit and then a heavy vehicle with a turntable ladder. He veered on to the verge to make room for them to pass. The crew in the first vehicle were getting ready, buttoning their jackets and strapping on their helmets. Wisting cast a glance in the rear-view mirror as he drove on, scanning the skies for smoke, but could see nothing.

There were plenty of parking spaces in the police station's back yard. He parked his car as close to the staff entrance as possible and let himself in.

In the basement he greeted a couple of summer temp workers whose names had slipped his mind. As he made his way up through the building, every floor was quiet, with nothing to indicate any breakthrough in the missing-person case, or any other kind of dramatic development.

At Bjørg Karin's office, he stopped in the doorway and said hello.

'Your case files have arrived,' she told him. 'They're on your desk.' She nodded in the direction of his office. 'And I have fresh coffee in the pot.'

Wisting thanked her with a smile. 'I'll get myself a cup,' he said.

Bjørg Karin was pouring out the coffee when he came back. 'How are things going here?' he asked.

'We're managing,' Bjørg Karin assured him. 'But Christine Thiis is on sick leave. She wasn't here yesterday either, so we don't have a police lawyer.'

Wisting remained on his feet, sipping from his cup. 'Anything serious?'

'I don't think so. She'd seen the doctor and was told to rest up for a few days. Hammer's at a meeting in Drammen, if you'd wanted to speak to him.'

'I've come to take a look at the old case files,' Wisting said.

As Bjørg Karin sat down again, she glanced at the computer screen.

'Do you know where the fire is located?' Wisting asked.

'It's the Kleiser house,' Bjørg Karin replied.

'Again?' Wisting asked, taken aback.

Bjørg Karin changed the screen image and opened up the log from the central switchboard. 'A message came in twenty minutes ago to say that the fire had flared up again,' she explained. 'It must have been smouldering for a long time.'

The blaze at Antonia Kleiser's home had been the last case he had investigated before signing off for holiday leave. The technicians had come to the conclusion that the cause of the fire had been the electrics in the old house, but the report was not yet complete. The fire had started overnight and Antonia Kleiser, an eighty-two-year-old widow, had been found dead on the floor near her bed.

Wisting thanked Bjørg Karin for the coffee before leaving to let himself into his own office. The desk was just as tidy as when he had left, apart from a large archive box.

Lifting the lid, he removed the contents, a total of six folders with green covers held together with rotting elastic bands. The name of the accused was written on the front of each document folder, the surname in block capitals, followed by the first name. MOMRAK, Dan Vidar.

Each folder was numbered in Roman numerals from I to V. Roman numeral II contained all the information about the victim, including the missing-person notification, the form that had set the ball rolling for the investigation.

Roman numeral III held the technical investigations, Roman numeral IV the witness statements and Roman numeral V encompassed everything to do with the accused.

Filed within Roman numeral I was a collection of different signed documents, from each time the set of files had been circulated around the system. There were also the judgements, firstly from the District Court and then following the hearing in the Court of Appeal. He leafed through to the final page to read the conclusion and the sentence.

The accused has demonstrated a clear motive of revenge and seems today to completely lack any sign of remorse. The act appears particularly selfish and to have been committed with ruthless aggression. His statement to the court has no credibility and nothing has been said in mitigation. The prosecutor has demanded that the accused be found guilty of the indictment and sentenced to imprisonment for 17 years with a deduction of 168 days for the remand period already served. The decision of the court is to accede to the prosecutor's request.

Wisting had anticipated that the anonymous sender would wish to draw his attention to an unsolved case or at least a case in which there was doubt about the question of guilt, but this judgement appeared thorough, clear and well founded.

But a sentence of seventeen years meant that Momrak would already be released on licence. The computer records could tell him where he was now and what he was doing.

As he switched on the desktop computer, he noticed someone at the door from the corner of his eye. He turned around to greet Maren Dokken with a smile.

'Back?' she asked.

'Just popped in for a few minutes,' he replied.

Maren Dokken had been redeployed from the patrol section after being severely injured in an explosion. A scar on her left cheek, close to her ear, was hidden when her hair was down. The most serious injury had been to her shoulder and she still had restricted movement in her left arm, making her unfit for active duty. It had been a matter of straightforward personnel policy for her to be trans-ferred to a job as an investigator, but at a time when reorganization bled them of local resources, she was a welcome addition to their team. Also, she was competent. More than thirty years ago, Wisting had worked alongside her grandfather. She shared his attributes of patience and precision. In addition she possessed the ability to keep track of major, complex cases, drawing out details and spotting connections.

'Is that the missing-person inquiry?' he asked, gesturing towards the papers she held in her hands.

Maren nodded. 'Everyone's working on it.'

'What direction is it taking?'

'Straight towards her husband.'

'What have you got?'

'Nothing specific, but there's something that doesn't add up.'

Wisting leaned back in his chair, keen to hear more.

'He's given a statement three times,' Maren began. 'First to the patrol that visited his home when she was reported missing, then in two separate interviews. It's the same statement every time.'

Wisting cocked his head. When a suspect began to change his statement, this was usually the first sign of guilt.

'I mean, word for word,' Maren continued. 'When you're telling the same story several times over, there are usually a few subtle variations. Tiny details are left out, and something else is mentioned instead. You express yourself a little differently, "around ten o'clock" becomes "tennish". That sort of thing. Erik Roll sticks to exactly the same testimony, as if it's a speech he's learned by heart. Do you get what I mean?'

Wisting knew what she meant. It was difficult to retell a fabricated story. The liar usually concentrated on sticking to the same account of a sequence of events. This made it tricky for investigators to challenge the statement, but it took a good acting performance in order to appear believable.

'What was their argument about?' he asked, referring to what he had read in the newspapers. 'The one that made her go home before him?'

'Money. It started with a disagreement about who would pay at the bar, and became a quarrel about all the family finances, which are strained.'

That was what these things were usually about, money or jealousy.

A phone rang further along the corridor. 'That's mine,' Maren said as she dashed out the door.

Concentrating now on the stack of papers facing him, Wisting took out the first document. Missing-person notification. It was always interesting to see where a case began.

The report was written by a local police officer called Kathe Ulstrup, who was unknown to Wisting. The actual report was brief and had been written in response to a phone call from Tone Vaterland's father. According to what he had found out, his daughter had last been seen when she left her work at half past eight the previous evening. By the time the report was logged, seventeen hours had elapsed.

The first interviews confirmed that she must have disappeared somewhere along the road between the snack bar where she worked and her home in Damstien, a stretch of only three kilometres. Her colleagues said she had left work as usual, but none of her neighbours had seen her come home.

It seemed, from the initial investigations, that Tone Vaterland had drowned. Information quickly emerged that she often stopped for a swim in a lake along that route. Nothing was found on land, no trace of clothing, bike or rucksack. Nevertheless, a search was initiated. Her body was not found until two days later and then it became clear that this was now a murder inquiry.

It was difficult to concentrate on reading. Something was bothering him. His eye strayed to the window, where a large sailing ship was moving into the fjord.

Pushing his chair away from the desk, he got to his feet and headed out to see Bjørg Karin. 'Have they put out the fire?' he asked.

She changed her computer screen to check. 'It's been

logged that the fire brigade have it under control,' she replied. 'No more than that.'

He gave her a brief nod of thanks and returned to his office. There, he closed the folders he had been reading, wrapped an elastic band around them and replaced them in the archive box. Then he took the box home with him.

6

He saw the smoke from a distance. A thin white plume, like a marker against the pale blue sky, that rose straight up and slowly dissolved into the still air. When the house had gone up in flames for the first time, he had spotted the smoke from his own home, dark and thick. The blaze was reported just before 6 a.m. and the house had already been burning for an hour by the time Wisting got up and looked out through his window.

It was only a week since the last time he had driven up the old gravel track. When Ingrid was alive, they had sometimes gone for a stroll in this area, past the Kleiser house. Close by, there was an old smallholding with a herb garden and farm shop where Ingrid had liked to buy tea, mixed spices and vinegar infused with herbs.

The Kleiser house itself was an old timber villa of two storeys and a basement, with verandahs, bay windows and an extensive garden. The property was situated in a forest owned by the Kleiser family for generations. When Antonia and Georg Kleiser had built the villa, it had been completely secluded. In the nineties, a property developer had persuaded the childless couple to hive off a large portion of land and a brand-new housing development was built, though none of it overlooked the old house.

Curious bystanders from the neighbourhood stood huddled together on the ground in front of the house when Wisting arrived. He drove up behind a police patrol

27

car and stepped out. After the first fire, half of the house had remained, but now it looked as if it would be completely destroyed. The entire roof had collapsed and only the south-facing wall still stood.

On his last visit, barriers had been set up around the fire-damaged house. Now these were scattered about, along with what was left of the police tape.

Although flames still flared here and there, the fire crew were taking no action to control them.

Wisting strode towards the chief firefighter for a briefing. 'It was well ablaze when we got here,' he explained. 'Last time we tried to save what we could of the house, but now we're conducting a controlled demolition.'

'That was a week ago,' Wisting pointed out. 'Could it really have flared up again?'

'Most likely that's what's happened,' the firefighter answered.

As the last wall slowly caved in, the burning timber creaked, followed by a deafening crash when it finally gave way. A stream of black smoke belched out and sparks were caught by the hot air and flew skywards.

Wisting ran his hand through his hair. 'I want you to extinguish it,' he said. 'As fast as possible.'

The firefighter looked at him. 'It's been cleared with your central HQ,' he said, glancing across at the two uniformed police officers. 'The technicians have done their investigations. It was an electrical fault. There's no residual value. The insurance company will have no objection if we let it burn down. Quite the opposite, in fact.'

'There are other considerations, though,' Wisting replied, taking out his phone to avoid any further explanation.

The chief firefighter looked at him with incomprehension

but shouted to a colleague and issued fresh instructions. The generator on the fire engine changed speed as the crew moved to the hoses and shot arcs of water at the flames. The timber sizzled and crackled and the air filled with ashy water vapour.

Wisting withdrew slightly and clamped the phone to his ear. Maren Dokken answered at the other end. 'I'm out at the Kleiser house,' he began.

'I heard it had flared up again,' Maren said.

'How far is it from here to Agnete Roll's home?'

Silence.

'You think she might be in the Kleiser house?' she eventually asked.

Wisting answered his own question: 'It can't be further than five or six hundred metres from here to her house if you go through the woods.'

'The search party checked it all out,' Maren objected. 'The woods, at least. They must have checked the house as well.'

'How carefully?' Wisting asked.

'That I don't know,' Maren replied. 'I'll have to talk to the officers who were there.'

'All the same, that was several days ago,' Wisting said. 'She could have been brought there later.'

One of the fire engines drew closer and a water cannon on the roof sprang to life. The jet fanned out into a broad carpet of water.

'It'll probably be completely extinguished here in the course of an hour or so,' Wisting went on. 'You can have the site of the fire examined some time this evening.'

Hearing Maren Dokken's hesitation, Wisting regretted not having called Nils Hammer instead. Maren was inexperienced and more used to following orders than taking decisions and instructing others.

'I'll get the patrol here to secure the site as soon as the fire crew are finished,' he said. 'Then you can take it from there.'

'I'll alert the technicians,' Maren said. Her tone became more decisive as they brought their conversation to a close.

Wisting skirted around the burning house outside the barriers. The grass was too long, but apart from that the garden contrasted starkly with the fire-damaged house. Lush and well tended, with paths and stone sculptures.

A black wrought-iron fence separated the garden from the forest. A gate lay half open. When Wisting pushed it with the toe of his shoe, the hinges made an excruciating noise. On the other side, an overgrown path led into the woods: he considered following it but dismissed the idea. Instead he strode back to his car.

7

'They're looking for the body,' Fredrik said. 'The dead woman,' he added, to make sure the other two understood.

The three local kids hung over the handlebars of their bikes as they watched the search party on the opposite side of the road, walking side by side, some with long poles in their hands, others with walkie-talkies. One had a dog. Altogether there must be almost a hundred people in red overalls and the search chain stretched from the edge of the ditch before disappearing in between the trees.

'They won't find her there,' Ida said. 'She's drowned.'

'They've already searched in the water,' Fredrik said. 'With divers. They didn't find her.'

An articulated lorry thundered past, whirling up dust from the road. The draught ruffled their clothes.

'Mum knows her,' Stian said once the vehicle had passed. 'She used to be her teacher.'

None of the three said anything for a while, until Fredrik proposed that they should search for her themselves.

'Whereabouts?' Ida asked.

Fredrik sat up straight in his saddle. 'On the old road,' he suggested, starting to pedal in the opposite direction from the Red Cross contingent.

It had been more than twenty years since the new motorway had been built, but part of the winding old road still remained. They had been there on their bikes lots of times before. The road was no more than three hundred metres in length and seemed to go nowhere. It just ended suddenly at a ditch.

Weeds had forced their way up through the cracks and holes in the grey asphalt. Bushes and trees had encroached on either side. In some places the branches formed a canopy above their heads so that it was like cycling through a green tunnel.

They agreed that Fredrik and Ida should search along the right-hand side of the road while Stian followed suit on the left. They had to be careful where they cycled. Shards of glass from broken bottles were scattered in a number of places.

Once when Fredrik and Stian had been on the old road, they had come across a group of teenagers there, drawing tags with spray cans on the asphalt, and on another occasion they had spotted a couple kissing in a car. But mostly there was nobody to be seen.

Pettersen's garage, an old grey brick building with two garage doors, was situated halfway along the old road. Olaf Pettersen lived two houses along from Fredrik. He was retired now, but had run a transport company in the past. When the motorway was constructed, he had been allocated a different plot of land by the roads authority and built himself a new, larger garage. The old one had just been left to rot. The walls were no longer straight. Most of the windows were smashed and the rest were spattered with bird droppings and dust.

Fredrik hopped off his bike. 'Maybe she's in there?' he said.

The sunlight slanted through the dense treetops, forming

patterns on the dark brick. Behind the woods they could hear the buzz of traffic out on the motorway.

'Maybe,' Stian said, 'but it could be dangerous in there.'

They had been inside before, all three of them, but that had been a long time ago. The first time, Stian's foot had plunged through some rotten planks and he had almost toppled into a cavity full of water, an inspection pit over which Pettersen could drive vehicles, enabling him to stand below and repair the undercarriage.

Ida set down her bike and edged around to the other side, where they could gain access. A broken window was covered with a panel of wood, but it was only attached at the top. If you levered it out from the wall, the gap was big enough to climb inside. On the ground beneath the window there was a pile of breezeblocks you could stand on, almost like a staircase.

The metal door beside the window had always been locked but Fredrik tried it and found it was now open. 'Someone's been here,' he said in a whisper.

As he pulled the door open wide, the light flooded in to form a square on the cracked cement floor. They stood outside, peering in, and Fredrik used his hand to swat a fly. He was nearest and had to lead the way.

Inside, the oppressive air was cold and raw and there was a horrible, acrid smell. The space was almost completely empty with only a workbench against one wall and a stack of old tyres in a corner.

When Fredrik glanced up, he saw holes in the ceiling and a variety of chains hanging from a beam. At the rear of the garage they spotted the room that Pettersen had used as an office, with his desk still inside.

The sound of their footsteps echoed off the walls as they

walked towards the desk. Beer bottles were strewn across the floor and the desk itself was littered with candle stumps.

Stian wanted to go out again. 'She's not here,' he said, making for the door.

'We have to check the pit,' Fredrik insisted.

As they gathered around it, they noticed that some of the planks were still in place, but the pit was almost filled to the brim with water.

Fredrik picked up a small lump of concrete that had loosened from the floor and tossed it in. It disappeared with a plop, sinking down into the dark water.

'Find a stick!' he said.

Ida headed outside and returned with a twig.

'That's too small,' Fredrik told her.

He stalked out with the others at his heels. Snapping off a little birch tree, he stripped it of branches and brought the slender trunk back with him. Stian and Ida stood by watching as Fredrik drove the stick down to the bottom of the inspection pit, swirling it around on the pit bed as he poked and prodded his way along.

'There's something here,' he said.

He used the stick to push what he had found up to the edge of the pit but lost it before he managed to draw it to the surface.

'You'll have to catch it,' he told Stian as he made a second attempt.

Stian lay prone on the dirty floor while the stick buckled under the weight of the unknown object on its way up. As it broke the surface of the water, Stian grabbed it.

It turned out to be an old quilted jacket, with water streaming off it, and Stian flung it to the floor. 'That's been there for a long time,' Ida told them.

Fredrik used the stick again, stirring it around in the water, but he could not find anything else. In the end he dropped it into the pit. 'Let's go,' he said.

As they mounted their bikes again, all three looked up in the direction of the noise from a distant helicopter. They failed to spot it through the trees but heard it approach, its pulsing rotor blades slapping through the warm air.

'Looks like they're going to use a helicopter to search for her as well,' Stian said.

The harsh thrumming sound intensified before the aircraft passed directly overhead, low in the sky. Fredrik cycled after it, following in the same direction. He jerked his bike up on to the back wheel and pedalled a few metres on one wheel before letting it drop.

Ida was the one who spotted it first, the handlebars of a bike protruding above a bank that flanked the road verge, almost entirely concealed by twigs. She would never have noticed it if it hadn't been for the sun twinkling on the metal.

She called the others over.

'It could be hers,' Stian said.

Fredrik dropped his own bike on the asphalt and hurried to take a closer look.

'It's a lady's bike,' he said. It was stuck fast in the twigs and he pulled and tugged at it to lift it free. 'It looks like an old wreck.'

Ida approached him to look around while Fredrik struggled with the bike. He succeeded in wrenching it out but lost his balance and stumbled. When he managed to regain his footing, Ida poked him in the side and pointed.

8

Driving up in front of the house, Wisting set down the archive box full of old case documents on the car roof while he checked his mailbox. It was empty.

He juggled the box as he let himself in and then laid it down on the kitchen table.

There was a pork chop in the fridge. He had actually intended to have a barbecue out on the terrace, but it was easier to use the frying pan.

While the meat was browning, he served up some potato salad and a few other accompaniments and set the table. Then he took out the five case folders and arranged them on the table in front of him. He saw that Chief Inspector Sten Kvammen had assumed responsibility for the investigation at some point. They had met sporadically throughout the noughties, not in connection with cases, but at conferences and courses. As far as Wisting knew, he had started working at Kripos, the National Criminal Investigation Service, a few years after this murder case.

Once the meat was ready, he dished it out, sat down and selected the folder containing all the technical investigations from 1999. He wanted to begin with the crime-scene report. This was one of the most important documents in all homicide inquiries, the one that described the technical evidence that would later link a perpetrator to the case and have them found guilty.

He read as he ate. The discovery of the body had been

called in on 6 July at 11.30 a.m., approximately twenty-one hours after the girl had been reported missing and forty hours after she had last been seen.

Tone Vaterland had been lying naked in the undergrowth when three youngsters found her. The scene was located along a deserted side road off the motorway. She had a contusion at the back of her head and several scratches on her back, legs and arms. Blood was detected on the surface of the old road and she had probably been raped and killed there before the perpetrator had made an unsuccessful attempt to hide the body. At the same place, five buttons with thread and torn fibres still attached had also been retrieved. Her bike was lying at the road verge, but her clothes were never recovered. A bag she always used when cycling to and from work was also missing.

The back wheel of the bike was damaged and the report suggested she could have had a rear shunt from a car, but no paint traces were discovered. The bike was also examined for fingerprints.

Wisting cut off a large slice of meat and chewed as he thumbed through to the report from the fingerprinting department. The prints found belonged to Tone Vaterland. In addition, some prints were discovered from a ten-year-old, one of the children who had come upon the body.

The plate in front of him was soon cleared. He pushed it aside and flipped through to the post-mortem report. In conjunction with other information, the time of death was fixed at some time between 20.30 and midnight on 4 July. The various injuries were described, most serious of which was a skull fracture at the back of the head with numerous rupture lines, but no internal head injuries were indicated. The cause of death was strangulation.

During the post-mortem examination, semen residue was found in the vagina. Wisting leafed further through to the analysis report. DNA from semen cells was identical to samples taken from the girl's former boyfriend, Dan Vidar Momrak.

Wisting leaned back. This appeared to be an incontrovertible case, and he still could not understand why someone would want him to take a look at it. It had gone through two courts and if there had been any irregularities that other people had failed to discover, then he would require more than a case number.

Once he had cleared the table, he continued his chronological review of the technical evidence. A separate folder of illustrations contained detailed photographs from the discovery site. Two maps were tucked in at the back of the folder. Firstly one of the Bamble district which showed the two urban areas of Langesund and Stathelle and the slightly smaller town of Rugtvedt, where both Tone and Danny lived. The E18 ran like a diagonal thread across the map, emerging from the north, moving across the bridge from Brevik to Stathelle, into the tunnel through the mountains to Rugtvedt and continuing south in the direction of Kragerø.

The second map was a segment of the first one, showing the discovery site in relation to the snack bar where Tone had worked. The distance between these two points was less than two kilometres.

Yet another report described the examination of the car belonging to Danny Momrak. A red Ford Escort, it had been towed in following his arrest. The most interesting find would have been discovering signs of rubber on it or something similar in keeping with a collision with Tone Vaterland's bicycle. Nothing of the kind was established.

However, both hairs and fingerprints from her were found in the car, but these had no evidential significance. A time-line indicated that the last occasion she had been a passenger in his car had been three days before she went missing. The car had not been cleaned, neither externally nor internally, but there was nothing to suggest that a vehicle had been used to transport the victim.

There was also a report of the search of Danny Momrak's room in the home he shared with his mother. A small quantity of hash was seized, as well as a mobile phone and a car stereo system reported stolen a fortnight earlier.

Tone Vaterland had not owned a mobile, even though the use of mobile phones was already widespread at the end of the nineties. Wisting had received his first service phone a couple of years before that.

The call data had been extracted from Danny's phone and another report gave details of his movements and the people with whom he had been in contact. At present Wisting knew too little about the case to spend much time studying that.

However, he devoted almost an hour to going through the technical investigations. Among other things, samples were taken from Danny Momrak's shoes, but it had proved impossible to establish whether they matched the soil at the crime scene. Fragments of broken glass were also discovered in the rubber on one of his tyres, but it could not be matched with any certainty to the shards of glass on the road where Tone Vaterland was found. Along the less than three hundred metres of cul-de-sac, seven cigarette ends had also been retrieved. These had been analysed to see if Danny Momrak might have dropped any, and matching DNA was found on one of them.

Also included in the technical evidence were a number of still images captured from the CCTV surveillance at a Shell service station. Wisting had stopped there himself a few times when he had been travelling south. Referring to the map, he saw that it was situated about three hundred metres as the crow flies from the discovery site.

The cameras seemed to have been installed primarily in order to film the petrol-pump area and secure registration numbers from the vehicles filling up with fuel. The resolution was poor, but good enough to identify Danny Momrak's red Escort. At 20.13 he drove by outside the pump area and stopped at a marked parking bay, where the car remained for almost ten minutes without him leaving it. That located him in time and place extremely close to the crime scene, at least if he was the driver.

The elastic band snapped when he returned the papers to the folder. The review showed an abundance of data pointing in the direction of Danny Momrak, but the single strand of technical evidence found against him was the DNA discovery.

Pushing the sheaf of papers across to the other side of the kitchen table, he picked up his tablet. The *Østlands-Posten* had now reported on the fire at the Kleiser house. It seemed to be cut and dried that the flames had flared up again after the fatal fire the previous week. Now they had been extinguished once more.

He saw no new articles about the missing-person case.

Wisting rose from the table to fill a glass of water before opening the folder marked with the Roman numeral V. The accused.

Danny Momrak was interviewed as a witness on the same day that Tone Vaterland was reported missing. By way of introduction, he explained about his relationship with her. How they got together and why it ended. They had known each other while growing up and attended the same schools, primary, junior and senior high. He had been one class ahead of her. The previous summer they had met up at a teenage party. Neither of them had any previous long-term or serious romances. She was the one who had ended it. He could not give the investigator who interviewed him any other explanation than the one she had given him: that they no longer suited each other. As far as he knew, she had not entered into any new relationship. The last time he had seen her was on the morning of Friday 2 July, the day she had dumped him.

In addition, he gave an account of his own movements on the day Tone Vaterland disappeared. The statement was fairly vague. He had stayed in bed sleeping until about one o'clock and stayed at home until four or thereabouts. Then he had driven to Langesund and met up with some friends. He had been with them until around seven o'clock, when he had gone home again and lounged in front of the TV in his room for the rest of the evening. He lived at his mother's and she had not come home until about eleven o'clock that night, but he thought their nearest neighbour could confirm when he got home.

During an interview on the evening of 6 July, Danny Momrak's status was changed from witness to that of accused, and he was told of the film footage from the Shell station. In the meantime, the charge was merely giving false information, but this provided the basis for detaining him at the police station, towing in his car and searching his room.

Cristian Bohrman was named as Danny Momrak's defence counsel. Wisting knew him. This must have been one

41

of the first major cases he had covered. Nowadays he was a lawyer with long experience and substantial expertise.

In the first interview with his lawyer present, Danny Momrak had changed his testimony. He had forgotten that he had also visited the Shell station before he went home. He hadn't had any business there apart from killing some time and seeing if he might meet someone he knew. He knew nothing about his ex-girlfriend's working hours and had no idea that she would come cycling past around the same time. In any case, he hadn't seen her.

Before the third interview, the police had obviously obtained a witness statement from someone who had observed a red car parked on the old road. The time fitted the murder. Danny Momrak explained that he knew the old road very well. As a little boy he and his friends had played in an old garage there, but he hadn't gone there for a long time.

The next day the charge against him was upgraded to that of homicide and he was remanded in custody. One week later he was interviewed again. Following the media coverage, several people had reported seeing a red car on the old road on the evening of the murder, and a number of these had testified that it was a Ford Escort and that there had been one solitary man in the vehicle. At the same time, a few of his neighbours had attested that Danny did not come home around 7 p.m. as he had stated and had in fact not turned up until approximately half past nine. The analysis of his mobile-phone use was also unambiguous, linking him to the crime scene around the estimated time of the murder.

Danny Momrak had immediately changed his statement for the third time, now admitting that he had been on the old road. He had stashed fifty grams of cannabis in the derelict garage and had obtained a buyer for it. Before he drove in to pick up the drugs, he had sat in his car at the Shell station to have a smoke. He named the buyer and confirmed that, true enough, he had not gone home until after he had delivered the hash.

Two days later, the results of the DNA analysis had obviously arrived. Danny Momrak was hauled in for another interview and for the first time confronted with the fact that his DNA had been found on a cigarette butt found on the old road. He insisted that this simply confirmed his last statement that he had picked up the hash from there.

When he was also informed that his semen had been found inside the victim's body, he had offered no explanation other than that this couldn't possibly be true.

Wisting screwed up his eyes tightly a couple of times and rubbed the bridge of his nose before reading on. By nine o'clock, he had devoured about a quarter of the documents. Nothing pointed to the existence of another perpetrator or suggested Danny Momrak's innocence.

He picked up his tablet again to take a break and at that moment his phone rang. It was Maren Dokken. 'You were right,' she said. 'There's a body in the charred ruins.'

As Wisting rose to his feet, thoughts of the forthcoming investigation forced their way to the front of his mind.

'Is Nils there?' he asked.

'He's on his way.'

'I'm coming too,' he said.

9

The search for Tone Vaterland was conducted from the car park outside a garden centre beside the E18 motorway. The local police officer in charge beckoned to the Red Cross leader. Ninni Skjevik aimed her camera lens straight at them. Two grainy, grey shadows materialized and she rotated the viewfinder to home in on the subject, making it sharp and clear.

She had no idea who the uniformed woman from the local police station was, other than her name was Kathe Ulstrup. The Red Cross man was the father of someone she had gone to school with and he was called something easy, Tom or Tore, or something like that.

The two figures in the picture were hunched over a map spread out on the bonnet of the police car. With only three photos left on her roll of film, she postponed the click until Ulstrup made a hand gesture, allowing her to capture some movement in the image.

The roll spooled back automatically, full of photographs from the search effort. After removing it, she wrote on the label and inserted a new one.

The pictures would not be published until tomorrow. There was less than an hour till the afternoon edition went to print and something significant had to happen soon if she were to succeed in having her story included.

The helicopter returned, flying in a semicircle above their heads. It appeared to have completed its inspection of the surface of Stokkevann lake. She had time to take a photo before it disappeared, heading east.

The sun was high overhead as she moved to her car, where she took some gulps of water and helped herself to a couple of strawberries from the punnet on the passenger seat.

A car turned into the car park. It stopped a short distance away and a man, seemingly at a loss, stepped out. He stood still and looked around.

Ninni approached him. 'Hello,' she said, giving her name and extending her hand. 'I work at *Porsgrunns Dagblad*, the local paper. Do you know anything about the missing-person case?'

'I think I saw her,' the man replied. 'She was cycling along the road.' He pointed.

Ninni nodded in response. The police had reported several similar witness observations. 'When was that?' she asked.

'About half past eight,' the man told her.

'So you could have been one of the last people to see her alive?'

The man looked at her. 'I don't want to be in the newspaper,' he said.

Ninni ignored him. With a little effort, she would be able to persuade him to come forward. 'Are you from around here?' she asked.

He nodded.

Ninni estimated his age to be around forty. 'Did you know her?' she pressed him. 'Or the family?'

'Everybody knows everybody around here,' he answered.

Something was happening over at the police car. Ulstrup had clambered in and was talking into the police radio.

Ninni raised the camera lens again and zoomed in closer. As Ulstrup re-hooked the microphone, she scrambled out of the seat and exchanged a few words with the Red Cross worker before folding up the map and returning to her car. Dust whipped up as she drove out of the car park, blue lights flashing and sirens sounding by the time she nudged out into the traffic on the E18.

Ninni weighed up whether or not to follow her. Instead she crossed to the man from the Red Cross, now busy on a walkie-talkie. Ninni heard him recall the search-party crew.

'What's going on?' she asked.

He looked at her as if judging whether or not to say anything. 'They've found her,' he said after a pause.

Ninni turned her eye in the direction in which the police car had driven off. 'Alive?' she asked carefully.

The man facing her shook his head.

IO

They had now passed Mjøsa lake. The radio was on with the volume turned low. Oda Vaterland looked across at her husband. She felt queasy and her stomach ached.

'I need the toilet,' she said.

Nodding, he glanced in the rear-view mirror.

They had driven all night, taking turns behind the wheel, but neither had caught much sleep.

It was not only that she needed the toilet, but also that it was more than two hours since they had spoken to anyone at the local police station. At that point, the search had resumed for the second day.

She had pictured various scenarios in her head. The previous day, her greatest fear had been that Tone had drowned. She was a good swimmer, but she might have hit her head on a rock or got caught up in water-lily stalks. It was said that drowning was a pleasant way to die, but Oda could not comprehend that. It must be absolutely dreadful. Holding your breath, only to run out of air and just draw in water. The panic. The fear of death. Knowing you were going to die.

But they had not found her in the lake.

Another possibility was that she had been struck by a car. Forced off the road by a vehicle that had simply driven on. Maybe even a huge lorry. That had given her hope for

47

a while, that Tone might be lying unconscious somewhere in a ditch. She didn't wear a helmet. But they hadn't found her along the roadside either.

Arne swung off the road into a petrol station.

'Will you phone?' she asked, turning to her husband. He responded with a nod of the head.

They walked together into the service station and Arne approached the cash desk while Oda headed for the toilets. A public phone was available on the wall outside.

It must have been quite some time since the toilets had been cleaned. The waste-paper bin was overflowing and there was a mess in the washbasin.

Oda pulled some paper from the toilet roll and arranged the sheets on the seat before sitting down. Her stomach was bloated with wind. A stress reaction.

Her stomach muscles clenched and she felt stabbing pains in her chest. Hearing footsteps, she realized someone was standing outside, but she refused to let that worry her. She released some gas, along with a low groan.

It must be Arne on the other side of the flimsy wall. She was aware of the telephone receiver in the call box being lifted and coins inserted, kindling faint hope within her that the uncertainty would soon be over. That everything would be all right.

Arne introduced himself and she heard him ask for Ulstrup, the local police officer. It was clear he had been told to hang on. Oda propelled herself forward on the seat, bowed her head and stared at a crack on the tiled floor.

Then Arne's voice was audible again, but the words were more difficult to catch. It sounded as if he was explaining where they were and how long it would take them to reach home. Followed by a pause while the person at the other end spoke.

Arne said something again, but she heard his voice give way so that he had to start over again.

Oda tugged at the toilet roll, making noise to avoid hearing any more, but took in that the receiver had been replaced outside.

She remained seated, with her head in her hands and her eyes shut while time ticked past. Arne knocked on the door and spoke her name. His voice was shaking.

Oda could not bring herself to answer.

Arne waited, knocked again. 'Are you there?'

She just sat there, not wanting to be.

11

Esther Momrak stood beside the kitchen window. It was now four hours since Danny had gone to the local police station and he had promised to come straight home afterwards.

Outside in the street, a car drove slowly past. It was Johnsen. He turned around in the driver's seat and peered up at the house.

Esther Momrak took a couple of steps back to avoid being seen and glanced down at the newspaper on the table. They were among the last to receive it. Their house was located at the end of the delivery route and in summer it seemed the paperboy started later than the rest of the year. It had been nearly half past four by the time it dropped into the mailbox.

A picture of Tone Vaterland was splashed on the front page. It said that a dead female had been found just before one o'clock. She had not yet been identified, but the search for Tone had stopped. There was not much more than that in print. The remainder of the article described the search effort, the divers in Stokkevann lake and the search crew combing the forest that flanked the E18.

She had liked Tone, a sensible, polite girl who had kicked Danny into some sort of shape. He had undoubtedly changed: he did not stay out until the small hours and no longer went to parties at weekends. He and Tone kept themselves to themselves, normally hiring a video and sitting in his room down in the basement.

Danny had not told her they had split up. Tone's parents were up north, and he had spent a lot of time at her house when she was not at work. But not in the last few days.

He refused to talk about Tone's disappearance. In the newspaper, it said she had last been seen on Sunday evening. Danny had not spoken to her since Friday. That was all she could get out of him.

The waiting was difficult to bear. She could go downstairs and tidy his room to make sure it was spick and span when he returned. Or if anyone else had cause to go in there.

Instead she decided to make a pizza for them to eat together that evening. She had what she needed and dug the food processor out of the cupboard to mix some dough. The police car arrived as she was measuring out the flour, an unmarked vehicle from the local police station. When the doors opened, a man and a woman emerged.

Esther Momrak could not understand. Danny was not with them. Hovering by the window, she watched them approach the front door. Not until they had rung the doorbell for a second time did she make a move to open up.

'Yes?' she said.

The two police officers introduced themselves. Kathe Ulstrup and Vidar Tangen. Esther Momrak nodded. She already knew who they were.

'Can we come in?' Tangen asked.

'Of course.'

She led the way into the kitchen. 'Where's Danny?'

'He's at the local station,' Ulstrup replied. 'Charged with giving false information.'

Esther Momrak was lost for words.

'I have here a warrant granting us permission to search the house,' the female officer went on. 'Primarily his room, but also other places where he has been.'

Esther Momrak stepped back, using the worktop for support. 'I don't understand . . .' she said.

The police officer handed her the formal papers. 'We don't believe your son is telling the truth about Tone Vaterland's death,' she said.

'You didn't need to come,' Maren Dokken said. 'You're on holiday.'

Wisting gave her a lopsided smile. 'It spares me from reading about it in the newspapers,' he replied.

Two technicians, wearing white hooded overalls and protective respiratory gear, were working in the midst of the charred ruins. Wisting was familiar with the layout of the house from the first fire. The spot where they were working had been one of the main bedrooms on the ground floor, but by now everything had completely caved in.

Daylight had faded, so floodlights had been erected on two sides of the ruined building. A strong smell of ash filled the air and in some places steam still rose from the carbonized timbers. Only a chimneystack and parts of one wall still stood, but apart from that, everything had collapsed into the basement.

Nils Hammer stood beside what was left of the foundations and they walked across to join him. The site examiners had removed several layers of blackened building materials and uncovered the contorted remains of a human body. All the skin and clothing had been burnt away, and the skull seemed to have cracked open.

'Do we know whether the house was checked out by the search party?' Wisting enquired.

Hammer said that it had. 'They scoured all the way along the path and through the woods,' he answered. 'There were barriers and police tape around the whole house, but two men came in. They went all through the house, but didn't go down into the cellar or up to the top floor. The stairs were destroyed in the first fire. Anyway, their search was not undertaken with the idea that Agnete Roll's body might have been hidden somewhere.'

'She could have been lying here the entire time,' Maren said. 'Or else the body was placed in here before the fire was started.'

'Has that been confirmed?' Wisting asked. 'That it was started deliberately?'

'We had a sniffer dog here just before you arrived,' Maren replied. 'It traced flammable liquid in a number of places. Samples have been taken for analysis.'

Hammer beckoned one of the technicians taking photographs. The man picked his way through the blackened ruins, mindful of where he put his feet. When he reached them, he lifted his respiratory mask from his face and hoisted himself on to the foundation wall – a young man Wisting had never seen before. He pulled off his gloves and introduced himself.

'David Eikrot.'

Wisting shook his colleague's hand and commented that they had not met previously.

'I started last winter,' the young man explained. 'But I haven't attended many crime scenes in this part of the district.'

Wisting nodded. Prior to the police reforms and re-organization, they had employed a crime-scene investigator at the station, but now all the technical expertise was centralized in a single unit at the other end of the jurisdiction. It created an excellent professional environment but meant that investigators working on the same case ended up being strangers to one another.

'What have you got for us?' Hammer asked.

The young technician sighed, as if warning that he had little to contribute. 'We assume that this is a woman,' he said in a formal tone.

Wisting glanced across at the physical remains. Intense heat had caused the skin and underlying organs to shrivel. Tendons and muscles had contracted so that the arms and legs were crooked and the body was contorted into a foetal pose. This had protected the pubic region from the worst of the fire damage so the sex was one of the only things that could be deciphered.

'She's wearing a ring on her right hand,' David Eikrot continued.

'A wedding ring?' Maren suggested.

'Presumably,' the technician replied. 'We haven't removed it or attempted to read any inscription as yet.'

'Prioritize that,' Hammer instructed.

Tilting his head, Wisting gazed at the discovery site. A fire scene was different from other crime scenes. Not only was the blaze destructive in itself, but also the work of extinguishing it caused considerable further damage.

'What floor was she lying on?' he asked.

Eikrot answered with the guardedness typical of crime-scene investigators. 'Most likely on the ground floor. We've worked down through the layers of rubble, removing the debris from the roof construction and the floor bracing between the ground and first floors, but we haven't reached the beams between the ground floor and the basement as yet.'

He pivoted round to gaze at the ruins.

'It may well be that she was concealed inside a cupboard,' he said. 'At least, we're finding detritus of that sort around her. Cupboard hinges and fragments of clothes hangers. It'll be easier to tell you more about that when we know the layout of the house and the room plans.'

Wisting took a few steps to one side, assessing the distances and working out the position of the body. From what he could remember, it must be around the same spot as where Antonia Kleiser was found. She had been sprawled on the bedroom floor, immediately in front of the door, and a row of fitted wardrobes had lined one wall.

'Whoever put her there must have walked through the fire-damaged part of the house,' he said, turning to face Maren Dokken. 'You should get hold of her husband's footwear. Examine his shoes for soot and ash.'

Maren nodded, as if she had already thought of that. 'It will have little evidential value, though,' she said. 'When he reported her missing, he told us he had searched for her off his own bat. That included checking the Kleiser house.'

Nils Hammer spat on the ground and used his finger to clear his inside upper lip of snuff. 'Slippery customer,' he commented.

Wisting thrust his hands into his pockets as he watched the insects swarming around the floodlights.

Maren Dokken broke the sombre silence. 'What about cause of death?' she asked. 'Can you say anything about that?'

The young technician shook his head. 'That will have to wait for the post-mortem,' he replied.

He headed off to the crime-scene vehicle, where he collected a black body bag before retracing his footsteps into the ruins. Once he had torn off the plastic foil around the bag, his colleagues helped him to unfold it and lay it out on a specific spot, and they then lifted the stiff corpse on to it.

A gust of wind blew through the foliage on the nearest tall tree. It was now close to 11 p.m. Wisting stood there for a while longer before returning to his car.

13

The phone rang down below. Cristian Bohrman, sitting in a chair near the bedside, glanced across at the bed and the small head on the pillow. Her deep breathing told him she had fallen asleep.

His wife, Torill, answered the phone downstairs. He could not catch what was said, but understood that she had asked the caller to wait.

Closing the book, he placed it on the bedside table and got to his feet.

A fly trapped behind the curtains was tapping on the window, desperate to escape. Cristian Bohrman used his fingers to part the blackout curtains. It wasn't a fly after all but a horrible four-winged insect with a large body. He opened the lower corner window and directed it out into the twilight.

There was a creak on the lower stairs. 'Cristian?'

He did not respond immediately but switched off the light, tiptoed out of the room and pulled the door shut behind him. 'She's sleeping,' he said, smiling at his wife.

'There's a phone call for you,' she said. 'From the police.'

He had a mobile phone, a brand-new Nokia 3210, but liked to turn it off in the evenings.

The receiver was off the hook and he raised it to his ear: 'Cristian Bohrman speaking.'

'It's Sten Kvammen from the police here,' the caller explained.

Cristian Bohrman was well aware of who Kvammen was: the man in charge of the Criminal Investigation Department at the police station in Porsgrunn.

'I'm at the local station,' the detective went on. 'We have a client here who would like to speak to you.'

'Who is it?'

'Dan Vidar Momrak.'

Bohrman sat down. He had assisted Danny Momrak a couple of times before. Mostly because he had helped his mother with a few matters. Firstly in a slightly complicated inheritance issue involving several children from previous marriages, and subsequently when the bank threatened to repossess her house. He knew Esther Momrak from their schooldays. They had been in the same class and he had dated her one summer.

'Is he charged with something?' he asked.

The first time he had met Danny, the boy had been stopped by the police after riding his moped along a footpath, without a helmet and with a pillion passenger. The other time, Danny had been caught stealing from a shop, but Bohrman had persuaded the police lawyer to drop the case. That had been more than a year ago.

'Breach of the criminal code, paragraph 163,' Kvammen replied.

Bohrman's eyebrows shot up. He understood there must be more to this.

'False statement?' he asked. 'Isn't that something that can wait until tomorrow?'

'He's requested a chat with you tonight, before we continue with the interview.'

'What's the background?'

'Tone Vaterland's disappearance.'

Cristian Bohrman felt a sudden contraction in his chest, a palpitation that deprived him of breath. 'I see,' he said. 'Where are you holding him?'

'Here, at the local station.'

Bohrman got to his feet again. 'I can be there in twenty minutes.'

After ending the conversation, he headed into the bedroom and put on the same suit and shirt that he had worn earlier to the office, but left off the tie.

Torill appeared at the door. 'What's it about?' she asked.

'Tone Vaterland,' he answered. 'They've arrested a man. He wants me to represent him.'

'A murder case? You've never had murder cases before.'

He refrained from telling her it was not officially a murder case as yet. But it was probably only a question of time before the charge against Danny Momrak was adjusted.

The thought brought a smile to his face. The disappearance had already hit the headlines, even in the national media. This could do something for his career.

Returning his smile, Torill planted a kiss on his cheek and followed him out.

The drive to the local police station took only ten minutes. All the office windows were brightly lit and the nearest parking spaces were occupied.

A car door opened and a young woman he recognized stepped out. Ninni Sjevik, a journalist from the local newspaper.

Slowing down, he took shorter paces to give her time to raise her camera and take his photograph.

'Are you here because of Tone Vaterland?' she asked.

Bohrman gave her a disapproving look. 'I'm going in to meet a client,' he replied.

'Danny Momrak?'

He nodded almost imperceptibly. She was obviously well informed. Maybe she had been standing out here when they brought him in.

'Is he suspected of the murder?' she asked.

Bohrman put his hand on the wide door handle. He wanted to point out that at present it had still not been confirmed that Tone Vaterland had been murdered, but he knew it was better to say as little as possible so early in a case.

'No comment,' was his response as he drew the door towards him.

At the public desk inside the police station, he was met by Sten Kvammen and a younger detective with an ID card on a lanyard around his neck. He shook hands with them both. 'Have you any documents for me?' he asked.

'I've prepared a set of copies,' Kvammen answered, grabbing the bundle of papers behind the counter. 'Do you want to read through them first, or meet Momrak right away?'

Bohrman weighed the papers in his hand. 'Give me half an hour,' he replied. 'Do you have somewhere I can sit?'

Kvammen nodded and the younger detective ushered Bohrman into a vacant office. The door was left open behind him. Bohrman pulled out a chair and sat down.

The case papers were not divided in any real order and were simply a chronological collection of documents produced in connection with the missing-person inquiry.

The formal charge sheet lay on top. It contained no information other than that Danny Momrak had given a false statement about his own movements.

Laying the charge sheet aside, he flicked past the report in which Tone Vaterland was registered as a missing person. He skimmed the report from the first police patrol to attend the discovery site, assuming that a more detailed crime-scene report with illustrations would follow later. Then he picked up Danny Momrak's first statement from the previous day, running to more than five pages. The initial three described his relationship with Tone, while the final two gave an account of his own movements the day she disappeared. The statement was fairly detailed, even though he had not done much. He provided times, places he had been, and people he had met.

The next interview had begun four hours later. Danny Momrak had repeated his statement, identical to the statement from the previous day in the main fundamentals. Then he was made aware of the footage of him and his car from a service station at a time when he had claimed to be in Langesund. When he was unable to provide any explanation for this, the interview was suspended and he was charged with giving a false statement.

Bohrman riffled through the papers and found some poor black-and-white photocopies of printouts from a video recording. The registration plate was legible in one of these, but it was impossible to make out the driver. That did not help much. Danny had already explained that he had gone to Langesund in his car at that particular time of day.

He returned to the report on the discovery of the body and realized that as the crow flies it was only a matter of a few hundred metres from where Danny had been caught on film. The timing was within the estimated time frame in which it was reasonable to assume that something had happened to Tone Vaterland. They were hemming him in.

Gathering up the papers, he stuffed them into his briefcase and pushed the chair out from the table.

The young investigator who had shown him into the room now appeared at the door and accompanied him to the office, where Danny Momrak was waiting.

They had let him smoke. A coffee cup in front of him was full of fag ends and the smell hung in the room.

Bohrman paid no attention to that. 'Hi, Danny,' he said, stretching out his hand. 'I'm going to help you with this.'

Danny took his hand but remained in his seat. Bohrman turned to face the detective. 'We need some time alone.'

'Shall we say half an hour?' the officer suggested.

'It will take whatever time it needs,' Bohrman replied, mainly to show Danny that he was calling the shots.

The door closed and Bohrman sat down. Danny looked across at him but did not say anything. 'How's your mum doing these days?' Bohrman asked.

'Fine.'

'She must be worried now,' Bohrman said. 'I can phone her afterwards, if that's OK with you?'

Danny nodded his head.

'I understand you've got yourself an Escort now,' Bohrman continued. 'What happened to the Mazda?'

'I sold it.'

Bohrman took out his notebook and asked a few more mundane questions in order to build trust, avoiding any mention of Tone Vaterland.

'Have you seen the pictures from the petrol station?' he asked.

Danny Momrak met his eye. 'I didn't do it,' he said.

Bohrman made no comment and merely produced the copy of the CCTV images. 'They're going to ask if you were the one who was driving,' he said.

'I'd just forgotten I went in there,' Danny answered.

'They want to know what you were doing there.'

'I did nothing. Just sat there. Had a smoke. Didn't have anything else to do. Then I drove home.'

'You didn't do anything else?' Bohrman probed. 'You have to think carefully. If other things crop up that you've failed to mention, then they'll use that against you.'

'What sort of other things?'

'The police are going to draw a timeline,' Bohrman explained, pointing at the time given in the corner of the image printout where the clock read 20.32. 'If you went straight home afterwards, your neighbours or passers-by may have seen you park your car outside the house. Then that would've been around quarter to nine, but if you stopped off in other places, it's crucial that you mention it, in case your neighbours didn't see you until later.'

Danny used his finger to draw invisible patterns on the table. 'Maybe I drove around for a bit first,' he said.

'Did you meet anyone or make any other stops?'

'No, not that I can remember.'

'If you don't recall or aren't sure of anything, it's also important to say so.' He leaned forward. 'Time is difficult to remember. Most people make mistakes when they have to cast their minds back. You have to appreciate it's better to estimate a time frame rather than give a precise time of day. For instance, that you were home between nine and ten, instead of saying it was half past nine.'

Nodding, Danny glanced at the door. 'Do you think they're going to let me go home afterwards?'

'That's not easy to say, Danny. They might need to check and double-check things. I think you should be prepared to stay here until tomorrow, at least.'

'Here?'

'They'll probably drive you to the detention facility in Porsgrunn.'

Danny Momrak sat bolt upright, propelling himself backwards into the chair. He looked panicked.

'But I don't know for sure, Danny,' Bohrman said. 'Anyway, I'll do all I can to assist you.'

'Do you think it'll go OK?'

Bohrman cleared his throat to camouflage a smile. 'It's too early to know,' he replied.

However, he knew how this was going to end. Danny Momrak's statement was far from credible. Unless something turned up to lead the investigation in a different direction, this was going to culminate in a court case and a prosecution for murder.

14

The documents from the case against Danny Momrak lay waiting on the kitchen table. Outside, the twilight was growing darker. After switching on the ceiling light, Wisting drew out his seat and stood with both hands on the back of the chair. The smell of the fire site still clung to his clothes. Thoughts of Agnete Roll had trailed him all the way home.

Before he read on, he skimmed through his notes. Danny Momrak had stated that he was delivering hash to a friend of the same age in Langesund when Tone Vaterland was cycling home from work. The customer was named as Jonas Haugerud.

Wisting found his name in the list of witnesses. He had been interviewed the next morning but could not confirm the transaction. It was true that he had met Danny Momrak on 4 July, but it had been in the afternoon. In any case, he denied that he had bought drugs from him and was unable to give him an alibi for the time of the murder.

As Wisting read through the notes, a clear picture of what had happened began to emerge. Several people had seen Tone Vaterland cycle along the road with a rucksack on her back, and she had also been spotted turning on to the old road. A canoeist had seen a solitary figure down at the bathing spot at the U-shaped rock, where she had gone for a dip on her way home. Everything indicated that Tone Vaterland had been attacked when she returned to her bike beside the road.

He took out the folder of photographs from the discovery site once again. A total of five buttons had been photographed, all that had been found of her clothing. White threads hanging from the holes told the story of how the blouse she had been wearing had been ripped off her.

Most of the statements given to the police were of little interest, but one was significant: Maria Strand. She had been Tone Vaterland's best friend since primary school. The person Tone confided in and talked to about everything. She was able to explain why Tone and Danny had split up.

It had been because Danny used to force himself on her. He had been keen for them to watch porn together and do things they had seen on film. He was rough and made her take part in things she really did not want to do. For instance, he had wanted her to masturbate him and perform oral sex on him while he was driving the car. They had also had sex in his car in a car park, where some of the thrill for him had been the risk of being seen. On the day they had broken off their relationship, Tone had come to see her. Danny had spent the night at her house ever since her parents had left, and they had the house to themselves. He had wanted them to sleep in her parents' bed, because there he could tie Tone to the bedposts. Danny had got his way, but it had been against Tone's wishes. The next morning Danny had come into the bathroom and forced her to have sex with him in the shower. Afterwards a quarrel had developed that ended with Tone ending their relationship, and Danny had stomped off in a temper.

The friend described Danny as sex-obsessed, aggressive, violent and jealous. These were descriptions repeated in interviews with a number of Tone's female friends.

A mosquito stung Wisting on the neck. He swung out his hand to swat it and discovered he had squashed it flat. Behind him, the fridge motor started up.

He shoved the bundle of unread witness statements aside, unable to see any point in continuing to work through them. Drawing his attention to Danny Momrak must have some other purpose than to prompt him to search for errors in these legal proceedings. He had been found guilty and had served his sentence. Maybe the anonymous sender wanted to make him aware that a murderer had been set free. What would then be of interest was where Danny Momrak was and what he was doing now.

He rose from the table, moved to the kitchen sink and filled a glass with water, but drank only two mouthfuls before putting down the tumbler.

He lingered beside the worktop in front of the window, watching the glow of the streetlamps cast shadows of the trees into neighbouring gardens. Line's house was shrouded in darkness. She and Amalie were away for another four days.

Line had been in a relationship for the last six months with Cederik Smith, who was two years younger than her. He was already divorced with a daughter the same age as Amalie. They had met in connection with a documentary film project. He lived in Bærum but had invited Line and Amalie to accompany him to his parents' summer cabin on the eastern side of the Oslo Fjord.

On the first day, Wisting had received photos on his phone. To start with, one of Amalie in a play tent erected on a patch of garden, then one of both of them at the water's edge on a beach. In the third photograph, all four of them were seated around a table.

Wisting had only met Cederik Smith twice, when he had visited Line. Most often she was the one who travelled to his house while Wisting took care of Amalie.

They had not had an opportunity to talk much, just the two of them together, and he had not yet formed a clear impression of Cederik. He seemed both vigorous and thoughtful and his appearance reminded him of the men Line had been involved with in the past. Dark hair and dark eyes. He was over thirty, and it was understandable that he was keen to find a relationship that would last.

The sound of a car made him turn his head and look up along the street. Wisting followed the dimmed headlights of the vehicle with his eyes until it disappeared at the other end of the street.

He had to admit it would soon be too late for him to find a partner to share his life. This summer marked ten years since Ingrid had died. Six years ago, he had met a woman who ran a café in Stavern and had thought their relationship would develop, but things had unfolded in a different direction. That was all. For the past five years he had gone to bed each night alone.

Tossing out the rest of the water, he cast one last glance at the documents on the kitchen table before turning off the light and heading to the bathroom.

Before bed, he opened the window and left it slightly ajar to air the room. The wind was rustling through the treetops outside. The forecast indicated a change in the weather later tomorrow, when the temperature would dip and there would be rain.

The mosquito bite on his neck was smarting now. He turned on to his side but struggled to find a comfortable position. Just then, he heard a noise at the front of the house, a metallic click, the lid of the mailbox falling back into place.

His body tensed. He lay there looking out into the room, waiting, but heard nothing more.

It was seventeen minutes past midnight.

He swung his legs out of bed and moved to the kitchen window to look outside but saw nothing.

Pulling on a pair of trousers and slipping on the clogs he kept handy in the hallway, he walked outside bare-chested.

The air was chill and dew speckled the grass.

Somewhere on an intersecting street, a car engine started up. It reminded him of the car that had driven by before he went to bed. The part of Herman Wildenveys gate on which he lived had little traffic. The street formed a crescent that emerged again on Signalveien. There was no through traffic. You accessed nowhere apart from the homes of the people who lived here. He had not recognized the car, a vehicle with square headlights.

Flipping up the lid, he saw a white envelope inside the mailbox. He stood there for a long time, looking around and then down at the envelope again before picking it up with two fingers.

The same stiff letters, but only his name this time. No address or postage stamp. He carried it inside, where he put on a pair of yellow washing-up gloves and took out a knife.

The last letter and envelope were still in separate plastic bags on the worktop.

He opened the new one and found contents similar to the last missive, a folded sheet of paper with a case number written on it.

11-1883/01 was what it said this time.

According to the old organization system, police district 11 was his. The case referred to was from 2001, two years after Tone Vaterland's murder. The sequential number indicated that it was from some time in late summer, around the middle of August.

August 2001.

It could only refer to one case. One for which he himself had had responsibility.

15

On Friday, 17 August 2001, seventeen-year-old Pernille Skjerven went missing. Two days later, she was found raped and murdered. After four intense days of investigation, Jan Hansen was arrested and six months later he was found guilty of her killing.

Wisting glanced across at the kitchen table where the old case papers lay. There were certainly similarities. Pernille Skjerven had also been cycling along a busy road when she vanished. She had been at the stables near Pauler, as she was almost every day. From there it was quarter of an hour to cycle home to Veldre, immediately outside Larvik town centre. She was picked up at a bus stop along the road. In fact, it was the same road on which Tone Vaterland had cycled just over two years earlier. At that time it was the main route to and from the south of Norway. If you followed it for thirty kilometres in a southerly direction, you would arrive at the spot where Tone Vaterland was found.

There were goose pimples on his bare torso. He thought about finding a sweater but was reluctant to waste any time. A thought had slowly entered his head, a dawning comprehension of what the anonymous letters were about.

Sitting down at the kitchen table, he took out the folder of witness statements. The names were given on the cover, on the front page and running to two pages, listed according to surname and time of interview. Wisting had skipped back and forth a little, finding names mentioned in other interviews that appeared interesting. Now he ran his fingertip down the list of names.

He found what he was looking for on the last page. *HANSEN, Jan* was entered on the fifth line from the top.

It was one of the commonest names in the country. This could be someone who just happened to have the same name as Pernille Skjerven's killer, but Wisting did not think so. There was a reason he had received these letters.

He flicked through to the interview and saw from the date of birth, address and employer inscribed that it was indeed the same man.

When Jan Hansen had abducted and murdered Pernille Skjerven, he was working as a driver and installer for a furniture company specializing in designer furniture. The company was based in Larvik but delivered to the whole of the Østland region. On the afternoon of Friday, 17 August 2001, he had been on the return journey after delivering a sofa and matching table to a cabin owner in Kragerø.

When Pernille was reported missing, two witnesses had been of central importance. The first was a man who had been driving in the car behind Jan Hansen. He remembered they had passed Pernille on her bike and that the delivery van had turned into a bus bay a short time after that. A second witness had seen a man standing at the bus stop talking to a girl and construed it as the man asking for directions. There were no witnesses to what had actually happened, but when they finally located the delivery van, it became clear that the empty cargo space had been the scene of the rape and homicide. Apparently Hansen had kept both Pernille and the bike lying there throughout the weekend before dumping the body in a remote spot. Just like Tone Vaterland, she had been naked when she was found. Her clothes, along with her bicycle, were not discovered until a week later.

Jan Hansen had never confessed, but the evidence had eventually become overwhelming. Pernille Skjerven's hair and fingerprints were found in the cargo space of the van and traces of his semen in her body.

So, two years earlier, Jan Hansen had been interviewed in another murder case. With the computer systems used nowadays, this would have been flagged up, but at that time there was nothing to connect the two cases. When the investigators in Bamble talked to him, he had no criminal record. His name was drawn into the earlier inquiry only because he had been a frequent customer at the snack bar where Tone Vaterland worked. On the day of the murder he had been one of the last customers she had served. He had been sitting in his driver's cab eating when she mounted her bike. A few minutes later he had caught up with her along the road and driven past. He was traced because he had used a bankcard as payment. The time recorded matched the time Tone had finished work for the day.

Jan Hansen had not noticed anything out of the ordinary and had no information to contribute to the inquiry. Kathe Ulstrup had interviewed him, the same local police officer who had received the report that Tone Vaterland was missing, and who had led the search effort. When the case had developed into a murder investigation, she had obviously been allocated more trivial assignments. Jan Hansen's statement was filed in the large bundle of routine work undertaken and never brought out again.

The evidence against Danny Momrak remained the same. He had been rejected and was temperamental and violent. Eyewitnesses and video footage placed him at the crime scene at the time of the murder. He had lied when interviewed and changed his statement, and not least he was linked to the killing via DNA traces.

Nevertheless, when Jan Hansen's DNA had been routinely added to the DNA register, they got a match with a five-year-old unsolved case. If the investigators had known that one of the last people to see Tone Vaterland alive was a brutal rapist, then the court case might well have looked quite different.

While Jan Hansen was in custody, a further six unsolved sexual assault cases had been reopened, but it had proved impossible to link him to any of them. The two cases on the indictment had, however, been enough to ensure he was given the severest punishment permitted by law.

Wisting scratched his neck.

Jan Hansen was the type of criminal who had to be stopped; otherwise he would simply adapt and move on like a hungry predator. The sentence was stiff enough to prevent him from injuring others and a year ago he had died behind bars.

16

Just before 3 a.m. it started to rain, and soon afterwards Wisting fell asleep. When he woke again, he still felt a grumbling disquiet. There was a blind spot in the case against Danny Momrak. Information the investigators, defence counsel and court did not have access to in 1999. Information that only time could bring to light.

He looked out. It was still raining and a fine veil of mist blanketed the ground.

What troubled him most was that the person who had discovered the latent potential in the flawed case was operating in secret. The motive was obviously to force Wisting's hand and make him reinvestigate the Momrak case.

Whoever lay behind this must be someone who would not be taken seriously if he raised the matter through normal channels. Someone with a personal agenda but who lacked the necessary credibility to be heard or taken seriously. The only realistic candidate had to be Danny Momrak himself.

Wisting tried to look him up on the Internet but found only a few old articles in which he was named as Tone Vaterland's killer. There was no information in the various directories. No phone number or address. No social media presence. Since the sentence pronounced had been seventeen years, he should have been provisionally released some time ago, but if so he had not left any electronic traces.

Before he ate breakfast, Wisting checked the online newspapers. The discovery of the body in the charred ruins of the Kleiser house had been made public and linked to the missing Agnete Roll.

Before he drove to the town centre, he checked his mailbox, but found it empty.

Once settled behind the wheel in the car, he switched on the fan at full blast to keep condensation off the front windscreen. Rainwater lashed the wheel arches as he drove.

Outside the police station, a man crossed the street with his jacket pulled over his head. After parking in the back yard, Wisting headed in through the basement car park to access the archives room. The fluorescent light tubes on the ceiling buzzed and blinked a couple of times before the bright, sterile light spilled on to the rows of shelving.

He located the year 2001 and found six boxes relating to Case 1883. They had gathered dust and did not appear to have been touched for a long time. Opening the first box, he took out the folder containing the signed documents.

He took out another folder and leafed through the introductory documents.

A detective in Oslo had informed him that Jan Hansen was dead. Wisting himself had broken the news of his death to Pernille Skjerven's parents, so that they no longer needed to dwell on the day when their daughter's killer would be freed.

Jan Hansen had received a diagnosis of prostate cancer while in prison, and when this came to light, it had already spread to his lymph nodes and skeleton. There had been repeated hospital stays and a lengthy period spent in the prison infirmary wing before the National Correctional Service had formally decided to grant him provisional release for transfer to a palliative care ward at Ullevål Hospital, where he died after a brief stay. That had been last summer. At the same time, Wisting had also learned that Jan Hansen had a girlfriend who had visited him regularly in prison during the past ten years. He had no idea who she was or how they had met, but it did not surprise him. He had come across this before. Some women found men who had committed serious crimes or were serving long prison sentences attractive. It seemed that the more callous the crime and the more sensational the headlines, the greater the attraction. Psychologists had a name for it: hybristophilia. *Hybris* was from Greek mythology and referred to the arrogance humans demonstrate when they attempt to rise above the limitations the gods have imposed on them.

Wisting returned the folder and pushed the box into place. There was really no way back for him. He had been sent the documents in Danny Momrak's case. It was like a Pandora's box – he had opened it and let what was inside escape. He was already involved.

A door slammed in the corridor outside and he heard rapid footsteps making their way along. Soon afterwards, he heard a car rev up and drive out of the garage, followed by the wail of sirens.

As Wisting let himself out, he bumped into two officers responding to the alarm. 'Road traffic accident,' they replied when Wisting asked what had happened.

He took the stairs up to the Criminal Investigation Department on the first floor. En route to his own office, he had to pass the one occupied by Nils Hammer. Maren Dokken stood in the doorway talking to Hammer at his desk. When he shifted his eyes to the door, Maren turned around.

Wisting could not simply walk on. 'Any news?' he asked.

'Could be,' Hammer said, looking across at Maren.

She glanced at her watch. 'A man's coming to see us in half an hour,' she said. 'Ole Lind. He just phoned me. His son cuts grass in their neighbourhood, including for Agnete and Erik Roll. He's fifteen and that's his summer job. With things as they are, with Agnete missing, the lad wasn't keen to go to their house. The grass was getting long and rain was forecast. So yesterday his father went over there to mow the lawn.'

Wisting scanned the corridor before taking a step forward.

'The lawnmower was in a shed,' Maren went on. 'He cut half the lawn before he ran out of petrol and had to refill the tank, but there was no petrol can in the shed. Although reluctant, he went to the door to ask Erik about petrol, but he wasn't at home.'

'When was this?' Wisting asked.

'In the morning,' Maren replied. 'Around eleven.'

'The fire at the Kleiser house was reported at 11.23,' Hammer commented.

Wisting nodded. He had encountered the fire engines around that time.

'Ole Lind went home to pick up some petrol to complete the job. Later that day he spoke to his son about it. The petrol can was usually left in the shed alongside the lawnmower.'

'You need more than that to bring in Erik Roll,' Wisting said. 'You'll have to find a chink in his statement.'

Nils Hammer nodded without saying anything.

'What are you doing here, anyway?' Maren asked.

'I'm just going to see to something in my office,' Wisting answered. 'I won't be long.'

Moving on, he let himself into his office and closed the

door behind him. He sat down without turning on the light and merely reached out for the computer switch and sat waiting for it to start up.

The rain beat against the windows. He watched as a container ship made its way out of the leaden fjord, but there were no other boats to be seen.

Once the computer was up and running, he took only a few minutes to find what he was looking for. Danny Momrak had been released two years ago. He had served his entire sentence at Ullersmo Prison. At the same time as his release, an address was registered for him at Oklungen, outside Porsgrunn. No one else was listed at the same address. According to the employment register, he had worked at a mechanical workshop but had been without permanent employment for the last six months. No listing in the vehicle registration records. The last source he checked was the criminal records. Danny Momrak had not been investigated for any new crimes since his release.

The only thing Wisting jotted down was the address. Sooner or later, he would have to talk to him.

17

The courtroom's side door opened and a handcuffed Danny Momrak was led inside. At first the crowded room fell silent, then whispered comments spread and chatter surged like a wave along the public benches.

Cristian Bohrman rose to greet the prisoner, who, pale and downcast, dragged his feet and let his eyes wander. Someone shouted something – Bohrman could not make out what, but turned to face the packed room. Tone Vaterland's parents both sat with heads bowed. The rows behind them were filled with what he assumed to be friends and family along with other curious members of the public. Danny's mother, in a drab sweater, sat almost at the very back. He hoped Danny would catch sight of her.

The press benches were crammed. He had already spoken to several of the journalists present, having made himself available for interviews and answered questions during the entire remand period. He considered some of them to be allies, but others he had written off as friendly to the police.

Having waited until the handcuffs were removed before shaking hands, Bohrman gave his client a solid handclasp.

'Are you ready?' he asked.

Danny Momrak responded with a whisper of confirmation.

Smiling, Bohrman nodded and released his hand and resumed his seat. Another three minutes crept past and it was now nine o'clock. The door behind the judge's bench opened and the District Court judge entered, followed by the two co-judges. Bohrman was one of the first on his feet and last to sit down after being requested to do so.

The judge declared the court in session and ran through the formalities, introduced the various parties, including himself, and rattled off the rules of impartiality.

'The accused, please stand.'

The chair scraped on the floor. Bohrman remained seated. This was the loneliest moment in the entire court proceedings. His client had to stand on his own before the judge with everyone's eyes fixed upon him. Bohrman could see that his knees were knocking.

The judge asked him to give his full name, date of birth, address and status before inviting the prosecutor to read the indictment.

Danny Momrak stood with his hands clasped in front of him. The Public Prosecutor stood up, raising the rostrum, straightening his papers and clearing his throat before launching into his speech. Cristian Bohrman sat with the document before him, following every word. The penal clauses were read out and the acts described in simple terms.

'You have heard the charges,' the judge continued. 'Do you declare yourself guilty, not guilty or partially guilty of the crimes of which you are accused?'

Danny Momrak answered in a surprisingly firm voice: 'Not guilty.'

18

Wisting looked up from his computer screen. A scud of wind hurled heavy rain against the office window; it sounded as if someone was throwing gravel at it.

He had also tracked down and investigated Danny Momrak's defence counsel. Cristian Bohrman had lost the case, both in the District Court and the Court of Appeal, but Tone Vaterland's murder had marked the beginning of a lucrative career as a defence lawyer. Even though he must have foreseen the outcome, he had made his mark as a forceful defence lawyer. His legal firm had expanded enormously and now employed a staff of eighteen, specializing in criminal law and child protection cases. Bohrman himself was based in the main office in Skien, but also had a branch in Tønsberg and another in Oslo. A couple of years ago, he had hit the headlines after his client was freed in a murder case in Fredrikstad. In a subsequent in-depth interview he was asked if he had defended cases that had ended in conviction but where he was equally certain of his client's innocence, as in this case. His answer was that all established lawyers had at least one case in that category, but did not reveal which case he had in mind.

Sten Kvammen had also advanced rapidly after the murder case. Even at that time, he had acted as head of the Criminal Investigation Department, but from what Wisting could see, today he was in charge of international police collaboration at Kripos. On his way up the career ladder, he had graduated in law, attended management courses and held positions of divisional head and chief superintendent. At present he was in the running for the post of Assistant National Police Commissioner and Head of the International Section in the Norwegian Police Directorate.

Wisting had managed to locate his phone number. He was keen to share and discuss his findings, and the closest relevant person was the investigator who had played such a central role in the inquiry.

Before he had a chance to dial the number, there was a knock at the door. Maren Dokken entered, carrying a laptop and a sheaf of papers.

'You're still here?' she asked.

'Afraid so,' he said. 'Are you finished with the lawn-mower man?'

'One of the others is talking to him now,' Maren replied. 'I'm searching for that chink.'

Wisting leaned back in his chair.

'I think I might have found it,' she went on. 'Have you got a minute?'

Wisting asked for details. Maren pulled a chair round to his side of the desk and set down the laptop so they could both view the screen.

'We have video footage of both Agnete and Erik Roll leaving the pub,' she said, showing him the still images. 'She leaves the pub at 23.52 and her husband follows just over half an hour later, at 00.24.'

Tapping the keyboard, she called up another photo. A woman in an ankle-length summer dress was walking along a narrow pavement with head bowed and arms folded across her chest. The image was grainy and it was impossible to recognize the face, but the clothing looked the same as in the photo of Agnete leaving the pub.

'There are few CCTV cameras around the streets in Stavern,' Maren continued, 'and we haven't found Agnete in any of them. This is from a dashboard camera on a car parked at the kerb in Brunlaveien. It records each time movement is detected. This is 1,100 metres from the pub. She's on her way home.'

Wisting squinted at the screen. The footage was recorded at 00.04. She had taken twelve minutes, assuming the clocks were synchronized.

'That's normal walking pace,' Maren said, as if she could read his thoughts. 'I walked the same stretch myself last night. If she goes straight home at the same speed, she would arrive in quarter of an hour.'

'Is anyone following her?' Wisting asked, gesturing towards the screen.

Maren Dokken shook her head. 'The next recording is a taxi, two minutes later.'

'What about her husband?' Wisting asked. 'Is he caught on film?'

'That's the chink,' Maren replied, showing him the next frame.

It had been taken at the same spot. A man was walking with both hands deep in his pockets. He was wearing a shirt with rolled-up sleeves, just like the picture of Erik Roll in the pub.

'Indeed – 00.49,' Wisting commented, doing the mental arithmetic. Erik Roll had taken twice as long as his wife on the same stretch of road. 'Didn't he go straight home?'

'He's stated that he hung about for a couple of minutes outside the pub, talking to a pal of his, but apart from that he spoke to no one. He didn't eat a baked potato or buy a hotdog or anything of that sort. We would have been able to check that.'

Maren Dokken thumbed through his witness statement. 'He doesn't remember when he left the pub, but claims he was home at about one o'clock,' she told him.

'He could have dawdled,' Wisting pointed out. 'Taken a piss, sat down on a bench to clear his head. Something like that.'

'He doesn't mention anything like that.'

'Was he asked?'

Maren Dokken shook her head. 'But we're talking about nearly twelve minutes,' she said. 'He wouldn't take as long as that to relieve himself along the way.'

Wisting admitted she was right. 'But he is behind her on the path,' he said. 'He can't have used the time difference to do anything to her.'

'All the same, I'd have liked to know what he was up to,' Maren said. She flipped down the laptop lid and got to her feet.

'It is a chink,' Wisting agreed. 'You'll have to prise it open. Find out what's hidden in there.'

Maren headed for the door. 'Sorry,' she said. 'I didn't mean to take up your time.'

Wisting smiled. 'Any time at all,' he said.

She shut the door on the way out and Wisting dialled the number he had jotted down. Sten Kvammen answered almost at once.

'It's about an old case,' Wisting said, after introducing himself. 'From the time you were an investigator.'

'What case?'

'Tone Vaterland's murder.'

There was silence at the other end, as if Kvammen needed time to cast his mind back. Wisting doubted this was true.

'Danny Momrak,' he said eventually. 'That's a long time ago. Why is that an issue now?'

'I've had a couple of approaches about the case,' Wisting replied. 'There may be circumstances surrounding it that were impossible for you to know of in 1999.'

'The case against Danny Momrak was investigated from every possible angle,' Kvammen said. 'It's one of the clearest convictions I've ever been involved in.'

'This is not something that directly alters the evidential situation,' Wisting said. 'It's more the way I've received the information that makes me want to have a chat with you.'

'Oh?'

'It's difficult to discuss over the phone. I really have to show it to you. Can we meet?'

'Whereabouts? I'm on holiday right now.'

'Are you away from home?'

'Yes, I'm at my cabin. In Bamble.'

'I can come there,' Wisting suggested. 'In fact, I can be there in a couple of hours.'

Kvammen hesitated. Wisting understood his reluctance. A meeting implied involvement. He had put the case against Danny Momrak behind him. If there were mistakes or deficiencies in the investigation, then that would be something he would want to distance himself from. But curiosity gained the upper hand.

'One p.m.,' he said. 'I'll send you directions.'

19

'Do you swear to tell the whole truth and not prevaricate on any point?'

Sten Kvammen raised his right hand. 'I solemnly swear to do so.'

The judge nodded. 'You may sit down.'

Kvammen cast a quick glance to one side, across to Danny Momrak, before drawing the chair towards him and sitting down in the witness box. He was always tense in court. It felt like going into an exam and having to give all the right answers. Everything he said would be weighed and judged – by the court, the defence lawyer and the media. He had a folder in front of him with the most important reports and his own personal notes, but was aware it would give a more convincing impression if he could cope without resorting to them.

The prosecutor was invited to speak and began with a few obligatory questions. Kvammen described his background and the qualifications his post demanded. Then he was led through an account of the investigation, from the time when the police had received the report that Tone Vaterland was missing until the charges were brought. They had gone through the questions the previous day. His answer was rehearsed and focused, and presented concisely so that the responses were easy to apprehend. After an

88

hour and twenty minutes, the prosecutor declared that he was satisfied.

The judge spent some time making notes before lifting his head and directing his gaze at the defence. 'Mr Bohrman. Do you have any questions for the witness?'

Kvammen turned his head and looked across at the defence lawyer.

'Yes, thank you,' Bohrman replied. He stalled for a moment as he completed a note and then looked up. 'When did Dan Vidar Momrak's name first crop up in the investigation?' he asked, twirling his pen between his fingers.

Kvammen hesitated, preparing to be duped into some semantic blunder. 'He was the deceased's ex-boyfriend,' he answered. 'They had split up a couple of days earlier.'

Bohrman laid down his pen. 'We're aware of that,' he said. 'I asked when his name was introduced into the investigation.'

Kvammen tucked his feet under his chair. 'If you're asking for a date and time, I can't answer that off the top of my head,' he said.

Someone in the room chuckled.

Bohrman picked up a sheet of paper. 'Isn't it correct that the deceased's mother gave his name when she reported her daughter missing?'

'That could be right.'

'I have it here,' Bohrman said, waving the sheet before glancing up at the judge. 'If I may be allowed to quote?'

The judge nodded.

Bohrman put on a pair of glasses and read aloud: 'The caller has been worried about the relationship her daughter has had with Danny Momrak, who is one year older than her. Her daughter backed out of the relationship on 2 July, but the caller is afraid he may have contacted her and been unwilling to accept the break-up.'

Removing his glasses, he looked towards the witness box. 'Do you recognize that, Kvammen?'

'Yes.'

'So from the very start,' Bohrman continued, 'from the initial telephone call, in the very first report that was written, my client's name was mentioned?'

Kvammen shuffled his feet under the chair.

'It's information pertinent to the case,' he replied.

Bohrman waved the police report in the air. 'Are any other names mentioned here, as being pertinent to the case?'

Kvammen drew the folder on the desk towards him but did not open it. 'I seem to recall that the mother described talking to her neighbours and friends before contacting the police,' was his answer.

'That's right,' Bohrman agreed. 'Erna and Torfinn Klausen, the retired neighbours. And Jenny, the woman she worked with at the Bamble Snack Shack. These are the names given in the missing-person report, in addition to Danny Momrak.'

The defence counsel paused for effect. 'What other people of interest came to your attention?'

'What do you mean?'

'I was wondering how widely you cast your net,' Bohrman said. 'How many other people had their alibis checked, for example?'

'We interviewed almost three hundred people,' Kvammen replied. 'The technical . . .'

He was not permitted to finish speaking. Bohrman held a ring binder up in the air. 'I have them here,' he said. 'All the interviews. Two hundred and ninety-four witnesses.'

He smacked the binder down on the desk. 'What did you do with the information that emerged?'

Kvammen's back began to feel clammy. 'Most of them were observations of Tone Vaterland,' he answered. 'From road users and others. They were logged and catalogued, but then we moved into a phase when this was no longer a search effort, but a murder case.'

'I see,' Bohrman said, donning his glasses again. 'Five of these witnesses claimed they saw a man with a rucksack walking along the E18 at the time Tone Vaterland disappeared. Did you do anything to find out who that was?'

'That assignment was allocated, yes.'

'Was he identified?'

'No.'

'Was he publicized in the media and encouraged to come forward?'

'No.'

'Why not?'

'It was not regarded as relevant.'

'In what sense?'

'At that point in time, other circumstances were prioritized.'

'Isn't it true to say that at that time you had prioritized Danny Momrak?'

Kvammen knew he was being provoked. 'Momrak gave a false statement the first time we spoke to him,' he replied. 'That was something we had to follow up.'

'False or incorrect?' Bohrman asked.

'What?'

'Was Danny Momrak's statement false or incorrect?'

'He was charged with giving a false statement,' Kvammen responded.

'That is not included on the indictment,' Bohrman pointed out.

'The charge was upgraded to that of murder,' Kvammen countered.

'But you do know the difference between false and incorrect?' Bohrman insisted.

Kvammen, realizing he was about to be inveigled into a bout of hair-splitting, refrained from answering.

'A false statement implies that it has been fabricated to replace what actually happened,' the lawyer went on. 'Whereas an incorrect statement can mean that you have made a mistake in timing or location, something has slipped your mind. Has that ever happened to you?'

Kvammen squirmed in his seat, fully expecting the prosecutor to break in with an objection to the question.

Bohrman pressed his advantage: 'Have you ever been mistaken, Kvammen?'

The prosecutor cleared his throat and interrupted with a plea to the judge. 'Your Honour. This does not concern the witness . . .'

Bohrman raised a hand, as if in apology. 'My mistake,' he said. 'Let's return to the witnesses. Four of them say they saw a man in camouflage clothing, isn't that correct?'

Kvammen gave an involuntary sigh, irritated by the inaccuracy of the lawyer's description, which made it sound as if someone had been hiding in the woods.

'A military jacket,' he corrected. 'That's right.'

Bohrman delved into his papers and read out one of the witness statements: 'A military-type jacket with patches of various green and brown colours, green trousers and black boots.'

He looked up again. 'That sounds like camouflage

clothing to me,' he commented. 'Almost as if someone wanted to avoid being seen.'

Kvammen's jaw muscles tensed. His answer had given the lawyer the opportunity to emphasize his point.

'It could have been the same man who was seen with a rucksack,' he replied.

The lawyer made a point of nodding, almost as if he were bowing. 'It *could* have been,' he said. 'But we don't know, do we? Because you never found out who he was.'

Kvammen steered clear of answering. He could guess what the defence lawyer's next move would be.

'There are also a number of witnesses who say they saw a man with a camera in the area where Tone Vaterland went missing and was later found murdered. Do you know the identity of this photographer?'

'No.'

'What steps did you take to find him?'

Kvammen swallowed audibly. His throat was dry.

'Traditional investigative work,' he replied.

'Was he announced to the media?'

'No.'

'Wouldn't it have been extremely interesting to get in touch with someone who had taken photographs in the area around the time of the murder?'

Kvammen had no choice but to agree. He well appreciated what the defence counsel was angling for.

'So there were at least three unknown men in the vicinity of the crime scene around the time of the murder,' the defence lawyer summarized.

'If you read the statements and descriptions carefully, you'll see that they were most probably one and the same person,' Kvammen said.

'Probably,' Bohrman repeated acerbically. 'Why wasn't more done to find him, in order to ascertain whether there were three or one?'

Kvammen seized the opportunity to broach a subject that would probably be less to the lawyer's liking. 'We were concentrating on the technical findings at the crime scene,' he said, picking up the tumbler in front of him. 'The two DNA traces that matched Dan Vidar Momrak.'

Pouring a drink, he glanced up at the judge, but could see in his peripheral vision that the prosecutor was happy with the avoidance tactic.

'Exactly,' Bohrman said. 'The two DNA traces . . .' He leafed through his papers. 'Referred to in the laboratory reports in the list of evidence.' He glanced up. 'Do you have them in front of you?'

Kvammen pulled the folder towards him. 'Yes,' he confirmed.

The lawyer addressed himself to the judge. 'Does the court have the reports to hand? I'm speaking of evidence documents seven and eight, the analysis of a swab taken from the victim's vagina and a cigarette end found approximately one hundred metres from the victim.'

The judge opened the folder of documentary evidence provided and directed the co-judges to do the same before giving Bohrman a signal to continue.

'Who conducted the analyses?' he asked.

'The Forensic Institute in Oslo,' Kvammen replied. 'There is analysis of semen found in the victim and of skin cells in saliva on the cigarette.'

'Yes, thank you,' Bohrman said, raising his hand to interrupt him. 'I meant which staff member at the Forensic Institute?'

Kvammen looked up at the judge. 'If it's of relevance, then I'd really have to look it up.'

He received a nod in response and, drawing the ring binder towards him, he thumbed through to the two analysis reports. 'Regine Mefjord,' he read out.

'Both analyses?' Bohrman asked.

Kvammen double-checked. 'Yes,' he confirmed.

'When were the analyses performed?' Bohrman asked.

Kvammen checked his paperwork. 'The seventh of July.'

'So the same lab technician analysed the two samples on the same day?'

'That's right.'

'Were any other DNA analyses conducted?'

'Yes.'

'Of what, then?'

'They included several cigarette butts and a few empty bottles found around and about the crime scene.'

'What was the result?'

'They were negative.'

'Negative,' Bohrman reiterated. 'What does that mean?'

'That there was insufficient trace material in the samples to generate a DNA profile, or that the profile was unknown.'

'Unknown DNA profile,' Bohrman commented. 'Is it not correct that in connection with these samples at and around the crime scene you found DNA from two unknown men? On a beer bottle and a cigarette?'

Kvammen was forced to admit this.

'So there may have been three other men at the crime scene?' Bohrman asked. 'Three unknown men?'

'Hardly at the same time,' Kvammen answered. 'It's not

possible to fix the time the items we found were left there. Both the bottle and the cigarette may have been lying there long before it became a crime scene.'

'That anyone at all could have thrown away at any time at all?'

'Yes, I suppose so.'

'But then I don't understand . . .' the lawyer went on. 'The Public Prosecutor has entered DNA from Danny Momrak's cigarette as evidence that he killed Tone Vaterland, but couldn't his cigarette have been lying there for a long time too?'

Kvammen was squirming now and failed to answer.

'Is that not also likely?' the lawyer pressed him. 'Danny Momrak has stated and admitted that he stored narcotics in the old garage near that spot. Can't his cigarette end have been one that he tossed on his way to or from his hash depot?'

'That has to be considered in conjunction with the other evidence,' Kvammen said, hearing the irritation in his own voice.

'I agree,' Bohrman said. 'Let us try to look at everything in conjunction.'

He flicked through the documents again. 'You examined Danny Momrak's car . . .' he began. 'Were any DNA analyses conducted in connection with that?'

'Yes.'

Bohrman gazed at him, waiting for him to continue. Kvammen began to get an inkling of where he was going.

'Among other things, a towel was analysed,' he replied.

'Has my client explained that at interview?' Bohrman asked. 'Has he said anything about how that towel was used?'

'It was used when he and Tone Vaterland had sex in the car.'

'When they were a couple?'

'Yes.'

'Was it used once or several times?'

'Several times.'

The prosecutor broke in. 'I don't see any point in this . . .' he said.

The judge spoke directly to Bohrman: 'Is there any point to this?' he asked.

'I'm coming to that, Your Honour,' Bohrman assured him. He took out a sheet of paper. 'I have the analysis report here. It is document 4/56.'

Kvammen watched the prosecutor open a ring binder. He did not have a duplicate of this.

'I have a copy,' Bohrman offered.

The judge nodded and a court usher moved forward and handed over the report.

'What is the conclusion of the analysis?' Bohrman asked.

Kvammen did not need the paper in order to answer. 'That Dan Vidar Momrak's DNA was found in semen on the towel.'

'Where was this analysis carried out?'

'At the Forensic Institute.'

'Who was responsible for the analysis?'

Kvammen located the name. 'Regine Mefjord.'

'When were the analyses conducted?'

'The seventh of July.'

Bohrman pushed a pen into his mouth and sat deep in thought for a moment. 'So the analysis of the swab from the victim's vagina, the cigarette end from the old road and the towel from the car were all analysed by the same technician, at the same place and at the same time?' he summed up.

Kvammen nodded. 'The Forensic Medicine Commission has not raised any objections to the result or the way the analyses were performed,' he commented.

'Are you familiar with the dangers of cross-contamination of DNA?' Bohrman asked.

'Yes.'

'You don't need to explain,' Bohrman said. 'I can illustrate this for the court with a case from the USA. The police there found traces under the fingernails of a victim of rape and murder that matched a man with a previous criminal record. There was only one problem. The suspect had been involved in a road traffic accident and was in hospital when the homicide occurred. It eventually emerged that the paramedics had transported the injured party from the accident to the hospital and then picked up the murder victim. The DNA from the injured man had been unwittingly transferred to the body.'

The prosecutor began to rise from his seat in protest. 'We are not in the USA,' he said. 'And this is not the time for conjecture.'

'I only have one final question,' Bohrman said before the judge had time to speak. 'I simply believe that this story demonstrates how vulnerable DNA traces are as evidence in criminal cases.'

'Go ahead,' the judge said. 'Ask your question.'

'Thank you, Your Honour.'

Bohrman leaned forward across the desk. 'We know, then, that a towel, stiff and covered in semen, was in the same laboratory environment as evidence items seven and eight. Is it not possible that DNA could have contaminated them during the course of the analyses?'

Kvammen lifted his glass. Cristian Bohrman had put forward exactly what he had wanted to, but it only showed how amateur he was. None of the three judges would allow themselves to be misled by his hypothetical theories. An experienced defence lawyer would not have played his cards in the District Court. He would have waited until the Court of Appeal, where a jury would decide the question of guilt. In a jury of one's peers it would have been enough to sow doubt, but now they knew the basis on which Bohrman would build his defence. They would be prepared and have their answers ready. Perhaps even conduct fresh analyses.

Gulping down some more water, he replaced his glass on the table in front of him as he trained his eyes on Bohrman. 'I'm no more qualified to have an opinion on that than you are,' he replied.

The judge waited for a moment before asking if Bohrman had any further questions.

'No, Your Honour.'

The prosecutor declined to ask follow-up questions. The judge looked across at his two colleagues, but neither had anything to add.

'Then we'll offer our thanks to Chief Inspector Kvammen. The court will take ten minutes' recess before calling the next witness.'

20

The front wheel plunged into a pothole on the gravel track and brown muddy water splashed sideward. Wisting had twice taken the wrong turning, but now he felt sure he was on the road Sten Kvammen had described to him. It led up a slope and wound down towards the sea before dividing in two. To the left there was a sign warning of private property with no unauthorized access. This was the route he should take.

The cabin was located down by the waterside, in a little hollow that provided shelter from the weather. It resembled an old sea captain's house, painted white, with blue shutters at the windows.

Kvammen was standing in the clearing in front of the cabin – it looked as if he had just arrived himself. He opened the boot of a four-wheel-drive Mercedes and released a smooth-haired black dog that sat down obediently at his feet. It must have been a puppy, though the size of the cage showed it was expected to grow into a large dog.

Wisting lifted the plastic folder in which he had placed the anonymous letters and jumped out of the car.

It had stopped raining, but the mist was thick along the coast, giving the nebulous landscape a silvery tinge.

'You found your way, then,' Kvammen commented.

Wisting smiled. 'Sorry to bother you in the holidays,' he said.

Kvammen brushed him off. 'I'm never totally on holiday,' he said. 'Something or other always crops up.'

They ambled round to the sea-facing side of the house and up on to a covered verandah. The oiled timber was wet and slippery in this damp weather. A sliding door into the cabin was half open, and the dog lay down inside.

'We'll sit out here,' Kvammen said, indicating the outdoor furniture. 'I'll get some coffee.'

Wisting remained on his feet. The air was heavy with mist and salt and he watched as the waves crashed on the shore.

From the verandah, steps led down to a small jetty where a dinghy was moored. As it rose and fell with the waves, the mooring rope creaked.

When Kvammen returned with a pot of coffee and mugs, they sat down. 'Fire away,' Kvammen said as he poured. 'You wanted to talk about Tone Vaterland's murder. What's on your mind?'

Meeting his eye, Wisting realized this was a man used to leading others and directing the conversation. As for himself, he had not found any way of stating his business other than asking the direct question: 'Is there any possibility of an alternative perpetrator?'

Lifting his mug, Kvammen shook his head firmly before taking a sip. 'It was a rock-solid case,' he said. 'We had DNA, CCTV footage, telecoms data and witnesses. Everything pointed to Danny Momrak. He had motive, time, opportunity and intent.'

The mug banged on the table when he set it down again.

'The requirements of evidence are more exhaustive now than in the past. The scope of electronic traces is far greater and DNA analysis much improved. In many old cases it's certainly possible to pose critical questions, but not in this one.'

'I see,' Wisting said, turning his eyes to the little cove.

The mist lay like a blanket of lead on the water. A pair of swans paddled towards the jetty with five grey cygnets in their wake.

'What makes you doubt it?' Kvammen asked.

One of the swans was now pecking beneath its wing with its beak.

'It began on Tuesday,' Wisting said. 'I received an anonymous letter.' He produced the envelope and the first letter, both encased in plastic.

The police officer opposite leaned forward as Wisting pushed the plastic bags across to him.

'It contained only a case number,' he went on, 'relating to the investigation of Tone Vaterland's murder in 1999.'

The dog rose from its spot and made a deep growling noise. Kvammen ordered it to be quiet.

'I got another letter today,' Wisting ploughed on. 'With another case number.' He laid it on the table. 'It's a case I investigated in 2001,' he explained. 'Jan Hansen was found guilty of the murder of seventeen-year-old Pernille Skjerven. There are many similarities.'

'Sexually motivated murders usually are similar,' Kvammen commented. 'Teenage girls attacked, raped and killed.'

'All the same, it made me take a closer look at the cases,' Wisting said. 'It seems Jan Hansen was listed as a witness in the Tone Vaterland inquiry. He was one of the last people to see her alive.'

Wisting had to explain how Jan Hansen had been a customer at the snack bar and driven away just after Tone Vaterland when she clocked off.

Sten Kvammen shook his head. It was difficult to say whether this was because these were details he did not remember, or because the information was so startling.

'Where did you get that from?' he asked.

'From the case files,' Wisting replied.

'And where did you get the case files from?'

'When I received the first letter, I requisitioned them from the archives.'

Kvammen raised his eyebrows. 'Have you opened a new investigation on your own initiative?' he asked. 'Of a case with a legally binding verdict?'

The raw summer air caught the back of his throat and Wisting turned aside to cough into his armpit. 'I've made a few enquiries,' he answered.

'Have you nothing else to do with your time?' Kvammen quizzed him. 'You have a missing-person case that has developed into a murder case. I was just reading about it.'

'I'm actually on holiday too,' Wisting replied. 'These letters arrived at my home.'

Kvammen's eyes narrowed. 'What have you found out?' he asked.

'Jan Hansen is dead,' Wisting told him. 'He was diagnosed with cancer in prison and died last summer.'

Kvammen took another swig from his mug. 'So you're chasing a ghost?' he asked. 'Surely there's nothing to take any further?'

Wisting leaned forward and drew the anonymous letters towards him. 'Someone obviously believes there is,' he said.

'Jan Hansen is no longer a problem,' Kvammen commented. 'He can't harm anyone again.'

'Danny Momrak served fifteen years in prison,' Wisting reminded him.

Kvammen pointed at the anonymous letters. 'He's had fifteen years to work that out,' he said. 'No doubt he's the one behind it.'

'That's possible.'

'Who else would it be?' Kvammen sniffed loudly. 'You're allowing yourself to be manipulated,' he said. 'If he thinks the verdict was wrong, he can take it up with his lawyer. We have systems for that. They'll have to put it before the Criminal Cases Review Board. Anyway, you can forget the whole shebang. You've already gone too far, far beyond the limits of your authority.'

Somewhere out on the misty sea, a ship sounded its foghorn to indicate it was entering the fjord. Kvammen downed the rest of his coffee. Wisting had not even tasted his.

The swans had reached the jetty, where the largest one stretched its neck, flapped its wings and looked around inquisitively.

Rising from his chair, Kvammen moved to the railings and grasped them firmly. 'What does Momrak do nowadays?' he asked.

'He's worked as a car mechanic,' Wisting replied. 'It's possible he got training in prison.'

'Where does he live?'

'In Oklungen. No fresh crimes are listed for him.'

Sten Kvammen turned to face Wisting and pointed at the anonymous letters. 'You probably know where all this comes from, don't you?' he asked. 'Why this has popped up now?'

The dog got up again and moved towards its master. This time it was left to do as it pleased.

Wisting made no response.

'The new regulation,' Kvammen explained. 'Regarding compensation for unlawful criminal prosecution. Momrak would be entitled to a minimum of 1,500 kroner per day for economic losses. How much would that amount to? Almost ten million. In addition, he would be able to claim the same amount in damages.'

The ship's foghorn sounded again. The deep, monotonous noise drifted slowly through the mist before it faded and died out.

'Have you had any contact with Tone Vaterland's parents?' Wisting asked. 'Since the trial?'

Kvammen shook his head. He seemed to consider this a strange question. Wisting thought of Pernille Skjerven's parents. He had not spoken to them since telling them of the death of their daughter's killer.

'So you don't know if they've been warned that Momrak is a free man?'

'I moved on to other assignments,' Kvammen said. 'Started work in Kripos, got assigned to overseas service.'

Wisting returned the bags containing the anonymous letters to the folder. 'When does the new appointment in the Directorate come up?' he asked, thinking of the vacant post that had been advertised.

'At summer's end,' Kvammen answered. 'There are a number of strong candidates.'

Any uncertainty surrounding the question of guilt in one of his old cases was probably what he wanted least of all at this particular time.

Kvammen glanced at his watch. Wisting had already received the message loud and clear that their conversation was at an end. He stood up and pushed the untouched mug of coffee across the table, aware that it had gone cold.

21

Wisting was already regretting his meeting with Sten Kvammen. It had been far from fruitful. On the way to the meeting, he had driven past the Bamble Snack Shack. It still existed. On the return journey, he drove in.

Two men in work clothes stood at the window. Wisting ordered a hamburger when his turn came. A mature woman took his order, old enough to have worked there at the time Tone Vaterland was killed.

He carried his food to an unoccupied picnic table at the rear of the snack bar, from which vantage point he could see the door used by staff when they came to and from work. In his mind's eye, he saw how Tone Vaterland's bicycle would have been propped up against the wall, and where Jan Hansen's delivery van must have been parked.

The hamburger was tasteless. As he chewed, he reflected on what had happened in 1999. The fact that Jan Hansen's name had cropped up did not automatically make him a suspect. The evidence had been solid enough to convict Danny Momrak. Perhaps Kvammen had been right when he said that he had let himself be lured into embarking on his own investigations But, if nothing else, he wanted to know who had sent the letters. He still had no candidate other than Danny Momrak.

Everything suggested that Danny Momrak was guilty, but the only person who could know for certain was the man himself. And if he were guilty, why would he drag the case back into the spotlight again? Bringing all the old stuff to the surface would not lead to any benefit, unless he was confident that he would emerge from the process having cleared his name.

Wiping his mouth with a napkin, he got to his feet and tossed the paper into a waste bin.

If Danny Momrak was innocent, there was of course one person who knew the truth – the real perpetrator. But Jan Hansen was dead.

The snack bar's back door opened and the woman who had served him stepped out. She gave him a smile before throwing a bin bag into a container and disappearing inside again.

Once settled back inside his car, Wisting turned out on to the main road and drove in the direction Tone Vaterland had cycled.

Mist swirled through the spruce trees that flanked the motorway. Summer had come to an abrupt end, or had at least been paused. It could not be very pleasant where Line was.

A car moved up behind him, using its headlights to signal that he should pick up speed. Wisting continued at the same rate and, locating the turn-off to the old road, swung in.

The trees had grown tall on both sides, narrowing the road. Roots had lifted the asphalt, forcing their way through and forming cracks and potholes. Farther on, a tree had fallen across the road, making it impossible to drive on.

As Wisting stopped and got out, birds flew off from the nearest trees.

Immediately in front of him, a track veered to the right.

He wondered if it might lead to the bathing spot where Tone Vaterland had gone swimming. He followed it, plucking wild raspberries from a bush along the path, and had his suspicions confirmed. The mist hung over the water, preventing him from making out the land on the opposite side. A towel someone had left behind told him that the locals still frequented this area.

When he returned to his car, he followed the overgrown road further on foot. Rubbish was scattered along the verges, and now and again broken glass crunched beneath his feet.

The old garage he had read about in the reports was still standing, surrounded by tall, spreading deciduous trees. Half the roof had collapsed, and the grey brick walls were crumbling beneath the proliferation of ivy and moss. Fragments of the vehicle entry gate were broken off and the narrow opening into the garage resembled the entrance to a cave.

Without pictures or map from the case folders, it was difficult to find his bearings, but he thought he located the bank of earth behind which Tone Vaterland's body had lain. Pushing aside a few branches, he climbed up and peered into the undergrowth on the other side. The old crime scene told him nothing. Nature had reclaimed it long ago.

He realized he should have used the toilet at the snack bar before leaving. He had no wish to take a leak where he stood, and instead moved further into the woods before unzipping his fly.

His phone buzzed as he stood there, and he finished off before answering the call. It was a media message from Line, a picture of Amalie holding a little shore crab in the palm of her hand, looking elated, caught in a moment of fear and delight. He texted back that she was a tough cookie, but had better watch out in case the crab bit her on the nose.

Before trudging back, he used his phone to take a photograph of the old crime scene. On his way back to the car, he also snapped the disused garage.

A new message ticked in. *We're coming home tomorrow*, Line wrote. *Nothing but bad weather here.*

The message was followed by an image of a little umbrella and a dark cloud with a zigzag line underneath. Wisting replied with a smiley face and a thumbs-up.

A branch scraped the side of his car as he reversed out from the old road. He turned, but delayed driving off. Instead he leafed through his notes and found the number for Danny Momrak's defence lawyer from 1999.

Cristian Bohrman answered almost at once. Wisting introduced himself and indicated that he was calling from the police.

'I'm on holiday,' Bohrman told him before Wisting had a chance to say anything further. 'I'll give you the number for our on-duty line.'

'Are you away from home?' Wisting asked.

'Why do you ask?'

'It's about one of your old cases,' Wisting explained. 'I'd hoped to meet you to discuss something that's come up.'

'What case is this about?'

'Danny Momrak.'

This was met by silence at the other end. 'I see,' he said finally.

'Could we meet today?'

'I'm at home,' the lawyer replied. 'Do you know the address?'

'Yes,' Wisting confirmed. 'I can be there in half an hour.'

Another silence.

'I've really been expecting someone to call,' the lawyer said at last. 'Things have kicked off now, I see that.'

22

10 December 1999, 13.30

The ballpoint pen had run out of ink and the end of the sentence was just blank grooves on the pad. Ninni Sjevik rummaged in her bag and produced another pen. This was the first trial she had covered. She had followed it every day in court and discussed what emerged with other journalists. They were all convinced of the outcome. Danny Momrak was guilty.

As for her, she was not so sure. The investigators, the experts and various specialists had appeared in the witness box, but unanswered questions still remained. She had voiced her misgivings to the others, but they had fallen on deaf ears.

Danny Momrak had DNA evidence against him, but all this discussion of DNA was difficult to understand. How long, for instance, could a semen cell live, and how easy was it for DNA to spread from one place to another? Neither did she have a clear picture of the actual chain of events. When the trial had started, she had tried to draw a timeline and place Danny Momrak's movements within that, but the exact time that Tone Vaterland had been killed was not known for certain. At least thirty-six hours had elapsed before she was found. This impeded the post-mortem work, and the police pathologist had given a time of death between 20.30 and 04.30, a window of eight hours. For most of that time, Danny Momrak had an alibi.

Ninni Skjevik scanned the room. This was the final day of the trial and there were even more members of the public than before. Danny Momrak's mother had also made an appearance, sitting on her own at the back of the courtroom.

The judge invited Bohrman, the defence lawyer, to speak. Adjusting his black cap, he raised the desk to give his closing remarks. He was the only person who had mentioned the three unknown men who had been spotted in the area. One man with a rucksack, a photographer and another man in camouflage clothing. She had reported on this in the newspaper and even included it in a separate story encouraging them to come forward. No one had been in touch, at least not with her or the newspaper.

'Your Honour,' Bohrman began, 'the claims made by the prosecutor in this case may appear convincing. What is most striking, however, is how inadequate this investigation has been. The police have made little effort to shed light on extremely significant elements of the case. They have obviously neglected to follow clues that did not conform to their pet theory. The prosecutor has therefore been able to sketch out only a limited picture for the court.'

Ninni Skjevik glanced across at the judge, who sat with an impassive face, leaning back with his hands folded over his stomach.

'Let me summarize these weaknesses,' Bohrman continued. 'We can begin with the main evidence. The prosecuting authorities often put forward DNA as conclusive evidence, but can we really trust the analyses?'

He drew out significant points he had elicited from the

various witnesses under cross-examination. Central to these was a new regulation aimed at the prevention of DNA cross-contamination in the laboratory, to the effect that items for examination should be separated and only disposable equipment used. The analyses in the case against Danny Momrak had been conducted prior to the introduction of this new regulation.

Two days earlier, the prosecutor had been forced to bring a lab assistant into the witness box. She assured the court that the analyses had been carried out in a secure environment and stood by the results. All the same, Bohrman had managed to sow some doubt, in Ninni's opinion.

He went on to talk about the three men the police had been unable to track down. 'The case against Dan Vidar Momrak originated because the police had not succeeded in finding any of those three men,' Bohrman argued. 'It came about because they did not succeed in finding the true perpetrator.'

His voice had grown fainter as he spoke, raspy and hoarse. There was water in front of him, but he did not touch it.

'From the witness box, we have heard friends and acquaintances of the same age as the victim put forward rumour and conjecture about Danny Momrak,' he added. 'Anecdotes they have heard and discussed. Some of those allegations are extremely coarse and serious. The police have failed to verify any of these claims. They have done nothing to try to discover the source of those rumours or the truth of them. They have simply left them hanging in the air, where they remain exactly what they are: idle talk and accusations, statements that cannot in any sense be accorded evidential value.'

The prosecutor sat immediately across from him, on the other side of the room, and Ninni had only a side view of him. He seemed completely unmoved by the criticism made by the defence counsel.

Bohrman was nearing his conclusion. 'The sum total of these weaknesses leaves room for doubt,' he declared. He ran through the various statutory provisions, explaining how they were applied in other cases and listing the rules stating that reasonable doubt should benefit the defendant.

'I therefore request that the defendant, Dan Vidar Momrak, be released,' he rounded off.

Silence persisted in the court even after he had resumed his seat. A strange atmosphere pervaded the benches, nothing visible or audible, but there was a definite hint of something indefinable in the air.

The judge leaned forward. 'Thank you, Mr Bohrman.' He cleared his throat. 'Does the prosecutor wish to reply?'

The Public Prosecutor declined with thanks and shook his head, as if what had been said was of no interest.

'The defendant is allowed a final word,' the judge continued. 'Does he wish to speak?'

Cristian Bohrman leaned to one side and whispered a few words in his client's ear. They exchanged a few more whispers before Danny Momrak stood up.

In a toneless voice, with a wooden expression on his face, he pleaded to be believed. His very last words could barely be heard: 'It wasn't me that killed her.'

23

Half of the wall in front of Cristian Bohrman's house was freshly painted, brilliant white against a faded shade of charcoal. A mobile platform had been erected beside the entrance, but no one was using it now.

The lawyer, having heard him drive up, stood in the doorway as Wisting stepped out of his car. Flecks of paint in Bohrman's dark hair showed that he was undertaking the work himself.

'I like to paint,' he said. 'You can see you're making progress the whole time, and it's easy to see the end result when the job is done. In contrast with many of the other things I do. But now the weather has put a stop to it for the moment.'

Bohrman ushered Wisting into a spacious home office in the basement, where ring binders, books and bundles of paper were strewn across all the shelves and tables. The venetian blinds were down, and the room was bathed in semi-darkness, reminiscent of a cave. There was a sitting area in one corner of the room and they sat down on opposite sides of the coffee table.

'Have you had any contact with Danny Momrak of late?' Wisting asked.

'Not for a year or so,' Bohrman replied. 'Maybe even a bit longer than that.'

'You said, though, you'd been expecting such an approach?'

The lawyer nodded. 'I reckoned something was going to happen,' he said, 'but I'd thought I might have received a letter.'

Wisting was confused, feeling that they might be speaking at cross-purposes.

'It's safe to say that not everyone will be happy to hear that the case has been taken up again,' Bohrman continued. 'I expected to get some kind of reprimand for having passed on the case papers.'

'You're referring to the killing of Tone Vaterland in 1999?' Wisting asked in order to clarify the situation.

Cristian Bohrman cocked his head quizzically but confirmed that they were talking about the same case. 'I think of it often,' he said. 'I always thought there was something that didn't add up, but never found the right way or the right time to get my teeth into it. It was easier to leave it to someone else, someone with a completely fresh pair of eyes.'

'Who was that?' Wisting asked.

Bohrman pursed his lips. 'Sorry,' he said. 'I just took it for granted that this was why you were here. That the journalist had got in touch with the police.'

Wisting shook his head. 'That's news to me,' he said. 'I'm here off my own bat. I may have come across information that wasn't brought to the attention of the original investigation, and that may well cast the case in a different light. I wanted to hear from you how it might fit into the picture you have of the inquiry. You're probably the one who knows it best.'

Bohrman sat up straighter. 'What information?' he asked.

'Let me hear about this journalist first,' Wisting said.

'So you haven't spoken to her?'

Wisting shook his head.

'She turned up unannounced at my office,' Bohrman said. 'Ninni Skjevik. Works freelance. I've had several enquiries from other journalists about other cases we've had. They all want to base something on actual cases these days. True crime. They're either going to write books or newspaper articles, or else make podcasts or TV series. But Ninni Skjevik is from hereabouts. She had a personal involvement. I remember her from that time. She was young then and perhaps a bit naïve. The experienced journalists laughed at her when she talked about there being aspects that pointed to Danny's innocence. But she followed the investigation closely and was in court every day. And just like me, she felt the entire time that we didn't get answers to all our questions.'

Somewhere inside the house, a phone rang, and Wisting heard a faint female voice but could not catch what was being said.

'She knew the case inside out,' Bohrman went on. 'We talked through the main points, and then I let her take the documents away with her.'

'The police documents?'

One corner of Bohrman's mouth moved up into a lopsided smile. 'You can call them that,' he replied, 'but they don't belong to the police. She received my copy of the case documents. I had kept them all. Six ring binders.'

Wisting nodded. That corresponded with the six he had at home. The idea that a journalist had gone through the same documents as the ones now in his possession opened up another possibility to help identify the sender of the anonymous letters.

'She phoned me a few times in the following weeks, after I had talked to her,' Bohrman added. 'What has made you take an interest in the case? You didn't work on it in 1999, did you?'

Wisting was not keen to tell him about the anonymous letters but felt forced to give the lawyer some explanation.

'I had a similar case in 2001,' he began. 'A young girl, about Tone Vaterland's age, who was abducted, raped and murdered. The perpetrator was Jan Hansen. Do you know the name?'

'Should I?'

'Jan Hansen died last summer, before he had completed his prison sentence,' Wisting continued. 'It appears he was interviewed as a witness in 1999. He was one of the last people to see Tone Vaterland alive.'

This made Bohrman sit up. 'You're telling me that a witness in the case turned out to be a killer in a similar case, after Danny Momrak had been convicted and sentenced?'

Wisting nodded.

'Is there a description of him?' Bohrman asked.

Wisting did not quite understand the question. 'Not in the documents,' he answered. 'But he was thirty-four at the time, about five nine in height, normal build. When we arrested him, he had cropped blond hair, but that was two years later, of course.'

'What about clothes?' Bohrman asked. 'Did he have a camouflage jacket?'

Now Wisting realized where his question was headed. There had been descriptions from witnesses of several men who had never been identified.

'I don't think that was mentioned in the interview,' he replied. 'I'd have to check.'

Bohrman had picked up a pen and was jotting something down on some spare paper. 'It's not,' he said. 'I would have spotted that.' He made a few notes before raising his eyes. 'What are you going to do now?' he asked.

Wisting shifted in his seat. 'I don't know if there's much more I can do,' he said. 'What I've done so far has been unofficial fact-finding. It must be up to our Head of Investigations as to whether this should become an official inquiry.'

'Sten Kvammen?'

Wisting nodded. 'And now you,' he added.

'Kvammen won't lift a finger,' Bohrman said firmly. 'It would damage his future career. He stands to get a senior post in the Directorate. The appointment process is underway now.'

Wisting agreed, but refrained from comment. There were currently three people in the running for the post, but on paper Kvammen appeared best qualified. He would probably be reluctant to do anything that would place him in an unflattering light.

'What are you planning to do?' Wisting asked.

Bohrman shook his head. 'I'll have to get hold of the journalist,' he replied. 'And hear from her what she's found out. Whether she's come up with something that, along with this, might lead to the case being reinvestigated.'

Wisting prepared to leave. 'You won't get round the fact that Tone Vaterland was found raped and killed with your client's DNA inside her body,' he said.

'We demonstrated in court that the samples could have been contaminated,' was Bohrman's response.

'All the same, it points to Danny Momrak,' Wisting said. 'With the atmosphere and situation the way they were at that time, he would have been convicted regardless,' Bohrman said. 'A positive DNA trace will always point to the perpetrator, while absence of DNA will not exclude him. That is simply explained by saying that the police were unable to find any.'

Wisting passed no comment. In court, it was the task of the defence to establish the probability that their client was not guilty, but for the case to be re-opened, you had to convince the Commission that he was innocent. This demanded far more, not least further fresh information than what had emerged so far, but he had a strong sense that there was more to come.

24

The day's newspaper had gone to press and would soon be on its way out to newsstands and subscribers. She had a splash on the front page about an elderly man in Eidanger whose garden fence had been destroyed by a snowplough. She had also written a piece about a pre-Christmas concert. That was how things were on a small local newspaper – all the minutiae of daily life.

Leaving her office desk, she headed out into the corridor to the editor's office and was called in when she knocked on the door.

Leif Grini stubbed out his cigarette and glanced up at her.

'The verdict in the Danny Momrak case will be delivered tomorrow,' she said, sitting down.

He nodded.

'I've written an opinion piece,' she said, indicating the printout in her hand.

The editor waved her across, keen to have a look. She handed it over.

'Just in case,' she said.

The title was *A Free Man*.

The editor frowned. He had read no more than the first couple of paragraphs by the time he opened his mouth. 'You could have saved yourself the bother,' he said, shaking his head. 'The question is not whether or not Danny Momrak will be convicted, but how many years he'll get.'

In the article, she had highlighted the weaknesses in the investigation and summarized what might lead to a verdict of not guilty. She criticized the police and expressed sympathy for Tone Vaterland's family, left without answers, and for Danny and his family, who had been dragged through the court system with all the strain that must have involved.

Rising from his seat, Leif Grini returned the paper to her without reading to the end.

'In this newspaper we use our working hours to write about what *has* happened,' he said, 'not what we hope or wish to happen. We write about facts, impartially and objectively. You've already made great strides in illuminating various aspects of the case. If this newspaper is going to come out with an opinion on it, then I'm the one who'll do that. I believe Danny Momrak to be guilty. He's a ruthless and cold-blooded killer. That's what I intend to write in the editorial tomorrow, after the verdict comes in.'

25

The rain began again while Wisting was driving home. He swung into the courtyard in front of his house, turned off the engine and sat watching the rivulets of rain trickle down the windscreen.

If Line was coming home tomorrow, he should really water her houseplants.

A sense of expectation took hold as he moved towards the mailbox.

Lifting the lid, he saw the box was half full of promotional leaflets and brochures. He picked up the bundle and noticed the white corner of an envelope. Another letter. His name was inscribed on the envelope in the same slanting letters. No address or stamp.

A few raindrops spattered it, soaking into the paper. He tucked the envelope under the other post and hurried inside.

The envelope contained only a single sheet of paper. It had been crumpled up and then smoothed flat again, just like the other two letters, but this time there were two lines of text. The first was a letter followed by a number, while the other line appeared to be an Internet address.

G-11
L2W.no/vi8

Although curious about what he might find on the Internet, he paused for a moment to look at the letter and number combination. This could be an evidence number. All trace material and potential evidence gathered by the police was registered with sequential numbers. In order to keep track of which material was stored where, the various discovery sites were allocated a letter. All the items marked 'A' were usually from the crime scene, whereas 'B' could be items a suspect had been carrying, 'C' evidence found in the vehicle, 'D' from an apartment, and so on.

The case papers were still on the kitchen table and he managed to locate the relevant report. The letter 'G' stood for everything collected in connection with the autopsy carried out on Tone Vaterland. G-11 was the swab taken at the gynaecological examination.

This was crucial evidence: Danny Momrak's semen sample.

His iPad had almost run out of battery power, so he rushed to key in the first part of the address. L2W.no was a web page that abbreviated lengthy Internet addresses.

He entered the whole address and was transferred to an American website comprising medical news and health information. The article he reached was a discussion of how long sperm could survive inside a woman's body. The life-span depended on the quality of the man's sperm, but investigations had shown that semen cells could survive for up to eight days after intercourse.

Without reading to the end, Wisting pulled out the sheet of paper on which he had drawn a timeline. Tone Vaterland had gone missing on Sunday, 4 July and was found murdered two days later.

He checked the post-mortem report and saw that evidence item G-11 had been taken on Wednesday, 7 July. Three days.

He picked up another folder and skimmed through to find the statement given by the secondary witness. Maria Strand, Tone's best friend, said that Tone had split up with Danny on Friday, 2 July. They had slept together the previous night and then had sex in the shower that morning, making five days. Five days from the last time Tone Vaterland and Danny Momrak had had intercourse until the semen was found.

The DNA trace could have had a totally natural explanation. A possibility that the defence lawyer could not have taken into consideration and which the investigators would have dismissed because it meant the perpetrator who had raped Tone Vaterland had not left any trace behind.

Wisting read through the article again. While sperm cells that ended up on a bed sheet, rug, paper or other places died as soon as they dried out, the damp, warm, dark female vagina was the perfect environment in which to survive. However, even when the cells died, the DNA would still survive. In the same way as the dead skin cells or dead blood cells from which a DNA profile could be obtained.

The screen went dark: the iPad was out of juice. Putting it down, he moved to the bathroom and flipped up the toilet lid. His urine seemed darker than usual, and the pain had returned. A faint burning and stinging sensation, and the itch persisted when he had finished. His GP was on holiday, but on Monday he would have to phone the surgery and speak to one of the other doctors.

The iPad charger was in the living room. Once he had connected it, he sat down with the iPad on his lap.

The numbering of the swab containing Danny Momrak's DNA was a detail that, strictly speaking, was hidden in the case documents. At the same time, it was one of the most central pieces of evidence, and of course it might be possible that the letter and number combination had become fixed in Danny Momrak's memory. Anyone else would need access to the papers in order to make a specific reference.

Ninni Skjevik was not difficult to find online. Now aged thirty-nine, she lived in Oslo. The photos showed a woman with a round face, blue eyes and a straight nose. Her hair fluctuated in length, style and colour. Many of the results were in articles she had written for a variety of media. It seemed she had worked as a freelancer, but for a period it looked as if she had permanent employment at the *Dagbladet* newspaper and later in one of the local offices run by NRK, the state broadcaster. She appeared to cover most topics, but some of the stories she had written had been crime cases. Now, she was obviously working for a TV production company, though he could not find any programmes listed that she had been involved in making. Perhaps Line would know who she was. They were in the same profession and had written for some of the same weeklies and magazines.

What he wanted most of all was to confront her. Her phone number was available online. But apart from asking whether she was the one who had been at his mailbox, he did not have much to say to her. Not yet, at least.

He dismissed the idea and checked the online newspapers. There were no developments in the Agnete Roll case. The body had been forensically examined, but it was too early to state anything about the cause of death.

The local newspaper had a picture from the site of the fire on the evening her body was found, taken after he had left: Maren Dokken in conversation with one of the technicians.

He thought of the camera on the parked car. He had come across similar footage in other cases. These cameras were small and compact, but he had no idea what they cost. He looked them up and saw that they came in all price ranges, the cheapest being about a thousand kroner. If he attached one to his own car, he would be able to film the mailbox.

He came to a sudden decision. The nearest electronics store was open until 8 p.m. By the time he left it, he was carrying a more expensive camera than he had envisaged, but one that possessed all the functions he required. He installed it while still in the car park outside, in case he needed help from someone in the shop. He had been rec-ommended to position it on the right-hand side of the rear-view mirror.

The installation was simple, and the same applied to its use. Footage was stored on a memory card. The operating buttons were on the back of the camera as well as a display on which the recordings could be played.

The camera automatically activated when the car was in motion. In addition, a function ensured that recordings were made if any movement was detected within the radius of the camera while the car was parked. It was recom-mended that this last function be activated to prevent other drivers getting away with causing damage such as rear shunts and side scrapes.

As soon as he began to drive, he noticed there was also a function to give his speed. He drummed his fingers on the steering wheel, happy with both his purchase and the fact that he had managed the installation single-handed.

26

The furniture firm where Jan Hansen had worked still existed, though by now it had moved and expanded. On his drive back from the electronics store, Wisting passed the new premises. Jan Hansen's social circle had been limited. Sometimes he had a colleague helping with deliveries when there were large, heavy items to be transported. The regular helper was a man of Polish origin who had probably been the person who had spent most time with Jan Hansen. The person who knew him best and might be able to say something about how Jan Hansen had been behaving around the time Tone Vaterland was killed. Wisting struggled to remember his name.

He considered calling in at the shop and asking for the man, but instead he turned into the back yard at the police station. Numerous staff cars were still parked there, as well as police vehicles from other stations, most likely belonging to personnel brought in to assist with the murder investigation.

At the staff entrance, he swiped his pass and tapped in the code. From there, he walked through the basement corridors to the archives and took out the old case.

Adam Dudek was the name he was looking for. Jan Hansen had been interviewed as a witness in the missing-person case in 1999. This should have been something they had both talked about in the cabin of the delivery van, something that would ensure Dudek remembered the episode.

He contemplated bringing all the old case files with him, but instead contented himself with taking a photo of the report containing the name and contact details for the Polish assistant.

Wisting had hoped to avoid meeting anyone, but on his way back he heard a door open behind him, followed by Maren Dokken shouting his name.

Turning on his heel, he took a couple of steps towards her. 'I heard the post-mortem was completed,' he said before she had a chance to ask what he was doing there. 'Could they say anything about the cause of death?'

'She had head wounds,' Maren answered. 'Probably from repeated blows.'

'Have you made any further progress?'

Maren shook her head. 'Not really,' she replied. 'But I may have discovered where Erik Roll was during the time missing from the footage.'

'Where, then?'

'We've specific teledata from Agnete's mobile, but not for Erik Roll. So far, he's not officially suspected of anything. But we do have teledata from all the phone traffic in the area, including his phone use.'

Wisting nodded. This was standard routine in any investigation into serious crime. The traffic data from the telecoms companies could tell them who had been inside the relevant area at the time the crime was committed.

'We see that on Saturday, Erik Roll starts to phone round mutual friends and acquaintances to ask after Agnete, as he has stated. I've gone through the list. One of the people he calls is Benedikte Lindhjem. Agnete has not been in touch with her by phone, at least not in the course of the past three months for which we have an overview, and neither have they made contact on Facebook or other social media. There's no reason for Erik Roll to believe she might know anything about where his wife is.'

'Great work,' Wisting commented, but he appreciated there was more to come.

'It appears Benedikte Lindhjem and Erik Roll are work colleagues,' Maren continued. 'She's a year younger than him and was divorced two years ago, but the most interesting thing is that she lives along the stretch between Stavern town centre and the spot where the dash-cam footage was taken.'

'He could have dropped in on her on his way home, then,' Wisting suggested.

Maren Dokken nodded. 'We can't be sure there's anything in it, but I'm on my way out to talk to her now.'

Wisting headed for his car and drove home, where he reversed into his driveway and parked slightly at an angle to ensure that the mailbox was in the centre of the camera image. He checked the mailbox, but it was empty.

The rest of the evening he spent in front of the TV. He began watching a film, but had trouble following the sequence of events and ended up channel hopping until he landed on a programme about a mortgage company in Las Vegas. This was followed by a historical documentary about George Washington. When it finished, he took it into his head to check the step counter on his phone. It had registered 3,616. He wondered how the device actually worked – the phone must use the inbuilt GPS in some way.

He gave some thought to going out for a walk, but decided the hour was too late.

Before bed, he checked the mailbox one more time and made sure that the camera was functioning. When he turned in for the night, he lay reluctantly listening to sounds from outside. Around midnight, the rain increased in intensity. At quarter to one, he paid a visit to the toilet. The time was 01.23 the last time he glanced at the clock on his bedside table.

27

Wisting woke with a tickle in his throat. The air in the room was chilly, and his chest felt tight. It was much later than he had thought – almost nine.

Coughing, he got out of bed, only to realize how cold the floor was. The bedroom curtain was fluttering in the draught. Outside, the weather was dry but still bleak.

He closed the window and padded barefoot out to the bathroom. It was still painful when he passed water, but not as bad as the day before. As soon as he had completed his ablutions, he got dressed and went outside.

The mailbox was empty.

Clambering into the car, he started the engine and checked the footage while the vehicle was idling, as recommended to prevent depletion of the camera battery.

The device had worked. At 00.32, a cat drenched by the rain had run across the road. In night mode, the recordings lacked colour and the cat became grey. One hour later, it was back in the picture.

At 03.37, a car appeared, entering from the left of the image. It drove past and continued down the street. Wisting played the recording one more time before shifting his gaze and looking out through the windscreen in the direction the car had travelled. A group of trees blocked his view.

As he stepped out of the car, he peered down towards Line's house. It had been her car. She had come home in the middle of the night.

His mind was filled with worried thoughts. The last ferry across the Oslo Fjord left just before midnight. She could not have taken that one. She must have driven the long way round or travelled through the tunnel. Something must have happened to make her unwilling to wait and to leave the cabin in the small hours. He wondered whether he should go down to see her, but she was almost certainly fast asleep.

There were three more recordings, all of seagulls at the crack of dawn, flying from the south and perching on fence posts before flapping their wings onwards.

Back in the kitchen, he was shivering with cold and had to pull on a sweater. Although he did not feel like coffee, he made a cup all the same and drank it while on his feet reading the online newspapers. There was nothing new. Even the weather was forecast to continue unchanged.

In case Line decided to drop in, he packed away the old documents from the Danny Momrak case. Afterwards, he felt exhausted. His plan had been to pay a visit to Adam Dudek at some point that day to find out if he had anything to tell him about Jan Hansen from the summer of 1999, when they travelled together in the delivery van. Instead he went into the living room and stretched out on the settee. He lay there reflecting that he had forgotten to water Line's houseplants. His whole body ached. He turned over, put his hand on his forehead and realized it felt hot and feverish. It could be a reaction to something he had eaten, or else he was coming down with a cold. He drew up the blanket that was draped over the armrest and tucked himself in.

He must have dozed off because a noise at the front door woke him abruptly. Little childish footsteps came toddling across the floor.

'Grandpa!'

Swinging his legs off the settee, he staggered to his feet and ran a hand through his hair.

'Hello there!' he shouted, taking hold of her. 'Are you back home again already?'

'Yes!'

Line followed after her. Wisting glanced at the clock and saw it was nearly noon. He had slept for two hours. 'When did you get back?' he asked.

'Early,' Line replied. 'Amalie wakes before seven. There was no need to drag things out.'

Wisting wondered whether to ask her why she came home early, but decided to drop the idea. Whatever had happened was none of his business. 'How did it go?' he asked instead.

Line came closer and held up a bottle of Calvados. 'We made a trip across the border into Sweden,' she said. 'I bought one of these for you.'

Apple brandy, aged in oak barrels. He took the bottle with a smile and a thank you.

Line stood looking at him. 'Aren't you well?' she asked. 'You look pale.'

'I might have a summer cold brewing,' Wisting replied.

Amalie was showing off a graze she had on her knee.

'I don't want her to catch it,' Line said.

'No, of course not,' Wisting said. He realized he now had a headache as well.

Line reached her hand out to her daughter. 'I really came to pick up my post,' she said.

'It's lying through in the kitchen,' Wisting told her. 'Have the houseplants survived? I was meaning to water them today.'

'I think they're OK,' Line said.

Wisting accompanied her into the kitchen. Line found the bag in which he had collected her mail.

'Do you know anything more about that Roll woman?' she asked. 'I heard she'd been found.'

'I went out there,' Wisting replied.

'Are you not supposed to be on holiday?'

'I was out for a drive and just called in to the site of the fire.' Setting the bottle down on the kitchen table, he rested one hand on the back of a chair. 'I had responsibility for the first fire,' he explained. 'When I went there on Wednesday evening, they'd just found her in the midst of the ruins.'

'Murdered?'

Wisting smiled. It was easier to talk to Line about such things now that she was no longer a reporter working for *VG*.

'I don't know much more than what I read in the newspapers,' he replied. 'But everything points to the corpse having been placed there and the fire set to hide the tracks.'

'It must be her husband,' Line said.

Wisting shrugged. Line took Amalie and headed for the door. 'Let me know if you need anything,' she said.

He went with them to the front door. 'By the way, do you know a journalist called Ninni Skjevik?' he asked.

'I know who she is,' Line told him. 'Why do you ask?'

Wisting put his hand to his brow and felt how clammy it was. 'She's sent an enquiry about an old case,' he explained. That was probably not far from the truth. 'I just wondered whether she was competent. Whether she can be trusted, if you understand what I mean.'

'What case was that?'

'I'm not entirely sure what she wants,' Wisting answered. 'It's about the murder of Pernille Skjerven in 2001.'

'Jan Hansen,' Line said. 'What about it?'

'I think she just wants to take a look at it, to see if it's a case she can make something out of. True crime. There are so many enquiries like that now.'

'I see,' said Line. 'I don't know her personally, but I can ask around about what she's done in the past.'

Wisting shook his head. 'Don't give it another thought. Anyway, as you said, I'm still on holiday.'

28

Wisting spent the rest of the day lying on the settee. Occasionally he got up to fetch some documents from the Momrak case files to find answers to questions as they crossed his mind.

He did not eat anything, apart from taking paracetamol. Now and then he felt a stabbing pain in the pit of his stomach, reinforcing his suspicion that he might have food poisoning. He had eaten an old pork chop, but that had been a couple of days ago. It was more likely to have been the hamburger from the Bamble Snack Shack. He was unused to eating that kind of food, and his stomach had become more delicate with age.

In the evening, he tried to watch some TV. Just before *Dagsrevyen*, the news round-up, he received a text message from Line to say that she had sent him an email about Ninni Skjevik.

He opened it right away. The subject was *Ninni Skjevik and true crime*, and it contained a collection of articles she had written. Line paid for access to a media archive comprising Norwegian and Nordic newspapers and magazines. This provided a completely different range of material from what he could find online for himself. She had downloaded several of them, but also included a link to a TV documentary on the Discovery streaming service. She had also sent her user name and password so that he could log in, and added a personal opinion: *Well made*.

Wisting stretched out on the settee, playing the programme on his iPad. It was part of a documentary series that sought out people, environments and places to which the majority had no access. He had seen some of these programmes when they were shown on TV. On the Internet, all the stories had been collected into an archive.

This episode was a few years old and featured the interior of Ullersmo Prison. Wisting sat up in surprise. Both Danny Momrak and Jan Hansen had been behind bars there around the time the programme was made. The blurb said that it took the viewers not only inside the jail but also into the minds of the inmates. Ninni Skjevik was listed as production manager. Wisting had no idea what this job actually entailed, but it meant she was somewhere behind the cameras.

It was the regular male presenter who brought the camera team into the prison to meet various inmates. Some of them appeared under their full names and allowed themselves to be filmed, whereas others were blacked out.

Ten minutes into the programme, he appeared, his face blurred when seen from the front. In the strapline beneath the picture, he was called *Dag (33). Sentence: 17 years.*

Dan Vidar Momrak. It had to be him.

This opened up fresh possibilities. Ninni Skjevik had met Danny Momrak in prison.

He worked as a trusty. That was the name given to inmates who helped the prison guards with a variety of tasks, including cleaning duties. In this scene, he was tidying and cleaning a visitors' room after a fellow prisoner had met his family there. He himself seldom received visitors. His mother had neither a car nor a driving licence, and came only once or twice a year.

Throughout the fifty minutes, inmates told their stories. The interviews were balanced and drew out several aspects of serving a prison sentence. The prisoners explained what they had done and talked about their lives under lock and key, touching on loss, regret, hopes and dreams. The conversations with Danny Momrak were different, however. He said nothing about guilt or innocence, and there was a continual undertone of bitterness as he spoke. Towards the end he put this into words: *'Helplessness has almost overpowered me, but the grudge I hold has kept me going.'*

It was possible to see him lower his blurred head, eyes downcast.

'Grudge is an insufficient word,' he continued. *'What I feel is even more intense. Hate is maybe more correct. Hatred towards everything and everyone who has destroyed my life, including myself.'*

Wisting struggled to interpret what he had said in light of what he knew. Deep feelings of hatred arose when someone was subjected to gross injustice, but this was an isolated statement plucked out of what had undoubtedly been hours of footage. It was difficult to know whether anything more lay behind it.

Jan Hansen did not take part in the programme. Even though he and Danny Momrak were serving sentences in the same prison, it was far from certain that they were in the same section. They might not even know of each other.

Feeling too warm, he pulled off the blanket but continued to lie there, contemplating what he had seen. Theories were forming, the most intriguing of which was that Ninni Sjevik could have met both Danny Momrak and Jan Hansen while they were scouting for prospective candidates to participate. Perhaps had even checked them out and interviewed them, gaining insight and knowledge of the crimes for which they had been imprisoned, and spotted the kind of opportunities that opened up for her.

Very quickly, he began to feel cold and shivery and had to wrap himself in the blanket again. This was how he spent the rest of the evening, feeling alternately hot and cold, but lacking the usual symptoms of a cold.

Around 11 p.m., he went out to check his mailbox again, but found it empty. He made sure that the dashboard camera was still functioning and let the car engine run for a few minutes.

There was an even more expensive version of the camera with a wifi connection, affording the opportunity to sit at home and watch the recordings or even live footage, and now he regretted not having forked out an extra few thousand kroner on that.

Wisting spent most of the next day in bed. The online newspapers reported that the police were making fresh investigations in Agnete Roll's house. Maren Dokken was pictured in one of the accompanying photographs, standing outside in the company of two white-clad crime-scene technicians.

By chance, he noticed the post arrive at twenty minutes past eleven. He was in the kitchen when the red van stopped in the street outside. As soon as it had driven off, he went out.

There was a letter in addition to two promotional leaflets. It appeared formal, a window envelope with his name and address that had clearly passed through a franking machine. No sender given. As well as the frank, it had a blue sticker emblazoned with the word *Priority*. Wisting had thought these were only used for letters sent from abroad. This must be something really urgent.

He waited until he was inside the house to open the letter. It was from the Police Privacy Protection Service. Wisting had not even known that such a service existed. It was a warning concerning a discrepancy registered.

The Police Service has received a report that you have conducted a search in the central data records likely to be in contravention of the law relating to access to information held in police records. Searches in the central police records may be undertaken only on the basis of the requirements of police duties and for the purposes covered by the law. Use in contravention of the rules will, following a specific evaluation, be considered a breach of official duties, cf Criminal Law §171, punishable by fines or imprisonment for up to two years.

Wisting blinked, screwing his eyes up tight before opening them again. He was flooded with irritation. The accusation that he may have done something to contravene the law sat like a lump in the pit of his stomach, a heavy queasiness. It was not spelled out in black and white, but this of course referred to the searches he had undertaken into Danny Momrak. Blinking again, he stood open-mouthed as he read on.

Your access to the central data registers has been suspended. You must make contact with your line manager if you require future authorization.

He put down the sheet of paper.

The rules for use of the records were rigid, but they were intended to prevent searches on colleagues, family, friends and acquaintances, or on celebrities. Before the use of the registers had been given a separate legal framework, he himself had searched the criminal records for one of Line's boyfriends and used the population register to find addresses of distant relatives, but this was not about that sort of thing.

The letter was signed by Eva Styrk, whose title was given as legal adviser. From the text at the foot of the page, he learned that the Privacy Protection Service was an organization under the auspices of Kripos, a section in their jurisdiction intended to maintain, quality-assure and supervise the various data registers. The letter bore all the hallmarks of a standard response, but Wisting doubted it had come as a result of routine enquiries. It had come from someone who did not want him to take a closer look at the case against Danny Momrak. If that were true, then the warning had worked against its intention. He now had a stronger suspicion that not everything in the case would bear close scrutiny. And the person with the greatest interest in keeping it under wraps was the former senior investigating officer, Sten Kvammen.

Folding the letter, he returned it to the envelope, aware that it had simply bolstered his motivation.

29

On Sunday, Wisting was feeling a little better. However, he had been up twice during the night, equally painful both times. He would phone the GP surgery the next day and request an appointment.

The weather forecast proved correct. The temperature fell a few degrees further and the summer's day continued in the shadow of rainclouds. Wisting spent his time going through the case against Danny Momrak once again. Murder cases were often named after the victim or the place where the crime had been committed. He had begun to think of the papers he had before him as 'the Momrak case'. Tomorrow morning, he would drive to work and send them back to the archives at the police station in Skien. If anything were to come of his investigations, he would instead have to go through formal channels and re-apply for the documents.

He could find no specific fault in the investigation material from 1999, but he was now reading with different eyes from when he had done so for the first time. In the light of what he had experienced in the past few days, it was easy for him to see that the work had been one-sided. The defence lawyer was right. Everything that had been undertaken in the inquiry had been directed at Danny Momrak. The investigators had not considered any other possibilities.

This made him think of Antonia Kleiser, the old

woman who had been burnt to death in her own bedroom. She had been found on the floor, immediately in front of the door, and had obviously tried to find her way out. The door was closed but not locked. And even though she had lived in that house for almost all her adult life, panic had blinded her to the fact that the door opened inwards. In desperation, she must have fought to push it open and get out.

The doorbell rang. Wisting got to his feet and glanced at the kitchen window. A silver estate car was parked in the street.

He was not expecting visitors. Instantly, he collected up the case papers and returned them to the box. The doorbell rang again. 'I'm coming!' he called out. He carried the box and deposited it in a cupboard in the hallway before opening the front door.

A woman stood outside, her hair soaked with rain. There was something familiar about her face, but he could not quite place her. She greeted him with a smile and a bright 'Hello!' as she held out her hand.

'I'm Ninni Skjevik,' she introduced herself. 'I'm a journalist working on a documentary about an old murder case.'

Wisting was lost for words.

'I got your name from Cristian Bohrman, the defence lawyer,' she went on. 'But no phone number. Apologies for calling in on a Sunday, but I have a few questions. Mainly out of self-interest, and in the first instance simply to gain some clarity on things.'

'I see,' Wisting said. He had some questions himself. 'Come in.'

Ninni Skjevik did not move. 'Is it OK if I bring my camera?' she asked.

Wisting peered above her head to her car. 'Let's have a chat first,' he said.

'Fine,' she replied. 'I just had to ask.'

He ushered her through the house and into the kitchen, where he drew out a chair opposite his usual place at the table.

'Coffee?' he suggested.

'Yes, please,' was her response.

Wisting took out cups and capsules for the coffee machine. Ninni Skjevik produced a notebook from her bag while the machine rumbled and did its work.

'Bohrman said you'd come across some interesting information,' she said.

Wisting pushed one cup across to her. He was loth to be the one who began the conversation, but assumed that Bohrman had passed on everything he had said.

'It could be just a coincidence,' he said. 'I had a case in 2001 with many similarities to the murder of Tone Vaterland. It seems the perpetrator in my case is registered as a witness in the Vaterland inquiry. He was a customer at the Bamble Snack Shack around the time she left.'

'Jan Hansen,' Ninni Skjevik pre-empted him.

Wisting nodded. 'I thought it might be worth taking a closer look, but we're not talking about a new investigation. Not an official investigation, at least.'

'What have you found out?'

'Actually, no more than that. I've talked to Bohrman and one of the investigators from 1999.'

'Kvammen?'

'Yes.'

'What's your opinion on the case?' Ninni Skjevik went on to ask. 'Do you think the evidence is sufficient?'

'They did conduct two court cases,' Wisting commented. As he drank his coffee, he realized this answer was not good enough for her.

'I'm from Bamble,' she said. 'I wrote about the case for the local newspaper in 1999. I followed the investigation and the trial, and spoke to people other than the ones the police interviewed. During the trial, the impression was given that Momrak was hot-headed, violent and sex-obsessed. No one asked why Tone had fallen in love with him. No one said anything about her thinking he was good, kind and easy-going, the sides of him that made him her first boyfriend. Everyone had turned against him and highlighted only the negative aspects of his character. The ones that suited the impression of a monster.'

'There was also technical evidence,' Wisting pointed out. 'He lied at interview and changed his statement.'

Ninni Skjevik said she did not disagree. 'But every single scrap of evidence can be explained differently,' she said.

'Explained away,' Wisting emphasized. 'The defence lawyer tried to do that in court.'

'No one was listening,' Ninni Skjevik said. 'There was neither the will nor the atmosphere to examine other solutions. At that time, everyone was focused on holding someone responsible. Society demanded revenge, balance had to be restored.'

Wisting said nothing more. The evidence was no different now, but Ninni Skjevik was right. Time had healed many wounds. Emotions had been set aside, and it was easier to see things clearly. Twenty years ago, confidence in the police, the prosecution authorities and the judicial system had been greater. Since 1999, there had been many examples of miscarriage of justice. The notion that mistakes had been made was easier to accept today.

'And even though the defence lawyer advanced alternative explanations, he lacked someone else to point the finger at,' Ninni Skjevik added. 'He did not come up with an alternative killer.'

'Jan Hansen,' Wisting said.

Ninni Skjevik sighed, looked down at the table and shook her head. 'He doesn't fit into my picture,' she said.

'No?'

The woman on the other side of the table put her cup to her mouth for the first time. She drank and then stared thoughtfully into it when she put it back down again.

'I lost my mother just after the trial,' she began. 'Three years later, I moved away from Bamble. By then people had stopped talking about the murder. Danny and Tone had been forgotten by most people.'

She stopped, as if unsure of how to continue.

'But not by you?' Wisting suggested.

'Yes, in fact. But Tone Vaterland's grave is just across from where my mother is buried. I have to walk past it every time I fetch water. I'm not there as often as I should be, but it has served as a constant reminder.'

She took another sip.

'The grave has always been beautifully tended, and is to this day,' she went on. 'Once I got in touch with her parents with a view to an article, about sorrow and loss and suchlike, but they weren't interested.'

Wisting let her talk without interruption.

'Now and then, when I'm in Bamble, I meet up with old friends. You know, catch up with the news. A bit of gossip. Who's left whom and that sort of thing. Last summer they were talking about the Kronborg girl, Janne. I don't really know how it came up, but probably because the brother of one of the girls had bought the house where she grew up. Her father had dementia and ended up in a care home, and her mother moved to an apartment. Anyway, I knew that Janne had taken her own life. That was in 2001. She was only seventeen. But I had no idea why. Now I learned that she had been raped a couple of years earlier, and that had been the reason.'

The story began to take on a shape that piqued Wisting's curiosity. 'A couple of years earlier?' he asked.

'In 1999,' Ninni Skjevik confirmed. 'They said it had been an American boy, an eighteen-year-old, here as part of an exchange programme organized by the Lions Club. Janne's father was president of the local branch. In the summer of 1999, they had a boy staying with them. He was to go to Norwegian school and live with them for a year, but all of a sudden he was sent home. Everything was obviously hushed up, but it was apparently because he had raped Janne. It wasn't reported or anything. They just packed him off back to the USA. What made me interested was that it happened the same day that Tone Vaterland disappeared.'

'The fourth of July,' Wisting said.

'Yes, or what I know is that he was picked up the next day and put on the first plane home,' Ninni Skjevik clarified. 'The rape took place the night before that.'

Wisting mentally inserted that information into the timeline. 'Would it be likely that he first raped and killed Tone Vaterland and then raped the daughter in the house only a few hours later?'

'It was never really established that Tone Vaterland had

been raped,' Ninni objected. 'She did have some minor injuries in the pubic area, but the conclusion was based on the fact that she was naked when she was found.'

'And the DNA evidence,' Wisting pointed out.

Ninni Skjevik smiled. 'Only if we can trust the analyses,' she said.

Wisting refrained from commenting that the DNA trace could also be explained in a simpler way, given that Danny Momrak was the last person to have sex with Tone Vaterland.

'But anyway, there's reason to believe it was a sexually motivated murder,' Ninni Skjevik continued. 'What if the American hadn't been able to get what he wanted with Tone Vaterland, but went home and finished it off there?'

Wisting was sceptical. 'There's a lot of ifs and buts in that theory,' he said.

'Well, in any case, that was what persuaded me to take a closer look at it,' Ninni Skjevik continued. 'I have an uncle who's in the same Lions Club as Terje Kronborg. Not then, but now. I got some help from him to investigate and had it all confirmed.'

She took a poly pocket from her folder. 'The American boy's name was Curtis Blair,' she said, producing what looked like a copy of the minutes of a meeting.

Wisting drew it towards him. It was recorded that the committee had met after receiving a report that Curtis Blair had behaved in an absolutely reprehensible way and in complete contravention of the organization's statutory objectives. It was out of the question to transfer him to another Norwegian host family, and after making contact with their sister organization in Connecticut it was agreed that he should be returned to his homeland as soon as possible.

The committee had therefore approved payment of 7,500 kroner for a flight ticket, and a named committee member had made sure he was taken to Gardermoen Airport.

'My uncle spoke to the man who had driven Curtis Blair to the airport,' Ninni added. 'What had happened became a kind of open secret within the club.'

Wisting was about to say something about how little she had to go on, and how flimsy her grounds for suspicion of the American exchange student actually were.

'I've managed to get hold of some photos,' Ninni said before Wisting had a chance to speak. 'They were taken at a sort of welcoming party when Curtis Blair arrived in Bamble, but they were never published anywhere.'

She took one of them out of the plastic folder and placed it in front of Wisting. It had been taken outdoors in early spring. The trees were bare. Several men and women, adults as well as children, were gathered around a bonfire, barbecuing sausages on sticks.

'That's Janne Kronborg,' Ninni said, placing her forefinger on a fair-haired girl standing with a soda bottle in her hand.

Moving her finger, she pointed out a slightly older boy wearing a jacket with green and brown patches on it. 'That's Curtis Blair.'

Wisting sat bolt upright, staring at him, before stating the obvious: 'Camouflage jacket.'

'It belonged to Janne's brother,' Ninni told him. 'He borrowed it frequently.'

She put down several more pictures, all taken at the same get-together. In one of them, Curtis Blair stood holding a camera with a long lens. 'He was interested in photography,' she said. 'He brought his equipment with him and took photos of the Norwegian landscape and wildlife. Animals and birds.'

Wisting nodded thoughtfully. 'It would have been useful for the police to have known this at the time,' he said. 'But I doubt whether it would have helped Danny Momrak. They could have checked out some of the witness statements, so that his lawyer had less to argue about in court. But it would not have set him free.'

Ninni Skjevik picked up the photographs. 'I know that,' she said.

Wisting's thoughts turned to the documentary filmed at Ullersmo Prison. 'Have you spoken to Danny Momrak about this?' he asked.

She looked across at him in surprise, as if unsure of what to say. The response was hesitant. 'I met him some time ago,' she admitted. 'We were in the prison, making a documentary.'

'Before you found out about the American boy?'

'Oh, yes, a long time before that,' Ninni said, nodding emphatically.

'Did you discuss his case?'

'Yes, but we didn't focus on that in the programme. That had more to do with the actual sentence. But I had to tell him I had written about the case and had been at the trial.'

'What did he say?'

'He said he hadn't done it, but nearly all the prisoners we interviewed in the jail claimed to be innocent. It was cut, out of respect to the victims, but mostly because it wasn't relevant.'

Wisting fixed his eyes on hers. 'Have you met Jan Hansen?' he asked.

She shook her head. 'I hadn't heard his name before yesterday.' She looked away. 'I've certainly read his interview, but there can't have been anything in it that attracted my attention.'

'He served time at Ullersmo,' Wisting said. 'He was there when you met the inmates.'

Her eyebrows shot up. 'I understood he was dead now,' she said.

Wisting agreed. 'What have you done with the information about Curtis Blair?' he asked.

Ninni Skjevik leaned back in her chair. 'I've tried to get hold of him,' she replied. 'I want to hear what he has to say, but it hasn't been easy. I haven't managed to track him down.'

She rummaged in her bag again and took out a copy of a newspaper cutting. 'All I actually know about him is this,' she said. 'It's from an old membership magazine. He and five other teenagers who took part in the exchange programme were introduced.'

She gave a loud sigh. 'To get any further, maybe I'll have to travel to the USA.'

'What next steps do you intend to take?' Wisting asked. 'Apart from travelling to the USA?'

Ninni Skjevik shut her notebook and placed her pen on top of it. 'We're in the pre-production phase,' she answered. 'Progress depends entirely on selling the project to a TV company. A couple have already expressed interest. The aim is not to show that Danny is innocent, but to demonstrate the existence of deficiencies in the investigation. Circumstances that should have been followed up to ensure Danny Momrak received a fair trial. We hope to make a start sometime this autumn. The plan is to reconstruct the chain of events and interview the people involved at that time.'

She picked up her pen again. 'What about you?' she asked. 'Would you be willing to take part and tell us about Jan Hansen?'

Rising from his seat, Wisting carried his cup to the worktop and put it in the washing-up bowl as a signal that he regarded the visit over.

'It won't be just up to me,' he replied, aware this was something he would prefer to avoid. 'I'll need to get back to you later.'

Ninni Skjevik also got to her feet. 'I'm staying at my father's in Bamble this summer while I work on the story,' she said. 'When do you think you'll know anything more?'

'Not until after the holidays at least,' was Wisting's gruff response.

30

It was almost five when Ninni Skjevik left. The clipping with the picture and description of Curtis Blair was left on the kitchen table. Wisting sat down to study it and ruminate on what he had discovered.

Ten minutes later, Line and Amalie arrived. Amalie raced into the living room and made a beeline for the toy box while Line stood leaning against the doorframe.

'Are you well now?' she asked.

Wisting put the news cutting in a drawer alongside the letter from the Privacy Protection Service.

'Much better, at least,' he replied.

'I was wondering if you could take Amalie for a few hours. I have to go to Oslo.'

'Now?'

'Yes,' Line said. 'I need to talk to Cederik. Without her in tow,' she added with a nod in her daughter's direction.

Wisting felt some stirrings of concern. 'Aren't things going too smoothly?' he asked.

She shook her head. 'I'm going to pick up the rest of my things.'

'Of course she can stay here,' he said. 'But it's already late. She will have to stay the night.'

'That would be great, if you can manage it. Did you have a visitor?' she asked.

'It was that journalist,' Wisting replied.

'What did she want?'

'It had to do with a documentary series. It's at a prelim-inary stage.'

'Did she need to come to see you at home? It's a Sunday and, in any case, you're on holiday.'

Amalie toddled in from the living room with a little horse figure, making it gallop between her fingers and ride onwards across the kitchen table.

'Do you ever talk to her father?' Wisting asked, casting a glance at Amalie.

Line followed his eye. Wisting could see that she didn't like the question. Amalie's father was John Bantam, who worked with the FBI and lived in Minneapolis. One of Wisting's cases with links to the USA had brought him and two colleagues to Norway and Larvik. As far as Wist-ing had understood, the short-lived relationship had not meant much to either of them. Neither was keen to cross the Atlantic, and they had parted on an agreement that Amalie's father would not share in her upbringing.

'No,' Line answered. 'Why do you ask?'

Wisting shook his head. He knew they had been in spor-adic contact.

'Apologies,' he said. 'I didn't mean it like that. It's just that I'm trying to find an American who was in Norway nearly twenty years ago.'

'Who is it?'

'A possible witness who was never interviewed,' Wisting replied.

'In the murder of Pernille Skjerven?' Line asked. 'Is this something that journalist came up with?'

Wisting nodded. 'He was apparently on an exchange programme,' he answered, without explaining the details.

'Can't you ask Maggie Griffin?' Line suggested.

That thought had already crossed Wisting's mind. She was the one who had led the FBI team and the one with whom he had worked most closely. 'Good idea,' he said.

'Do you need anything?' Line asked, gesturing towards her daughter. 'She's just had dinner.'

'No, we'll be fine,' Wisting reassured her.

Line thanked him, said cheerio to Amalie and disappeared out the door.

Wisting took out his laptop. He had kept in contact with Maggie, and she had invited him several times to come over on a visit – before this summer he had been on the point of accepting. She had been transferred twice since her spell in Norway, and now she worked at the New York branch. She wouldn't be in the office until the next morning, but she would pick it up then.

He began writing an email, making it clear that his approach concerned preliminary enquiries in connection with a 1999 homicide. His information was limited, but he knew that Curtis Blair had been eighteen in 1999. In the clipping with the boy's picture in the members' magazine, it stated that he hailed from Waterbury in Connecticut. That should be sufficient to allow Maggie to trace him.

One of the things Amalie enjoyed most was building tall towers of wooden bricks from her toy box, only to knock them down again. They kept this up for half an hour before she demanded that he read to her. She sat in front of the TV with two slices of bread and butter and, by 9 p.m., she was fast asleep. Wisting carried her to bed in what had been Line's bedroom.

The most prominent stories in the online newspapers had to do with the weather. Apparently summer would return in seven days' time.

At half past ten he checked on Amalie before heading outside. The weather was dry but cold.

He looked down towards Line's house but saw that her car was still gone. If she intended just to drive to and from Oslo, she should be back soon.

He thought about the email he'd sent Maggie. Even if she had picked it up, it would be optimistic to expect an answer so soon. Besides, what he had asked her to do, strictly speaking, was something for which he himself had already received a written warning. Snooping in the registers.

He checked anyway. He had received a reply.

Call me, she wrote. Nothing else.

He gathered that she had found something but was reluctant to send a written response. Formal rules were in place for the exchange of information across national borders. Wisting had already broken them.

In his head, he calculated that it would be nearly 6 p.m. in New York. He went into the bathroom, took a hard look at himself in the mirror and saw that he should have shaved.

On previous occasions when they had talked, they had used Skype because the cost of ordinary phone calls between the USA and Norway was exorbitant.

As he sat down at his laptop to make the connection, he appreciated how glad he was to see her. Her eyes radiated warmth and it felt good to be on the receiving end of her friendliness. She had the same hairstyle, short dark hair with soft curls, and the same genial smile.

'Hi,' she greeted him. 'Great to see you. How are you?'

'Fine,' he replied. 'What about you?'

'Good, thanks, it's busy. Mostly routine work.'

They made a few more polite exchanges, with Wisting

telling her about the weather and her telling him about a heatwave.

'I think I've found the person you asked about,' she said. 'What kind of case are we talking about?'

Wisting explained about the two cases, without mentioning the anonymous letters sent to him.

Her smile vanished. Instead, a worried frown appeared on her smooth forehead.

'The Curtis Blair I've found is in Hartford Correctional Center,' she said.

'Correctional Center?' Wisting repeated.

'In prison,' Maggie explained. 'He was convicted of homicide.'

Leaning closer to the screen, Wisting took a sharp intake of breath. 'What sort of homicide?'

'I don't have any details, but it happened fourteen years ago.'

The idea had lain dormant. This was what had made him get in touch with Maggie. Curtis Blair had raped once and got away with it. He could have done so again.

'Are you certain it's him?' he asked.

'I need a few details to verify it, but then it will have to go through official channels. Will that be a problem?'

'I don't know,' Wisting replied. 'I don't quite know how to move on with this.'

31

Wisting began the day by calling the GP surgery. Luckily, they could fit him in that morning, and asked him to prepare a urine sample.

When Amalie woke, he took her out into the back garden, where some strawberry plants grew. He had been keeping an eye on them and thought some would be ready to eat. They picked a few of the best ones. Mashing them up with sugar in a dish, he divided the resulting mixture on two bread rolls he had thawed in the microwave. Amalie devoured both. Wisting wanted to ask her about her mother's boyfriend, but let the idea drop.

Once they had cleared the table, he went outside and looked in the mailbox. Empty.

Line's car was parked in her driveway. Wisting sat in his own car and scrolled through the footage on the dashboard camera. She had not arrived home until almost 2 a.m.

Switching the camera to record mode again, he went back inside. After an hour or so, Line came to collect Amalie.

'Is it all over?' he asked.

She seemed annoyed that he had asked. 'I don't know for sure,' she said.

He was keen to ask more questions, in that case, about what this meant with regard to her job. Line was not a permanent employee, while Cederik Smith had a senior post.

Wisting hated to see her unhappy, but at the same time it meant he no longer had to worry that she and Amalie might move away.

When he was on his own again, he moved to the bathroom and got himself ready for his doctor's appointment.

The locum was a young woman and, after twenty minutes with her, she was able to tell him that his urine sample showed an infection.

'Cystitis?' he asked. 'I didn't think men could get that.'

'It's rare,' the doctor replied, going on to say that a course of antibiotics would most probably have him well again by the end of a week.

Wisting was relieved. He had googled the symptoms and found the worst possible causes on the Internet. 'How did I get it?' he wanted to know.

'It's bacterial,' the doctor replied. 'It can be transmitted by sexual intercourse.'

Although he nodded, Wisting knew that could not possibly be the reason in his case.

'There could also be underlying illnesses,' she went on. 'Is it long since you had your prostate checked?'

'Yes.' The truth was that he never had.

The examination was quickly over and done with. 'Completely normal,' was the conclusion.

Wisting sat down again.

'If the antibiotic doesn't work, you must come back and get a referral for a bladder scan,' the doctor went on. 'It might also be a good idea to empty the bladder with the use of a catheter, to see if there is any residual urine.'

She turned to the computer screen. 'You can have a sick note,' she said.

'It's OK,' Wisting replied. 'I'm on holiday.'

'You work in the police,' the doctor said. 'A state employee. You have the right to another holiday period.'

Wisting shook his head. 'As long as I'm healthy for going back to work, that's fine,' he said.

'I'm writing a prescription,' the doctor answered. 'You should notice an improvement in the course of the next couple of days. In a week's time, you'll probably be good as new.'

Wisting thanked her and paid at the card machine.

The GP surgery was located on the first floor of the shopping centre at Fritzøe Brygge. Since there was a pharmacy in the same location, he collected his medicine, bought something to drink and swallowed the first tablet.

His next errand was the police station. Before he drove into town, he had taped up the box containing the Momrak case files and written a return address on it. Bjørg Karin was not in the office, but he put the carton on her desk and scribbled a message on a yellow Post-it note.

Nils Hammer was not in his office either, but Maren Dokken was at her desk. She pushed aside the papers she was working on when he greeted her.

'Are you any closer to a resolution?' Wisting asked.

She smiled. 'I thought you were keeping yourself updated from home,' she said. 'And logging into the computer system from there.'

He shook his head. 'There's something wrong with my login,' he said. That was true, to a certain extent. 'Anyway, I'm really on holiday,' he added.

'Well, it turned out I was right about those twelve minutes missing from the dash-cam footage,' Maren told him. 'He'd been at his colleague's house. Benedikte Lindhjem. I interviewed her. They've had an affair. It was broken off six months ago, but he's visited her a couple of times since. She'd gone to bed when he arrived and just spoke to him through the window.'

'What did he want?'

'To come in. She told him to go home.'

Wisting sat down on the chair opposite her. 'Have you spoken to Erik Roll about that?' he asked.

'Hammer thought we should wait,' Maren replied. 'It's a possible motive. That his wife stood in the way of another relationship.'

'The most usual route in that case is to get a divorce,' Wisting commented.

'All the same, I think it's right to wait,' Maren said. 'Until we have more evidence against him.'

'You have the missing petrol can,' Wisting pointed out.

Maren agreed. 'We haven't asked him about that either,' she said. 'Not yet.'

'Have you anything else?' Wisting asked. 'I saw you paid a visit to his home.'

'We've taken his shoes. There is ash on them, but of course he's already explained that he'd been inside the Kleiser house searching before it went up in smoke for the second time. So it doesn't really have any value as evidence.'

'Anything else?'

Maren smiled again. 'A witness has come forward,' she said. 'A secondary witness.'

'Who?'

'A friend of Agnete Roll. She was on holiday in France, but phoned earlier today. Agnete confided in her about an affair with another man.'

'Do you know who it was?'

163

'Jarle Schup. He lives in Stavern.'

Wisting shook his head; he did not know the name.

'It was news to us too,' Maren said. 'They kept in touch via WhatsApp, so he didn't turn up on her phone list.'

'Does he have an alibi?'

'We're planning to interview him now. In fact, we're bringing him in this afternoon.'

Wisting nodded.

Maren picked up her pen again as Wisting prepared to leave. 'I won't make any more of a nuisance of myself,' he said.

'You're never a nuisance,' she assured him.

With a smile, he moved to the door, but lingered there for a moment, trying to think of something to say. In the end, the only thing he could think of was to smile encouragingly.

On his way out, he let himself into the archives room again. The last time, he had been reluctant to take the case folders with him, and had made a note of the details of the Polish assistant who had accompanied Jan Hansen in the delivery van from time to time. Over the weekend, he had come to the conclusion that he would have to read through the entire case to see if there was anything pointing back to 1999. If he were to do that thoroughly, it would take a week, but it was his case. He had been responsible for it at that time, and still was. He would have no difficulty explaining why he had taken out the files.

It was dark for a second or two before the fluorescent light tubes on the ceiling flickered into life. One of them continued to blink. He strode across to the bookcase but stopped before he reached it.

The six archive boxes were gone.

Phone coverage in the basement was poor, but he would have to try to call Bjørg Karin. The number connected and rang for a long time, but she did not answer.

Wisting stood with the phone in his hand, a knot twisting deep down inside his gut, where anxiety and foreboding had a tendency to gather.

32

Shirley Bassey was playing on the car radio, but Wisting was not listening.

Before the weekend, he had found it difficult to imagine that two killers had been in the same place at the same time as Tone Vaterland's murder. Danny Momrak and Jan Hansen. Now an American, subsequently convicted of homicide, had become a third candidate.

The evidence against Danny Momrak still tipped the scales. The only thing pointing to Jan Hansen and Curtis Blair was their presence near the scene. But what had now emerged did expose the weakness of the police work in 1999 and was more than enough to raise doubt about the leadership of the investigation. About Sten Kvammen's acumen and judgement.

Kvammen was obviously behind Wisting's exclusion from the central data registers. Wisting was being drawn into some sort of power play. A game of pulling rank. Sten Kvammen was in the running for one of the most powerful positions in the Norwegian police force. As boss of the International Section in the National Police Directorate, he would report personally to the National Police Commissioner. From there, it was only one step up to leadership of the entire force.

He tried to ring Bjørg Karin twice more as he drove, but received no answer.

En route into his own street, he encountered the mail

van. Farther along, he spotted another car parked in the street outside his house. A dark-grey estate car, a typical government service vehicle.

The car was unoccupied and he could not see anyone in the vicinity.

Reversing into his driveway, he parked and positioned the camera. He also tried to phone Bjørg Karin for a third time before getting out.

A man came walking up the street – it looked as if he had been at Line's house. Wisting recognized him as Adrian Stiller, from the Kripos Cold Cases Group, formally the section for old and unsolved cases. Old, unsolved cases had brought them together earlier, and Wisting guessed this unannounced visit was not through sheer chance. Line had also worked for him in the past, taking photographs for use as illustrations in several internal Kripos publications as well as documenting a number of crime reconstructions.

Stiller acknowledged him with a wave.

Wisting nodded his head in return as he walked to his mailbox, where he found the usual junk mail, but also a white envelope, another letter with the same distinctive handwriting. Only his first and second names, no address or postage stamp, but this one was slightly thicker than the previous three missives.

'You're on duty, I see,' Wisting commented, gesturing towards the grey estate car.

'I happened to be in the area,' Stiller answered. 'Have you time for a chat?'

Wisting tucked the letter under the rest of his mail. 'Come on in,' he said.

After taking a briefcase from his car, Stiller followed.

Wisting considered him to be an ambitious investigator. Beneath a veneer of joviality, he was a calculating man, happy to mislead others as long as it was to the advantage of a case. However, he was certainly efficient and Wisting appreciated his often controversial methods. After all, his work was rather different from normal police assignments, with no crime scenes, just folders and archive boxes.

'It's been a poor summer,' Stiller said as he sat down at the kitchen table.

Wisting put down his post and started up the coffee machine. 'They say it's to improve next week,' Wisting answered, taking out two cups. 'What's brought you to this neck of the woods?'

Stiller folded his hands on the table. 'I've been asked to look at a couple of old cases,' he replied.

Wisting stood with his back to the kitchen worktop, resting his arms on the surface behind him, waiting for him to continue. 'What cases are they?'

Stiller smiled. 'You've probably guessed,' he said. 'One of them is yours. The murder of Pernille Skjerven in 2001. The other is two years earlier. Tone Vaterland's killing.'

'Why?' Wisting asked. 'Who's asked you to do that?'

'My boss,' Stiller replied.

'But why?' Wisting insisted. 'Both cases were solved. There are legal convictions. They're not the kind of cases you usually take up, unless there's a very special reason.'

'I expect whoever has given me the assignment does have a very good reason,' Stiller said. 'Why, though, have you taken an interest in these cases?'

Wisting carried the cups to the table without answering. It crossed his mind that Stiller usually liked water with his and so he filled two glasses.

'You've left a few tracks behind you,' Stiller continued. 'When I requisitioned the Vaterland case from the archives in Skien, I learned they had just been sent to you by courier.'

'I've returned them now,' Wisting told him.

Stiller leaned back. 'What did you discover?' he asked.

Wisting did not reply. They had started going round in circles, a ploy devised to avoid showing too much of the cards you held.

'They won't be collected by the internal courier service until tomorrow,' he said instead. 'You'll be able to pick them up at the police station if you get there before twelve.'

Stiller nodded as he sipped his coffee. Wisting took hold of his own cup.

'Have you taken out the Jan Hansen files?' he asked.

'I have them in the car,' Stiller replied.

'When were you given the assignment?' Wisting queried.

'On Friday.'

Wisting had visited Sten Kvammen's cabin on Thursday. Friday made sense, but only if Stiller was telling the truth. Through the other cases on which he and Wisting had collaborated, Stiller had revealed his usual investigative strategy. Instead of going through old evidence again, he tried to provoke something new. His methods were generally unorthodox.

Wisting drank his coffee. 'So you're not the one who's written the letters?' he asked.

'What letters?'

Wisting gave him an appraising look.

Stiller understood that he was not going to get an answer. 'Is there some connection between these two cases?' he asked. 'Apart from the superficial similarities?'

'Have you not been given any information?' Wisting asked. 'Were you just sent down here to talk to me?'

Stiller shrugged. 'That was more or less how things went,' he replied. 'You must have uncovered something that's made waves. Someone has talked to someone else. What was said must have been of sufficient interest that they felt the need for an official investigation. Hence my involvement.'

'You realize you're being used?' Wisting asked.

'You're thinking of the vacant post in the Directorate,' Stiller said. 'There are two applicants under consideration. Thore Kvande, who's acting in the post at present, and Sten Kvammen. Kvande represents the establishment, the safe pair of hands. Kvammen has the best formal qualifications, is keen on development and change, and will get the job if nothing turns up to discredit him.'

'I met Sten Kvammen before the weekend,' Wisting told him. 'If anyone has spoken to anyone, then it's him. But he won't benefit from any new reassessment of the case. It's more likely he doesn't want to rock the boat.'

'He didn't succeed, then,' Stiller said. 'Kvammen intervened to prevent you from taking action but was intercepted by someone whose interests did not coincide with his.'

Wisting nodded. This was more or less what he had thought must have happened behind the scenes.

'Anyway,' Stiller went on. 'As far as you and I are concerned, this is about something other than digging up dirt on Sten Kvammen. It's about finding the truth. Is that something we can work on together?'

It had to be true, Wisting thought. He himself had no authority to re-evaluate the Momrak case. It was outwith his formal duties. If he was to continue what he had embarked upon, then it must be with one foot inside the Cold Cases camp.

'There's no direct connection between the two cases,' Wisting said. 'But Jan Hansen was in the area in 1999.'

He explained how the 2001 murderer had been interviewed as a witness in the 1999 case, and about the deficiencies he had found in the evidence built up against Danny Momrak. For the present he omitted mention of Ninni Skjevik's involvement and the American behind bars in the USA.

'What made you start looking at this?' Stiller asked.

'I received a letter.'

'From whom?'

Wisting got to his feet and crossed to the kitchen drawer where the three letters lay. 'I don't know,' he answered as he brought the letters back to the table.

Stiller sat up straight.

'First this,' Wisting explained, laying down the bags containing the first letter and the envelope it came in. 'It was sent through the post.'

He pushed the other two letters across. 'These were hand-delivered to my mailbox.'

'What is G-11 and the Internet address?' Stiller queried.

Wisting told him about the medical article providing a scientific basis for an alternative explanation of the semen sample that had been critical evidence.

'I received another letter today,' he rounded off, glancing across at the worktop. 'I haven't opened it yet.'

33

Wisting picked up the fourth letter from the kitchen worktop.

Stiller rose from his chair. 'I can have them examined for fingerprints,' he said.

Wisting drew on washing-up gloves, took a knife from the drawer and cut open the envelope to find it contained a sheet of paper with coordinates and a picture.

N 59°2'27.6"
E 9°40'38.9"

The image looked as if it had been developed in a photographic shop, probably a self-service machine where you could insert a memory stick or transfer photo files from a mobile phone.

To begin with, the picture, of a grey brick wall covered in moss, taken from a distance of about a metre, was meaningless. A rusty metal plate was propped up against the wall and nettles and weeds grew around it.

Stiller had already taken out his phone and was keying in the coordinates. Wisting had no idea where these would lead them.

'It's the crime scene,' he said when Stiller had called up the map reference. 'Where Tone Vaterland was killed. There's an old brick garage there.'

'Is that where the photo was taken?'

'I assume so.'

Stiller took a closer look at the photograph. 'It looks as if something is scratched on the metal plate,' he said.

Wisting went into another room to find a magnifying glass before taking the photo across to the worktop to study it in better light.

'Just looks like some scratches,' he decided.

'Maybe there's something on the back of it,' Stiller suggested.

He checked the map on his phone again. 'It's only half an hour from here. We can take my car.'

Wisting peered out at the weather and saw that it was raining again. 'I have another appointment,' he said.

'What's that?'

'A Polish guy,' Wisting replied. 'Adam Dudek, the regular assistant in Jan Hansen's delivery van. They were working together in 1999 as well. I'm going to meet him at the warehouse at two o'clock. We'd have to do that first.'

'Fine with me,' said Stiller.

Moving to the kitchen drawer, Wisting took out the roll of freezer bags and tore off three. 'That's exactly what he wants us to do,' he said, as he divided the envelope, letter and picture into the three bags.

'Who?' Stiller asked. 'Danny Momrak?'

'If he's the sender,' Wisting replied. 'He points out what he wants us to find. It's manipulation. I don't like it.'

'Do you really think he's the one behind this?' Stiller asked. 'He's certainly had plenty of time to plan it.'

'I just can't get my head round it,' Wisting answered. 'It seems so unnecessarily complicated. If he believes there's something that could clear his name, then he should take it up with his lawyer and put together an appeal petition. Not hide in the shadows, pulling the strings.'

'He lacks the necessary credibility to get a hearing,' Stiller said. 'Now he's made sure of your total attention and forced both you and me to doubt the legal procedure. Call it manipulation if you like, but he has at least succeeded.'

Wisting nodded.

'Besides,' Stiller went on, 'who else could it be? Someone who's out to harm Sten Kvammen?'

He gathered up the freezer bags. 'I'll drive in with these this evening,' he said. 'We should have the fingerprint results sometime tomorrow.'

Wisting returned to the kitchen drawer and took out another bag. This one contained the clipping from the Lions membership magazine in which Curtis Blair was introduced as an exchange student.

'Ask them to check this too,' he said, handing it over.

Adrian Stiller immediately asked: 'Who is Curtis Blair?'

Wisting explained about Ninni Skjevik and the American now serving a sentence for homicide. 'The journalist's fingerprints are on the cutting,' he recapped. 'Get them to compare the others with this.'

Stiller was full of questions. 'What kind of homicide are we talking about?'

'I don't know,' Wisting replied, outlining his conversation with Maggie Griffin of the FBI. 'I won't receive any further details until we initiate an official investigation. But I guess we have that now.'

As they headed out to the car, a heavy drizzle hung in the air.

'No matter who's behind it, that person must have been keeping an eye on you,' Stiller said, once they were settled inside the vehicle. 'You received the first letter on Tuesday. It must have been posted on Monday, maybe even as early as the weekend. Whoever sent it must have known you hadn't gone away on holiday.'

He turned on the windscreen wipers and moved out on to the road. 'Everything seems carefully thought through and planned,' he went on. 'They must have been watching you. Driven past your house, maybe even stood watching you at the mailbox.'

Nodding, Wisting told him about the car he had spotted on the night he had received the second letter. 'I doubt anything will come of testing the fingerprints,' he said. 'But I think the letters were written with an iPad. The paper laid over the screen and the text traced off. There will always be a lot of cell material on a screen, from being touched by fingers. That may have transferred to the paper.'

Stiller agreed. 'DNA takes longer,' he said. 'But I'll get that checked out too.'

They were almost twenty minutes early when Stiller drove up in front of the furniture warehouse where they planned to meet Adam Dudek. Wisting rang him from the car, and soon afterwards one of the vehicle entrance gates swung open and Dudek waved them in.

Just inside the building, there was a small reception room with a settee and two chairs. Wisting and Stiller sat side by side on the settee.

In 2001, Adam Dudek had been interviewed about Jan Hansen. Now Wisting wanted him to cast his mind back to 1999.

'What is this actually about?' Dudek asked. 'I heard that Jan was dead.'

'Where did you hear that?' Wisting asked.

'They were talking about it in the shop,' Dudek replied. 'He's buried in the churchyard in Hedrum. Someone in the office had seen the grave.'

'Did you have any contact with him while he was in jail?'

Adam Dudek shook his head. 'Why would I? I didn't owe him anything. We worked together, nothing more than that.'

'Did you also work with him in the summer of 1999?'

'I've been here since 1997,' he answered. 'I went with the van driver nearly every time a customer had arranged for something big and heavy to be carried in. A sofa or a wardrobe. That sort of thing.'

'Did he ever tell you he'd been interviewed by the police?'

'I don't think he'd have said anything like that to me.'

'Not because he'd done anything illegal,' Wisting continued. 'We're thinking about a girl who was reported missing. Jan Hansen was one of the witnesses who saw her before she disappeared.'

'Do you think he did that too?' Dudek asked.

'It's not exactly like that,' Wisting replied. 'Another man was arrested for her abduction. We're just interested in whether it was something Jan Hansen talked about.'

Adam Dudek could not recall anything of that kind. 'But it's years ago,' he pointed out. 'Where did it happen?'

'In Bamble,' Wisting told him.

'We've delivered a lot of furniture to Bamble,' Dudek said. 'All the way down to Kragerø, in fact.'

Wisting made a few more attempts to jog the man's memory. He told him about the Bamble Snack Shack and that the girl had been cycling along the road. It might have been natural for Jan Hansen to mention it the next time they passed that way.

'He used to whistle at them, you know,' Dudek said. 'Every time we drove past a girl cycling or walking along the road. He hung over the steering wheel and whistled. Sometimes he honked the horn as well, so that they had to turn round and look at him.'

Stiller broke into the conversation. 'Do you remember anything else?'

Adam Dudek told them about other episodes from the trips they'd made and things that Jan Hansen had told him, including a story about a dog that had been knocked down and a car that had driven off the road and ended up on its roof. He had talked about this incident a number of times, every time they had driven past the spot where the accident had occurred. In the end Wisting felt convinced that Jan Hansen had never mentioned the day Tone Vaterland had been murdered.

A bell rang somewhere in the building, and Adam Dudek had to leave to attend to a customer collecting something.

'We're all done here,' Wisting said as he got to his feet.

They headed straight back to the car.

'What do you think?' Stiller asked as they drove on. 'Being called in for interview in what turned out to be a murder inquiry isn't exactly an everyday occurrence. Normally you'd think it would be something you'd talk about.'

Wisting agreed. The fact that Jan Hansen had not done so gave him food for thought.

34

The rain had eased off and the shape of the clouds had changed. From being only a murky blur they had built up into dark towers, augurs of heavy rainfall to come.

Wisting felt he was being lured into some kind of trap. The feeling grew stronger by the minute as they neared the crime scene in Bamble.

They arrived after twenty-five minutes and Wisting indicated where Stiller should drive to reach the old cul-de-sac. They parked at the same spot where Wisting had left his car before the weekend.

The air was dank and oppressive, saturated with moisture, and there were puddles in the cracked asphalt. A frog hopped into the grass at the verge.

Stiller took a camera from the car and Wisting led the way. They rounded a gradual bend before the old garage appeared on the right-hand side. Faded graffiti that had once covered the grey brickwork was becoming overlaid with moss and creeping plants that clung to the crevices.

'Tone Vaterland was found two hundred metres further on,' Wisting clarified. 'The garage was not thoroughly searched in 1999.'

'The picture must have been taken round the back,' Stiller said.

Stinging nettles and other weeds grew tall and thick around the old building, attaching themselves to their trouser legs as they waded through.

The sloping terrain was uneven. Wisting had to use the wall for support as they made their way round to the rear. In the middle of the main wall they spotted the rusty metal plate, propped up against the wall, exactly as in the photograph. They advanced all the way and took up position beside it. The surrounding trees were dripping with rainwater and they heard a bird make a low whistling sound.

They had left the picture enclosed with the letter in the car, but there had been less greenery when it was taken. Wisting wheeled round to gaze back at where they had come from. There were no tracks through the vegetation to suggest anyone other than them had walked here. The photo he had been sent must have been taken earlier that summer or perhaps even the previous year.

Stiller snapped a photograph as Wisting drew on plastic gloves before moving across and tilting the metal plate. Behind it, there was a hole in the brick and a square wooden frame cemented into the wall. The gap measured about twenty centimetres square and was covered with netting.

'An air vent,' Stiller commented.

Wisting used the torch function on his mobile to light up the interior. A spider's web glistened as a spider scurried into hiding, but apart from that there was not much to see. It was a crawl space. The height between ceiling and floor was about half a metre. The beam of light did not reach very far inside, but at the extreme end of the cavity he could see a strap or belt.

He had to lie on his stomach to get a better view and the dampness on the ground soaked through his clothes. Clamping his cheek against the brick wall allowed him to see obliquely across to the opposite side.

'There's something lying there,' he said. 'At the far end, on the inside.'

The netting in front of the hole was attached to the wooden frame with nails that had large, flat heads. Fragments of the cement around the frame had crumbled away. Wisting grabbed hold of the frame itself and found it loose. There was a shower of plaster and disintegrating flakes of concrete when he jiggled it out.

Glancing across at Stiller, he was given the nod before he stretched his arm in through the opening. The air inside was dry, still and odourless.

Feeling his way forward, he came across a soft, shapeless bundle. He took hold of the corner of something and pulled out a dusty piece of cloth. When he held it up he saw that it was a purple sweater, discoloured and faded. On the left of the chest, *Bamble Snack Shack* was embroidered in yellow lettering.

'It's hers,' Wisting said. 'Tone Vaterland's. She was naked when she was found.'

He peered down into the small cavity in the brick wall. 'There's more in there,' he said.

Stiller knelt down to look inside for himself. 'We'll have to leave the rest to the others,' he said.

Wisting agreed. There was every chance that the clothes had been hidden there by the killer. They could have lain there untouched since 1999 and still bear traces to reveal something about what had happened.

Stiller put back the iron plate to protect the cavity in case the rain came on again.

Wisting folded up the sweater and carried it back to the car. Stiller ripped out a few sheets of paper from a notebook and used them to cover the rear seat before Wisting carefully placed the sweater on top. Then, phoning police headquarters, he explained the situation and asked them to send out a team of crime-scene technicians.

The two men sat in the car to wait. Condensation covered the interior windows. Stiller switched on the air conditioning and let the car engine idle.

A huge raindrop smacked the front windscreen, followed by another and then several in succession. Wisting's eyes flitted to and fro to catch one splat after another until they were too numerous and fast.

'Who could know of this?' Stiller asked. 'After so many years?'

Wisting was frantically struggling to order his thoughts. To start with, there was only one person who could know about the clothing. 'The person who put them there,' he replied.

'The killer,' Stiller concluded.

Wisting could not see any realistic alternative, but was struggling to find a logical explanation for why he had been led to this discovery so many years afterwards, and who on earth could be behind it.

If it had been Danny Momrak who had murdered Tone Vaterland and placed her clothes under the garage, there was no reason for him to lead the police to further evidence, unless he wished to confess. On the contrary, it would be more rational to remove the last traces in order to be able to continue protesting his innocence.

Jan Hansen was dead, but the most likely hypothesis was that he had at some point confided in someone who did not want to get involved. The same applied to the American.

As the windscreen blurred with rain, Stiller activated the

wipers. 'Did you say the crime scene is actually two hundred metres further on?' he asked.

Wisting confirmed this.

'Then why hide the clothes here?'

The question was left hanging in the air when a police patrol car swung in behind them and drove alongside. Stiller rolled down his window and gave their particulars.

The van with the technicians should not be far behind, they were informed.

The two uniformed officers got out of their vehicle and put on rain jackets. The tree trunk blocking the road was dry and brittle and they managed to lift it aside so that they could drive all the way up to the old garage.

The technicians arrived twenty minutes later. Their first action was to erect a work tent at the rear of the garage in order to work in shelter from the rain. It had open sides but space enough for Wisting and Stiller beneath its canopy without obstructing the technicians.

The rain drummed on the hard plastic cover. The technicians set up a small table and began to work systematically. The opening in the brick wall was measured and photographed before the earth beside the wall was covered with a tarpaulin. Before they moved anything inside, they inserted a probe with a camera attached at one end and a small, powerful light. The images captured were transferred to a hand-held screen. All four gathered round and Wisting caught a glimpse of a shoe before the camera moved aside. Although the image was indistinct, the lens quickly adjusted focus. There was a little fabric bag with straps and buttons. The other items were difficult to identify, except that they were various items of clothing.

The first item to be brought out was a blue canvas shoe

with laces and flat soles. The eyelets were discoloured and covered in verdigris, but otherwise the shoes were in good condition.

'It's dark and dry in there,' one of the technicians commented. 'Good ventilation, no rot or damp. With no great fluctuations in temperature either. A bit like a storage cellar.'

The shoe was photographed, packed up and labelled.

The next item the technicians brought out was the rucksack. Plaster from the edges of the air vent drizzled down it as it was dragged out.

The bag was stained with mildew and the top cord was open. It too was photographed and recorded before the contents were removed: a shampoo bottle, bathing costume, pair of socks, T-shirt, small bag with a clasp and a wallet.

The technician let Wisting open the wallet. It clearly belonged to Tone Vaterland and contained a student ID card, a bus pass and a customer card for video rental. One pocket held two hundred-kroner notes from the previous, outdated banknote series and two receipts from a clothes shop.

The bag contained make-up, headache tablets and a pack of contraceptive pills.

Next was a bath towel with a floral pattern, covered with fungus and black mould. It had obviously been damp when it was stowed away.

A car door slammed at the front of the garage and they could hear voices in the distance.

An overweight woman in her late forties was picking her way down the wet slope. She slid and slithered, trying to catch hold of a tree branch, but fell flat on her back.

Wisting rushed to help her up, but she had struggled to her feet by the time he reached her. A police ID dangled around her neck.

'Are you OK?' Wisting asked.

The woman wiped her hand on her thigh before holding it out to him. 'Yes, fine, thanks,' she answered, and went on to introduce herself: 'Kathe Ulstrup.' She had a dirty mark on her cheek.

Wisting recognized the name from the case papers. She worked at the local police station and had been in charge of the case until Sten Kvammen took over.

'Is this to do with the Vaterland case?' she asked.

Wisting confirmed this.

'It stated in the log that technicians had been sent here to assist the Cold Cases Group, but didn't mention what case it had to do with,' Ulstrup said. 'It could hardly be anything else. I worked on it at the time.'

'We've found her clothes,' Wisting told her, guiding her towards the rear of the garage.

She nodded to the two technicians and said hello to Stiller. 'I worked on the case,' she explained. 'I was first on the scene when she was found.' She gestured with her head to point out the direction.

They huddled around the opening. A torn white summer blouse with buttons missing was now lifted out.

Kathe Ulstrup took a step forward. 'The buttons were scattered around the crime scene,' she said. 'That was all we found.'

The white blouse was placed in a brown paper bag, labelled and put in a box. The next item out was a bra.

Kathe Ulstrup turned to face Wisting. 'What made you search here?'

'A tip-off,' he said. 'Anonymous.'

'An anonymous tip-off,' Ulstrup repeated. 'What did it say?'

'Nothing more than an indication of where we should search.'

The local officer took a step back, looking up at the grey garage wall. 'We searched in here,' she said. 'It wasn't a forensic examination, but the garage was searched and the ditches fine-combed. In the end we concluded that he had taken the clothes with him and got rid of them somewhere else.'

She turned now to Stiller. 'Does this mean the case has been reopened?' she asked.

'A few additional reports will have to be written, at the very least,' Stiller answered evasively.

Ulstrup stepped forward, crouching down and squinting into the opening in the wall while the technicians removed the second shoe.

'How long have you been working on the case?' she asked, glancing up at Wisting. 'How deeply have you gone into it?'

'I received the case documents last Wednesday,' he replied.

'Have you read through them?'

He nodded.

Ulstrup stood upright again. 'What do you think?' she asked.

Wisting hesitated to answer. 'This find doesn't change anything,' he said. 'Maybe the opposite, in fact. Danny Momrak knew his way around here. He used the garage as a drugs depot. He's most likely the one who put the clothes in there.'

'So you don't envisage there could have been a different killer?'

The question took Wisting by surprise. 'Do you?' he asked.

Kathe Ulstrup did not reply. 'Is the message telling you to search here the only tip-off you've had?' she asked instead.

'Why do you ask?'

Ulstrup smiled. Her round cheeks had deep dimples. 'If you received the case documents last week and have managed to read them, I mean. If I'd had a tip-off about the clothes belonging to a murder victim, I wouldn't have waited a week. I would have gone straight out to see if there was anything in it. So there must have been something else that made you reopen the case.'

Wisting returned her smile. He liked her reasoning.

Ulstrup continued before he had a chance to answer: 'I don't need any details,' she said. 'But if the name Curtis Blair has turned up, then it's possible I can be of help.'

Nodding, Wisting realized he would have to take her completely into his confidence. 'We'll have to talk elsewhere,' he said.

'We can go to my office,' Ulstrup suggested.

A phone rang and it took a while for it to dawn on Wisting that it was his own. A call from an unknown number.

He failed to reach it in time. At that very moment, one of the officers who had been guarding the front of the garage appeared.

'A journalist's been here,' he said. 'She arrived just before Ulstrup.' He waved his hand in the direction of the local officer. 'She went away again, but her car's still parked there,' he continued. 'It's possible she'll try to make her way round.'

They turned and looked at the dense woodland behind them, but no movement was to be seen.

Wisting's phone rang again. This time he managed to answer in time. It was Ninni Skjevik. 'We're in the same location,' she said. 'Have you time for a chat?'

'Where are you?' Wisting asked her, squinting through the trees.

'I'm sitting in my car, up on the old road,' she replied. 'I wasn't allowed to come down to where you are.'

'It's not convenient.'

'I've spoken to Danny Momrak,' Skjevik went on.

Wisting knew it would be only a matter of time. 'I see,' he replied. 'I'll come up to you.'

35

The car engine was running. Ninni Skjevik waved him into the passenger seat and Wisting clambered in. She was soaked to the skin, and a twig and some grains of grit were tangled into her hair.

'Is it OK for me to film this?' she asked, nodding in the direction of a camera tucked all the way into a corner of the dashboard.

Wisting peered at it sceptically. The lamp was already glowing red.

'I'd like to document everything to do with Danny Momrak,' Skjevik continued. 'It's not definite that I'll make use of it. It's more instead of making notes. You'll get the opportunity to approve it anyway.'

Wisting did not answer. 'Have you already been filming us?' he asked instead.

'A brief recording,' she confirmed, picking the grit from her hair. 'There's a serious mobilization going on here. Crime-scene technicians dressed in white and a forensics tent. What have you found?'

'How did you know we were here?' Wisting asked.

'I was driving past and saw the police car from the road.' She pointed at the patrol car. 'It couldn't have been a coincidence,' she added.

A convoy of trucks passed on the motorway and they felt the draught in the car. Ninni Skjevik leaned against the steamed-up side window.

'What are you doing here?' she asked.

'Investigating something,' Wisting replied.

'It looks as if you've found her clothes,' Ninni Skjevik said. 'I've got footage of it.'

'What did you and Danny Momrak talk about?' Wisting asked.

'His lawyer had already informed him,' Skjevik replied. 'Told him about your visit and about Jan Hansen.'

Wisting shook his head, feeling vexed with himself. He had started at the wrong end. He should have gone straight to Danny Momrak so that he could witness his reaction first hand.

'He remembered Jan Hansen well from prison,' she went on. 'But he hadn't anything nice to say about him. I doubt there's been any kind of exchange of information or cooperation between them, if you were thinking in that direction.'

He had been thinking in that direction. 'Did you tell him about the American?' he asked.

She nodded. 'I was afraid it might be too much for him all at once, but the most important thing for me was to persuade him to take part in the documentary. The discovery of two major flaws in the original investigation certainly aroused his interest.'

'Did you get the impression this was something he'd heard about earlier?' Wisting asked.

This gave Ninni Skjevik pause for thought. 'It didn't seem so,' she responded.

'How was he?' he asked.

'What do you mean?'

'What did he think of it all?'

Ninni Skjevik took time to reflect again. 'I noticed a

certain unwillingness in him,' she answered. 'At first he wouldn't talk to me either. But now I think your chances are better. He became enthusiastic. It was clear that he felt he was innocent and he seemed keen to fight to clear his name.'

'Does he live alone?'

'Yes, extremely isolated. No neighbours or any other signs of life around him.'

'Work?'

'No.'

In front of them, Adrian Stiller and Kathe Ulstrup emerged through the rain from the rear of the garage and got into their vehicles. Ninni Skjevik let the wipers slide across the windscreen. They snagged on a broad crack, probably caused by a spray of gravel.

'Who is that man there?' she asked, peering out beneath the crack, where condensation had not formed.

'Adrian Stiller,' Wisting told her. 'From the Cold Cases Group.'

'So they've been brought in?'

'They're here, at least.'

Skjevik's eagerness increased visibly. 'Does that mean the case has been officially reopened?' she asked.

'It means they're exploring the possibilities of that,' Wisting replied.

'What are you going to do with the clothes?' Skjevik asked. 'Is it possible to find DNA on them, after so many years?'

Wisting had posed the same question to the crime-scene technicians. They had been optimistic, since the clothing had been lying on dry stone.

'That remains to be seen,' he said.

Skjevik shifted in her seat. 'With everything that's kicking off now, I expect a decision about the production will be taken in the course of this week,' she went on. 'Have you thought any more about whether you'll participate?'

Wisting took hold of the door handle. 'If you must have an answer now, then it's no,' he said.

Ninni Skjevik lifted the camera down and held it in her lap. 'What about offscreen?' she suggested. 'Can you keep me posted if there are any developments in the case?'

Wisting shook his head. 'It's not my case,' he replied. 'It's not up to me. You'll have to talk to Stiller.'

Ninni Skjevik looked at the car in front of them. 'Can you introduce me to him?'

'I've told him about you,' Wisting said, pushing the door open. 'He knows who you are.'

Stepping out, he stood for a moment in the rain with his hand on the door. 'You'll have to get that front windscreen replaced,' he told her before he shut the door and jogged across to hop into Stiller's car.

'What did she want?' he asked.

'She wants to make a TV documentary out of it,' Wisting answered. 'She's apparently got Danny Momrak involved.'

Kathe Ulstrup manoeuvred her car round on the old cul-de-sac and managed to turn the vehicle. Stiller drove off after her. Ninni Skjevik was left sitting in her car, wiping condensation from the front windscreen.

'How did she know we were here?' Stiller asked.

'She was driving past and saw a police car,' Wisting told him. 'She was here in 1999 too, when the body was found. Twigged that it must have something to do with Tone Vaterland.'

Stiller glanced in the mirror. 'Do you believe that explanation?' he asked.

Wisting twisted round in his seat and looked back. Ninni Skjevik was following them.

36

The local police station was located inside a shopping centre. Kathe Ulstrup ushered them in through the staff entrance and up to the top floor. Her office overlooked the murky Frier fjord and they watched as a tanker passed beneath the Grenland bridge.

Wisting and Stiller both sat down.

'Was that Ninni Skjevik?' Kathe Ulstrup asked. 'The journalist in the car?'

Wisting confirmed this.

'I thought I recognized her,' Ulstrup said. 'I had a lot of dealings with her when she was working at the local news-paper, the *Porsgrunns Dagblad*. She reported on all the police cases. What does she want now?'

'She's making a TV documentary,' Wisting told her. 'About Danny Momrak and the Vaterland case.'

Kathe Ulstrup produced a ring binder from the bottom shelf of an open-plan unit and set it down on the desk.

'Well, she did write about it at that time, but I wouldn't trust her, really,' she said as she began to leaf through the binder.

'To be honest, I trust very few journalists,' Wisting commented.

'Did you have a bad experience with her, Kathe?' Stiller asked.

Kathe Ulstrup gave a fleeting smile. She was about to say more but had found what she was looking for in the folder. 'What do you know about Curtis Blair?' she asked instead.

'He was here on an exchange in 1999,' Wisting replied. 'His stay was cut short. He was sent home, I believe.'

'That's right,' Ulstrup said. 'It was all organized by the Lions. He stayed with the Kronborg family. Terje and Mona and their children, Peder and Janne.'

Wisting nodded but held back from telling her anything more.

'In 2001 we received a report that Janne Kronborg had drowned in her bathtub. I went out with a colleague. It was her mother who'd found her and phoned us. Janne was still lying in the bath when we got there. She had put on a long dress. The water had turned cold. Seemingly, she had got into the bath straight after her mother had left for work.'

Ulstrup glanced at the papers before continuing: 'The doctor came fifteen minutes after us. Janne had cut both wrists, there was a knife on the floor, but the post-mortem showed she died of drowning by overdosing on her mother's sleeping tablets. Rohypnol. It was still on sale at that time.'

She thumbed through to the photographs.

'The bathroom door was locked from the inside,' she continued. 'The mother had broken it open. Her daughter left no note, but it was rumoured that she'd been depressed. We didn't take any further action. The case was quickly closed, but the suicide led to a great deal of gossip. It was said that she'd been raped by Curtis Blair. He was sent back to America. Terje Kronborg refused to discuss the case and that was that.'

Ulstrup's phone rang. She checked the display and switched it off.

'You know how it is,' she went on. 'It takes a long time to get results from the forensic toxicology tests. The final post-mortem report with details of the active ingredient in the sleeping tablets didn't reach us until two months after the funeral. But it gave me the excuse to visit the family again, and I managed to ask them about Curtis Blair. They confirmed that their daughter had been raped and linked that to the suicide. The rape took place on the same night that Tone Vaterland disappeared.'

She sat back in her chair. 'But maybe you already knew all that?' she asked.

'Not the details,' Wisting replied.

Ulstrup leaned forward across her desk again. 'There are people mentioned in the Vaterland case who were never identified,' she went on. 'A young man with a camera was spotted, as well as a man in a camouflage jacket and a man with a rucksack.'

She put down one of the photographs that Wisting had already seen of Curtis Blair in a camouflage jacket with a camera slung over his shoulder.

'I got this from someone in the Lions,' she said. 'Janne's family hadn't followed the Vaterland case. They went away. Took their daughter to their cabin in the mountains to shield her and left her brother on his own at home.'

'What have you done with this information?' Wisting asked.

'I wrote a report and submitted it to Sten Kvammen,' Ulstrup replied. 'He was the one in charge of the investigation in 1999. I thought it would be interesting to take a closer look at the American. Check him out.'

'What did he do with it?'

'Nothing as far as I know. I asked him when I had a

chance later. Apparently it wasn't worth squandering resources on.'

'Have you done anything more?'

'I talked to someone in the Lions, as I said, as well as some of Janne Kronborg's friends. It didn't lead anywhere. She hadn't talked to them about what had happened.'

'Did you make any attempt to track down Curtis Blair?' Wisting asked. 'Find out where he is and what he's doing now?'

Ulstrup smiled and shook her head. 'The world has become smaller since 1999, of course,' she answered. 'We've got Facebook and Google now. I've tried to look him up but haven't succeeded in finding him. Apart from that, I've neither the contacts nor the clout to take it any further.'

She looked across at Stiller as she answered.

'Have you spoken to anyone else about this?' Wisting asked.

Kathe shook her head. 'For everyone else here, the case was done and dusted the day Danny Momrak was arrested,' she replied. 'But I followed it from the start. I lived with it. I know all the details. I know where the loose threads are. I wanted to find all the answers.'

Adrian Stiller leaned forward in his seat, clasping his hands and resting his elbows on his knees.

'Don't you believe Danny Momrak was the one who killed her?' he asked.

Kathe Ulstrup was browsing through the ring binder. 'I've always believed that,' she answered. 'Everything adds up. Everything fits. Not least the DNA sample. But ten years ago I received this.'

She took a sheet of paper from the ring binder and handed it to Stiller. He and Wisting read it together. It was a letter from the Forensics Institute recalling DNA results for three cases because the samples had been mixed up or contaminated.

'I assume that mistakes can happen,' Ulstrup commented.

Wisting said nothing about how the DNA sample from Tone Vaterland could have stemmed from voluntary sexual intercourse with Danny Momrak five days prior to the murder.

'Then, of course, there's the question that has haunted me ever since Danny Momrak was arrested,' Ulstrup continued. 'A question I asked myself during the trial: who else could it have been? If Danny Momrak was not the one who killed Tone Vaterland, then who could it have been?'

She paused for a moment, looking from Wisting to Stiller and back again.

'Since you're taking up the case again, there must be some reason for it,' she said. 'If Curtis Blair isn't the reason, then he does at least deserve a place in the new investigation.'

37

They drove a few kilometres in silence. Stiller moved the car out into the left-hand lane and passed a motorhome.

'What's the name of your contact in the FBI?' he asked.

'Maggie Griffin,' Wisting replied. 'New York office.'

Stiller drummed his fingers on the steering wheel. 'There's a morning flight tomorrow at eleven,' he said.

Wisting smiled. 'To the USA?' he asked. He laughed before it dawned on him that Stiller was not joking. 'Were you thinking of going over?'

'Not me,' Stiller said. 'You're the one who made the initial contact. You should follow it up.'

Wisting shook his head. 'It's not in my jurisdiction,' he said. 'I had nothing to do with the case in 1999, and formally don't have now either. Anyway, strictly speaking, I'm on holiday.'

Stiller's eyes were nailed straight ahead on the traffic. 'You could have a temporary appointment with us,' he said.

'With Kripos?'

'With my unit,' Stiller said. 'I've already had the Vaterland case assigned to me.'

Kripos was the National Criminal Investigation Service and the contact point for international police cooperation. Temporary transfers of personnel were not unusual.

'FBI can just send over the information we need,' Wisting objected all the same.

'It would be quicker to nip across and pick it up than if

we submit a legal request,' Stiller pointed out. 'Anyway, you know the case. I'd like you to travel across and talk to Curtis Blair yourself.'

'We don't even know if it's the right Curtis Blair,' Wisting began. 'I can't —'

'Is your passport up to date?' Stiller broke in.

'Yes.'

'Then I'll organize the tickets and establish formal contact,' Stiller said.

No matter how far technology had advanced, face-to-face conversation would always be the investigator's most vital tool.

He sat lost in his own thoughts for the rest of the journey — first circling around how he would approach Curtis Blair and eventually looking forward to meeting Maggie Griffin again.

They remained seated in the car outside Wisting's house. Stiller agreed to take care of the technical side of things, ensuring that the anonymous letters were examined for fingerprints and DNA and that the lab technicians were given the clothes belonging to Tone Vaterland.

'I'll keep the Jan Hansen case files,' Stiller said, tossing his head in the direction of the car boot. 'I'll read up on them. I expect you'll want to keep the Vaterland case?'

Wisting nodded. 'But it's at the police station now,' he said.

He would have to call in there later and take copies of the most significant documents so that he could take them with him to his meeting with Curtis Blair.

'What names do you have on your list?' Stiller asked. 'Who do you want to talk to?'

'Jan Hansen had a girlfriend while he was inside,' Wisting

said. 'We should speak to her and the prison guards who had most contact with him.'

Stiller agreed, adding, 'Do you have the name of the girlfriend?'

'No.'

'I can try to find that out.'

Grabbing the door handle, Wisting prepared to exit the car. 'Danny Momrak named an alibi witness in 1999,' he said, but was unable to recall the man's name. 'Someone he delivered hash to around the time of the murder. He denied it then. We should talk to him again.'

He stepped out of the car, reflecting that names slipped his mind more and more often these days. It had begun to bother him.

'Aren't you going to check your mailbox?' Stiller asked, pointing.

With a smile, Wisting slammed the car door and headed for the gatepost where the box hung, but found it empty. As the lid dropped shut, Stiller started the car engine and drove off.

Once indoors, Wisting's first port of call was the toilet, and it occurred to him that he should take one of the prescribed tablets. Then he looked out his passport and a small suitcase. He did not need any more than hand luggage, as it would be a short trip: one overnight stay and the night flight back home.

Maggie had told him about a heatwave along the Eastern Seaboard. As Wisting folded a short-sleeved shirt, it crossed his mind that he would have to tell Line he was going to be away for a couple of days.

After he had finished packing, he looked out an umbrella and made his way down to her house.

Amalie barrelled towards him in the hallway and he swept her up, tickling her, before she dragged him along to show him a cabin she had made of blankets.

Wisting knelt down and peeked in while Amalie babbled enthusiastically about all her dolls and teddies that lived in there.

Line stood watching them. 'What did Stiller want?' she asked once her daughter had finished talking. 'Was it to do with Pernille Skjerven's murder?'

Wisting got to his feet. He had told Line about the case after Ninni Skjevik's visit, but he had not spilled all the beans.

'Among other things,' he said. 'I have to go away for a day or two.'

'But you're on holiday,' Line commented.

'I can take time off again later,' Wisting replied, 'when the weather improves.'

'Where are you going?'

'To the USA.'

Line looked surprised. 'The USA?' she repeated. 'Have you tracked down that American you were talking about?'

'Yes,' Wisting answered, but left off telling her he was in prison, convicted of homicide.

'Have you talked to Maggie?' Line asked.

Wisting nodded in response.

'Are you going to meet her?'

'I don't know yet,' Wisting replied. 'Stiller's arranging the practical side of things with the police over there.'

He crouched down to the opening of the blanket cabin. 'I'll be back on Thursday,' he said as Amalie gave him a hug.

'You should stay for a few days, since you're travelling anyway,' Line said.

'That'll have to be left for another time,' he said, giving his daughter a hug too.

She walked with him to the door. 'Should I take in your post or anything?' she asked.

'It's only a couple of days,' he replied. 'It'll be fine.'

Out on the steps, he changed his mind. 'Or maybe, yes. Do that, please,' he said. 'Send me a message if any letters arrive for me.'

Opening the umbrella, he dashed out into the rain before she had a chance to ask anything further. 'Have a good trip!' she called after him.

He checked the mailbox again before getting into his car. During the course of the day he had neither read the online newspapers nor followed the case concerning the Agnete Roll murder. When he parked in the police station back yard, he saw lights in several of the windows in the Criminal Investigation Department, but apart from that, all seemed quiet.

On the way in he checked the news on his phone. No developments.

The box containing the Vaterland case files sat where he had left it and he took it into the photocopy room. Wisting wanted to take copies of documents describing the crime scene and the witness statements observing a man in camouflage gear carrying a camera.

He riffled through the bundles, removing staples and placing the relevant documents on the automatic feeder. The machine ran smoothly for the first five reports before the paper jammed.

Maren Dokken appeared as he stood with the cover up, trying to free the trapped paper without causing too much damage.

'Sorry,' he said. 'I'll soon be finished.'

'No problem,' she assured him.

Once he had managed to free the paper, he removed the other papers from the feeder before restarting the machine.

'Be my guest,' he said, letting Maren Dokken take her turn.

'Thanks.'

'Any news?' Wisting asked. 'You were going to bring a man in? Her lover?'

Maren Dokken started up the photocopier. 'Yes, Jarle Schup,' she confirmed. 'Agnete was with him on the night of the murder.'

'Aha,' Wisting said.

'It was tricky to winkle it out of him, but he confirmed they'd had a relationship. Agnete Roll sent him a message on Snapchat when she left the town centre. He didn't answer, but half an hour later she appeared at his door. They sat in the kitchen. He's recently divorced and had his children staying that weekend, so there was nothing more to it than that. The youngest child woke up, so she left after half an hour or so. She wanted to get home before her husband.'

'Is he credible?'

'Difficult to say, but he understands the situation. He's agreed to the crime-scene technicians carrying out investigations in his home.'

Wisting leaned against a bookcase. 'How long had the relationship been going on?' he asked.

'Six months or so,' Maren Dokken replied. 'They'd been childhood sweethearts.'

'Could her husband have known about it?'

'She had suspicions about his relationship, at any rate. She had told both Jarle Schup and a friend in France.'

She finished with the photocopier and handed over to him. 'What are you working on?' she asked, gesticulating towards the old document folders. 'Aren't you on holiday?'

'I've landed myself a summer job,' he answered with a smile.

Maren Dokken cocked her head and gave him a quizzical look.

'I'm looking through an old case,' Wisting explained. 'At the request of Kripos.'

'Have you found anything?'

'I don't know yet,' was Wisting's honest answer.

Maren Dokken pulled a face before returning to her own office, as if she knew all about how difficult a case could be.

Wisting filled the photocopier again and stood watching the papers slide out at the other end. This case was like a labyrinth, he mused. It seemed impossible to find the way out.

38

The bus drove into the terminal seven minutes late. The large vehicle shook and rattled before the engine stopped. Curtis Blair sat for a few seconds staring at the Lions emblem on the top of his rucksack. After sliding out of his seat, he hoisted the bag over one shoulder and walked up the centre aisle. He hesitated on the bottom step, watching while the bus driver opened the luggage hatches beneath the bus. Curtis hauled out his luggage.

He had called home from the airport in New York and spoken to his mother, but his father was the one who had come to collect him. He was sitting behind the wheel of the Chrysler and made no move to come out.

Dragging his cases behind him across the diesel-speckled asphalt, Curtis skirted around the car and heaved them into the boot.

His father did not utter a word when Curtis got in. Nor did he meet his son's eye as he simply swung out on to the main road, his jaw muscles twitching.

Curtis wondered what he had been told. What he had learned about the events in Norway. He wanted to tell him his version, but knew that no matter how he expressed himself, he would not be believed.

It was dark by the time they arrived home and his mother greeted them in the kitchen. She had always come between the two of them when his father intended to punish him for something. He had hoped it would be easier for her when he was gone. From the time he was little, Curtis had felt it was his fault that his father hit her, as if he wanted to punish her for having brought him into the world. But he could see that she had paid dearly in the months he had been absent. She was paler and thinner than when he had left and her bruises looked fresh.

The blow came before he had a chance to say a word, as soon as he had turned his back on his father. An open hand struck him above the right ear and sent him flying into the kitchen table. Curtis felt sure his eardrum had burst. Sparks flickered in his eyes and a buzzing noise shot through his brain.

'What were you thinking?' his father roared at him as he hit him again.

Finding a chair, Curtis slumped down on it with the Lions rucksack on his knee.

'It's not –' he began, but a third blow interrupted him.

His mother was sobbing. She took a step closer but did not come between them.

'Do you understand what you've done?' his father spluttered. 'How shameful this is for your mother and me?'

Curtis knew better than to contradict him. He simply raised his arms to protect himself from the next blow.

'Are you aware of how we've slogged to achieve all this?' his father continued. 'How much it's cost us?' He struck him again. 'Do you?'

His father jerked the rucksack away. 'Have you any understanding at all?' he went on. 'You know I can never go to meetings again? That I'll have to resign my position?'

A guttural growl followed. 'You realize this will be

reported throughout the entire organization? That even the international president will find out about it?'

He had grabbed the rucksack. Now he turned it upside down and shook out the contents. The camera fell to the floor. His father picked it up, ripped off the lens and hurled it at the floor again so violently that it exploded into pieces.

Curtis curled up and closed his eyes. He had spent all his savings on that camera before he left.

'To hell with you!' his father bellowed. 'Ungrateful bastard.'

Seizing hold of him, he yanked him out of his chair and flung him from the room. 'You should have stayed over there!' he yelled. 'Rotting in a Norwegian jail!' He kicked Curtis in the small of his back and knocked him to the floor.

'Robert,' his mother said tentatively. 'No more, Robert.'

Curtis hauled himself up on all fours and crawled in the direction of his room. Another kick struck his side, just below the ribs.

'Get away from me,' his father shrieked after him. 'I don't want to see you ever again!'

His mother said something Curtis did not catch. Staggering to his feet, he lurched into his room, closed the door and lay thinking of what his future would hold.

39

Wisting sat watching as his plane flew in. He was taken aback by the skyscrapers and landmarks he had only ever seen on TV. The Statue of Liberty, the Empire State Building, Central Park and Brooklyn Bridge.

The vista soon vanished as the cabin crew prepared for landing. Wisting fastened his seatbelt. He always felt sleepy on flights and had slept for half the journey. Now he felt refreshed.

As soon as the wheels hit the runway, he switched on his phone. It took a while for it to find a network and adjust the clock to American time. It was afternoon, quarter to four. At home in Norway it would be quarter to ten.

Two messages ticked in while the plane taxied towards the terminal, both from Adrian Stiller. The first told him that Maggie Griffin would meet him at the airport and it had been arranged that they would drive straight to the prison for a meeting with Curtis Blair. The second related to the fingerprint analysis of the letters he had received. The result would not be available until the following day.

He returned a brief message to say his flight had landed.

The air inside the terminal building was surprisingly cool. An enormous American flag covered the wall behind passport control. Even though Wisting was one of the first off the plane, the queues were lengthy.

People moved slowly forward until a man in a well-pressed uniform with a pistol in his belt emerged from the side and picked him out of the line.

'Mr Wisting?'

'Yes?'

'Come with me, please.'

Wisting followed him forward to a control desk reserved for flight personnel and public employees on official business. Maggie Griffin stood on the other side with her hands on her hips, wearing a black trouser suit and a white blouse. Her jacket lapels hung in such a way that he could see the FBI ID attached to her belt.

'Welcome to the USA,' she said with a smile. 'How was your journey?'

'Thanks,' he replied. 'I managed to catch some shuteye.'

They chatted as she led him through customs into the terminal building. Her service vehicle was parked immediately outside. Only when they were settled inside the car did they begin to discuss the case.

'They're expecting us at the prison,' Maggie Griffin said. As she fired up the engine, the air conditioning kicked in. 'The trip usually takes a couple of hours,' she added, 'but we're going to land in the middle of rush hour through the Bronx.'

'Have you found out anything more about him?' Wisting asked.

'I have a folder for you,' Maggie Griffin replied, reaching into the back seat. 'He's serving a sentence for killing his own father,' she added.

'His father?' Wisting repeated as he took the folder.

'Shot with a rifle,' Maggie said, turning on to a road marked I-78.

The folder was slim. It contained a judgement from the Connecticut Superior Court in Waterbury and a few print-outs from criminal records.

'He received the minimum sentence, twenty-five years,' Maggie went on. 'His father had been violent towards him and his mother for many years.'

Wisting skimmed through the final verdict. Forty-eight-year-old Robert Blair had been shot with his own hunting rifle. It was described as an act of self-defence. The son had moved between his parents to ward off a violent attack on his mother. The court had criticized him, however, for not contacting the police and reporting his father straight away.

'What has happened in your case?' Maggie asked. 'There must have been a development after we spoke, since Kripos is now involved and you've come over at such short notice.'

Wisting gave an account of what had taken place. The heat shimmered on the road ahead of them.

Once they had driven across the Hudson River, they had Manhattan on their right. The towering buildings soared towards a hazy sky. On the other side, the traffic was queued up and diesel exhaust belched out of gigantic trailer trucks.

Maggie Griffin had to summarize what he had said to be sure she had understood him correctly. 'So the case has been settled in the court system, and no one has challenged the verdict?' she queried. 'And yet you've chosen to reopen the case?'

'There are a few unanswered questions,' Wisting commented.

The car radio was on and a commercial singing the

praises of mattresses and beds cut through their conversation. Maggie turned down the volume.

'Officially I'm the one leading the interview,' she said. 'But *you* must ask the questions.'

Wisting agreed. The procedure was the same as when the pursuit of a wanted American killer had led her to Norway five years earlier. Formally, the FBI had been present as observers and had to stay on the sidelines. Now the roles were reversed.

When they passed the state boundary to Connecticut, the traffic eased off and the road narrowed into two lanes, with dense leafy forest on either side.

An hour and a half later, they stopped at a highway restaurant for a bite to eat. Wisting calculated the time as past midnight in Norway.

He took one of his antibiotic tablets while Maggie was still using the restroom.

He ordered a chicken fillet from the extensive menu and had it served with far too many trimmings. Maggie chose a fish dish.

'I understood you're returning as early as tomorrow,' she said, 'that there's no time for anything other than work.'

'Not this time,' Wisting replied with a smile.

'Where are you staying the night?' she asked. 'Thinking of the time difference, I assume you'll want to get to bed as soon as we've finished here.'

'At an airport hotel,' Wisting told her. 'I can take a taxi out there on our return.'

'I'll drive you,' Maggie assured him.

Half an hour later they were back in the car. Just before 8 p.m., they drove into Hartford, a medium-sized city with a network of ramrod-straight streets. The prison was situated in an industrial area on the northern side. The relatively low building, encircled by a massive wall, was also surrounded by a wire-mesh fence topped with barbed wire.

Hardly any cars were parked in the car lot and Maggie Griffin drew up as close to the entrance as possible. There was not a breath of wind and the heat remained as oppressive as ever.

Inside the building, a vast space opened out with an X-ray machine and an arch-shaped metal detector. A bald prison guard sat behind a counter of solid concrete and thick security glass. Maggie showed her ID and introduced Wisting before producing the documentation granting them access for a meeting with Curtis Blair. Removing her service weapon, she pushed it through a small metal lock chamber. The guard disappeared and emerged at the other side of the security control desk. Maggie Griffin helped herself to two grey plastic trays and handed one to Wisting before emptying her pockets.

Wisting sent his passport, wallet and keys through the conveyor belt on the X-ray machine. On the other side of the metal detector, another guard took over. He led them through corridors of drab linoleum flooring and mint-green walls with harsh fluorescent light tubes on the ceilings. Eventually, as they walked further into the building, they could hear the muffled howls and shrieks of the inmates as well as thumping on metal and concrete.

In the middle of a long corridor, they were shown into a box-like room furnished with four wooden chairs and a table on which a handcuff clamp was fitted at one side. They sat on their own for a few minutes before Curtis Blair was escorted in.

His hands were chained together and he was wearing the same type of orange boiler suit that Wisting had seen in American films.

Wisting and Maggie stood up and Maggie requested the handcuffs be removed. Once the guard had unlocked them, Curtis Blair rubbed his wrists and stayed on his feet until they were left alone.

'You knew we were coming,' Maggie Griffin began once they were all seated.

Curtis Blair looked across at Wisting. 'I don't know why, though,' he said. 'It's a long time since I was in Norway. It must be too late to come up with anything now.'

Maggie Griffin explained that their visit had not been arranged because he was suspected or accused of anything, but because the Norwegian police wanted to speak to him about his stay in Norway.

'This is voluntary,' she clarified. 'Are you willing to talk to Mr Wisting?'

'That depends on what they've said about me,' Curtis Blair replied.

'Well, all the same, we're interested in hearing what *you* have to say,' Maggie answered.

Curtis Blair held up his palms. 'What do you want to know?' he asked.

Wisting was reluctant to begin by letting Curtis Blair discover that Janne Kronborg was dead if he did not already know of it. It was important that he believe what he had to say about his stay in Norway could be checked against information provided by her.

'Have you been in touch with anyone in Norway since you returned home?' he asked.

'I received a letter from Janne,' he replied. 'I wrote a

number of letters in return, but I don't think they reached her. At any rate, I never heard anything back.'

'What happened to force you to leave?'

Curtis Blair slumped into his seat, as if wondering where to begin.

'Janne and I got on well the minute I moved in with her family,' he said. 'She was bubbly, funny and outgoing. Her brother was the same age as me. We shared some of the same interests, but he was more introverted. He had hardly any friends and mostly sat at home in his room. Janne had a zest for life. We could talk to each other about everything. Perhaps it was because she was eager to practise her English and wanted to learn more. I don't know.'

He paused. 'It developed into a kind of relationship,' he continued. 'When her parents found out, they didn't want me there any longer. I was sent home.'

'Couldn't you have changed to another host family?' he asked.

Curtis Blair shifted in his seat. 'I think the whole situation was misunderstood,' he replied. 'Janne's father made it out to be an assault, but that was far from the truth.'

Janne Kronborg had been fifteen years old. Wisting had no idea what the age of consent was in Connecticut, but in Norway having sexual relations at that age was a criminal offence, even if it had been consensual.

'Can you tell us about when you were discovered?'

The man opposite took a deep breath and let the air blow slowly out through his nose. 'I went to her room after everything went quiet in the house,' he began. 'She slept in the basement, as far away as possible from her parents' bedroom.'

He sat up a bit straighter. 'It wasn't the first time,' he

went on. 'We usually lay chatting about all sorts of things until I sneaked back to my room. This time we both fell asleep. I woke when I heard her father in the room. He chased me out, back to my own bedroom. Then I was told to pack. I spent the next few hours getting ready to leave. That was it.'

Wisting took notes, unsure of whether this was a doctored version of what had happened, or whether the Norwegian version had been overdramatized. 'What did you do earlier that evening?' he asked.

Curtis Blair took another deep breath, held it in for a moment and then let it out. 'I can't remember,' he said. 'I probably read, or else I was out taking photographs. I took loads of photos while I was in Norway.'

'Do you still have those photos?' Wisting asked.

'I expect my mom has them,' Curtis answered. 'It was a digital camera, a brand-new model. I had a laptop with me that I uploaded the photos to. I don't know what's become of that, but I transferred the pictures on to CDs.'

'Did you take photos near Stokkevann lake?' Wisting asked.

'Yes, I think so,' Curtis Blair replied. Wisting produced a map and pointed out the lake and where Janne Kronborg had lived. Curtis Blair nodded in recognition.

'There's a road here that's no longer in use,' Wisting explained, running his finger along the map. 'There's an old garage here too. Do you remember that? Have you been there?'

Nothing suggested that Curtis Blair recognized the area Wisting was describing. 'Maybe,' he said.

Wisting took out a photograph of the garage and laid it down, but it failed to help jog his memory.

'What kind of clothes did you wear when you were out with your camera?' Wisting ploughed on.

Blair shook his head. 'It's hopeless to try to remember that sort of thing,' he replied. 'Why are you asking?'

'Did you borrow clothes from Janne's brother?'

Curtis Blair shook his head again. 'I had my own clothes,' he said in a hesitant voice.

Wisting had brought the pictures from a barbecue at the Lions Club. He showed him a picture that did not include Janne Kronborg.

'Is that you?' he asked, pointing to him in the photograph.

'Yes,' Curtis said, nodding. 'That's his camouflage jacket. Peder, that's his name. I borrowed it now and again.' He took a closer look at the picture and smiled, as if it brought back good memories.

'Is there anyone else you know there?' Wisting asked.

'That's Charles Wright,' Curtis said, pointing out a man with a thick white moustache. 'He's from Massachusetts. Boston, I think. But he's lived in Norway for years and is married to a Norwegian woman. We were to celebrate the fourth of July with them, but nothing came of that. He was the one who came to pick me up after . . . I spent the night with them until the flight tickets were organized and then Charles drove me to the airport.'

Wisting retrieved the photograph and replaced it in the folder. Curtis Blair had had almost two decades to fabricate a story if he had anything to do with Tone Vaterland's murder. He would know what to say if anyone ever came and asked him. So far his answers had been vague and marked by the sense that time had erased most of his memories of his time in Norway.

He brought out a picture of Tone Vaterland and spoke her name aloud. 'Did you know her?' he asked.

Curtis Blair studied the photo but shook his head. There was nothing but confusion on his face.

'She disappeared at the time you left Norway,' Wisting told him. 'She was found dead a few days later.'

'In Bamble?' Curtis asked.

Wisting recounted a few details of the case. Curtis Blair's body was pressed into the back of his chair.

'Shit!' he groaned. 'I didn't hear about that. Wasn't anyone arrested for that?' He raised his voice without waiting for an answer: 'Surely you don't think I had anything to do with it?'

'A man was convicted, but cases can be reopened,' Wisting replied. 'I'm trying to find answers to a few questions that have remained unanswered since the original investigation.'

'Like what?'

'Among other things, a man with a camera was seen on the day she was killed,' Wisting answered. 'The police never found out who he was. We're wondering if it might have been you.'

'Why . . . ? Am I suspected of something?'

'This is really because the police never had a chance to talk to you at the time,' Wisting tried to explain. 'Since you left Norway before the investigation began.'

Curtis Blair seemed far from convinced. Maggie Griffin leaned forward a little.

'Can I ask you one thing?' she said.

Wisting nodded, keen to hear what Maggie had picked up on.

'You said you were meant to celebrate the fourth of July

at Charles Wright's house, but nothing came of it,' she said.

'Yes.'

Maggie glanced across at Wisting. 'The fourth of July is American Independence Day,' she explained, before turning back to Curtis again. 'Why did nothing come of it?'

Curtis Blair seemed not to understand the question. 'Because of what happened,' he replied.

Maggie leaned across the table. 'Let me just understand this correctly,' she said. 'In the early hours of the morning you were discovered in Janne Kronborg's bed. You had to leave the house and were collected by Charles Wright before lunchtime. The fourth of July celebration that evening was cancelled, and the next day you were sent on a flight back to the USA?'

'That's right.'

Maggie sat back and stole a glance at Wisting. His throat felt dry. The timeline had unravelled. Tone Vaterland had been killed on the evening of 4 July.

'Could you have planned to celebrate the fourth of July on another day?' Wisting asked.

'What do you mean?' Curtis Blair asked in return. 'The fourth of July is the fourth of July.'

Wisting realized how pathetic his question had been. Norway's national day was not celebrated on any day other than 17 May, neither in Norway nor anywhere else in the world.

'Were you at Charles Wright's house the whole evening on the fourth of July?' he asked.

'Yes.'

'You didn't go out?'

'No.'

Putting down his pen, Wisting was suffused with a feeling of annoyance and embarrassment. He understood what had happened. Speculation that the American exchange student had something to do with the Vaterland case could have arisen in 1999, and then died down when Danny Momrak was arrested, only to flare up again when the Kronborg girl had committed suicide. What had been idle gossip had been given a breeding ground in the unanswered questions following the trial and then sustenance by the family's silence about both the suicide and what had happened to cause Curtis Blair's sudden departure for the USA.

He had experienced this before. When a rumour began to do the rounds, reality became distorted. Details were altered, the chronology was misaligned and the facts changed to fit the story more exactly.

All the same, he would have to check this information and talk to Janne Kronborg's family as well as Charles Wright. Maybe he could check the actual flight details. He could have done all this before he travelled to the States. It could have been done as early as 2001, when the rumours had reached Kathe Ulstrup and she took it up with Sten Kvammen.

Maggie Griffin sat with her notebook on her lap, the FBI emblem embossed on the cover. Wisting felt like an amateur. He really wanted to wrap things up now, but spent almost another hour in the cramped interview room pinning down the details in Curtis Blair's statement.

When he closed his notebook, Maggie Griffin got to her feet, moved to the door and called the guard. Curtis Blair pushed his chair back a little from the table.

'Have you spoken to Janne?' he asked.

Maggie sat down again and looked across at Wisting,

who moved his head slowly from side to side. 'Janne Kronborg is dead,' he said, and went on to explain how she had taken her own life.

Curtis Blair's jaw muscles twitched. 'Why?' he asked. 'What about her father?'

'What about him?' Wisting retorted.

The American's eyes flickered. 'Why do you think he had come into her bedroom in the middle of the night when he found me there?' he asked. 'Do you think that was the first time?'

Keys rattled outside the door.

'Why do you think she had her bedroom at the other end of the house, where no one could hear anything?' Curtis went on. 'I never slept with her. She wasn't ready for that. I just spent the night with her. When I was there, he couldn't do anything to her.'

The interview room door swung open. A prison guard entered and ordered Curtis Blair to stand up.

'Why do you really think I was sent home?' Curtis Blair demanded.

Wisting stood up at the same time. Curtis was told to hold out his hands so that the guard could attach the handcuffs.

'Don't you get it?' he asked.

There was a metallic click.

'He wanted to have her for himself.'

'I see,' Wisting said, asking the guard to wait.

He now understood why Janne could not bear to go on living. Before Curtis Blair was led out, he managed to tell him that Terje Kronborg was suffering from severe dementia and would spend the rest of his life in a closed nursing-home ward.

It was dark by the time they left the prison.

Wisting felt the need to apologize for wasting the time of Maggie and the FBI, following a trail that had ended in nothing.

'That's our job,' she said, getting into her car. 'We check people of interest in and out of cases. If you hadn't come here, you wouldn't have been able to exclude Curtis Blair from your enquiries. Now you can concentrate on the other evidence.'

She was right, but all the same he felt as if the trip had been a waste of time.

The GPS showed the hours they had ahead of them in the car. For the initial stretch, the conversation flowed freely, and then Wisting began to feel tired. His chin dropped on to his chest a couple of times before he laid his head against the side window and fell fast asleep.

40

From his hotel window, Wisting watched the planes land and take off. It was ten hours until his departure.

Before he had gone to bed, he sent a message to Stiller explaining the conversation with Curtis Blair, but had not received a reply.

Plugging in his laptop, it took him some time to log in to the hotel's Internet connection. When he was eventually up and running, he saw that Stiller had sent him two emails, the first of these a response to his text. Stiller said he would try to find out if it was possible to get hold of passenger lists from 1999. Wisting was doubtful but planned to make contact with the treasurer of the Bamble Lions Club. The ticket had been purchased with the organization's money and he had more confidence that it might be possible to find a departure date in their accounts.

The second email had been sent four hours ago. It contained the result of the fingerprint analysis of the anonymous letters. On three of them, several prints from one person had been found, but a search had been conducted in the fingerprint register without success. That excluded Danny Momrak. Ninni Skjevik had also been ruled out through the prints found on the newspaper cutting she had brought him.

He checked the online Norwegian newspapers, but there were no developments in what the media had now dubbed 'the Stavern case'.

It was almost nine o'clock and he still had just over an hour left for breakfast. At home in Norway the working day would be in full swing.

He called Adrian Stiller from his computer. His face soon appeared on the screen. Wisting repeated several more details of what had emerged in the conversation with Curtis Blair. 'I'll write a synopsis in the course of the day,' he rounded off.

'What do you make of the fingerprints on the letters?' Stiller asked. 'Have you any other potential candidates for the sender's identity?'

'It has to be someone who has intimate knowledge of the case,' Wisting replied. 'Someone familiar with the numbering of the evidence items and the case documents.'

'You've met the lawyer,' Stiller commented.

Wisting shook his head. 'I'm more inclined to think it's an accomplice in the circles around Danny Momrak, or else it's just a coincidence,' he said. 'The paper used could have been taken from a workplace, and any marks on the paper could be from another employee who placed them in a photocopier or something like that.'

'When were you thinking of having a chat with Momrak?' Stiller asked.

'Soon,' was Wisting's terse reply.

His mobile was vibrating on the desktop and he reached out for it. It was a message from Line. *Letter for you*, was what it said.

A picture accompanied the message, with Line holding the envelope up to the camera. This time, only his name, in the familiar, sloping handwriting.

'Another letter has arrived,' he said, glancing up at Stiller. 'I'll have to call you back.'

He disconnected Stiller and rang Line, who was in the

kitchen when she answered – it looked as if she was preparing a meal.

'How's the USA?' she asked.

Wisting smiled. 'Just like it looks on TV,' he replied.

'Have you managed to do what you planned?'

'Yes, I'll be home early tomorrow.'

Line was stirring a pot as she spoke. 'Did you meet Maggie?' she asked.

'She's been showing me round,' he replied.

'This letter looks a bit unusual,' Line said as she drew the pot from the hotplate. 'Shall I open it?'

'Yes, but you'll have to use gloves.'

'Do you think it has something to do with the case?' Line asked. 'The one you're working on?'

'Yes,' he said. 'I received a similar letter last week.'

'From whom?'

'I don't know. There's no sender's name given.'

Line had produced a pair of washing-up gloves. 'It's a bit gross,' she said. 'After all, someone must have put it in your mailbox.'

'I know,' Wisting agreed, thinking of his car parked at the airport with the camera on the front windscreen. 'You've not seen anyone? Noticed a car or anything?'

'No. Amalie and I went out about noon. We've been to see Sofie and Maja. I checked the mailbox when we got back.'

She had taken out a fruit knife. In the background, Wisting could hear Amalie singing. Line stole a glance in the direction of the living room.

'Could it be something dangerous?' she asked. 'White powder, or something?'

'No,' Wisting answered. 'It's probably just a message.'

'Wait a minute, then,' Line said. She put down her phone

in order to use both hands but tilted the device, so that Wisting could see.

The engine noise from a large, heavy aircraft taking off from the runway reached in to him as Line cut open the envelope, laid aside the knife and peered inside before removing the contents.

Wisting was unable to see what it was.

'It's some Christian guff,' Line said.

'Let me see,' Wisting asked.

Line picked up her phone and held the camera above the kitchen table as she opened out a sheet of paper that looked as if it had been torn from a magazine.

'It must be from some Christian maniac,' she said.

The light reflected off the glossy paper. At the top, to one side, there was a picture of an elderly man with grey hair and beard in a purple shirt and black leather waistcoat with a large cross on a chain around his neck.

Faith, Hope and Charity was the headline. The text in the four columns below was too small for Wisting to read, but he could see a couple of the words highlighted with a yellow marker pen.

'What's accentuated there?' he asked.

'His name,' Line told him. 'Thorleif Fjellbu. It's from an interview with him in some sort of church journal. He's worked as a prison chaplain for thirty years.'

'Whereabouts?' Wisting asked, though he already knew the answer.

'Ullersmo,' Line replied. 'He talks about having been the spiritual guide of killers and other prisoners. Does that tell you anything?'

'Yes,' Wisting answered. 'It tells me who I need to talk to when I get back to Norway.'

41

The plane landed at the scheduled time. Wisting had slept for most of the flight and ate breakfast on board.

Although it was not raining outside, the runway was wet and the sky still overcast.

As soon as he had switched on his mobile phone, two messages from Adrian Stiller arrived. The first was brief: *Thorleif Fjellbu is able to meet you*. In addition, his address was given. It would be a mere half-hour's detour on his drive home from the airport.

The second message referred to Jan Hansen's girlfriend. Her name was Hanne Blom and she was younger than him. Jan Hansen had been fifty-one when he died, whereas Hanne Blom had recently turned forty-seven. She lived in Sketten, just outside Oslo, and had published three books of knitting patterns. For a time she had also run a yarn shop but had changed to online selling, an enterprise she now operated from her home. She had a grown-up daughter from a brief marriage who no longer lived with her.

Wisting drove straight to the clergyman's house. Less than an hour after leaving the plane, he was sitting in Thorleif Fjellbu's home office.

The man's beard, long and straggly, had grown since the time the photograph had been taken. A half-full pot of coffee sat beneath a filter funnel on his desk. Without asking, he pushed a mug across to Wisting's side.

'I understand this has to do with Jan Hansen,' he said, filling the mug.

'I was the senior investigating officer in the case against him in 2001,' Wisting explained. 'In the past fortnight I've received information that he may have committed another serious offence earlier in his life. A crime for which he may have needed to seek forgiveness when he became ill and died.'

Thorleif Fjellbu nodded. 'The work of a prison chaplain is founded to a large extent on trust,' he replied. 'I learned that early in my career: if I was to persuade the prisoners to open up about their inner torments, then they had to be able to trust that their confidences would remain with me.'

'What if you learned that someone was serving a sentence unfairly, for a crime someone else had committed?' Wisting probed. 'If somebody had been unjustly convicted? Wouldn't you have a moral duty to put things right? Pass on your information?'

The old prison chaplain drank the coffee he had poured for himself. 'That depends on whether it would be possible to put right the injustice that had been perpetrated,' he replied.

'What do you mean?' Wisting asked.

'If the innocent party had completed his sentence,' the chaplain explained, 'there's no chance of replacing lost time. Atoning for the sins of others can be a privilege.'

He shifted slightly in his seat before going on: 'If I were told such a truth, it doesn't change anything. To me, it's a matter of seeing the big picture. Trust is not something that's handed out with the clerical collar, it's something that's created and has to be fostered.'

'You're retired now,' Wisting broke in. 'You no longer work in the prison.'

'But I'm just as much a man who wishes to keep his word,' Fjellbu replied.

Wisting said he understood. 'I'm not actually asking what he confided in you,' he said. 'I just want to know if he did. If he'd done something that had gone unpunished.'

Thorleif Fjellbu sat nodding thoughtfully. Wisting took this as confirmation.

'Jan Hansen destroyed many people's lives,' the chaplain finally said. 'He had a deep inner need to talk. But what he confided to me were circumstances he didn't want known, not even after he was gone. I can't pass that on.'

When Jan Hansen was convicted, he had also been suspected of six cases of assault and rape. They were all shelved. It could be these cases he had wanted to discuss, but it could also have been the Vaterland one. However, Wisting would not be able to take this further.

'Did you speak about his girlfriend?' he asked instead. 'Hanne Blom?'

'I understood he'd been contacted by a woman and this had developed into a relationship,' the chaplain said. 'I was happy for him. Everyone may well need such an anchor in life, but we didn't talk about her. I don't know what she brought to his existence.'

Leaning forward in his chair, Wisting asked, 'Can you show our discussion the same discretion as your conversations with the inmates? You won't repeat it to anyone?'

'I'd have no interest in doing so,' Fjellbu reassured him.

Wisting nodded. 'This is to do with Danny Momrak,' he said. 'He served about fifteen years in Ullersmo. Did you ever meet him?'

The old prison chaplain took a firm grasp of his coffee mug and drank deeply before setting it down again. 'I know of him,' he replied. 'But he wasn't someone who sought the kind of comfort I could give.'

His hand was still wrapped around the coffee mug and he tapped his fingers lightly on the side.

As Wisting took a sip from his own mug, the notion began to form in his mind that Thorleif Fjellbu might be the anonymous letter-writer. This could well be a device for him to direct attention towards an injustice without breaking the bonds of trust.

'Have you a Post-it note?' he asked, gesticulating towards a block on the desk.

Fjellbu seemed surprised, but tore off the top sheet and handed it over.

Accepting it, Wisting opened his notebook and stuck it inside before scribbling something on the part of the note he had touched.

'You never spoke to Danny Momrak about guilt and innocence?' he asked, mostly in order to avoid further questions from the chaplain.

'No.'

Wisting shut his notebook. He could make no further headway here.

42

Danny Momrak splashed soapy water on the floor and drew the mop across the linoleum in a slow, practised movement, swabbing from side to side.

The door to number six was open a crack. The cell had been unoccupied for two days and he was keyed up about who would be allocated to it. Usually it took no more than twenty-four hours for a vacant cell to be filled.

He was missing Tom already. They had been inmates together for nearly eight years, but Tom's days in prison were numbered. As for himself, he had far too long left for it to be worthwhile counting.

The floor was actually spotless, but his hour of cleaning duties in the middle of the day had become part of everyday life for him.

He moved down the corridor, using his foot to remove the mop head, then tossing it in the bucket and attaching a new one before setting to work in the common room.

He could hear raucous laughter from the guardroom. Frankmann and Lasson.

When Danny had finished his chores, he pulled the cleaning trolley across to the guards and positioned himself half a metre from the door.

'I'm done,' he said.

Keys rattled as Frankmann got to his feet. Danny

followed him out into the corridor, where the visitors' rooms were located.

This was the worst part of the job. Cleaning up after other prisoners and their visitors. He seldom had visitors himself. His mother came on his birthday and just before Christmas, and that was that. A few years ago, he had met up with someone from the Red Cross befriending service, but it felt artificial and strange. All his friends had broken off contact. To be honest, it was reciprocal. He had not written or sent a single letter.

He changed the rubbish bag and began to wipe down the leather furniture.

It felt as if no one knew he was here.

Geir Atle in cell eight had been interviewed by *Det Nye* magazine. He had told them about his life in prison and about the man he had killed. In the weeks that followed, he had received more letters than he could answer. Danny too had been asked for an interview, both by a journalist from his hometown and from *Vi Menn* magazine, but he had not even responded to the enquiries. Geir Atle had been abused by his grandfather throughout his childhood, almost up to the time he was at junior high school. When he was nineteen, he had shot the dirty old pervert with his own rifle. This was a story that aroused compassion and sympathy. Danny's story was very different. It was difficult enough to gain acceptance among his fellow prisoners with a conviction for rape and murder. And no one was interested in hearing that he hadn't done it.

The interview in *Vi Menn* was for a series about *what actually happened*. He had read some of the published stories. Inmates who had denied in court that they had committed robbery, blackmail and murder finally told the truth. That was not something he could take part in. He had already given an account of what had happened.

Frankmann's radio crackled: a message about a new inmate waiting in reception who had to be escorted to the section, a transfer from Skien Prison.

Frankmann told Danny to hurry up. When he had completed his duties, he was returned to the common area to lock away the cleaning trolley.

The heavy metal door leading into the section slammed noisily. A man in jogging trousers and a white T-shirt, a black bin bag slung over his shoulder, was led in by two guards.

Lasson emerged from the guardroom with a slim blue folder in his hand. 'Jan Hansen?' he asked. The newly arrived prisoner said yes and put his bin bag down on the floor.

As Danny hovered in front of the cell door, Jan Hansen's eyes swivelled round and met his.

Frankmann rattled his keys. 'Lock up,' he said, consigning Danny to his cell.

43

Hanne Blom featured in countless photographs on the Internet, usually depicted in a sweater knitted from her own design. Slightly plump, her appearance was fairly ordinary – blonde hair, blue eyes and glasses with thick black frames. Nothing about her suggested she would have problems finding a partner outside prison walls.

Wisting arrived unannounced. The door leading into a cavernous double garage was wide open when he turned into her driveway. Hanne Blom was busy carrying packages for the post to a small delivery van. The garage appeared to function as a storeroom.

She gave him a quizzical look.

Wisting introduced himself, keen to see how she would react. 'I've come because of Jan Hansen,' he said. 'I was in charge of the inquiry against him.'

She nodded as if she had immediately realized who he was and what role he had played in Jan Hansen's life.

'Have you time for a chat?' he asked.

'We'll have to go inside,' she answered.

Sliding shut the side door of the delivery van, she closed the garage door and led the way into her house.

'I understand you visited him a lot in prison,' Wisting began once they were seated at the kitchen table.

'We were a couple,' Hanne Blom declared without a blush. She gathered up some scattered magazines and stacked them neatly. 'But I don't understand why you've come here now,' she said. 'It's more than a year since he died.'

'His name has cropped up in another old case,' Wisting replied.

'A murder case?' the woman facing him asked. 'Is he a suspect?'

Wisting moved his head slightly to one side.

'A man has already been convicted in this case,' he clarified. 'But accusations have been made against Jan Hansen that I'm obliged to look into.'

It seemed as if Hanne Blom quickly appreciated what this was all about. 'So this other man may have been unjustly convicted?' she asked.

'That's what the allegations claim,' Wisting said.

Hanne Blom rose from her chair and moved towards a coffee machine. 'He was a different man before I met him,' she replied. 'Coffee?'

Wisting accepted with thanks. 'How did the two of you meet?'

'I answered a lonely-hearts personal ad,' Hanne Blom explained. 'At that time there were personal ads in the weekly magazines. Now they're all on the Internet. They don't have online access in our prisons.'

As the coffee machine began to rumble, Hanne Blom hovered beside the worktop. 'We exchanged letters for a while before I started visiting him,' she went on. 'At that point he was incarcerated in Skien. Eventually he applied for a transfer to Ullersmo, to move nearer to me.'

'Was he open with you about who he was and why he was under lock and key?' Wisting asked.

'From the very start.'

'Did he make any kind of admission or acknowledgement to you?'

'What do you mean?'

'To me he always stuck to his story that he was innocent,' Wisting said. 'But you had a different kind of relationship with him, I'm sure.'

Hanne Blom set cups down on the table. 'Our relationship wouldn't have worked unless we were honest with each other,' she said.

'Does that mean he confessed to you?' Wisting asked.

'It means I had no reason to doubt what he told me,' Hanne Blom replied.

Wisting took a gulp of coffee and felt his stomach protest against it.

'Did he talk about cases other than the ones for which he was convicted?' he asked.

Hanne Blom's answer was evasive: 'What he did and didn't do will have to remain between him and Our Lord,' she said. 'I won't be the one to hang him out to dry in any circumstances.'

Wisting's mind strayed to the prison chaplain. 'Did he change much when he became ill?' he asked.

'He was ill long before the prison took action and he was diagnosed,' she said. 'By then it was too late. Things moved fast towards the end.'

'Did he say anything to you about the other inmates?'

'Sometimes,' she replied. 'There was someone he played chess with. Ingar. And a Spanish chef who rustled up a lot of food in the section he was in.'

'What about Dan Vidar Momrak?' Wisting went on. 'He was known as Danny.'

She shook her head quickly. 'I don't recall that name, but there was a neo-Nazi there he kept his distance from. I don't know what his name was.'

'Have you had any contact with the other inmates?'

'Why should I?' Hanne Blom replied.

'I was thinking that some of them might have attended his funeral, or something along those lines.'

She shook her head again. 'The chaplain held a special service in the prison chapel.'

Wisting's phone rang. He took it out, saw that it was Stiller and clicked it off.

'Tell me about this other case,' Hanne Blom said. 'What is Jan accused of?'

Hanne Blom had been reticent in her answers. If she knew anything, she seemed unwilling to share it. Wisting saw no need to go into any details on the background for his visit.

'I'll have to come back to that later,' he said, using the phone call from Stiller as an excuse for ending their conversation. 'I have to leave, sorry.' He pushed his coffee cup across the table. 'Thanks for sparing me the time to talk.'

She accompanied him to the front door and stood at the top of the steps with her arms crossed as he reversed out of the courtyard.

He drove a couple of hundred metres before turning at the first intersection, where he stopped to return Stiller's call.

'Forensics have completed their DNA analyses,' Stiller told him. 'They've found both blood and semen on the clothes from the garage cellar. They have a satisfactory DNA profile that's being relayed to the register as we speak. We may have a name by the end of the day.'

'Blood as well?' Wisting asked.

'Smaller amounts,' Stiller replied. 'Possibly from her. They've prioritized the semen sample.'

Wisting felt elated by this information. The bag and clothing had been well preserved, but even though they did not seem degraded in any way, they had been exposed for many years. His hopes that the tests would yield results had been limited.

'Where are you now?' he asked Stiller.

'Kripos,' Stiller replied. 'The office at Bryn.'

'Then I'll head for there,' Wisting said. 'I've some fingerprints to be checked.'

They wound up the conversation and Wisting sat for almost another ten minutes, using the time to read the online newspapers. No news about Agnete Roll.

He made a U-turn and had to reverse twice to turn the car in the narrow street. Then he drove back to Hanne Blom's house and saw that the small delivery van was gone.

Parking in the street, Wisting took out a pair of latex gloves and left the car engine running as he approached two rubbish containers beside the fence. One was for paper, cardboard and boxes. Wisting lifted the lid and saw it was almost full, with a couple of customer leaflets and advertising flyers on top. He had to search for a minute or two before finding what he was looking for, a weekly magazine printed on glossy paper. A summer edition of *Hjemmet*. The top-right-hand corner was emblazoned with *Three magazines in one*.

He glanced over his shoulder before snatching it up. No one seemed to have noticed.

44

Adrian Stiller met him down in reception inside the Kripos building. 'You should have had your own pass,' he joked. 'Now that you're employed here.'

Wisting followed him through the security doors and up in the lift to the sixth floor. The silent corridors and deserted offices testified to the holiday period.

Stiller's office was impersonal: a few bookcases of ring binders and an almost clear desk with a computer screen. An abstract art print hung on one wall.

Wisting placed the magazine he had taken from Hanne Blom's recycling bin on the desk. He had removed the prison chaplain's Post-it note from his notebook and stuck it inside on page three.

Pulling out a drawer, Stiller took out an evidence bag and labelled it. 'I'll take them down to the labs,' he said.

'Both the chaplain and the girlfriend are in a position to know something but be unwilling to come forward,' Wisting remarked, and went on to give an account of the two conversations.

Stiller's phone rang. Checking the number, he cast a glance at Wisting. 'The DNA registry,' he said, as he answered.

After speaking in words of one syllable to the person at the other end, he turned to his computer screen and logged in to read the analysis results. 'Exactly,' he said, nodding. 'I see. Thanks.'

Wisting leaned forward but was unable to read the results on the screen from where he sat.

Stiller put down his phone and turned to face Wisting again. 'Jan Hansen,' he said. 'Positive result on five out of five samples.'

Wisting's throat became dry. He stood up and walked towards the screen as Stiller moved aside to make room for him.

There were five simple lines in the space for the conclusion, one for each of the samples. They were all *identical with the person recorded in the ID-register as HANSEN, Jan.*

He could scarcely remember ever seeing such an unambiguous result. 'Tell me about the samples,' he requested.

Stiller had printouts in a cardboard folder. He took them out and handed them to Wisting. 'These are just the preliminary analyses,' he said.

Wisting read while Stiller explained. Several stains on Tone Vaterland's white blouse had reacted positively to an acid phosphatase test. Three samples had tested positive for semen, while in two others there was a mixture of semen and blood. All five tests had produced DNA profiles, four of these from semen while the fifth was from a microscopic quantity of blood.

The rest of the clothing had also been tested and several samples taken, but these yielded negative results.

According to the report, two of the positive samples were taken from the bust of the blouse, one from the stomach area, one from the right side and another from the back. The absence of semen on the other items of clothing and the way the semen was distributed around the garment made Wisting conclude that Jan Hansen had used it to wipe himself. Used it as a rag when he was finished.

'Do you have photos of the clothing found?' Wisting asked. Stiller called them up on the screen and Wisting drew his chair closer.

The first photographs were overview images of the garage and the opening in the brick wall. The ones he was particularly interested in were the pictures taken from the interior of the crawl space before the rucksack and clothes had been lifted out.

The white blouse lay at the very back, as if it had been thrown in with greater force than all the rest. A layer of what looked like dry cement dust was scattered over it along with some dust and debris from the ceiling.

'Can I have copies?' he asked. 'Of the photos and the reports?'

Stiller picked up an envelope from the desk and handed it to him. 'User access restored,' he said. 'New password.' Wisting accepted it with thanks.

'Is something wrong?' Stiller asked.

'I don't know,' Wisting said. 'I just find the analysis results overwhelming. Far more conclusive than I'd imagined they'd be.'

He clicked further into the file, studying details. 'This entire case has been rigged from the start,' he said. 'Staged with the anonymous letters. It gives me a feeling that something doesn't add up. If something is too good to be true, then it's usually false.'

'All the same, we'll have to circulate the information,' Stiller said. 'The Public Prosecutor and local police authorities will have to be told. Danny Momrak's lawyer should also be sent word.'

'Let's hold back for a bit,' Wisting suggested. 'Danny Momrak's conviction has given the victim's relatives peace of mind for many years. If we do anything to disillusion them, then we really must have all our ducks in a row first. All the answers.'

'I'm obliged to alert the Public Prosecutor before the day is out,' Stiller said. 'I'm not sure how long we can allow ourselves to drag our feet.'

Wisting rose from his seat. 'We ought to find out the identity of the anonymous letter-writer before we broadcast anything,' he said.

Stiller picked up the evidence bag containing Hanne Blom's magazine. 'What about Danny Momrak?' he asked.

'I'm going to speak to him,' Wisting replied.

45

The wet road surface had dried and Wisting drove home with the sun in his face. He could feel how the change to his normal daily rhythm had affected him. He was tired and jet-lagged, but rest was not an option.

He turned up the volume on the radio as soon as he heard the news bulletin and hunched over the steering wheel when they spoke about the killing of Agnete Roll in Stavern. Someone who had been charged with giving false information to the police was now in police custody. The police prosecutor refused to make any further comment but indicated there would be a press release in the course of that afternoon. *Agnete Roll was found murdered eight days ago after being missing for five days*, the newsreader ended.

Driving on until an exit road appeared, Wisting turned off and found a convenient lay-by, where he took out his phone and sent a message to Hammer: *The husband?*

There was no immediate answer, so he returned to the motorway, immediately regretting his message, an inappropriate intervention.

His phone rang five minutes later, a call from Hammer. 'Yes, it's Erik Roll,' he confirmed. 'We brought him in yesterday, but I think he's slipping through our fingers.'

'What have you got on him?'

'He gave a false statement about when he went home on the night Agnete disappeared. He's admitted he didn't go straight home from the town centre but paid a visit to a female colleague he used to have a relationship with.'

Wisting remembered the name: Benedikte Lindhjem.

'That might well furnish him with a motive, but it doesn't link him any closer to the murder.'

'What about the petrol can?' Wisting asked. 'Maren told me the can of fuel for the lawnmower was missing.'

Hammer gave an audible sigh. 'Erik Roll claimed it must have been stolen,' he said. 'It's not particularly believable, but the shed was left unlocked and, in fact, other thefts of petrol were reported in the locality.'

'He's got a defence lawyer?'

'Reidar Heitmann.'

Wisting nodded to himself. This was one of the local lawyers. 'Do you have anything else on him?' he asked.

'Maren is working on a couple of leads,' Hammer replied. 'She's found ash on Erik Roll's shoes.'

'He said he'd been at the site of the fire when he was searching for his wife,' Wisting reminded him.

'She's working on something that will nail down the date for that.'

Wisting cast a glance at the microphone on the car roof. 'Date the ash?' he asked. 'Is that possible?'

It sounded as if someone had entered Hammer's office. 'She can explain that for herself,' he said hurriedly. 'Her hypothesis is that Erik Roll hid his wife's body at the fire site and came back later to set it all ablaze again.'

The car radio kicked in once more when their conversation ended. Wisting switched it off and tried to focus his thoughts on Danny Momrak. All the evidence, both circumstantial and physical, had pointed to him. At the final verdict he had been described as completely lacking in trustworthiness. However, criminal cases were not about either trust or worthiness, they were about pinning down the truth.

It was nearly three o'clock when he turned into his own driveway. He needed a bite to eat and a couple of hours to prepare for his meeting with Danny Momrak.

His mailbox was empty and he noticed the grass on the lawn was overgrown. He would have to cut it while the weather was fine.

He carried his suitcase in and, as he unpacked, it crossed his mind that he had not taken the tablets, as his doctor had prescribed. Morning and evening had merged into one on his trips to and from the USA. He rushed to swallow one and left out the blister pack with the rest of the pills beside the bathroom basin.

A limited choice faced him in the fridge and he ended up heating a portion of frozen meat and potato hash, frying two eggs to have on the side. Line made an unexpected appearance while he was eating.

'Welcome home,' she said with a smile, setting his post down on the kitchen table. The anonymous letter was in a transparent plastic bag.

'Thanks,' he said.

Line sat down. 'How are you feeling?' she asked. 'You look tired.'

Wisting finished chewing. 'My body's telling me I've been on a long journey,' he said.

'Was your trip productive?' Line asked. 'Did you manage to speak to the American?'

He nodded. 'It's apparently all been a misunderstanding,' he said. 'It's not certain he was even in Norway at the time in question.'

'And you had to travel to the States to find that out?'

He shrugged. 'It remains to be seen if it all stacks up,' he told her.

Wisting, having finished his meal, began to clear the table. 'We'd thought he fitted into the timeline,' he added, glancing at the clock.

He had not told Line about Danny Momrak and did not do so now either. She still thought everything focused on Jan Hansen and the murder of Pernille Skjerven in 2001.

'Where's Amalie?' he asked.

'With Sofie and Maja,' Line replied. 'I'm going to pick her up now.'

'I need to leave now too,' Wisting told her.

He saw her to the door but returned to the kitchen to find his notes. One of the most important aids in an investigation was the timeline.

Something had tugged at him when he was telling Line that the American did not fit into the timeline. He could not think of what, though.

The timeline he had drawn extended over almost twenty years. The starting point was the murder of Tone Vaterland in 1999. Two years later, Pernille Skjerven had been killed. In 2005, Jan Hansen became romantically involved with Hanne Blom, and in 2012 he had been transferred to Ullersmo Prison. Until the time of Danny Momrak's release, they had served time in the same section. Last year, Jan Hansen had died. One year later, Wisting began to receive letters pointing to Hansen as the real perpetrator in the Vaterland case.

Between these main points on the timeline, there was a whole series of events, minor and major. Janne Kronborg had taken her own life, Curtis Blair had been convicted of killing his father, Ninni Skjevik had made a documentary inside the prison, Sten Kvammen had carved out a career, Thorleif Fjellbu had retired as prison chaplain and Bohrman the defence lawyer had lent out his case documents.

A network of threads and lines of connection, but he still had no idea who was pulling the strings.

46

The paper, faded and fragile, crackled in Danny's hands as he unfolded it.

Moving across on the leather settee, Ninni peered out through the bars on the small window. Snow had added to the height of the wall outside by almost half a metre.

The opinion piece, one of very few things she had taken with her when she finished up at the local newspaper, was dated the day prior to Danny's conviction. She had worked there for nearly six years, submitting two or three stories daily, but there was no cake or speeches on her last day. All she was given was a testimonial stating when she began and when she left, along with a list of a few simple character traits. Independent and persistent, with an immense capacity for work and excellent writing skills – that was the best she could take out of it.

'I don't understand,' Danny said, glancing up.

'I believed you to be innocent and prepared this article in case you were freed,' she told him.

Danny looked down at the paper again.

'I still do,' she said, 'and I think it's possible to convince others of that too.'

'How?'

Leaning forward, Ninni lowered her voice, as if someone

might be able to hear them. 'By finding out who really did it,' she replied.

'In what way, though?'

She explained how she would make a special documentary about his case. Bragged about how good he had been in front of the camera in the production currently under way, and exaggerated her personal experience in investigative journalism. 'I already have a name in mind,' she concluded. 'A rapist who lived in Bamble at that time, but who was never interviewed.'

'Who was that?'

She refused to give him the name until she had persuaded him to participate, to prevent him from going straight to his lawyer with the information.

'An American exchange student,' she said. 'He left Norway the very next day after the murder. I'm working on tracing him on the other side of the Atlantic.'

Getting to his feet, Danny paced back and forth across the floor, but stopped when Ninni began to rummage through her bag.

'This was taken in Norway, three months prior to the murder,' she said, handing him a photograph of Curtis Blair. She saw that he understood what this meant. The man with the camera and camouflage clothing the police had never tracked down.

'If I'm to go on with this, I need your cooperation,' she said. 'You mustn't talk to anyone else at all about it. Not to your lawyer and not to any other journalists. Not to anybody, in fact.'

Danny was full of questions, which she carefully answered. 'Do we have a deal?' she asked.

He agreed. 'Just tell me what you want me to do.'

47

The visit to Danny Momrak was the kind of encounter Wisting had no wish to call and announce in advance. A great deal could be lost or slip through the cracks in a telephone conversation. Facial expressions and emotions. Nuances.

He had used an online map to familiarize himself with the area. Danny Momrak lived beside the old railway track between Larvik and Porsgrunn. It had been decades since Wisting had been in the area and he found little left of the sparsely populated village. The school had closed down and a number of houses had been abandoned.

According to what Wisting had discovered, Danny Momrak had taken over a house left unoccupied after his uncle's death four years previously. He found what had to be the correct turn-off and bumped along a gravel track ending at an isolated house on the very fringes of the forest. Ochre yellow with scaffolding lining the walls. Three car wrecks sat in the yard beside an old grey Volkswagen Touran. Wisting made a note of the number plate.

As he stepped out, he heard clicking noises from the car engine. A black cat, sprawled on the gravel, rose and stood staring at him with its tail in the air.

Danny Momrak appeared at the door in work clothes – a few years older, but still very like his photographs.

Wisting greeted him with a nod as the cat sauntered

across the yard. Danny Momrak took a few steps back. 'You're from the police,' he said. 'William Wisting. My lawyer said you'd been to see him.'

'That's right,' Wisting said. 'There's been a development since I paid him a visit. Can we sit down somewhere for a chat?'

Danny showed him round to the back of the house, where he had been busy working on a patio. Slabs of slate were stacked high, but alongside the house several squares had already been laid. Wisting commented on the scale of the job.

'I do a little at a time,' Danny said. 'My uncle worked at the quarry.' He used his hand to point. 'These slates have lain here for as long as I can remember.'

Two birds alighted on the edge of a rusty wheelbarrow full of rainwater but soon took off and flew away. The cat did not bat an eyelid.

They sat down on either side of a rickety garden table.

'I'm sure it will look great when it's finished,' Wisting commented.

'The birds shit all over the place,' Danny complained, wiping dried bird droppings from the table.

The cat curled up at his feet as Wisting took out his notebook.

No matter what questions a laboratory analysis answered, the most important thing was to talk to people. This was the heart of all investigation. Statements from witnesses and suspects were the fundamental source of insight.

Momrak shifted slightly to avoid having the glare of the sun in his eyes. 'Does this mean you're working officially on the case now?' he asked.

Wisting confirmed this and explained about his

appointment to the Cold Cases Group. 'Is it OK for me to tape this?' he asked, finding the record function on his phone.

'So this is an official interview?' Momrak asked. 'Should I have my lawyer present?'

'I think we're on the same side in this,' Wisting told him.

With a nod, Momrak crouched down and stroked the cat's neck. 'Was it Jan Hansen who did it?' he asked.

Wisting started the recorder. 'It's too early to say at the moment,' he replied.

'But have you found any new evidence?' Momrak asked. 'Apart from him being there when Tone was killed?'

Wisting was reluctant to mention Tone Vaterland's clothes and the DNA analyses. 'Everything's been complicated by Jan Hansen's death,' he answered.

'But it's not too late, surely?' Momrak asked. 'You can find things out even though he's dead? DNA and fingerprints and that sort of thing, I mean. Surely they don't get deleted from the records because he's dead?'

'Not for a few years afterwards,' Wisting reassured him.

Momrak dug a pack of cigarettes from his pocket, found a lighter and lit up.

'You were in prison together,' Wisting said. 'What kind of contact did you have?'

'No more than necessary,' Momrak replied. 'I realized what he was like right from the start. A sly bastard. He always wangled things for himself, never shared anything. He was the oldest in that section and thought he knew best.'

'Did you ever discuss your cases?'

'No.'

'So he didn't know what you had been convicted of, and you didn't know about his crime either?'

'I knew he was in for murder. There were rumours

about a few other rapes as well. I kept my distance from him.'

'Who talked about other rapes?'

'One of the lads, but I don't know anything more. After all, it's not as if we can use Google to do a search while we're behind bars.'

The tiny birds had returned to the barrow, perching on the rim, pecking at the water with their beaks. The cat got up from its comfortable spot but just stood staring at them.

'I saw the documentary you were in,' Wisting said. They chatted a little about how Danny Momrak had come to take part in the recording. He had been reluctant at first, but had been pleased with the final result.

'I understand you've spoken to the woman who put it together,' he said. 'Ninni Skjevik. She was here on Monday. She covered the whole case in 1999. I didn't follow the newspapers at that time. When I sat in prison, I wasn't allowed to read anything, but my lawyer took care of most of it. I read everything before the appeal court hearing. Most of it just made me angry and frustrated, but what she had written was OK. She didn't take sides.'

The cat ambled to the edge of the forest and moved along a path. At the other end, Wisting could make out the glitter of water.

Danny Momrak tapped ash from his cigarette to the side of his chair. 'What about the American?' he asked. 'Have you checked him out?'

'We're working on that,' Wisting replied, before turning the conversation on to a different path: 'Can you tell me about the day Tone Vaterland was killed?'

Danny Momrak heaved a sigh. 'I've been through that

so many times before,' he complained. 'You can read about it. My story is no different now from that time.'

'Begin with you sitting in the car outside the petrol station,' Wisting said, picturing the footage from the CCTV surveillance in his mind's eye.

Danny Momrak pinched his cigarette between two fingers and dropped the stub on the slate slabs. 'I drove along the old road,' he said. 'As far as the garage, picked up my gear and drove out again. That was it.'

'Your gear?'

'The hash.'

'How long did you take?'

'Quarter of an hour max.'

'That's a long time,' Wisting commented.

Momrak shrugged. 'I had nearly fifty grams there,' he said. 'I divided it up into fives. Weighed and packed. That took time.'

'Whereabouts in the garage had you hidden the hash?' he asked.

Momrak hesitated for a moment.

'Not in the actual garage,' he replied. 'There were some old car tyres on the slope beside it. I stored it in one of them.'

'What about the scales?'

'I brought them with me.'

Wisting nodded thoughtfully. That was listed in the evidence report from the examination of his car.

'Jan Hansen drove a small white delivery van with an elevating gate,' Wisting said. He knew it would be impossible to remember, but had to ask: 'Did you see a vehicle like that?'

'Not on the old road,' Danny Momrak replied. 'It's in

253

the interviews. I saw neither Tone, nor her bike, nor anything else, for that matter. But you know . . .'

He paused for effect, as if collecting his thoughts.

'I sat in the car watching the traffic before I drove on to the old road. Sometimes cars turned off there or someone arrived to go down to the shore for a swim. I wanted to make sure I'd be on my own and there were no police in the vicinity. From time to time, the emergency squad met up at that petrol station. Sometimes unmarked cars as well. So I took a good look round.'

He paused again. 'I've thought about this a lot,' he said when he picked up the thread. 'After all, it's an evening I've gone over numerous times to try to remember more of it. I can sort of see it all before me and think there was a van like that at the petrol station, while I was parked there. There was a name on the side of it. I don't recall what it said, but there was a picture of a chair.'

Wisting looked down at his mobile to make sure it was recording.

Jan Hansen had driven the same delivery van when he abducted and murdered Pernille Skjerven two years later. *Larsen Furniture* was written on the side and the image was of a Stressless armchair.

The cat had returned from its stroll and sat licking its fur.

'I can't say for certain, of course,' Momrak went on. 'But it is at least something I can picture in my head. From where it was parked, it would be only a matter of crossing the motorway and you'd be at the turn-off for the old road when Tone came cycling along.'

Wisting jotted down a couple of key words. It could be false memory, or something Danny Momrak had invented to support the suspicions against Jan Hansen. When Hansen had been arrested, a photo of the delivery van had appeared on TV and in the newspapers. In some but not all of these images, the registration plate and company name had been obliterated.

'What do you know about the murder Jan Hansen was convicted of?' he asked.

'Not much more than what Ninni Skjevik has told me,' Momrak answered. 'It's not so easy to find anything about it on the Internet. It's getting to be a long time ago.'

'Did you know he had a girlfriend?'

Momrak nodded. 'She visited him in prison,' he replied. 'Everyone knew when she was about to arrive. The stink of aftershave wafted all through the section when he was getting ready to see her. Sometimes we could hear them too – the noise carried all the way back to where we were.'

'Have you had any contact with her?' Wisting asked.

'Me? Why would I have any contact with her?'

Wisting made no response. What he was after was lines of connection, to give a picture of who was in cahoots with whom and who might be behind the anonymous letters.

'What about Thorleif Fjellbu?' he asked instead. 'The chaplain?'

Danny Momrak shook his head. 'I'm not religious,' he said. 'I had nothing to say to him.'

The sun had shifted while they were speaking and Danny Momrak had to move his chair to avoid the sun in his eyes.

'The person you should speak to is Jonas Haugerud,' he said. 'He chickened out at that time. Didn't dare admit he bought hash from me. It's time-barred now, and from what

I've heard, he's been convicted of far more serious things since then. Maybe he can man up and be honest now.'

The cat vanished beneath the table again. Wisting felt something rub against his legs as he gazed at the man opposite. He tried to imagine what a sentence of seventeen years in prison had done to him. His eyes looked confident and assured, but the expression around his mouth was somewhat cynical, as if something had been left unsaid at the corner of his mouth. At the same time, there was an obsequious air about his demeanour. Some kind of indifference or even contempt for other people that could result from years spent in prison. Something obstinate and spiteful.

48

Reinstatement of his data access was a painstaking process. Wisting had to log in to every single database with the passwords automatically generated for him, and then choose new ones. By the time he had negotiated all the systems it had grown dark outside. He lingered in the blue-grey light from the computer screen, reading through the report that confirmed the discovery of Jan Hansen's DNA on five samples from Tone Vaterland's blouse. He understood that the tests had been more comprehensive than he had initially realized. They included DNA with female sex markers found on underwear. Tone Vaterland's DNA was not held in the computer system, and in order to confirm that the DNA was hers, her profile had to be extracted from the Forensics database.

He picked out the report on the examination of biological trace material in 1999. The list of the material tested was lengthy. Samples had been taken from the vagina and vulva, anus, chest, throat, mouth cavity, arms, hands, feet, fingers and nails. The only site to produce a positive result was the internal examination.

He noted the name of the lab technician who had conducted the re-examination of the clothing. Analysis conditions were completely different nowadays compared to 1999, but he had questions for her nonetheless. It would be interesting to have the old samples analysed using modern methods.

Before he logged off, he looked up the case against Erik Roll. From what he could see, the man was still detained in one of the cells at Tønsberg police station.

Several new interviews had been recorded in the course of that day. Wisting clicked into the file and opened the last of these. A sixteen-year-old boy had been interviewed with both his parents present. Jan Ove Bergene Larsen. From the introductory preamble, Wisting figured out that he was the last of a group of four boys to be interviewed. His friends had already admitted stealing petrol for their mopeds. They had sneaked out at night and trawled the neighbourhood in search of petrol cans, rummaging through garden sheds and garages. In some locations they had taken cans, and in others they had poured the petrol into half-full cans they were already carrying. The raid had been pulled off the night before Agnete Roll went missing. The shed at the house belonging to her and her husband was one of the places they had visited.

Wisting also read the statements of the other boys, one of them a friend of the lad who mowed the lawn at Erik and Agnete's home. He had accompanied him one time when he was cutting the grass at an old woman's house in Vardeknausen and spotted a ten-litre can in a garden shed. That was how the idea for the entire enterprise had struck him. Litres of petrol, easily accessed. Very few householders would notice a few litres missing, and it was doubtful that anyone would go to the bother of reporting it to the police if a can went astray.

A separate report pointed out a locus behind the junior high school where three of the empty petrol cans had been discarded. Two of these were the same type as the one Erik

Roll claimed had been stolen. They had been taken in for DNA and fingerprint testing.

The case was shifting direction. Erik Roll's credibility had been reinforced and he would be released the following day. What could have proved a breakthrough had turned out to be a setback.

49

As the forensics section did not open until 8 a.m., Wisting ate and read the online newspapers while he waited to place a call.

Most of the time taken on the phone was spent hanging on while the lab technician at the other end tried to find out whether the original samples from 1999 were still stored there. They would comprise swabs with samples taken from the body, nail clippings and strands of hair. When she returned, she was able to inform him that all the material had been returned to the originating police district after the verdict had been delivered in court.

Adrian Stiller had phoned twice during this conversation, so Wisting called him back.

'Any new letters?' the Kripos investigator asked.

Wisting had been out to the mailbox just after seven o'clock. 'No,' he answered. 'When will you get the fingerprint results?'

'Before lunch.'

Wisting walked out on to the verandah and picked up one of the chair cushions. Having forgotten to bring them inside, they were soaking wet after three days of rain. He propped them up to let the sun dry them.

'I've spoken to the Public Prosecutor and sent him a preliminary report,' Stiller told him. 'He'll pass it on to the local police today, but he's of the opinion that we can't wait too long before informing the other parties. Specifically, Momrak and Hansen's lawyers.'

Wisting's mind strayed to the former senior investigating officer in the case. 'That means Sten Kvammen will also be informed,' he said.

'Would you rather talk to him yourself?' Stiller asked.

Wisting mulled this over. He wondered how *he* would react if he received a message that everything he had done in a case had been faulty. The reopening of old cases worked both ways. For the Cold Cases Group it was a victory, but for those with responsibility for the original investigation, it represented a defeat.

'Not today,' he replied. 'I've a couple of other things I want to do more work on.'

He told Stiller about the previous day's visit to Danny Momrak and that this would have to be followed up with a new interview of his alibi witness from 1999. 'I was thinking of dropping in on Kathe Ulstrup at the local police station first,' he said. 'I think she should be kept up to date.'

'Do you want me to come down?' Stiller asked.

'No need,' Wisting said. 'I can take Ulstrup with me. She knows the case.'

He packed his laptop and notes in a briefcase while he spoke and brought the conversation to a close as he settled into the driving seat of his car.

Kathe Ulstrup had already answered a message that Wisting wanted to meet up with her to update her on developments in the case. She was free and agreed to meet him at her office.

Wisting sat down in the same chair as last time. Kathe Ulstrup had prepared a pot of coffee and must have gone down to the bakery in the shopping centre below to buy some cake.

'We've found Curtis Blair,' was his opening remark.

'Have you spoken to him?' Ulstrup asked.

Wisting nodded. 'He's actually in prison in the USA,' he replied. 'Convicted of killing his father.'

He saw that this information triggered a host of questions in her, but did not give her time to voice them. Without mentioning that he had gone to the USA, he explained that Curtis Blair had been interviewed and claimed he had left Bamble the day before Tone Vaterland was murdered.

'Kripos has been in touch with the airline company, but they don't retain passenger information from that time,' he said.

Kathe Ulstrup pushed the slices of cake across to him.

'I wonder whether it might be possible for you to check that out with the Lions treasurer?' Wisting continued. 'He probably bought the flight tickets. Maybe he'll still have some documents?'

Ulstrup nodded and made a note.

'When Janne Kronborg committed suicide . . .' Wisting went on. 'Were there any indications that things were not as they should be within the family?'

She looked at him. 'If everything had been in apple-pie order, I don't suppose she would have taken her own life,' she answered.

'You said she had taken her mother's sleeping pills,' Wisting added. 'Do you know how long her mother had been taking them?'

'I got the impression it had been a long time,' Ulstrup said. 'What's on your mind?'

He told her what Curtis Blair had insinuated about Terje Kronborg.

'That's news to me,' Ulstrup said. 'But it wouldn't surprise me. Terje Kronborg was a domineering man. He's got Alzheimer's now and lives in a care home.'

She helped herself to a slice of cake. 'When will you get the results of the examination of the clothes you found?' she asked.

'They came yesterday,' Wisting told her.

'And?'

'DNA was found in semen and blood,' he said.

Kathe Ulstrup looked bewildered. 'Do they match Danny Momrak?' she asked.

'It doesn't originate from him, but another match was found in the ID register.'

'Who was that?'

Wisting did not answer immediately. Instead, he produced a copy of the report from the interview Kathe Ulstrup had conducted with Jan Hansen in 1999 and pushed it across the desk to her.

'You interviewed him,' he said, presenting her with the printout.

Kathe Ulstrup picked it up and read the name aloud. 'Jan Hansen . . .' She skimmed through the statement she had written down. 'I remember this,' she said. 'He saw Tone leaving the Bamble Snack Shack.'

'Two years later he was arrested for the murder of Pernille Skjerven in Larvik,' Wisting clarified.

Kathe Ulstrup's lips slid apart.

'I remember that case,' she finally said. 'Pernille Skjerven. She was out cycling, exactly like Tone. Wasn't his name publicized in the media?'

'They held it back until after he was convicted, but Jan Hansen is, after all, such a common name,' Wisting said. 'There's no reason you or any of the other investigators should have made the connection.'

'So what are you doing now?' Ulstrup asked. 'Have you spoken to him?'

'Jan Hansen died last summer,' Wisting told her. 'Prostate cancer that spread rapidly.'

Ulstrup cleared her throat and searched for words. 'But how . . . Was his name mentioned in the tip-off you got? Did you know about him when you were at the garage cellar?'

Wisting said yes and went on to tell her about the anonymous letters.

Ulstrup leaned back in her seat. 'So Danny Momrak is innocent,' she summarized. 'Does Sten Kvammen know about this?'

'We haven't concluded yet,' Wisting replied. 'Kvammen will be brought up to speed by the Public Prosecutor, and we're waiting to tell Momrak and the Vaterland family.'

'What remains to be done?' Ulstrup asked.

'First and foremost, I'd like to know the identity of the anonymous letter-writer,' Wisting answered. 'But I'm also keen to have the old samples re-tested, using today's technology.'

He explained that they had been returned by Forensics to the police in Porsgrunn. 'Can you find out if they're still stored somewhere?'

Ulstrup agreed. 'Of course. Is there anything more I can help you with?'

'Yes, do you know where we can find Jonas Haugerud these days?' he asked. 'Danny Momrak insists he'll now confirm his story about the sale of hash.'

'In Langesund,' Ulstrup replied. 'He's been involved in buying and selling ever since that time. It's no more than a few weeks since we last had him in here.'

'Can you come with me?'

Ulstrup sprang to her feet. 'Count me in,' she said.

50

They took Wisting's car out to Langesund and Kathe Ulstrup directed him into one of the back streets.

'He lives with his father,' she said, telling Wisting to stop outside a two-storey villa with decorative carving.

A small black dog was barking loudly behind a gate, but they let themselves in without letting it escape.

At the rear of the house, a bare-chested man rose from a garden chair. Wisting realized this must be Jonas Haugerud. There was something tense about him, as if he were unsure whether or not to flee.

He remained on his feet while Ulstrup introduced them. Then she handed over to Wisting.

'It's to do with an old case,' he began. 'Danny Momrak.'

Immediately appearing more relaxed, Jonas Haugerud instead took on an irritated expression.

Wisting pulled out a chair and sat down, encouraging Haugerud to follow suit. He was skinny and sinewy, and his skin had a deep suntan. 'Have you spoken to him since his release?' Wisting asked.

Jonas Haugerud made a snorting sound. It was difficult to interpret what that might mean.

'He still claims he had nothing to do with what happened in 1999, and has asked us to talk to you again,' Wisting said.

'I've no more to say than I did at that time,' he said. 'Neither to you nor to Danny, nor anyone else, for that matter.'

'Does that mean you've spoken to Danny about it?' Ulstrup asked.

'He stood where you're standing now,' Haugerud replied.

Kathe Ulstrup now sat down too. 'When was he here?'

'A few weeks ago.'

'What did he want?'

Haugerud spat on the gravel ground. 'He said there was a TV woman who wanted to talk to me. I told him I didn't want anything to do with it, but she came here a couple of days later anyway.'

Wisting glanced across at Ulstrup. 'Did you speak to her?' he asked.

'Yes, but I didn't have anything to say, really. I've nothing to say to you either.'

'Can't we just go through it all the same?' Wisting asked.

He took out copies of Haugerud's statement from 1999, in which he described how he knew Danny Momrak and that they had indeed met on 4 July, but it had been several hours before Tone Vaterland left her work at the Bamble Snack Shack. In any case, he had not bought hash from him.

'I've nothing more to add or take away,' Haugerud insisted.

He hawked and spat again. Thick green slime that slid down between the tiny stones.

Refusing to give up entirely, Wisting carried on asking questions, but Jonas Haugerud stuck rigidly to the same story he had told in 1999. If it was a lie, then it had taken root. He had lived with it for a long time and had nothing to gain by going back on his word.

'Who else could it have been?' he asked in the end, flinging out his hand for emphasis. 'She had just dumped Danny. He wouldn't put up with that.'

'You've been charged with using, buying and selling on drugs since then,' Wisting said. 'Were you also the one who ran that business then?'

Jonas Haugerud cast a glance up towards the windows on the upper floor.

'My mother died when I was five,' he answered. 'I've mostly had to manage by myself ever since. I started smoking when I was twelve. Tried hash when I was fourteen.'

Wisting's phone buzzed and he saw the call was from Stiller. He switched off the sound and let it vibrate in his pocket.

'Was it Danny who got it for you?' he asked.

'There was never a problem getting hold of it. This town is not as blameless as it looks.'

'But you did buy from Danny?' Wisting pressed him.

Jonas Haugerud began to pick at a loose thread on the cut-off jeans he wore as shorts. 'Sometimes,' he admitted.

'What about on 4 July?'

The thread came loose from his shorts as Haugerud shook his head. 'Not on that day.'

'You're absolutely certain?'

The man opposite gave a loud, demonstrative sigh. 'He raped and murdered her,' he said. 'There was DNA and all sorts. I don't understand why you've come here asking about this now.'

Wisting repeated his question: 'Are you absolutely certain you didn't meet that evening?'

'Yes.'

The answer was blunt, but his body language suggested something different. His eyes wandered and his fingers had returned to the fringes of his shorts.

'Listen!' he said. 'I've never been ruled by the clock.' He

raised his left arm and shook his wrist. 'I know for sure we met up that day, but not what time it was. It was the middle of summer and it's light almost twenty-four hours a day. It could have been five o'clock or seven o'clock, or even nine o'clock, for that matter. I haven't a clue.'

He stood up. 'I told that to the lady with the camera too,' he added. 'And that's all I have to say.'

They could not progress any further. 'OK,' said Wisting, getting to his feet. Jonas Haugerud stood, watching them leave.

Wisting's phone buzzed again. Once again Stiller calling.

'I've received the results from the fingerprint section,' he said. 'I know the identity of the anonymous letter-writer.'

51

After almost three hours behind the wheel, Wisting was back at Hanne Blom's house in Skjetten. Her fingerprints had been found on three of the five anonymous letters. Adrian Stiller was of the opinion that this allowed all the pieces to fall into place. Towards the end of his life, Jan Hansen must have confided in her what he had done. She could not keep the knowledge to herself, but neither could she be the one to come forward with the information.

Wisting was unable to argue against it. Admittedly, one of the letters had referred to G-11, the police evidence number allocated to the swab from the gynaecological examination of Tone Vaterland during the post-mortem. This should mean that the sender had sight of the case documents, but the number had been mentioned both in the court judgement against Danny Momrak and several newspaper reports.

He was about to turn off the ignition, but the start of the news bulletin made him wait. The newsreader was reporting that the police had changed the charge against Agnete Roll's husband.

Wisting turned up the volume on the car radio.

Erik Roll was now charged with the murder of his wife and an application had been made for him to be remanded in custody. His lawyer was surprised by the development and insisted his client was at a loss to understand how he could be suspected of killing his wife.

This was all that was said. The information confused Wisting. He had taken a fleeting look at the Roll case the night before and there was nothing to provide a basis for jailing the husband. Fresh evidence must have turned up, but he could not imagine what that might be.

Collecting himself, he strode up to the front door and rang the bell. Hanne Blom appeared from the side of the house. 'You again?' she said. 'I thought I heard a car.'

'Something else has turned up,' Wisting replied. 'Do you have a minute?'

With a nod, she led him round to the garden, where her knitting lay on a chair. She moved it and sat down. Wisting sat opposite and came straight to the point: 'I didn't tell you when I was here yesterday, but I've received some anonymous letters that point to Jan Hansen as the killer in a case from 1999.'

Hanne Blom seemed neither surprised nor alarmed. She opened her mouth to speak, but Wisting carried on. 'The letters have been examined for fingerprints,' he went on. 'Your prints are on them.'

She shook her head. 'There must be a mistake.'

Wisting countered: 'They've been double-checked.'

The purpose of this conversation was to make Hanne Blom admit she was the sender, and persuade her to tell what more she knew. He had to avoid being too confrontational.

'It's not illegal to send anonymous letters, as long as the contents are not threatening,' he told her. 'I entirely sympathize with this method of going about things.'

'I haven't sent anyone letters,' Hanne Blom insisted. 'There must be some kind of misunderstanding. Some sort of mix-up, perhaps.'

She moved her head slightly, as if she had just thought

of something. 'Where did you get my fingerprints from?' she asked.

Wisting was reluctant to tell her he had helped himself to her waste paper but appreciated this meant there was a possibility that the prints did not in fact stem from Hanne Blom.

'We can do this formally,' he offered. 'In that case, we'll have to go to the police station and register them officially.'

She ignored this. 'Was it from my passport?' she asked.

Wisting shook his head. The police did not have access to biometric data from the passport database.

'But it must be a mistake,' she said. 'A mix-up, surely. I send out several hundred packages in the post every week. Patterns and yarn.'

She gestured in the direction of the garage, where she had her store, as if the fingerprints could have transferred from one shipment to another.

'We're talking about a number of letters,' Wisting pointed out, even though her explanation was absurd. 'The prints were found on the actual sheets of paper, the letters themselves.'

Hanne Blom was still unwilling to admit she was behind this. 'Where were they sent from?' she asked.

'There's no frank mark with the location of posting,' Wisting answered.

'Didn't they come in the post?'

Wisting explained that the first letter had arrived in the post, but the others had been hand-delivered to his mailbox.

'When did you receive them?'

'The first one came last Tuesday,' Wisting told her.

'Last week,' Hanne Blom repeated. 'I was in Bergen last week. Went there on Monday and came home on Friday.'

'Bergen?' he asked.

'I have a friend there,' she said. 'You can check with her.'

She produced the name and phone number. Wisting had no doubt her story was true. This meant Hanne Blom was either in cahoots with whoever had delivered the letters, or she was being used in some other way.

It crossed his mind how easy it had been for him to get hold of a magazine with her fingerprints on it. 'Could anyone have got their hands on writing paper with your prints on it?' he asked.

Hanne Blom shook her head. 'What do the letters say?' she asked, but then, before waiting for Wisting to answer, she rose from her chair and slapped her head. 'The notes!' she exclaimed.

'What notes?' Wisting asked.

'It was a few months ago,' Hanne Blom began to explain. 'Someone attached notes to my van windscreen. I discovered it for the first time when I was coming out of the post office. I thought it was a flyer or something, but it was just a blank sheet of paper.'

'What did you do with it?'

'I threw it away.'

'Where?'

'I had parked near the door and there was a bin there. I scrunched it up and tossed it in.'

The letters Wisting had received had been covered in creases and folds.

'How many times did this happen?' he asked.

'Seven or eight times. It began to feel unpleasant. Someone must have been following me. I was in and out of several places and, each time I came out again, there was another note on the windscreen.'

'Did you tell anyone about it?'

Hanne Blom nodded. 'I told Nora in Bergen, for one,' she said. 'The last time it happened, I took a photo of it.'

She brought out her phone and swiped through to a photograph. A blank sheet of A4 paper was tucked behind the windscreen wiper of her delivery van. The picture was dated 3 April.

Wisting sat staring at it before slumping back into the chair. This tallied with the overall scheme. Everything had been well planned and prepared in advance for a very long time.

52

The low evening sun shone straight through the windscreen. Wisting stepped on the gas and flipped down the sun visor. He drove another twenty or so kilometres, lost in his own thoughts, before calling Adrian Stiller and relating the story of the fingerprints. Stiller's first comment echoed Wisting's own assessment.

'That was three months ago. It's too late for us to get to the bottom of it.'

According to investigative theory, it would be possible to discover who had placed those sheets of paper on Hanne Blom's windscreen. Wisting had spent half an hour drawing up as exact a summary as he could of where and when the notes had turned up. They could use telecoms data to find out which mobile phones had been active at the same time and place and compare that information to the list of people involved in the case. However, after three months these electronic traces were automatically deleted.

'It could be a coincidence,' Wisting said.

'Or calculation,' Stiller commented. 'The first letter appears exactly three months after the data has been deleted. I think there's a great deal in this case to suggest that whoever is behind it knows how the police operate.'

A dead animal that looked like a badger lay on the roadway. Wisting swung out to avoid it.

'We've come as far as we possibly can,' Stiller went on

over the phone. 'If this had been any other case, we'd have handed it over to the Public Prosecutor with a request to press charges. We have a suspect, Jan Hansen. His semen was found on the victim's clothes, he was in the vicinity of the crime scene at the time of the murder and he has subsequently committed other similar crimes.'

Wisting did not feel convinced. 'It's all a bit too easy,' he replied.

'Difficult or easy,' Stiller said, 'the result is the same regardless. That's the conclusion we've reached.'

'But that's exactly the point,' Wisting said. 'From the very first letter, it was all set up to achieve this result.'

'When even the fingerprints can't be used to rule out the sender, who's your suspect, then?'

'The obvious candidate is Danny Momrak,' Wisting said. 'He has the most to gain.'

There was silence at the other end.

'It sounds as if you believe there could be something wrong with the DNA evidence?' Stiller said after a while. 'Something that doesn't add up.'

Wisting moved out to the left-hand lane and drove past a car towing a caravan. This idea had crossed his mind, but it was obvious that Tone Vaterland's clothes had lain beneath the garage since 1999, and Jan Hansen had been dead for more than a year. All the same, he could not shake off the idea.

'I need this weekend to go through everything again,' he said.

The phone alerted him to another incoming call, from Kathe Ulstrup this time. He took a few minutes to end his conversation with Stiller and had to return her call.

'I've spoken to the Lions treasurer,' she told him. 'He's

just phoned back and had found the supporting documentation. Curtis Blair's story checks out.'

'Good to have it confirmed,' Wisting commented. 'What about the original evidence?'

'That was destroyed in 2008,' Ulstrup explained. 'Apparently in connection with the centralization of the Porsgrunn and Skien police when they transferred to a new building. There's a note on the form to say it had been cleared with Sten Kvammen, the grounds being that there had been a lawful conviction.'

Wisting turned into a petrol station. No rules existed about the retention of evidence in confirmed cases. In 2008, any new investigation would not have yielded different results, but since then the technology had improved significantly. New methods of analysis could have linked Jan Hansen even more closely to the murder.

'I'll send you a report about both of these,' Ulstrup promised.

'Thanks.'

After filling the tank, he bought a hotdog and a bag of buns. While he was in the shop, he had received a message from Line, wondering when he would be home. The dashboard clock was at quarter to eight.

He rang her up and said that he would be home in half an hour. 'Why did you want to know?'

'I wondered if you wanted to come here and eat with me?' Line replied. 'I've made a salad and have sausages left over from Amalie's dinner.'

Wisting glanced at the bag of buns in the passenger seat and accepted. He realized he had spent far too little time with his daughter and grandchild of late.

Amalie had gone to bed and was asleep when he arrived.

Line had set the table outside. 'Did you check the mailbox before you came?' she asked.

Wisting shook his head. A road accident on the E18 had meant he had taken longer than estimated. He had driven straight to her house and parked in the street outside.

Line fired up the gas barbecue and put on some sausages. 'Have you found out who sent the letters?' she asked.

'It's complicated,' Wisting told her.

He had only relayed parts of the story to her, and now he explained about Danny Momrak and the case from 1999. He saw how this left her both flabbergasted and fascinated. 'This is the story Ninni Skjevik is making a documentary out of,' he concluded.

'Well, that's an incredible story,' Line said. 'I'd give my right arm for a scoop like that.'

'How's your job going, anyway?' Wisting asked, thinking of how Cederik Smith was also one of her bosses.

'I'll have to look for something new,' Line replied. 'It won't work if we have to cooperate on the same project.'

She did not seem keen to tell him anything more about what had gone wrong between them. Instead she shared her thoughts and reflections on the Danny Momrak case. 'He really must be the one who's behind it all,' she said. 'It's easier to pay attention to an anonymous letter-writer than a convicted killer.'

'But in that case, where did he get the information from?' Wisting mused. 'Someone must have told him where the clothes were hidden.'

'Could he and Jan Hansen have talked to each other in prison?' Line suggested.

'Nothing suggests they had any significant contact,' Wisting answered.

'Jan Hansen could have told other inmates about it and they've passed it on to Danny,' Line said.

'That's a possibility.'

'Have you spoken to the prison and the men he served his sentence with?'

'Not yet.'

Line sat deep in thought. 'Maybe it has something to do with his lawyer,' she said. 'Maybe Jan Hansen told his lawyer everything, and when Hansen died, he went to Danny's lawyer and told him about it. Then they found a way to pass on the information without being accused of breaking confidentiality.'

Wisting's thoughts had not gone in that direction.

'Who are their lawyers?' Line asked.

'Danny Momrak uses Cristian Bohrman,' Wisting replied. 'Jan Hansen had Reidar Heitmann.'

'The same one that Erik Roll is using now,' Line commented.

Wisting nodded. He had not read the news in the past few hours. 'Do you know if he's been remanded in custody?' he asked.

'For four weeks,' Line told him. 'They haven't said anything more about the grounds for that.'

She began to clear the table, heading inside with the dirty plates and emerging again with a bowl of chocolates. 'Do you have plans for Sunday?' she asked.

'I don't have any appointments,' Wisting said, guessing what she was after: 'Do you need someone to look after Amalie?'

'Just for a few hours in the evening. I need to get out of the house for a while. Sofie has tickets for a summer concert. Is that OK?'

Wisting picked a chocolate. He had the weekend ahead of him to sort out all the elements around Jan Hansen. Something might well crop up, but he had no wish to put her off. 'Of course,' he replied.

They lingered for a while, chatting. The air grew cooler and Line wanted to go inside to fetch a couple of blankets, but Wisting rose from the table. 'I have to get home,' he said.

She accompanied him around the house and out to the car. Wisting drove the less than one hundred metres up to his own house, where he reversed his car into the driveway and checked that the dashboard camera was working.

The mailbox was half full, mostly junk mail. No new letter but, at the front door, a note had been inserted between the doorframe and the door.

Wisting snatched it up and unfolded it. It was from a young boy offering to mow the lawn and tend the garden. Wisting cast a glance at the grass, realizing that the boy must have cycled around the neighbourhood ringing doorbells where it looked as if work was needed.

He went inside and sat down in the living room with his laptop on his knee. The remand decision for Erik Roll had piqued his curiosity and he wanted to find out what the police had on him. He logged on but was unable to access the casework system. He wondered whether he could have done something to cause him to be barred again, but he was able to delve into all the other registers and databases. It could be a temporary glitch, but in the meantime he had to content himself with reading the newspaper reports about the developments in the case.

The remand meeting had taken place behind closed doors. Christine Thiis, the Police Prosecutor, had beaten about the bush in her communication, claiming there were circumstances in the accused's statement that failed to agree with the rest of the inquiry. Reidar Heitmann had been vehement on behalf of his client, as he had also been at the time when he had defended Jan Hansen.

Photographs had been taken of him outside the courtroom. Heitmann could be regarded as arrogant and often came out with patronizing, pontificating comments about the police, but Wisting had always considered him honourable. He hoped Hammer and the other investigators had something solid on his client.

Late that evening, the wind picked up. Wisting lay in bed listening to the cord on his neighbour's flagpole flapping in the gusts.

Around 4 a.m., he woke and had to go to the toilet. It dawned on him that he had again forgotten to take his medicine. Once he had finished, he pressed a tablet out of the blister pack. They had not had the desired effect, but then he had not taken them regularly. He counted the tablets left in the pack and the total did not tally. He must have forgotten them once or twice earlier as well.

When he returned to bed, the birds had begun twittering outside his window, and he knew he would find it impossible to go back to sleep. A car drove slowly past in the street outside. It sounded as if it had stopped and been left with the engine running for a minute or two before the engine was switched off.

Raising his head from the pillow, Wisting listened for the sound of a car door slamming shut. It did not come.

He flung aside the quilt, planted his feet on the floor and pulled on his trousers. The car was visible from the kitchen window, but there was no one inside. It was a black

SUV, a BMW. That must have been what he had heard. It had not been parked there earlier that evening and was not a vehicle that belonged in the street. If it had parked, then the driver must have sneaked out and closed the car door quietly to avoid disturbing anyone. From where he stood, he could not make out the registration number.

He stood watching it for a few minutes before putting on a sweater and shoes and heading outside. When he reached the steps, he heard a car door slam. The car had started up and driven away by the time he reached the street.

He checked his mailbox. It was empty. Then he fetched his car keys and inspected the dashboard camera. The car had been caught on film as it drove along the street. Wisting stopped the playback. It was impossible to see the driver, but the registration number was legible. He found a pen in the console between the seats and jotted it down on a notelet.

From the living room, he linked up to the police system and logged in to the vehicle register. The car owner listed was Cederik Smith. Line's boyfriend until last weekend.

This disconcerted him. It was a bad sign that this guy had turned up in the middle of the night. It made him go out again and walk down the street. Her house was silent, but there were tracks in the dew on the grass from someone who had walked round the house. His pulse rate climbed higher.

He walked up the steps and checked the door, which was locked. Then he skirted around the house himself. Line's bedroom window was open slightly for air, but the curtains and blinds were undisturbed.

Trudging on, he was able to make out wet footprints on the terrace where they had been sitting only a few hours earlier. Their empty glasses were still on the table. The tracks led up to the terrace door. Wisting carefully checked that it was also locked.

There was something unsettling about this.

He peered into her mailbox before going home to check his own. It was still empty.

Before he moved inside again, his thoughts had veered off to something Stiller had said about the anonymous letter-writer. How they had kept Wisting under surveillance to make sure he was not away on holiday. Maybe even stood watching as he had carried in the post.

It was a logical conclusion. The entire project hinged on Wisting receiving and reading the letters, ideally in the intended order.

He sat down again with his laptop. All the telecoms data for the night Agnete Roll had been killed had been provided by the telephone companies. It was a standard step in every major case in which they were searching for an unknown perpetrator. The data was vast and included everyone who had used a mobile phone in the Stavern area, whether the phone was used to make calls, send messages or consume data.

He entered the database and saw that data had been secured from four hours prior to the last sighting of Agnete Roll until twenty-four hours afterwards.

The first letter had arrived in the post the Tuesday before last and must have been posted the day before at the latest. It was not inconceivable that the sender had spent the weekend checking whether he was at home.

He first made an attempt with his own phone number and received several hits of messages sent to and received from Line.

Opening his notebook, he located Ninni Skjevik's contact details and keyed in her mobile number. No results.

On the next page he had noted the information he had on Danny Momrak. He tapped the number into the search field and got a result — a total of twelve lines of data traffic.

He had not spoken or communicated with anyone but had charged eight megabytes to his subscription. The first entry was just before midnight and the last was logged at 1.47 a.m.

Wisting sat back in his chair. It was impossible to place him any closer than within the area of the mobile-phone mast covering Stavern town centre and its environs, but all the same: Danny Momrak had been in town the night Agnete Roll was murdered.

53

Wisting assumed that Hammer and the other investigators would be at work from early morning onwards. At half past eight he let himself into the police station. Up in the Criminal Investigation Department, he met a steady stream of investigators making their way from the conference room. Some of them were unknown to Wisting, most likely detectives who had been brought in from other stations to help with the inquiry in the days following an arrest and remand-in-custody order.

Nils Hammer and Maren Dokken were still seated at one end of the conference table, faced with piles of case documents.

'Congratulations on the breakthrough,' Wisting greeted them.

Hammer thanked him but said: 'Maren's due the credit.'

The young investigator beside him smiled but seemed slightly embarrassed.

Wisting moved to the cupboard in the kitchen corner and took out a cup. 'What have you got on him?' he asked.

'A number of things,' Hammer replied. 'But the most important are the soil samples and an analysis of his electricity use.'

'Analysis of electricity use?' he asked. This was an expression he had not come across before.

Hammer nodded. 'Maren can clarify,' he said.

As Maren Dokken drew a bundle of folded papers

towards her and smoothed them out, Wisting filled his cup from a coffee pot on the table and edged round to her side.

The strip of fanfold paper Maren had laid out was almost two metres in length and divided into hours and minutes.

'This is the timeline for the night of the murder and the previous evening,' Maren explained. 'Based on electronic traces and Erik Roll's statement.'

She pointed to a red horizontal line. Several fixed points were marked, such as when Agnete and Erik Roll had gone out that evening, when they had left the pub, and when they had been filmed by the dashboard camera.

Above the red line, a blue contour rose and fell in steep curves, but also lay flat for prolonged periods. 'What's that?' Wisting asked.

'It's the analysis of electricity use,' Maren spelled out. 'It's based on data from the digital smart meter in the house.'

Wisting got the picture. The electricity network had been modernized, and all householders now had new smart meters installed that registered consumption on an hour-by-hour basis.

Maren continued: 'Here the consumption is level at around two hundred watts,' she explained, drawing her finger along the blue line from four o'clock in the afternoon. 'Some lights are on, a phone is charging and suchlike.'

Wisting took a sip from his cup.

'At 7 p.m., the consumption takes a leap,' Maren went on, using her finger to point. 'First by 2,200 watts, then by another 1,000 watts, before dropping again. That fits with Erik Roll's account that he cooked a frozen pizza while Agnete was in the shower. We can see the use of the electric oven and hot water kicking in.'

'Electronic traces,' Hammer commented. 'Quite literally.'

Maren ran her finger further along the blue line. 'Here, they've gone out into town,' she clarified. 'There's nobody at home. The consumption is continuously low. Only the underfloor heating in the bathroom and a few lights are turned on.'

At 10 p.m., a slight increase was registered. 'That's the exterior lights switching on automatically,' Maren told him. 'A total of six bulbs. Forty watts.'

By now Wisting had understood the significance of the electricity analysis. According to his last statement to the police, Erik Roll had arrived home around 1 a.m. That chimed with the dash cam and Benedikte Lindhjem's explanation that he had been at her door around half past midnight. But there was no fluctuation in the use of electric power at one o'clock. Not until almost 3 a.m. did anyone appear to come home and switch on lights. After that there was a jump that indicated the hot water had connected up again, followed by an increase of 2,500 watts that lasted for two hours.

'Erik Roll has stated that he arrived home just after 1 a.m.,' Maren said. 'When Agnete was not there, he assumed she had gone to a friend's house. He tells us in the interviews that he went straight to bed.'

'What's he doing here?' Wisting asked, pointing at the final steep curve showing consumption of 3,500 watts.

'He's putting on the washing machine.'

Wisting nodded in appreciation. 'So he comes home two hours later than he said at interview, takes a shower and turns on the washing machine?' he summarized.

'Spot on,' said Maren.

'How does he explain that, then?' Wisting asked.

'He changed his story at the remand-in-custody hearing,' Hammer told him. 'Said he sat down on a sun lounger outside the house to wait for his wife. Drank some beer and fell asleep. When he woke, he went inside and took a shower. He'd spilled some drink on his clothes and chucked them in the washing machine. It's plausible, but not particularly believable.'

'You had some soil samples too?' Wisting asked.

'From his shoes,' Maren answered. 'Ash, bacteria and soil with a high nitrogen and potassium content were all found.'

'From poultry manure,' Hammer interjected. 'As well as tramping around in the fire ruins, he's stepped in some chicken manure.'

'We know about the ash,' Wisting said, 'but where does the chicken manure come from?'

'From Anne's herb garden,' Maren told him. 'It's on the neighbouring property.'

Hammer leaned forward. 'He could explain the ash by saying he'd been inside the Kleiser house when he was out looking for Agnete on the Monday,' he said. 'It's not so easy when it comes to the chicken shit.'

'It's a natural route, going through the herb garden,' Wisting commented.

'He says that's what he did,' Maren agreed. 'He explained that he walked across the bottom of the nursery, where no one could see him from the houses.'

Wisting could not understand the point of this.

'Have you seen *Gladiator*?' Hammer asked him.

Wisting nodded.

'In one of the fight scenes at the Coliseum, a passenger aircraft flies past,' Hammer explained. 'It can hardly be noticed, but all the same, it shouldn't have been there.'

'The herb garden was not fertilized until Tuesday,' Maren said. 'The day after he claims he was there, but before the second blaze at the Kleiser house.'

'He wouldn't have had chicken manure on his shoes if he was telling the truth,' Hammer pointed out.

'When was the last time it was fertilized?' Wisting asked.

'In April, just after the snow melted,' Maren replied. 'But according to the experts, the nitrogen values are too high to stem from that time.'

'Aren't both potassium and nitrogen elements?' Wisting asked. 'Could they have originated anywhere else?'

Neither Hammer nor Maren could answer that question.

'In addition, traces of petrol were found on the soles of his shoes,' Maren continued. 'But in all probability, that's also true of everyone who's ever been in a petrol station. There's often a lot of spillage between the pumps.'

'What does he say himself?'

'That he must have gone somewhere that had been recently fertilized when he was searching for Agnete,' Maren replied. 'He went around the whole neighbourhood. Checked in all the gardens, under bushes and other places to see if she might have been taken unwell and lain down somewhere.'

'Plausible, but not believable,' Hammer said again.

'So you've nothing concrete on him?' Wisting asked.

'This *is* concrete,' Hammer broke in. 'Men have been convicted on flimsier evidence than this.'

Wisting agreed. 'You're right,' he said, drinking his coffee. 'What CCTV footage do you have?'

'Hours of it,' Hammer answered.

'Can I take a look?'

Hammer cocked his head. 'What are you looking for?' he asked.

Wisting hesitated. He was reluctant to tell them that a previously convicted killer had been in town on the night Agnete Roll was murdered. 'It's a side issue,' he said. 'I can explain later.'

Neither of the two asked any more questions.

'The footage is stored on a separate disc,' Maren said. 'I can show you.'

Scooping up the papers, she accompanied him into the media lab. Wisting sat down on the chair in front of the large screen while Maren took hold of the computer mouse.

'Don't you think it's enough?' she asked. 'To get him convicted?'

'In isolation it should be sufficient,' Wisting replied. 'You have motive, he has no alibi and has been caught lying. It depends on whether there could be other explanations for what happened. Whether there's a potential alternative perpetrator.'

Once she had accessed the system, her gaze lingered for a moment on the screen before she turned her head towards him. 'Is that what you're looking for?' she asked.

Wisting refrained from replying. Instead, he asked: 'Have you checked out the man she was with on the night of the murder?'

'Jarle Schup?'

'He's one of the last people to see her alive,' Wisting reminded her. 'It's only a few hundred metres from his house to the spot where she was found.'

'Well, he certainly wasn't the person who set the Kleiser house on fire,' Maren told him. 'He went to Denmark with his kids on Monday morning. Came home on Friday.'

Wisting looked thoughtful as Maren straightened up.

'But we've examined his shoes,' she added with a smile. 'No ash or chicken manure on them.'

She left the screen to him and closed the door behind her.

The fans in the computer housing on the wall whirred as Wisting drew his chair closer to the screen. Video footage had been collected from six cameras operating in public places and, in addition, the raw material from the dashboard camera in the car parked in Brunlaveien was stored on the disk.

Wisting began with the footage from the petrol station. This was situated at a crossroads in the small town, but the camera did not capture any traffic other than the vehicles that drove past the pumps on the forecourt.

The camera at the pub entrance showed footage of when Agnete and Erik Roll entered and when they left. The street outside was a one-way route and the camera caught all the vehicles passing through.

Wisting had the plate number of Danny Momrak's grey Volkswagen Touran, registered in his mother's name, written on a note.

He put the note down in front of him but had already memorized the number. At four times the normal playback speed, it took him an hour to run through what he reckoned to be the time span of interest. Momrak's car had not passed by.

The other recordings were from the entrance to the Justice Department's Conference and Training Centre in Helgeroaveien, from the Staverntunet shopping mall where the off-licence and pharmacy were located, from the Wassilioff Hotel, from a private residence in Prinsensgate and the waterside marina. The only camera that could have filmed traffic to and from the residential area where Wisting lived was the dash cam that had recorded Agnete and Erik on their separate ways home from town.

He began the playback at 11 p.m. and was able to recognize the section from the stills Maren had shown him. The car was parked facing oncoming traffic and only caught the front of vehicles driving past, not the traffic travelling in the opposite direction.

There was little traffic. Almost the same number of vehicles as cyclists and pedestrians. The car headlights dazzled the camera and made it difficult to read the number plates. The registration number on Momrak's car ended in zero one, and Wisting concentrated on the last two digits of the vehicles that drove past. Twice he had to stop the playback to check if it was the right car, but each time it was not.

At 00.04, she moved into the picture. Agnete Roll, walking with her head bowed and her arms crossed over her chest. Seven seconds later she was out of the picture again.

Wisting expected that Maren Dokken or some of the other investigators had studied the same footage. Vehicles passing within the next half-hour would have been potential witnesses who had probably been contacted and interviewed.

He crossed off every car that passed. The first was a taxi. He had drawn three lines when he paused the film and leaned closer to the screen. In the frozen image the registration number grew even more indistinct, but it looked as if it ended in 801. The last three digits of Momrak's plate number.

The picture was taken at an angle and it was possible to make out the contours of someone behind the wheel, and there also seemed to be another person in the passenger seat.

He played it back again, backwards and forwards, without being able to say for certain, but he grew convinced that the car number ended in 801. The backlight from the headlamps made the initial numbers and letters impossible to see, but above the registration plate he could make out the 'V' and 'W' of Volkswagen's logo.

The exact time of transit was 00.09, five minutes after Agnete Roll had walked past. Taking a printout of the screen image, he folded it up and crossed the corridor to Maren Dokken's office.

She glanced up from her papers. 'Did you find what you were looking for?' she asked.

'Maybe,' Wisting replied. 'Do you have data from the toll stations?'

'Of course.'

There were automatic toll stations on the motorway on either side of town. In a murder case it was a routine step in the investigation to obtain an overview of all the comings and goings in case they might be dealing with a perpetrator travelling through.

'Could you do a search?' Wisting asked.

Maren Dokken positioned herself in front of the computer and called up the file. Wisting read out the number.

'Two instances.'

Although it did not come as a surprise, Wisting still felt the information hit him like a punch in the gut.

He edged round the desk and stood beside her to see for himself. An Excel sheet filled the screen with columns for car number, time of transit, sum debited, chip number and other technical data.

'Transit on E18 Sky in the northbound lane at 23.47 hours,' Maren read out.

'Coming from Porsgrunn,' Wisting concluded.

Maren clicked her way through to the next instance. 'Returning in the southbound lane at 02.11.'

Wisting put down the still image from the dash camera. Maren craned forward to look at it but left it there, as if this was something from which she wished to distance herself. 'Who is that?' she asked.

'The driver's name is Danny Momrak,' Wisting answered. 'He was convicted of murder in 1999. Released on licence a couple of years ago.'

Maren Dokken slumped into her chair with a look of surprise and disbelief on her face. 'How have you . . .' she began, but broke off. 'Do you mean he could have killed Agnete Roll?'

Wisting returned to the opposite side of the desk. 'There's no reason to believe that,' he replied. 'But I'd like to know what he was doing here that night.'

'Me too,' Maren said. 'We can bring him in and ask.'

'Do that,' Wisting told her. 'Let me know when the interview is taking place.'

54

Wisting stood at the office window waiting for Stiller to answer, watching a plane's white vapour trail disperse into the bright sky. He wondered whether he had in fact seen that *Gladiator* film Hammer had mentioned, but the aircraft was a detail he had not noticed.

'Any news?' Stiller asked when he picked up the call.

Wisting sat down. Formally he was working for Adrian Stiller on this assignment, and it felt strange to report to a boss almost two decades younger than himself.

'I think I know the identity of the sender,' he said, and went on to explain what he had discovered.

Silence was the only response at the other end.

'They're bringing him in for a routine interview in connection with Agnete Roll's murder,' Wisting added.

'Her husband's been charged, hasn't he?' Stiller asked.

'We're talking about a witness interview, though,' Wisting replied. 'In theory he may have seen both Agnete Roll and her husband, but it's mostly a cover to get him to tell us what he was doing in this neck of the woods. It will put us in a position to confront him with the anonymous letters.'

'I see,' Stiller said.

'He wasn't alone,' Wisting went on. 'It looks as if there were two people in the car when it was caught by the dash cam. He has an accomplice.'

'Who could that be?'

'I've no idea. It could be a friend, his mother or anyone

else. I know too little about him to guess, but the most obvious candidate is Ninni Skjevik.'

'The journalist?' Stiller asked. 'Wasn't she working on the America angle?'

'Yes, and I've checked that out for her,' Wisting reminded him. 'Anyway, it'll be interesting to know who he gets in touch with when he leaves here.'

'You're thinking of surveillance?' Stiller asked.

'There's no legal basis for that,' Wisting answered. 'I was wondering if we might turn out a team to tail him.'

Adrian Stiller took a deep breath. 'We've no surveillance operatives available here at present,' he said. 'They've been wound down for the holidays.'

'I'll see what we can manage with the folks from here,' Wisting said.

'I can come down,' Stiller offered. 'Let me know when it's happening.'

Once they had rounded off the conversation, Wisting lingered with the phone in his hand, thumbing through his contact list, searching for a name that had slipped his mind.

When he had begun as an investigator, he could call up any administrator whatsoever and receive information over the phone. Now personal privacy protection measures were stronger and the procurement of information had become bureaucratic, but down through the years he had built up a clutch of personal contacts to oil the wheels of the investigation process and to which he could turn when something important cropped up.

He found the name. Gustav Bolk. They had never met, only spoken on the phone or corresponded via email.

Gustav Bolk worked in the toll company responsible for the collection of levies on the motorway through

Vestfold and Telemark and could provide information about whether the transits made by Danny Momrak's vehicle could be linked to the times when he had received the anonymous letters.

Bolk obviously had Wisting's number stored on his phone and answered by asking how he could assist.

'I need to know whether a particular car passed between Larvik and Porsgrunn the Wednesday before last,' Wisting told him.

The man at the other end hesitated before responding. 'I appreciate it must be urgent,' he said, 'since you're phoning on a Saturday.'

Wisting had lost track of what day it was. 'Do you have access to the systems from home?' he asked.

'To some extent,' Bolk confirmed. 'But this is the kind of unauthorized search that could be questionable.'

'I don't need to know a car number or owner's name,' Wisting told him. 'I have a chip number and I'm looking for a transit time.'

'Wait a minute,' the other man said.

Wisting understood he was logging in to a computer and prepared to give him the subscription number on the Autopass chip.

'Fire away,' Bolk said when he was ready.

Wisting rattled off the sixteen digits.

'There we have it . . .' Bolk murmured. 'What day are we talking about?'

'The night of Wednesday, 13 July,' Wisting said, leafing back through his notebook.

'Then I have a transit on the northbound lane of Sky station at 00.02, and back on the southbound carriageway at 00.34.'

Wisting had noted hearing the metallic clunk at 00.17. It tallied.

'What about later the next day?' he asked.

The third letter had been in his mailbox when he came home the following afternoon after visiting the crime scene in Bamble.

'There are several registrations in the course of that day at various stations, but I can see a corresponding transit that afternoon,' Bolk replied. 'The E18 northbound at 16.38. Return on the southbound carriageway at 17.05.'

Wisting let his finger run down the page of notes. The fourth letter had been in the mailbox when Adrian Stiller had joined him outside his house on Monday 18 July, while the last letter to date had been picked up from the mailbox by Line on Wednesday 20 July.

He received the required confirmation. 'Can you send me a full list?' he asked.

Gustav Bolk hesitated again, but promised to do as requested.

The phone beeped to indicate that someone was trying to ring him. Wisting was about to wind up the call when he suddenly thought of something else.

'What about Wednesday, 13 July? Was he in Vestfold that day?' This was the day the Kleiser house had been set on fire for the second time.

'No,' Bolk replied. 'Not in that vehicle, at least.'

Wisting thanked him and ended the conversation before checking who had tried to phone him. It was Sten Kvammen. He was disinclined to return the call, but a text message from him pinged in before he got that far.

Can we meet?

55

An awkward atmosphere quickly developed when Wisting met Sten Kvammen outside the police station. They were sizing each other up but neither uttered a word about what had happened after their previous meeting.

'We'll go upstairs,' Wisting said, leading the way up to his office.

Kvammen took a seat. Something deferential about his manner made Wisting feel ill at ease.

'The Public Prosecutor has briefed me,' Kvammen began. 'I understand that new evidence has come to light with significance for the question of guilt.'

'No conclusions have been drawn as yet,' Wisting said.

Kvammen shook his head. 'All the same, I'm the first to apologize,' he said. 'I had well-meaning investigators who worked conscientiously on the case. I had complete confidence in the crime-scene technicians, the forensics experts and the court, but I want you to know that if there's anything I can do to help put this right, then I'll put everything else aside. The way the system has let us down has kept me awake all night long. This is going to be a wake-up call for the entire force. Something we really must learn from.'

Wisting gave him a long, hard look. When an investigation went awry, it was often a matter of inquiries being steered by a self-assured leadership with unwavering self-belief. Kvammen made it sound as if what had happened was just one of those things and his purpose in coming here began to sink in. Kvammen had realized the direction this case was going to take and now he was trimming his sails to the prevailing wind. This would inevitably be a major media story and he was in danger of being identified as the scapegoat. He had come to allocate the blame squarely on the system and at the same time create the impression of personal dynamism.

'It's my duty to put things right,' Kvammen continued. 'I'd like to be the one to inform Danny Momrak and Tone Vaterland's family.'

'It's too early for that,' Wisting answered.

'But when the time comes,' Kvammen insisted. 'I've raised the matter with the Public Prosecutor.'

'It's not up to me,' Wisting reminded him. 'The Cold Cases Group at Kripos is in charge of this.'

'I've arranged a meeting with the Kripos top brass next week,' Kvammen told him. 'But I was keen to talk to you first. You're the one who can take the credit for this.'

'We've not drawn things to a conclusion yet,' Wisting said. 'Some unanswered questions still remain.'

Sten Kvammen leaned forward slightly and asked: 'Is there anything that could change the state of play as it is now?'

Wisting hesitated. 'Have you seen *Gladiator*?' he eventually asked.

'The film?'

'The action takes place around the year 180 after the birth of Christ,' Wisting explained. 'But in one of the scenes, there's an aeroplane in the sky.'

Kvammen did not say anything. Wisting produced the analysis report concerning the positive result on Jan Hansen's DNA and the photos of the clothing found under the garage on the old road.

'There's no doubt that this is Jan Hansen's DNA,' he went on. 'Neither is there any doubt that this is Tone Vaterland's blouse. It had five of eight buttons missing. The rest of them are of the same type as the ones found at the crime scene. The manufacturer has been traced and the blouse went out of production as early as 1998. Everything we found in that cellar bore signs of age and has most likely lain there since 1999.'

Sten Kvammen studied the images. 'I ordered a search of the whole area,' he said. 'Both manually and with the use of sniffer dogs. I can't comprehend how this was overlooked.'

'Jan Hansen's DNA was found in semen on the blouse,' Wisting explained. 'In addition, microscopic traces of blood were detected.'

He pointed to the description in the report. 'Blood in semen can in itself be a symptom of cancer,' he continued. 'But the most common cause is that a tissue sample has been taken from the prostate gland in connection with medical examinations.'

Sten Kvammen seemed not to understand. 'Jan Hansen died of cancer, didn't he?'

Wisting crossed his legs under the desk. 'He had it diagnosed two years ago,' he replied. 'It's like the plane in the film. The blood shouldn't have been there. Not if the traces originate in 1999.'

The former senior investigating officer licked his lips. 'What are you saying now?' he asked. 'Do you mean that the DNA trace could have been planted later?'

'It's too early to say,' Wisting told him. 'There could be other natural explanations for the blood being there, but we're carrying out further analysis with a view to detecting cancer cells or toxins we know Jan Hansen had in his body when he was ill.'

'But Jan Hansen died over a year ago, surely?' Kvammen objected.

'Everything about this case seems carefully planned,' Wisting said. 'A lot of time has gone into the preparations. If the DNA trace was planted, then the dust in the cellar under the garage has been given time to settle again, and the grass allowed to regrow along the walls. Furthermore, Jan Hansen had to die before the plan was put into action. It's always easier to blame a dead man.'

'Who could be behind something like that?' Sten Kvammen demanded.

'Strictly speaking, only one person,' Wisting replied. 'The person who knew where Tone Vaterland's clothes were. The true killer.'

Sten Kvammen took a deep breath and sighed. 'Danny Momrak,' he said.

56

A black Mercedes swung into the car park in the back yard as Wisting was walking to his car. Reidar Heitmann, the lawyer, sat behind the wheel.

The marked spaces were reserved for staff and patrol cars, but Wisting made no comment on that when the lawyer stepped out.

'Have they brought you in too?' he asked. 'They said you were on holiday.'

Wisting shook his head. 'I was just popping in,' he replied. 'I've nothing to do with the Roll case.'

The lawyer took off his suit jacket and placed it on the back seat. 'That's probably just as well for you,' he said, rolling up his shirtsleeves. 'It's a thin case.'

'Are you going to be in on the interview?' Wisting asked.

Heitmann shook his head. 'I'm going to meet Hammer,' he replied. 'Pick up the latest documents.'

Wisting took the opportunity to turn the conversation to his own case. 'I heard Jan Hansen had died,' he commented.

'He passed away last summer,' Heitmann agreed. 'Cancer.'

'Did you have any contact with him towards the end?'

'Yes and no,' the lawyer answered. 'He did keep in touch in the years after he was convicted. Rang up and wrote letters. Demanding that the case be reopened and wanting his case taken to the Court of Human Rights in Strasbourg. I really just dragged things out. His case had no business there. Eventually he went quiet. You know, he never admitted anything and didn't claim to be innocent. He simply felt he had been unfairly treated.'

'Why is that?'

'He had a list,' Heitmann explained. 'Your name was mentioned in most of the points. It had to do with the interviews, among other things. That you had asked questions you already knew the answer to. Misguided him, interpreting misunderstandings and inexactitudes as lies. But it wasn't only you, it was the entire system. He felt violated, felt he had been found guilty in advance and that he never received a fair trial.'

Wisting failed to recognize himself in that description.

'I told him to get in touch with a journalist or a writer,' Heitmann went on. 'Get someone to write his whole story, seen from his side.'

'And did he do that?' Wisting asked.

'I don't think so,' Heitmann replied. 'He didn't have a high opinion of journalists. No one had written anything positive about him. He may well have been right in that, of course. The coverage of the case at that time was pretty one-sided.'

'It could have been interesting to hear his whole story,' Wisting said. 'I understood he had a lot of contact with the prison chaplain near the end. That there were things he needed to talk about.'

'I can imagine that,' Heitmann answered. 'He got in touch with me too when he got sick. It had to do with practical matters. I wrote a petition for an interruption of his sentence and drew up a simple will and a future power of attorney for him.'

'I heard he had a girlfriend,' Wisting said.

Heitmann gave a broad smile. 'There wasn't much to inherit from him, but the prison did at least get a place where they could send his effects.'

A patrol car drove into the back yard and up to the garage doors. Reidar Heitmann checked his watch.

'Jan Hansen died a bitter man,' he rounded off. 'I'll have to get moving.'

They parted and Wisting got into his own car. He drove out on to the E18, northwards in the direction of Oslo. An hour and a half later he drove into a neighbourhood comprising spacious new terraced apartments in Bekkestua.

The opulent BMW was parked in the street. Wisting drove up behind it and sat for a while before getting out. He then walked up the path and rang the bell.

Cederik Smith seemed taken aback when he opened the door.

'I'm Line's father,' Wisting said, in case the man had not realized that. 'You've been in my home. I invited you to dinner.'

The figure in the doorway nodded, but said nothing and made no sign of asking him in.

'She doesn't know I'm here,' Wisting went on. 'And I don't know why you split up, but I need to have a word with you.'

'I've nothing to say to you,' Cederik Smith answered. 'Neither to you nor to Line.'

Wisting took a step closer. 'I don't sleep well at night,' he said. 'I'm usually up about five in the morning. Last night I saw your car out in the street. I didn't like that. I've come to ask you to stay away from Line.'

'Your eyes must have deceived you,' Cederik said.

'Besides, the relationship between Line and me is none of your business.'

'I'm her father,' Wisting said. 'And the relationship is over. I know what I saw, and you'd better keep your distance.'

'You're mistaken,' Cederik said. 'Maybe you should get your eyesight checked or something.'

Wisting merely shook his head.

Cederik Smith took a pace forward. 'I want you to leave,' he said.

'I'll leave as soon as we agree that you're going to stay away from Line,' Wisting replied. 'That you're not going to contact or visit her again.'

Cederik Smith's face had darkened. A few wrinkles had appeared on his forehead and his lips were tightly compressed.

'Get lost!' he said, placing his palms on Wisting's chest in an attempt to push him back.

Wisting shoved them away, a practised move from the days when he had patrolled the streets.

'Calm down,' he said. 'I don't know what's happened between you and Line, but –'

The punch was unexpected, but he did have time to react. He tilted his head to the side so that the clenched fist merely grazed his left ear.

Wisting used the force in the misplaced blow to his own advantage. Stepping to one side, he grabbed Smith's wrist with his left hand, using his right to put pressure on his opponent's elbow, and knocked Cederik off balance. He jerked him further in the direction of the punch and pushed him down. His face hit the gravel. Cederik Smith shrieked with pain when Wisting twisted his arm behind his back and planted his knee on it. With his free hand he pressed his opponent's head into the tiny stones, then held tight and crouched down to put his mouth to the young man's ear.

'You don't need to admit anything,' he said through gritted teeth. 'You don't need to apologize or ask for forgiveness. I just want you to agree to keep away.'

He remained crouched over him as Cederik Smith gave a loud moan. Flecks of spittle hung from his lips but no answer came out.

Wisting pressed the guy's arm further up behind his back.

'OK,' the man beneath him groaned. 'I've lost interest anyway.'

Cederik Smith might as well have the last word. Wisting had no need to challenge him any further. Nothing good would come of that. He released his grip, staggered to his feet and strode to his car without a backward glance.

57

Wisting's neck muscles protested when he pulled on his seatbelt. He must have given himself a crick.

The encounter with Cederik Smith had not gone quite as anticipated, but he felt certain that Smith would stay away from Line and Amalie from now on.

His phone buzzed. A call from Maren Dokken. 'Danny Momrak's coming in for interview tomorrow afternoon at two o'clock,' she told him.

'No objections or arguments?'

'He bombarded me with questions but bought the idea that it was a matter of routine.'

'Good,' Wisting said. 'I'll come in at noon, so we can go through what I'd like you to ask him.'

'Where are you now?' Maren asked.

'On my way to Ullersmo,' Wisting replied. 'I'm going to meet one of the guards who had most contact with Momrak during his sentence. I just had to attend to some personal business first.'

'I'll be at work for a few hours longer if anything crops up,' Maren said.

'Is there any news in the case against Erik Roll?'

'Both good and bad,' Maren told him.

'What's the bad news?'

'Heitmann has engaged a researcher from the Norwegian University of Life Sciences to take a closer look at the fertilizer evidence on his shoes,' she said. 'He's the best in his field, apparently. It's not certain the evidence will be so incontrovertible afterwards. The analysis of electricity consumption may also be weakened. Following the installation of the smart meter, their household consumption has risen. Agnete Roll was the one who paid the regular bills. She'd complained to the power company several times that there must be something wrong with the meter.'

Wisting envisaged how these two pieces of seemingly solid evidence could crumble away in a courtroom.

'What's the good news?' he asked.

'We've done an activity analysis,' Maren replied.

Wisting had to ask her what that was.

'We've obtained the data from the activity monitor in the health app on Erik Roll's mobile phone,' Maren explained. 'Between one and three that night, almost five thousand steps have been recorded.'

Wisting glanced down at his own phone on the centre console. This was a new type of electronic trace. 'Do you know where he'd been?' he asked.

'No,' Maren answered.

'But isn't it possible to find out when you know he'd been on the move?'

'There's no GPS tracker function activated, sadly,' Maren told him. 'The step counter uses the gyroscope and accelerometer to record steps and movement.'

Wisting had no idea what she was talking about, but appreciated that this was something she had researched thoroughly, and the conclusion was clear. Erik Roll had undoubtedly been in motion at the time of the murder.

'What about her phone?' he asked.

'That was found in the ruins of the fire, but unfortunately the data can't be restored,' Maren replied.

'I see,' he said. 'Are you planning another interview?'

'I'm going to finish work on the petrol traces first,' she said. 'If his own petrol can was stolen by the moped boys, then he must have got his hands on petrol somewhere else. We're checking all the petrol stations for the sale of cans and purchases of less than ten litres.'

'Excellent,' Wisting said. He was on safer ground when it came to understanding such a traditional investigative method. 'I'd have done the same myself,' he added.

He ended the call before checking the clock and knew he had plenty of time.

His appointment at the prison was with an employee called Arild Frankmann. He would start the afternoon shift at 3 p.m., but had a number of regular duties to attend to before he could meet Wisting.

At three thirty he parked in the extensive car park outside the grey circular prison wall and headed straight for the visitors' entrance. He had to wait before someone answered on the gate telephone. He stated his identity and the name of the staff member he was there to meet. He had to wait a few minutes longer before he heard a click at the turnstile and he pushed the bar forward as he made his way through.

He had to wait even longer before the massive sliding gate began to open with a loud buzz. As soon as the opening was large enough, a man in a uniform shirt with rolled-up sleeves appeared on the other side.

'I'm Frankmann,' he said. 'I've arranged for us to use an office in the admin block.' Keys rattled as he walked on ahead and showed Wisting the way. 'You said it had to do with Danny Momrak and Jan Hansen,' he said just before opening the office door.

'As far as I understand, they were both in the same section,' Wisting said.

'I dealt with both of them,' Frankmann confirmed. 'Jan Hansen died last year. He wasn't here at the end. Whereas Momrak was released on licence two years ago.'

They had entered a cramped office space where Frankmann had already logged on to the computer and had called up a page with a photo of Momrak.

'What was he like?' Wisting asked.

Frankmann shrugged. 'We have all sorts of inmates here,' he answered. 'Most of them manage to accept the situation they're in and adapt in various ways. Danny Momrak became a manipulator.'

'How so?'

'He used others to his own advantage. But he was not the only one. Manipulation is a natural consequence of being incarcerated. It's the only means of power they have.'

'What does that mean in practice?' Wisting asked.

'Just small things, really,' Frankmann replied. 'He could worm his way to phone time outside the regular times, having his clothes laundered more frequently, being allowed to take part in more leisure activities than the others, and he got the jobs he wanted. He worked in the prison shop as well as working as a trusty on cleaning chores.'

'Are they attractive jobs?'

'The ones who work in the shop usually eat the goods if a crisp packet tears open or something like that. Also they have control of the tobacco sales. They often help themselves to some cigarette papers from the packets before they're sold and usually pick open the packs of loose tobacco and take out a pinch or two before closing them up again. Five or six packs can give you two or three roll-up fags. The trusty cleaning function is well paid for little work. It consists of cleaning the toilets, the common rooms and the floors inside the cells. It usually takes no more than two hours, while the other prisoners are hard at work all day. Immediately after roll call in the morning he can more or less go back to bed again. The only requirement is that the work is done by the end of the day. Besides, you have the opportunity to take things from the others, to help yourself from the fridge and snoop around in the other inmates' cells.'

'Did Danny do that?'

'All the trusties get accused of stealing from the cells. I don't think Danny was ever caught doing it, though.'

Wisting made some notes. 'Did he say anything about his case?' he asked.

'Precious little,' Frankmann answered. 'Of course, we're well aware of why they're in here, but it's not something we talk to them about, or that the inmates discuss among themselves. They all know who was convicted of murder, or who is in here for narcotics or robbery. Murderers have a bit of status, but they lose that once the others find out it was the murder of a young girlfriend they'd broken up with.'

'So he never claimed to have been a victim of a miscarriage of justice?'

Frankmann smiled. 'Most of them in here claim to be innocent,' he replied. 'Momrak was no exception.'

'How did that manifest itself?' Wisting asked.

'I perceived him as bitter and malicious, with a grudge against the system in general and the police in particular, though that didn't make him any different from the other inmates. But I remember one evening shift when almost all the prisoners in this section were gathered in front of the TV in the common room. There was a news broadcast and a piece with a policeman commenting on an ongoing investigation. Danny Momrak got up off the sofa, walked up to the TV set and spat at him. It was the detective who'd been responsible for his case.'

'Sten Kvammen?'

'I don't know his name. The others cheered him to the rafters. I asked him to clean up after himself, but he downright refused. It ended with him being locked up and two days of black TV screens.'

'What about Jan Hansen?' Wisting asked.

'He was more introverted,' Frankmann told him. 'But I think he was one of the ones who cheered loudest when Momrak spat at the TV. He also had an obvious grievance against the police, but there was something manic about it.'

'In what sense?'

'He didn't directly protest his innocence, but he felt the police had been dishonest. He took cuttings and collected cases in which the police had made mistakes. He was obsessed with miscarriages of justice and took an interest in other prisoners' cases as well.'

'Did he and Danny Momrak have any contact?'

'Well, they were both held in the same section, serving long sentences. We're only talking about a total of twelve inmates. They all have contact with one another.'

'Did he take an interest in Momrak's case?'

The prison guard shrugged. 'Not in any way that involved any of the people who work here, at least.'

'Jan Hansen refused to take part in the TV documentary that was produced while he was here,' Wisting said.

Frankmann nodded. 'That's right. I don't know why. They talked to all the inmates in this section before they began filming, but ended up choosing a couple of prisoners to profile. Danny Momrak was one of them.'

'Did you have any dealings with the production folk?'

'No, Peter Lasson was responsible for that and he kept in touch with them, but I do remember it was a woman who was in and out of here.'

'Did you speak to her?'

He shook his head. 'I kept my distance from all that.'

'What about visitors?' Wisting asked.

Frankmann turned to the computer screen. 'I have an overview here,' he replied. 'I can give you a printout if you like.'

Wisting accepted with thanks. Frankmann navigated through the computer system and a printer beside the wall sprang to life.

'It was Jan Hansen who had the most visits,' he said as they waited for the documents. 'He had a lady friend who came here every week. Danny Momrak only had an occasional visit from his mother, not much more than that, I think.'

He reached out for the paper tray and handed the printouts to Wisting. Frankmann was right. Two names recurred. Hanne Blom and Esther Momrak. A few other individual names were listed as researchers, students or representatives of various organizations.

'No lawyers,' he remarked.

'Visits from lawyers and police wind up on a different list,' Frankmann told him.

'How is a visit conducted?' Wisting asked.

'The inmate must agree to a visit and they draw up a visitors list with up to four people they wish to visit them,' Frankmann explained. 'Anyone who wants to come in has to send an application. Their background is checked and the visitors are searched before they enter. There's a visitors' room in every section. Each inmate can receive one visit per week lasting up to one hour.'

'Does much supervision take place?'

'That depends,' Frankmann answered. 'If both the inmate and the visitor have previous dealings with narcotics, then the visit may take place with a guard present. In some cases a room with a glass wall is used.'

'What about Jan Hansen and his girlfriend?'

'No supervision.'

'So they could be together in private? Have sex?'

'They would have, almost certainly.'

'In the visitors' room?'

Frankmann smiled. 'There's lubricant and condoms in the cupboard there,' he replied.

Wisting made more notes. 'Are the visitors checked again on the way out?'

'No. All personal belongings – bags, watches, keys, phones, medicines, have to be left behind. In addition, the visitors have to pass through a metal detector. Jackets and shoes are checked in the X-ray machine.'

A call came in on the radio Frankmann carried on his belt. A voice crackled and spoke about a delivery of goods. Wisting understood he had to wind things up.

'Just one more thing,' he said, stealing a glance at the computer. 'Do you have a list of leaves of absence?'

Frankmann set the printer going again and handed the

printouts to Wisting. His radio sounded again. 'I really have to go now,' he said.

Wisting gave a brief nod. An idea about what could have happened began to take shape in his head.

58

Standing by the window in the spacious conference room, Wisting gazed down at the square in front of the police station. Danny Momrak parked his car nose-first in one of the vacant spaces and strode up to the main entrance. Wisting carried his notes to the control room, where he could watch the transmission of the interview on a computer screen.

Hammer was already seated and had set up the recording. They had to wait almost five minutes until they saw Maren Dokken enter the interview room with Danny Momrak behind her.

Momrak scanned the room before they sat down on opposite sides of the table. Maren explained the formal framework.

'You're aware that Agnete Roll's husband has been charged and remanded in custody for the murder,' Maren began. 'But as I explained on the phone, we're still reviewing all movements in Stavern around the time of the homicide and looking for potential witnesses.'

'How do you know I was there?' Momrak asked.

'We have in our possession all the telecoms traffic from the night of the murder,' Maren replied. 'That's one aspect of our review. Your number appeared there.'

'I was there,' Momrak admitted. 'But I didn't use my phone.'

'You don't need to have spoken to anyone or sent a

message,' Maren told him. 'Data traffic was registered. That may be because you checked your email or surfed the Internet or even took photos that were automatically uploaded to the Cloud.'

Momrak nodded, as if this rang a bell for him.

'You don't actually need to have actively used your phone either,' Maren continued. 'It can also be from background updating.'

'Are you talking to everybody, or are you particularly interested in me?' Momrak asked.

'I know you have a murder conviction,' Maren answered. 'That makes it especially important for us to speak to you. We want to avoid Erik Roll's lawyer being able to point a finger at you later and make insinuations. So we're required to do an extra-thorough job. We have to know why you were in Stavern and what you were doing there.'

Danny Momrak did not seem to have any problem understanding that. 'There was no special reason, and I didn't do anything much,' he replied. 'I've difficulty sleeping and often drive around at night, especially at the weekends, when a lot of people are out and about.'

Maren Dokken asked first about his car. Who owned it and whether anyone other than him drove it. She went on to ask him to tell her in greater detail about when he set out from home and when he left Stavern. This matched the transit information from the toll station.

'Why did you drive to Stavern?' Maren queried. 'Could you not have driven around in your own locality? Porsgrunn, Bamble or Skien?'

'I don't know anyone over here,' Momrak told her. 'I'm spared having to talk to people.'

'Were you alone in the car?' she asked.

Wisting moved slightly closer to the screen. Momrak's Adam's apple wobbled above the neckband of his T-shirt. 'Not the whole time,' he answered. 'A woman came up to me when I was parked near the town square and asked if I could give her a lift to her friend's house.'

'So you did that?'

'Yes.'

'When was this?'

Momrak shrugged. 'Around midnight.'

'Where did her friend live?'

'I don't know. She gave me directions as we drove. It was a residential area, five or six minutes away.'

'Could you find your way back there?'

He shook his head. 'I didn't drive her to the door,' he said. 'She asked me to drop her off at an intersection.'

'Could you find it on a map?'

'Maybe.'

Maren Dokken had brought a map with her. She unfolded it on the table in front of them and Hammer used the video control to zoom in.

'It must have been somewhere here,' Momrak told her, using his index finger to circle the area where Wisting lived. 'I was struggling to find my way back.'

'Did she pay you?'

'I got a hundred kroner.'

'Cash?'

Hammer had zoomed out again. Danny Momrak nodded.

'Can you describe her?'

Danny Momrak gave a vague description of a dark-haired woman in her forties.

319

Maren Dokken drew back the map and studied the area Momrak had pointed out.

'Did you get out of the car at any point?' she asked.

Momrak pondered this. 'Not that I can recall,' he said finally.

Hammer turned to face Wisting: 'What do you think?'

'We can't verify any of that,' Wisting replied. 'He could have done anything at all in the hours he was here.'

The conversation in the interview room moved into another phase. Maren Dokken set down the photo of Agnete Roll taken with the CCTV camera as she left the pub in the town centre. The same picture had been used in the media.

'Did you see this woman?' Maren asked.

Danny Momrak took a long time to answer, as if it was important for him to show that he was giving this his serious consideration. 'No,' he answered in the end. 'At any rate, she wasn't the woman I drove.'

Maren laid down the pictures from the dashboard camera, both of Agnete Roll and his own vehicle. 'You could have passed her along the road,' she said.

Momrak studied the new photographs. 'That could well be,' he replied. 'But I can't remember it.'

Maren had a few more routine questions before going back through the statement again. They were the same questions, but phrased in a slightly different fashion. Danny Momrak's answers remained the same.

'Have you been over here on any further occasions since the night of Friday, 8 July?' Maren ploughed on.

'Why do you ask?' Momrak demanded, suddenly seeming surly. 'Does that have anything to do with this case?'

'It may have,' Maren answered. 'I would at least ask that

question if I were Erik Roll's defence counsel. Four days after the murder, Agnete was found dead in the ruins of a house fire. There is reason to believe that the person who killed her also set that fire.'

Wisting sipped his coffee. It had gone cold, but he stayed on his feet with the cup in his hand as he kept pace with the pair on the screen. Maren, reclining in her chair, looked relaxed. She was making inroads into something that should make Danny Momrak feel uncertain and provoke him into getting in touch with an accomplice after the interview. His telephone use had led him here so he would probably avoid calling or sending a text. He would most likely pay a personal visit to his sidekick.

'I've made a number of trips into this area,' he answered. 'What day was the fire?'

'It was reported on Wednesday morning.'

'The days all seem to run into one another,' Momrak told her. 'But I'm pretty sure I haven't been here on any morning.'

'What about during the night?' Maren persevered.

Momrak looked ill at ease. A tendon in his neck tensed as he balled his fists and opened them again before answering: 'Am I suspected of something?'

Ignoring this, Maren picked up the map again. 'Were you back in this area?' she asked, circling Wisting's neighbourhood.

'I've no idea,' Momrak replied. 'I don't know these parts.'

'Were you ever out of your car when you came back here again?'

Momrak clenched and unclenched his fists. Wisting thought he could see confusion in his eyes. The sender of the anonymous letters must be aware that he may have been observed, and denying he had ever been out of the car could rebound on him later. In the 1999 case, he had been caught out lying several times, and the outcome of that had certainly been to his disadvantage.

'Maybe,' he replied in an irritated tone. 'I can't see how that has any relevance for this case.'

Wisting released the police radio he wore on his belt and called up Adrian Stiller. 'The interview's nearing an end,' he said. 'We've got him where we want him.'

'Copy,' Stiller acknowledged. 'I'm in position.'

59

Danny Momrak had only taken a few steps outside before he stopped, fished out a pack of cigarettes and shook one out.

Wisting was watching from the window.

After a couple of deep drags he walked to his car and got in behind the wheel.

'Leaving,' Wisting announced over the radio.

'*Copy*,' Stiller replied.

Kathe Ulstrup also acknowledged receipt of the message. She was waiting in a car much further south and would take the lead if Momrak drove in her direction.

Nils Hammer would soon head out on his motorbike. Maren Dokken also intended to follow on, but as she had just sat face to face with Momrak she would have to steer clear. Wisting was also exposed. Momrak was apparently very aware of the kind of car he drove. He had swapped vehicles with Line and would lead the others at a suitable distance. He had transferred the dash cam, but apart from that they had no electronic aids, no tracking devices to tell them at any time where Momrak's car was located. This was old-school surveillance, the kind he and Hammer had often undertaken.

Momrak reversed out from the parking spot, turned around and drove down towards Storgata.

Half a minute later Stiller had picked him up and hung two cars behind him in the direction of the E18.

Wisting went downstairs to his car and drove out.

Momrak was driving south on the E18 motorway. Stiller reported his position as still two vehicles behind him and that they were following the flow of traffic.

Hammer was one kilometre further back, but could quickly catch up. Wisting was third in line, while Maren Dokken let them know she would also soon be en route.

At regular intervals, Stiller reported the landmarks they passed: the Pauler tunnel, the Vassbotn bridge, Solum and Langangen. Kathe Ulstrup was waiting at the Public Roads Administration's roadside checkpoint in Solum.

'*Passing,*' she reported. '*I'm taking over.*'

Wisting was almost five minutes behind. As he accelerated, he felt his pulse rate soar. Ulstrup confirmed that Momrak was on his way down the rocky descent at Lillegårdskleivene. A couple of kilometres further on, he would either turn off towards Porsgrunn or continue straight on for Bamble. If he turned off, that could mean he was heading home.

'*Continuing straight ahead,*' Ulstrup told them.

Nils Hammer's voice broke in. The connection to his motorbike helmet crackled and the traffic noise could be heard through it.

'*What contacts does he have in that direction?*' he asked.

'Ninni Skjevik,' Wisting told him. 'The documentary-film-maker.'

He had found her father's address, where she had told him she would be staying that summer. 'Rådhusbakken 9 in Stathelle,' he added.

Kathe Ulstrup remained a few vehicles behind and gave

her positions. They passed the tunnel beneath Hovet and Brattås.

'*Continuing straight on past the intersection for Heistad.*'

They passed the Grenland bridge, drove into the Bamble tunnel and approached the 1999 crime scene.

'*He's turning off from the E18,*' Ulstrup announced. '*I'll lose him at the first intersection. Who'll take over?*'

Stiller spoke up and they made a manoeuvre in which Ulstrup and Momrak drove in different directions while Stiller followed him towards Stathelle.

'*I'm coming up,*' Hammer's crackly voice spoke from his motorbike.

'*Right at the first roundabout,*' Stiller told them. '*I've got a shopping centre on my left. Brotorvet. Heavy traffic.*'

All of a sudden the surveillance became more challenging now that they had left the motorway.

'*It's going on into Sundbyveien,*' Stiller continued. '*Towards Langesund.*'

'*I can take over,*' Hammer announced.

'*Who do we have in Langesund?*' Stiller asked.

Kathe Ulstrup answered before Wisting had a chance to speak: '*Jonas Haugerud. His childhood friend.*'

Momrak continued in the Langesund direction. Wisting had managed to make up speed and turned off from the E18. Maren Dokken reported that she was two minutes behind him.

'*He's turning off to the left,*' Hammer announced, holding down the send button until he had read out the road sign: '*Towards Ekstrand.*'

Wisting did not catch the place name: 'Repeat,' he requested.

'*Left to Ekstrand,*' Hammer reiterated. '*To Ekstrand. I'll have to drop off, driving on.*'

Stiller announced that he was taking over. Ulstrup was just behind him.

'His lawyer lives there,' Wisting informed them. 'Cristian Bohrman.'

Ulstrup broke in with her local knowledge. '*It's a huge residential area, but only two roads lead out,*' she told them. '*I'll cover the lower exit.*'

Stiller announced that he had to drop off from the tail because Momrak had driven into a side street. Wisting was struggling to recall the lawyer's address. He remembered that the streets had names of Norwegian monarchs and it dawned on him that Bohrman lived in the one named after Håkon the Good.

'*I'll take a drive by,*' Stiller said.

Immediately afterwards he reported that Momrak's car was parked outside number 44.

'*No sign of activity outside the house.*'

A radio discussion ensued, speculating why Momrak had paid a visit to his lawyer.

'*He must have felt under suspicion in the interview,*' Maren Dokken suggested.

Nils Hammer had jumped off his motorbike and obviously moved closer on foot. '*What part has his lawyer played in the new information that has come to light?*' he asked.

'A passive one,' was Wisting's response, and he went on to give an account of how Bohrman's involvement had been limited to allowing Ninni Skjevik to borrow the case documents.

They waited, two units at each exit road, while Maren Dokken kept her distance. Every five minutes, they took turns to drive past to make sure that Momrak's car was still parked there.

Almost forty minutes went by before Ulstrup suddenly announced that she had spotted the car at the lower exit.

Hammer was covering that road with her, but he lagged behind because he had to take time to don his helmet again. Stiller and Wisting were positioned at the other side of the residential area.

'*I had to let a bus come in between us, so I don't have visual contact,*' Ulstrup reported.

Wisting passed a speed bump at full throttle and had to grit his teeth. Hammer gave notice that he was weaving his way through the traffic and had caught sight of Ulstrup and the bus.

'*Catching up with him.*'

The message almost disappeared in the background noise from acceleration and high revs. A few minutes elapsed and then Hammer was back on the radio: '*I'm right behind him,*' he said, and swore under his breath. '*He's pulling into the side and inviting me to overtake. I'll have to pass him.*'

It would not be a problem to have one unit in front of the object under surveillance if the others had been in position, but the fact that Momrak was letting Hammer pass meant that Hammer was now burned. Momrak had noticed him and, even if he had no suspicions at present that he was being followed, they could no longer use Hammer.

'*I can't get past the bus,*' Ulstrup reported.

Hammer was obviously watching in his mirrors. '*He's continuing on towards Stathelle,*' he said. '*I've got an intersection with a churchyard on the left-hand side. I'm continuing straight ahead.*' There was silence for some time before he gave a further report: '*He's taking a left turn. Repeat: left turn at the churchyard.*'

Wisting called on Maren Dokken: 'He may be coming your way.'

'*Copy.*'

Kathe Ulstrup estimated he would reach her in less than two minutes.

'*I've passed the bus now,*' she said. '*I'm one minute behind him.*'

Wisting spotted the bus up ahead. It turned into a bus bay to pick up passengers and he pushed on, noticing in his mirror that Stiller was doing likewise.

More than a minute elapsed before Maren reported that she could see Kathe Ulstrup approaching in her car. Momrak must have driven a different route.

'Stay in position,' Wisting told her. 'Keep a lookout.'

Ulstrup said she had taken up an observation post at what would be a natural point from which to drive back out on to the E18.

Wisting keyed the address of Ninni's childhood home into his GPS. He followed the directions and became ensnared in a network of narrow, steep streets of white-painted timber houses. The house he was looking for was at the top of a hill. He had hoped to find Momrak's car parked there, but it was not. They had lost him.

60

Wisting and Amalie sat on the steps eating ice cream, Amalie chattering and singing as she ate. Her cone had disintegrated and melted ice cream trickled down her arms and dripped on to her legs. Wisting was struggling to use a paper napkin to wipe her when Stiller phoned.

They had also checked whether Momrak had visited his mother, but his car had not been there. Once they had ascertained that they had lost him, everyone except Stiller had driven back. Wisting had given him directions to Momrak's house and told him to park some distance from the side road and continue onwards on foot, but Momrak had not been there either. Afterwards, Stiller had continued to sit in his car, waiting while he kept an eye on the road leading to the house.

'He's arrived here now,' he said.

Wisting demolished the rest of his ice cream and checked the time. Almost four hours had gone by. He wanted to ask Stiller to stay and see if he received any visitors or drove out again, but could hear from the traffic noise in the background that Stiller was already making his way home.

'Don't you have a contact in the toll company?' Stiller continued. 'It would be interesting to know which direction he headed after we lost him.'

'I can check,' Wisting replied.

Amalie had finished her ice cream, though most of it

was spattered on the steps. Wisting kept his phone tucked between ear and shoulder as he dried her fingers.

'Then I'll hear back from you after that,' Stiller said. 'We ought to have a full briefing. There's a lot hanging in the air.'

After they ended their conversation, Wisting took Amalie inside to the bathroom and helped her to wash.

'Shall we go for a drive in the car?' he asked her. Amalie's face lit up. Wisting shut the verandah door and took her outside.

Line was in town with a friend and would not need her car for a while. Letting himself into her house, he found her keys and sent her a text message in case she was alarmed when she came home and saw that her car was gone.

He strapped Amalie into her car seat and, as they drove, he rang Maren Dokken to tell her that Momrak had arrived home. 'Are you still at work?' he asked.

'I'm just finishing up,' she replied. 'Why do you ask?'

Wisting squinted at the camera on the windscreen. 'I've bought myself one of these dash cams,' he said. 'I was thinking of parking the car in Oklungen, so that I can film the traffic to and from Momrak's house.'

'Got you,' Maren said.

'The car will have to be left there,' Wisting went on, 'so I need someone to pick me up and drive me home again.'

'No problem,' Maren said. 'I can collect you.'

Once he had given her directions, he and Amalie played a game as he drove. She counted all the red cars they passed, while he counted all the yellow ones. By the time they reached their destination, the score was 8–0 in favour of Amalie.

Wisting turned into the lay-by he imagined Stiller had used as his observation post. The distance from here to the side road was almost 150 metres. The camera had a digital zoom function, so that the picture was in close-up. The traffic to and from the turn-off came from the opposite side. All the same, there was a danger that Momrak would notice the car if it was parked there for too long, and possibly even discover the camera if he took a closer look, but in that case he would have footage of it and at least be aware that Momrak had grown suspicious.

Maren Dokken turned up after quarter of an hour. They transferred the child seat and Amalie into the rear of Maren's car and drove back.

'Anything new on Erik Roll?' Wisting asked.

'I may have found something interesting,' Maren replied.

'What's that, then?' Wisting asked.

'The petrol traces,' Maren told him. 'The moped boys confessed to stealing seven cans. We found three of them in the woods beside the junior high school.'

Wisting nodded. He had read that in the report.

'We've done more door-to-door enquiries,' Maren went on. 'Eight petrol cans were stolen.' She glanced across at him and smiled. 'Erik Roll may have taken the eighth can and used it to set fire to the Kleiser house,' she said.

'The boys' memories may be faulty,' Wisting told her. 'Seven or eight . . .'

Maren shook her head emphatically. 'The eighth can was stolen from a shed in the herb garden,' she said. 'The boys are adamant they did not go there.'

Wisting nodded again. Maren was right. She may have found something that was very interesting indeed.

61

Amalie fell asleep in the car on the way home. Wisting carried her in and put her to bed. Afterwards he sat outside on the verandah with his laptop.

An email from Gustav Bolk with an overview of Danny Momrak's transits through the toll stations lay unread in his inbox. Opening it, he wrote back to thank him and ask if there had been any transits that day.

In the attached file, there were more toll transits registered than Wisting had asked for and been told of on the phone. The transits were timed to the second. He scrolled through the list to see if there was anything of particular significance, but did not notice anything untoward.

He marked the transits that could be linked to the delivery of the anonymous letters and studied the remaining entries.

On Thursday, 14 July, Momrak had virtually operated a shuttle service: there were transits before and after Wisting had received letters, one after midnight and another in the afternoon of the same day, when the third letter had turned up.

Between these marked transits, there were four others. Danny Momrak had passed on the northbound carriageway just before 8 a.m., but did not return until quarter past twelve. After that there were two transits at the brand-new toll stations on the newly opened motorway in West-Bamble.

It was difficult to figure this out in any meaningful way, but one idea occurred to Wisting.

When he had bought a new car and transferred the toll chip from the old one, he had had to log in to *My Page* on the toll company's website and register the change. On the same page, there had also been a list of his transit journeys and the amounts for which he had been charged.

On Thursday, 14 July, he had driven to Bamble, where he had met Sten Kvammen at his cabin, paid a visit to the 1999 crime scene and also visited Cristian Bohrman at his home.

The overview showed that he had passed the Sky station on the southbound carriageway of the E18 at 12.19.43.

He looked across at Danny Momrak's list. He had passed seven seconds later.

Wisting screwed up his eyes and opened them again. It felt as if a muscle or nerve had begun to pulse somewhere at the back of his neck.

Danny Momrak had initially visited him late the previous evening and dropped off an anonymous letter. Then he must have returned the following morning and kept him under surveillance. He had been following him.

In order to reach Sten Kvammen's cabin, Wisting had also driven past the toll station in Bamble. The transit was registered at 12.46.23. Danny Momrak had passed through at 12.46.27.

He must have been right behind him.

The meeting with the former senior investigating officer had lasted almost an hour. The return journey in the opposite lane was at 14.04.23. Danny Momrak had passed five seconds later, but on the way back to Larvik he had passed through five minutes ahead of him. Probably he had picked up speed, raced past and managed to leave the third letter before Wisting arrived home.

Momrak had followed him all day long, without Wisting noticing a single thing.

He checked whether this had also happened on other days, but it had not.

Before he could call Stiller to tell him what he had discovered, he received a message on his phone from Maggie Griffin.

Call me when you get a chance.

He linked up to Skype and phoned her at once. She sat close to the computer and her face filled almost the entire screen. What little could be seen of the background was anonymous but looked like a hotel room.

'Hi,' she greeted him. 'Lovely to see you when you were here. How's it going?'

Wisting thanked her for her help, told her he was fine and apologized for having had so little time when they were together in New York.

Maggie leaned even closer to the screen and camera. 'Are you sitting outside?' she asked.

Wisting told her about the warm weather and that he was at home on his verandah. 'We've received the results from the DNA samples on the clothing we found,' he went on. 'They gave a positive result for Jan Hansen.'

'So is Curtis Blair out of the picture now?' she asked.

'We also got confirmation of the date he left Norway,' Wisting replied.

'Checked and double-checked,' Maggie commented. 'I'm back in Connecticut and have met with his mother.'

They had arranged for her to follow things up with a

statement from Ann Blair, but Wisting had assumed Maggie would get a local agent to talk to her.

'She remembered that the message that came, telling them Curtis was being sent back to the USA, had spoiled their 4 July celebrations,' Maggie continued.

Wisting nodded. 'We now know it all adds up,' he said. 'I should have informed you.'

He heard her phone ring – Maggie checked it but just laid it aside. 'She had the CD discs with his photographs,' she said. 'I took them with me and have been busy looking through them all.'

He realized she must have found something, since she had contacted him. 'Anything interesting?' he asked.

'There's no time stamp to say when the photos were taken, just when they were transferred to CD,' Maggie explained. 'But they're obviously from Norway. There are lots of landscape images.'

Wisting waited for her to come to the point.

'I'm sending a photo over to you so that you can take a look at it,' she said. 'It's one of a series of almost identical photographs, but this is the best one.'

Almost as soon as she had said this, the laptop pinged with an incoming email. He opened it and the photo attachment. It was of a young man in a camouflage jacket holding a camera in his hand.

'Have you managed to open the photo?' Maggie asked.

Wisting was no longer looking at her. 'Yes,' he replied.

'Who is it?' Maggie asked. 'I thought at first it was Curtis Blair. After all, the picture is almost twenty years old and he could have changed a lot.'

'It's not him,' Wisting told her.

Maggie Griffin agreed. 'It must have been Curtis who

335

took the photo,' she said. 'But who, then, is this other man with the camouflage jacket and the camera?'

'The brother,' Wisting replied. 'It must be Janne Kronborg's brother.'

He could not think of his name. 'Curtis Blair used to borrow his jacket,' he added.

He tried to remember what he was called, but something else struck him, something that Curtis Blair had said about him when they were talking to Blair in prison. They had shared interests, but nonetheless did not have much contact. Wisting had not asked what these common interests were, but they might well have included photography.

'I think his name is Peder,' Maggie said. 'Could that be right?'

'That's it,' Wisting said. 'He was three years older than his sister.'

He got to his feet. 'Wait a minute,' he said, and moved to fetch his notebook from the kitchen.

He leafed through to the point where he had drawn a timeline for Tone Vaterland's murder in 1999. He had used a colour code. Black for what was confirmed and blue for the timings and events that could not be corroborated. The suggestion that Curtis Blair had been forced to leave the Kronborg house and was picked up by Charles Wright had originally been noted in blue but had been overwritten in black.

He stood thumbing through his notes from the very first conversation with Kathe Ulstrup. He had not jotted it down, but thought she had said something about Janne's parents not having followed the Vaterland case. As soon as Curtis Blair was out of the house, they had taken their daughter to their cabin in the mountains and stayed there for a week, but the brother had remained alone at home.

'What are you doing?' Maggie asked.

He sat down in front of the laptop again and explained the connection. 'There are still one or more unidentified people in the vicinity of the crime scene,' he said. 'A man with a camouflage jacket and camera. He could have been Peder Kronborg.'

Maggie leaned back in her chair. 'If not for the new DNA evidence, you could have had a new suspect,' she commented.

Wisting did not have time to answer before her phone rang again. 'I really have to take this,' she excused herself. 'Keep me posted.'

'Will do,' he promised.

As the call disconnected, Peder Kronborg's photo replaced her on the screen.

Wisting opened the police database and looked him up. Unmarried with no children, he lived in Skien. Only a traffic offence was listed in criminal records, but Maggie was right. If it had not been for the DNA result, they would have had a new suspect.

62

Amalie was helping herself. The breakfast cereal over-flowed the rim of the bowl and scattered all across the table. Line, first out of her seat, dashed to the worktop for a cloth to wipe up the mess.

'Did you have a late night?' Wisting asked her.

'Later than intended, anyway,' Line replied.

The arrangement had been that Wisting would take Amalie for a few hours the previous evening, but he had offered to keep her overnight. Line had come to eat breakfast with them.

Amalie began to wriggle once the bowl was half empty. Wisting let her leave the table and began to clear away the dishes.

'I have to go to Skien,' he said.

'When will I get my car back?' Line asked.

'When do you need it?'

'Not until tomorrow, really.'

'I'll bring it back before that,' he assured her.

Line was chewing a slice of bread. 'What are you planning to do in Skien?' she asked. 'Is there another development in the case?'

'Could be,' Wisting answered, and went on to tell her what Maggie Griffin had discovered about Janne's brother.

'What about you?' he asked. 'Any developments in the Cederik Smith saga?'

He had not really meant to ask.

'Well, at least I haven't heard from him for a couple of days,' Line told him. 'That makes a change.'

Wisting had stacked the dishwasher and sat down again. If his daughter ever intended to tell him what had happened, then it would be now.

'I've done something stupid,' she said, cradling her coffee cup in her hands.

Wisting felt a twinge of anxiety in his chest.

'I lent him some money,' Line continued. 'He'd come out of his divorce badly. Child maintenance and starting over again. I was supposed to get it back after a month, when he received the dividends from the production company. That was less than expected and he spent it on other things, but then he was to get a bonus in connection with a production being sold abroad. I didn't see any of that either. There were always apologies and excuses. When I checked, I found out that he owes money all over the place. There are a number of debt-recovery proceedings and talk of repayment enforcement. I couldn't be part of that, though. I just can't have that sort of thing in my life. I need to have order around me, in every way.'

'I see,' Wisting said. He was wondering how much money she was talking about, but held off asking straight out.

'He refused to accept me ending things,' Line went on. 'He's kept calling me and sending messages. Hassling, threatening and begging, but now it's gone quiet.'

She looked out at her daughter playing on the grass. 'Amalie has stopped asking for Pia too,' she said. 'His daughter.'

'Sounds like an expensive experience,' Wisting said. 'But it seems as if you're on your way to putting it behind you and are ready to move on.'

Line smiled. 'The last time I met him, I got him to sign an IOU with twelve per cent interest and a payback plan,' she told him. 'It could be a long time until I'm completely finished with him.'

Glancing across at her father, she realized there was a question on his mind: 'It was 130,000 kroner. All my savings. And now I've no income, because it's become impossible to work alongside him.'

Wisting put his hand on her arm and sat for a while without saying anything. He had saved a solid economic buffer, his mortgage was paid off and he was in a well-paid job, at least for the police force. He spent no money on anything other than regular expenses.

'Let me know if you need any cash,' he said as he rose from his chair. He could see from her face that she appreciated the offer, but knew she would put it off for a long time before ever asking for help.

'I don't want to hold you back,' she said.

She crossed to the dishwasher with her empty cup and called Amalie. Wisting headed out with them and climbed into his car.

The GPS directed him to a terraced apartment with drawn curtains on the outskirts of Skien. Wisting had to ring the doorbell twice before the curtain on the window nearest the door was tugged aside. The face of a man with cropped wiry hair appeared and Wisting gesticulated to signal that he should come to the door.

'Peder Kronborg?' he asked.

The man in the doorway nodded. Wisting identified himself and asked for permission to come inside.

'What's this about?'

'A number of new questions have come up in an old

case,' Wisting replied. 'Tone Vaterland was killed in 1999. Danny Momrak was convicted of her murder but not all of the questions in the case were answered.'

They sat down at the kitchen table. A faint, indefinable food odour lingered in the air. Peder Kronborg cleared away two dirty plates. 'Wasn't it Danny who did it, then?' he asked.

'You knew him?' Wisting asked.

'He was in a parallel class to me at primary school and junior high, but we didn't hang out together.'

Wisting asked a few questions about what sort of impression Danny Momrak had made on him, but did not really receive any satisfactory answers. 'In cases such as this, the police chart all movements around the crime scene,' he went on. 'Do you remember the day it happened?'

'Not really,' Peder Kronborg replied. 'There was a helicopter flying low in the sky, but I didn't know why until I was down at the shop. They were searching for her.'

'The search didn't start until the day after she was killed,' Wisting clarified. 'We're talking about 4 July.'

Peder Kronborg nodded as Wisting shifted in his seat. He was forced to ask a leading question. 'Do you remember when you were on your own at home that day? Whether your parents and Janne had left, or if they were still at home?'

'I was on my own,' the man opposite answered. 'The others had gone to the cabin.'

Wisting realized this matched the timeline. 'I understand an American boy was staying with your family at that time,' he continued.

'Curtis,' Peder Kronborg confirmed. 'He went back.'

'Why did he go back?'

'There was a bit of a rumpus,' Peder replied. 'He tried it

on with my sister. She was only fifteen. Dad didn't like that, so Curtis had to go back before his time was up. It happened at the same time as all this other stuff, with Tone Vaterland and the helicopter and all that. When I got up that morning, Charles had already picked him up. Mum, Dad and Janne went to the cabin.'

Wisting had a few more questions but eventually arrived at the conclusion that Curtis Blair had left before Tone Vaterland went missing.

'I've gone through the whole case again,' Wisting explained, 'but I can't find any mention of the police speaking to you at that time?'

'Why should they?' Peder asked.

'They talked to everyone,' Wisting told him. 'Especially anyone who'd been out and about in the area where she disappeared.'

Peder Kronborg did not really seem to understand the logic of this.

'Several people reported seeing someone in a camouflage jacket with a camera on the afternoon and evening of 4 July,' he added. 'Could that have been you?'

Peder Kronborg looked perplexed. 'Maybe,' he replied.

'Because you did take photographs that summer?' Wisting asked.

'Yes, so what?'

'And you went about in a camouflage jacket at that time?' he continued his questioning.

'Well, I did at least have a jacket like that,' Peder Kronborg answered. 'It was something Dad had bought at a military surplus sale.'

Wisting put down the picture Maggie Griffin had sent him. 'That's you,' he stated rather than asked.

'I haven't seen that before,' Peder Kronborg commented.

'Curtis Blair took this photo in 1999,' Wisting explained. 'Did you also wear a rucksack when you were out taking photographs?'

Peder Kronborg nodded. 'Sometimes,' he replied. 'The kind of rucksack that's combined with a fold-up stool. It was great to set it up when I sat waiting for a good shot.'

'Fine,' Wisting said. He had now established that the man with the camera, camouflage jacket and rucksack who figured in the witness statements could have been Peder Kronborg.

'You were spotted,' he said. 'What I'm wondering is what you saw. Whether you might have seen Tone Vaterland or Danny Momrak or have noticed anything else.'

Peder Kronborg shook his head.

'Where are your photographs from that time?' Wisting continued.

'I've no idea,' Peder Kronborg replied. 'Not here, at any rate. Mum might still have them, or else she threw them out when she moved house.'

Wisting now shifted to a more comfortable position and changed the subject. 'Certain accusations have been made against your father,' he said.

'What kind of accusations?'

'They have to do with Janne.'

Peder Kronborg's jaw tensed and a truculent expression crossed his face. 'My father's not well,' he said, without asking for any clarification. 'You can't talk to him about this. Not Mum either. She's troubled with nerves. Always has been.'

'But what do *you* have to say about it?'

The atmosphere in the room changed imperceptibly.

Peder Kronborg shook his head. 'I've nothing more to say,' he answered, getting to his feet. 'It's a long time ago. Talking about it now changes nothing. None of what happened can be undone.'

Wisting fixed his gaze on the table and decided to let things lie. What Janne Kronborg had been subjected to did not impinge on his case.

He got up to leave, not entirely satisfied with the outcome of his visit. A lot was still left up in the air.

63

The car had been parked in the sun while he was in Peder Kronborg's house. Wisting had to open all the windows before driving off. Once he had got rid of all the stifling air, he closed them and called Adrian Stiller to bring him up to speed.

'I think we can almost certainly draw the conclusion that Peder Kronborg was the person a number of people reported seeing on the day of the murder in 1999,' he ended. 'Some spotted him with a camera and others saw him in a camouflage jacket and with a rucksack.'

'Have you told Sten Kvammen about this?' Stiller asked.

'No,' Wisting replied. 'I don't see any reason to. Not yet, at least.'

They went on to discuss their next moves.

'I'd like to have the results from Forensics of the expanded analysis of Tone Vaterland's blouse first,' Wisting said. 'I've also found out he was following me on the day I paid a visit to Sten Kvammen. I really think we ought to arrange a meeting with Danny Momrak and his lawyer and confront them with what we know.'

Adrian Stiller agreed. 'The Public Prosecutor wants a resolution,' he said. 'My superiors too. When do you think you'll know more?'

'Today.'

Stiller asked to be kept informed and they ended the call. Wisting considered phoning Sten Kvammen all the same. The numerous witness observations of a man with a camera must have given him quite a headache in 1999. He would probably be interested in knowing that the person had now been identified. If nothing else, Wisting had to admit to himself that he would derive considerable satisfaction from telling him he had discovered something they had failed to pin down at the time.

The number was stored in his phone but, although he let it ring out, Kvammen did not pick up.

The phone call from Forensics did not arrive until the end of the day, when Wisting was back at home. Line had left Amalie with him again while she was out shopping. She was thirsty and he had mixed a glass of squash for her.

'We've analysed the blood in the original sample, and it looks as if you're right,' the lab technician told him.

Clutching the phone between his ear and shoulder, Wisting moved out on to the verandah with the tumbler.

'This gets technical,' the lab technician continued. 'But we've found elevated values of ALP. That can come about when cancer spreads through the body. In addition, there's a striking number of bodies resembling Auer rods in the cytoplasma. That's another strong indicator.'

Wisting put the tumbler down on the terrace table, but Amalie was too preoccupied with her games to come and drink.

'So the samples derive from a man suffering from cancer?' he asked.

'I can't make a definite diagnosis,' the lab technician replied. 'But at the very least they derive from a man who was far from well.'

Wisting swatted a wasp that was circling the squash glass.

'I see,' Wisting said, taking a seat. 'Will I receive a written report today?'

'You can have a printout of the various analysis results, but I need a bit more time to write a conclusion,' the woman at the other end of the line told him. 'We've also made another discovery that might be of interest to you.'

'What's that?'

'A foreign substance has been detected in the samples.'

Amalie came up to him and used both hands to grab the tumbler of squash.

'A foreign substance?' Wisting repeated. 'What do you mean by that?'

'Something from neither the body nor the textiles,' the technician explained. 'It's a synthetic compound that contains silicone, among other things.'

'Do you know where that comes from?' Wisting asked.

'We've come across incidences of this before, of various types,' she said. 'It's probably traces of silicone-based lubricant from a condom.'

Wisting was glued to his seat. He let his eyelids close and pictured in his mind's eye how Jan Hansen's DNA had been conveyed from the visitors' room at Ullersmo.

'We don't often come across it along with semen,' the lab technician went on. 'It's usually something we look for in cases of rape where there's an absence of biological traces, in order to prove that the perpetrator has used a condom.'

Wisting wanted to be sure this discovery would be included in the report.

'Of course,' the lab technician assured him. 'You'll find the values in the analysis report you receive today, but I'll explain this in more detail in my final report.'

'Thanks.'

Amalie shouted to him, wanting him to watch as she performed somersaults on the lawn. Only now did he notice that the grass had been cut. Line must have seen to it while he was away.

He cheered in response as she rolled around, before phoning Stiller and telling him what he had just heard.

'Hanne Blom,' was Stiller's initial reaction. 'The girlfriend.'

Wisting's thoughts had gone in a different direction.

'I think Danny Momrak could have smuggled out semen from Jan Hansen,' he said. 'One of Momrak's duties was to clean the visitors' room. He could have taken a used condom from there and smuggled it out. I've compared the list of his home visits with Jan Hansen's visitors list. One of Momrak's last pre-release furloughs was the day after Hanne Blom had paid a visit. That was a short time after Hansen's cancer was diagnosed.'

There was silence at the other end as Stiller absorbed this reasoning.

'That makes sense,' he said. 'But why go to the bother of putting her fingerprints on the anonymous letters?'

'To be able to point in another plausible direction if the plan misfired for some reason.'

'Well, it has done now,' Stiller declared. 'We have what we need to charge him with fabricating evidence.'

'I don't think those legal provisions can be used,' Wisting said. 'What he's done is to plant false leads in a case that's already been investigated and decided in a court of law. From a legal point of view, it's more a case of an attempt at criminal deception. A reopening of the case and acquittal would mean he has a right to compensation.'

Stiller grew thoughtful again. 'How much do you think the lawyer knows?' he asked.

'I don't know,' Wisting replied. 'But I think we have to turn the tables.'

'How so?'

'It's too early to arrest Momrak,' Wisting said. 'We can prevent him from progressing his plans, but as things stand, it would never lead to a prosecution. The whole matter would simply evaporate. Not until Jan Hansen's DNA is cited as fresh evidence and grounds to reopen the case will Danny Momrak have stepped over the line. He's been playing a game with us, but now we have the upper hand.'

'What do you want to do?' Stiller asked.

'Exactly what would be expected if the new DNA evidence were genuine,' Wisting answered. 'I want to call Danny Momrak and his lawyer in for a chat and let them know about the new developments in the case against him. Then I want to wait until they submit a formal application for the case to be reopened. And at that stage it would be a fully-fledged case of deception.'

Stiller liked what he was hearing. 'I'll have a word with the Public Prosecutor,' he said. 'I'll let you know when you can go ahead.'

Amalie tumbled over on the newly mown lawn. Wisting checked his step count on his phone. He had only just passed one thousand.

64

'Did you put sunscreen on her?' Line asked. 'I left some high-factor cream.'

The blanket where Amalie was playing had been in shadow when Line left for the shops. Now it was in the full glare of the sun.

'No,' Wisting answered, squinting at the sky. 'Sorry.'

Filling her hands with sun cream, Line brought her daughter over and rubbed it in.

Wisting headed indoors, where he mixed a jug of squash and carried it out with a couple of glasses.

An hour had now elapsed since he had talked to Stiller. He was keen to call Bohrman, Momrak's lawyer, to arrange a meeting before the working day was over.

'Thanks for cutting the grass,' he said as he sat down.

'It was about time it was done,' Line replied.

At that moment, the message ticked in. A text from Stiller to say that the on-duty Public Prosecutor had approved the course of action he had proposed.

He waited until Line had left with Amalie before calling Bohrman. The lawyer sounded slightly tense when he answered, as if he had been busy with something. Perhaps he was still on the scaffolding, painting the house.

'I'm glad you called,' Bohrman said. 'I heard you had visited Momrak at his home. I think it would be best if all further communication was made through me.'

'That's part of the reason for my call,' Wisting replied. 'I need a briefing meeting. If it would be possible for you to do that around now, during your holidays, I'd really appreciate it.'

'No problem,' Bohrman answered. 'I understood from Kvammen that there had been a certain development in the case.'

'Kvammen?'

'Yes, it was an informal chat,' Bohrman explained. 'I understood he had come straight from a meeting with you. It seems remarkable, this whole business.'

Wisting felt irritation wash over him as he wondered how much Kvammen had revealed. 'Sten Kvammen is not working on this case,' he said. 'That would not be normal process. A lot of what we've done is to track down any possible errors in the original investigation.'

'That's probably what he needed to talk about,' Bohrman said. 'To maintain that he hadn't made a mistake.'

'In what sense?'

Bohrman hesitated. 'He told me that Tone Vaterland's clothes had been found and Jan Hansen's DNA was on them, but that it must have ended up there recently. After he became ill with cancer.'

Now Wisting understood why Sten Kvammen had not picked up the phone and was reluctant to speak to him. He had not only broken the latest news from the ongoing investigation, but also jumped to conclusions. However, the fault was really Wisting's. He should never have let Kvammen know.

'He was extremely determined that any potential errors from 1999 should be corrected,' Bohrman went on. 'But between the lines there was an unequivocal warning that this would backfire on Momrak if, for example, he decided to take part in Ninni Skjevik's documentary.'

'Why is that?' Wisting asked.

'The only person who would have anything to gain by planting false DNA evidence would of course be Momrak,' Bohrman told him.

Wisting clutched his head in despair and felt something sink within him. 'Have you talked to Danny Momrak about this?' he asked.

'He was here with me yesterday,' Bohrman replied. 'He came directly from an interview with your lot.'

'The Roll case,' Wisting confirmed.

'I would have preferred to be informed in advance,' Bohrman pointed out.

'I'm not familiar with the details of that case,' Wisting said. 'But I understood he was a potential witness.'

Bohrman cleared his throat. 'That's what I understood too,' he said. 'Since you're talking now about a briefing meeting, can I suggest we hold it at my office?'

Wisting was keen to have the meeting the following day, but in the end they agreed on a day towards the end of the week.

'I'll arrange it with Momrak,' the lawyer said before they ended the call.

Wisting sat cradling the phone in his hand, considering whether to ring Kvammen or let it drop, but in the end he decided he had to find out how bad the damage was and precisely what Kvammen had revealed.

The call went straight to voicemail so he called Stiller instead. He was too incensed to sit still and paced around the room as he relayed the details.

'That could have been a calculated act,' Stiller felt. 'Sten Kvammen is desperate to have the least possible fuss and attention on the case. By circulating the story that the

DNA evidence is false, Bohrman and Momrak have been given the chance to reverse their plans. He's forced them into silence.'

Wisting had not considered that possibility, but Stiller was right. It could have been a deliberate leak to kill off the whole case.

'I need some time to collect my thoughts and find out what we can do,' he said, sitting down again. 'I'll call you tomorrow.'

Moving to the kitchen sink, he filled a glass with water and stood at the window. A man with a panting dog walked past on the warm asphalt. In the distance he could hear the sirens of an emergency vehicle. The noise rose and fell before being suddenly cut off.

Wisting wondered whether to get into his car and drive down to see Kvammen, but dismissed the idea. Instead he sat down at the kitchen table and flipped up his laptop lid. He saw he had received the analysis results from Forensics. Among other emails of little significance, there was also a reply from Gustav Bolk at the toll company.

The phone rang before he had time to examine them more closely. It was Kathe Ulstrup calling. If he answered, he would feel obliged to tell her about the fake DNA evidence. What they were planning had to be kept on a need-to-know basis, but he could not really exclude her. At the very least, he could not avoid taking her call.

'There's one thing I thought you should know,' she told him. 'Jonas Haugerud was caught with amphetamines this morning. He has a number of previous charges that have not been dealt with yet, and there's some talk of a remand in custody. He asked to speak to you.'

'Oh, and?'

'I've just come from the cells,' Ulstrup went on. 'He wants to cut a deal to avoid custody and had something on Danny.'

'What was that?'

'That he's carrying a gun.'

Wisting sat bolt upright. 'A gun?'

'Danny had a pistol in the waistband of his trousers when he was at Jonas's house a few weeks ago,' Ulstrup explained. 'He didn't draw the gun, but it was obvious Danny wanted Jonas to clock it and understand that he had to change his statement from 1999.'

Wisting took a moment to let this information sink in.

'Normally we would react to that kind of information,' Ulstrup added. 'Arrest Danny Momrak and search his house, but not if it would upset your plans.'

Wisting explained about the developments in the case and the arrangement they had made with Momrak's lawyer.

'This information is already a few weeks old,' Ulstrup said. 'No harm in letting it lie for a few more days. Jonas Haugerud is not a particularly reliable witness, anyway. He would have said anything to avoid jail.'

Wisting went for a walk after they had brought the call to a close, out on to the terrace and back to the kitchen table again. His laptop had gone to sleep and he fired it up, clicked on the file attachment from Gustav Bolk and took a look at the list of Danny Momrak's toll transits the previous day.

Eight minutes after they had lost sight of him, his car was recorded on the southbound carriageway of the E18. Just over an hour later, it made the return journey.

Slowly but surely, Wisting's pulse rate began to climb. The last time Momrak had driven through that same toll station had been when he had followed Wisting to Sten Kvammen's cabin.

Picking up his phone, he tried yet again to call the former senior investigating officer, but once more received no answer.

A nagging feeling had lodged in his gut. He gripped the car keys that lay on the table and sat squeezing them before he got to his feet. It was mere supposition, a dawning suspicion that was insufficient grounds to sound the alarm or alert anyone, but nevertheless he felt he had to do something about it.

65

The cramped visitors' room was not an ideal place for filming, but she had no alternative.

'Have you found out anything more about him?' Danny asked as she adjusted the light and focus.

Ninni shook her head. She had discovered there must have been a misunderstanding somewhere. It looked as if Curtis Blair may have left Norway before Tone Vaterland was killed, but she was unwilling to tell him that. Not yet.

'I'll probably have to fly over there,' she said, mainly to impress him.

'To the USA?'

'Yes, but something else has turned up.'

Danny paused his questions. He knew she was keen to capture everything on film and had grown used to her not saying much until the camera was rolling. She was desperate to tell him, but it was important to record all of his responses, and what she was about to say was guaranteed to trigger a reaction.

'What have you found out?' he asked once the recording lamp was lit.

'I've received the case documents from your lawyer,' she said, sitting down. 'I've read them all and have uncovered something interesting.'

'Something new?'

She shook her head. 'It was there the whole time,' she replied. 'But no one has understood its significance.'

She opened a folder and picked out Jan Hansen's interview. 'Just one thing,' she said before handing him the papers. 'When you go back to your section, you have to act as if nothing has happened. Behave normally.'

She glanced up at the camera. This admonition would have to be edited out. 'Got that?' she asked.

'OK,' Danny answered as he reached for the printouts.

He began to read but did not seem to have grasped the point. That was how she too had read through the first interviews. She had skipped over the details of names and other formalities and moved straight to the witness statements. The person who had given the affidavit was of little interest to begin with. What had been observed was the main focus. But in this case, it was the opposite.

'The solution may be closer than we'd imagined,' she said.

Danny still did not get the picture.

'This is a statement given by Jan Hansen in cell six,' she said. 'He was there when Tone was murdered. He was one of the last people to see her alive.'

Danny sat still, and then the reaction followed, a jolt through his body, followed by an incessant tremor. Violent shaking.

She captured it on film before telling him what she knew about Jan Hansen. Danny listened, tight-lipped. When she had finished, he fixed his gaze on the camera. 'Switch it off,' he said.

Ninni stood up and did as he asked. She realized she

had something. She had discovered something that offered immense opportunities. If she managed to land this catch right, she would be noticed, and it would be of enormous significance for her.

66

The black dog sprang up but remained in the shadow cast by Sten Kvammen's car. Wisting drove forward and parked his vehicle in the same spot as last time. The gravel crunched under his feet when he stepped out. The dog hovered in the background as Wisting approached the cabin and edged round to the sea-facing side. A cool breeze wafted the salt tang of the sea across the land as it stirred the air.

A newspaper lay on the table where they had sat on his previous visit and the sliding door leading into the living room was open. The gauze curtains in front of the opening fluttered in the draught.

'Hello?' Wisting shouted.

A gull took flight from one of the jetty poles. He heard the beating of its wings, but apart from that a remarkable stillness enveloped the place.

'Kvammen!' Wisting called out again, but there was no answer.

He went to the doorway and drew aside the gauze curtains. The wooden floor planks creaked as he walked through the empty living room. In the hallway, a bedroom door lay open. The bed was not made, but otherwise the room was tidy.

Wisting called out again as he looked through the other rooms, the bathroom and the kitchen, but the cabin was deserted.

He returned to the verandah. The heat of the sun had

soaked up much of the colour from the grass on the slope down to the jetty where the boat was moored, rocking in the rhythm of the gentle waves.

The dog loped towards him. It sat down and stared at him with his mouth hanging open and his tongue lolling.

'Are you thirsty?' Wisting asked.

He went back inside the cabin, turned on the kitchen tap and let the water run until it was cold before filling a bowl and carrying it outside.

The dog greedily lapped up the water. Wisting walked down to the jetty but found the boat empty. He looked intently into the depths of the water, where he could see clumps of bladderwrack drifting with the swell of the waves. He used his hand to shade his eyes from the sun and gazed far out along the smooth rocks and pebbles on the shore. The pair of swans from last time appeared behind an islet, but nothing else could be seen.

Something was wrong.

Plodding back up to the cabin, he took a walk around it, all the while searching for signs and tracks, but found nothing to provide any inkling of what had happened.

The heat made him feel sticky and his shirt clung to his back. He moved across to Kvammen's car and tugged at the driver's door, but it was locked.

He could see nothing on or between the car seats, but he thought he could smell some kind of foul odour in the air around it. As if driving it hard had damaged the catalyser.

The back seat was also tidy. He moved to the rear of the vehicle and peered into the boot space, where condensation had formed on the window. Cupping his hands on the glass, he gazed in and took a few seconds to comprehend what he was looking at. The sight made him instinctively draw back, as if he had been burned. He had to steel himself to take two steps forward again to double-check what he had seen.

Sten Kvammen was trussed up, a lifeless bundle, trapped in the dog cage.

Wisting struggled to open the rear hatch, tugging and tearing at the handle, but the car was locked. He picked up a stone and threw it at the driver's side window, but it bounced off, triggering the car alarm.

Wisting grabbed another stone, slightly bigger and sharper this time. He hammered it against the window and, after three attempts, the glass cracked. On the fourth, it imploded and shattered.

The heat and stink from the baking-hot car belched towards him. Leaning inside, he managed to open the door from the inside. He was unfamiliar with the make of car, but assumed there would be a lever somewhere he could use to open the rear door from the driver's seat. Finally locating it, he pulled and heard the mechanical click through the wailing of the alarm.

Sten Kvammen sat with his knees drawn up to his chest, his head hanging down between them. One leg slid out when Wisting opened the cage door. Grabbing hold of the other one, he dragged Kvammen halfway out through the opening. His head flipped back, mauve-coloured, covered in burst blisters and open sores.

Wisting grasped one arm and hauled him all the way out, lugging him across the yard into the shade, where he laid him flat on the ground.

Aware that the switchboard operator would ask, he placed two fingers on the man's neck. His skin was warm. Soft and clammy, but without a pulse.

67

One of the men in the first patrol car had opened the bonnet and removed the battery leads to silence the alarm. Thereafter, crime-scene tape was set up in anticipation of the arrival of the technicians.

Wisting had trudged round to the other side of the house, facing the sea and overlooking the jetty. Adrian Stiller had leapt into his car and was making his way down from Oslo. He phoned again, eager to hear the latest news.

'The technicians have just arrived,' Wisting told him. 'But as I see it, he's been threatened and manhandled into the cage and left there.'

'It must have happened yesterday,' Stiller said. 'While I sat waiting for Momrak to come home. That's twenty-four hours ago.'

'He could have survived overnight,' Wisting suggested. 'But he must have been dead long before I got here.'

Stiller exhaled – a protracted, audible sigh.

In the past, Wisting had investigated an accident with a similar fatal outcome. A Romanian seasonal worker had been picking raspberries at one of the farms in Brunlanes. He had put on rainwear to avoid being scratched by the branches although the temperature was almost thirty degrees Celsius that day. At some point he had succumbed to heatstroke and collapsed, but he lay for several hours before he was found. When he was admitted to hospital, his core body temperature was 41.8 degrees. Most of his organs had already failed and he died after twenty-four hours in intensive care.

Inside Kvammen's car, the temperature must have soared to at least ninety degrees. It was like an oven. Everything inside must have reached the same temperature at some stage.

'Did I tell you that Momrak once spat at the TV screen in prison when Sten Kvammen appeared on a news broadcast?'

'No,' Stiller replied.

Wisting related the story. 'He must have projected all the blame for his own situation on to Sten Kvammen,' he concluded. 'Built up an intense hatred.'

'Yesterday he heard from his lawyer that his plan would not succeed,' Stiller said. 'That the fake DNA evidence had been detected. He must have seen red at that.'

The pair of swans came paddling in towards the jetty with their young in tow. They had grown bigger and their feathers were paler.

'I've spoken to Kathe Ulstrup,' Wisting said. 'She's preparing to move into action. The local emergency squad will bring him in.'

He glanced at his watch. 'The meet-up is beside the old railway station in Oklungen, eight hundred metres from his house.'

'I'm on my way,' Stiller said.

68

The squad leader had sent up a drone. At first it rose so high that it took in all the surroundings of the deserted spot. The nearest neighbour was on the other side of a small ridge covered in dry conifers, so far away that there was no need to take anybody into consideration during the raid.

Wisting looked up. Unable to hear the drone, he did not catch sight of it until it was a couple of hundred metres up in the air, filming at an angle down to Danny Momrak's house.

His car was parked in the yard. The drone dropped even lower and circled the house. Both front and side doors were closed. The outdoor area where Wisting had sat four days earlier was deserted.

A brief order was barked over the police radio: 'Action!'

Wisting, Stiller and Ulstrup were able to watch on the drone operator's screen. A cloud of dust shot up behind two black off-road vehicles as they accelerated along the gravel track and up in front of the building. The doors sprang open before they drew to a halt. Eight men from the local emergency squad stormed out and took up position around the house. Four of them advanced towards the front door.

The drone moved in closer and the radio transmitters were switched to open dialogue. They could see one of the police officers slam his fist on the door, heard the blows and Danny Momrak's name being shouted, ordering him to come out.

Five seconds passed and then the door was levered open and the four armed officers charged in. Short messages were spat out as they moved through the rooms in the house.

'*Clear.*'

'*Clear.*'

Another three rooms were cleared before two men were sent up into the attic.

'*Clear,*' was also the report from that area.

'*Copy,*' was the response. '*Pull out.*'

The drone closed in as the four police officers emerged, swinging their machine pistols round to their backs and tugging off their helmets.

The leader had stayed at the rearmost vehicle. Now he came forward and asked for a situation report.

'*Empty,*' was the response. '*No one home.*'

The open radio link was disconnected and the drone recalled. Wisting moved to his car.

The cat came padding across from the edge of the woods as he swung up in front of the house. Wisting wanted to go inside to see for himself. Adrian Stiller followed on his heels.

The house was not only empty, it seemed to have been abandoned. In haste.

Flies were buzzing around a plate of leftovers from a half-eaten portion of some kind of stew and there was similar activity above a pot on the stove. An open cola can sat on the table beside a cigarette packet, a lighter and a bunch of keys.

Wisting peered more closely at the keys. One of them was for a Mercedes. 'Sten Kvammen,' he said, pointing.

They moved on through the house, room by room, but found nothing to suggest where Danny Momrak might have gone. On the way out, Wisting stopped in front of the fuse box in the hallway. He opened it and took a photo of the smart meter.

The lead officer was rounding off a phone conversation when they re-emerged. 'I've initiated tracing of his mobile phone,' he said. 'We'll have his location in quarter of an hour.'

Wisting moved back to his car and invited Stiller and Kathe Ulstrup to hop in.

'Where are we going?' Stiller asked.

'Not far,' Wisting replied.

69

Wisting was seated at the wheel of Line's car with Stiller by his side. Kathe Ulstrup leaned forward between the seats. The car had been parked in the shade beneath tall trees, but the cabin was still warm. Wisting turned on the ignition and ran the air conditioning at full blast.

The inbuilt screen on the back of the dash cam was small, so they had to put their heads together. There was a lengthy list of recordings. All the vehicles that had passed on the main road had been caught on film. The first footage was of Maren Dokken's police car driving off with Wisting and Amalie the previous evening.

They worked their way through the list of film clips. Cars drove past in both directions, but not so many that scrolling through the footage became unmanageable.

Less than an hour after Wisting had parked the car and camera at the road verge, a silver estate car had arrived and turned off towards Danny Momrak's property. The time on the recording showed 18.34.

Wisting recognized the car. The onscreen image was too tiny to make out the registration number or whether there was a blemish on the front windscreen, but he still recognized Ninni Skjevik's vehicle. A cloud of dust kicked up behind it.

He fast-forwarded through the list of recordings. The time on the footage now indicated that one full hour had elapsed the previous day.

Kathe Ulstrup's radio transmitter crackled. It was the squad leader. 'The phone is no longer active,' he reported. 'The last position looks to be a spot east of the residence. We're searching the terrain.'

Wisting glanced at Ulstrup, uncertain of that information's import.

'Copy,' she signed out.

Wisting skipped forward in the recordings. A roe deer with two calves crossing the road had also triggered the sensor. Not until 21.02 did Ninni Skjevik's car reappear. It stopped at the junction and waited until a timber lorry had passed before swinging out.

'Nearly two and a half hours,' Stiller calculated.

Wisting wound back the tape and froze the image as the car waited at the crossroads. He fumbled with the controls to zoom in. Despite the reflection on the windows, it was possible to make out one person alone in the car.

The squad leader announced himself on the radio again, now reporting that a mobile phone and clothing had been found at a bathing spot beside Farris lake.

Driving back, they followed the track that led through the woods and down to the lakeside.

The squad leader handed the phone to Kathe Ulstrup, who dropped it into a protective plastic bag. 'It was inside the trouser pocket,' he said, pointing at the clothes lying on a rock – a pair of torn jeans, a T-shirt, boxer shorts and socks. A pair of trainers lay on the ground beside the boulder.

Wisting scanned the area as the waves splashed on the shore. A layer of yellow pollen dust outlined the water's edge.

The squad leader ventured out on one of the wobbly

stones and pointed to a spot where discolouration was obvious. 'Probably blood,' he said. 'The divers have been called in. They'll be here within the hour.'

'I want crime-scene technicians as well,' Wisting said.

'Can't it wait till we find him?' Ulstrup asked.

'It's deep out there,' one of the other police officers commented, gazing out across the lake. 'It's not certain we'll ever find him.'

'I want to know what happened here in the last twenty-four hours,' Wisting said, heading off along the path back to the house.

'Where are you going?' Ulstrup asked.

'I want a word with Ninni Skjevik,' Wisting replied.

Kathe Ulstrup nodded. 'I'll come with you,' she said.

70

The gravel scrunched under the tyres and sprayed up into the wheel arches as Wisting drove out of the yard.

Kathe Ulstrup put the unspoken into words: 'You don't believe it was an accident? That he went for a swim?'

'Not in the middle of a meal and without a towel,' Wisting told her.

The tyres gripped the asphalt on the main road. Wisting connected his phone and made a call to Maren Dokken. 'What do I do to arrange an analysis of electricity consumption?' he asked.

'For what purpose?' she queried.

He gave her an update on the situation. 'I need to know when the stove was switched off and the stew was ready,' he told her.

'The simplest thing would be if you could get me the meter number,' Maren replied. 'I have a contact who can give you what you're after sometime this evening.'

'Thanks,' Wisting said. 'I'll send you a picture.'

He handed the phone to Ulstrup and asked her to send the photo of the fuse box in Danny Momrak's house.

'I said Ninni Skjevik wasn't to be trusted,' Ulstrup remarked as she put down the phone.

'You never said why,' Wisting commented.

'She's callous,' Ulstrup answered. 'Ruthless, even.'

Wisting asked her to explain.

'I once investigated a head-on collision,' Ulstrup began.

'A delivery van had smashed into a passenger vehicle. An elderly couple died. It happened on a secondary road west of Frier fjord where there's little traffic. Ninni Skjevik was first on the scene, but she wasn't the one who sounded the alarm. One car had gone up in flames and she was busy taking photographs.'

They had overtaken a lorry. Wisting drove past on a level stretch of road.

'The next car arrived after a minute or two,' Ulstrup continued. 'The police were called and she helped to get the delivery van driver out. They couldn't do anything for the married couple in the other car.'

'But all went well with the man they saved?' Wisting asked.

'Not really,' Ulstrup replied. 'He had sat too long without getting any air. The lack of oxygen caused major brain damage. He's probably still in some kind of institution. If only Ninni Skjevik had tipped his head back before she started taking photographs, he would have been able to breathe. And he would be a healthy man today.'

'Tragic,' Wisting commented.

'In the pictures printed in the newspaper, you can see that she broke off a few branches from the bushes at the side of the road to fit both vehicles into the frame,' Ulstrup went on. 'To get a better picture.'

'Were there any consequences?' Wisting asked.

'The idea of bringing charges for breach of duty to provide assistance was considered, but it didn't go that far. Maybe because the van driver was to blame for the accident. He was well over the limit and had wandered across into the oncoming lane. But both she and her editor were challenged about it. Not long afterwards, she moved on and started a new job. I don't know if there was a connection.'

They sat in silence for the next few kilometres.

Ninni Skjevik was standing beside her car when they arrived. Wisting parked behind her.

'Has something happened?' she asked as she put her bag in the boot.

'I'm glad I met you here,' Wisting said, with a nod towards her car. 'Are you going somewhere?'

'I'm going home to Oslo for a few days,' she replied. 'Is there any news?'

'Danny Momrak is missing,' Wisting answered.

Ninni Skjevik glanced down at the camera in the boot, but left it there and shifted her gaze back to Wisting. 'Missing?' she repeated. 'How on earth?'

'The house is unlocked, his car is in the yard, and his phone is dead,' Wisting told her.

Kathe Ulstrup had edged around the car and taken out a notepad, but let Wisting do the talking.

'When was the last time you had contact with him?' he asked.

'Yesterday,' she replied. 'I visited him at his home.'

'When was that?'

'Early evening.'

'When did you leave?'

'Sometime around nine. We'd intended to do some filming, but he wasn't in the mood.'

'Why not?' Wisting asked. 'Did he say anything about what was wrong?'

Ninni Skjevik pulled down the boot lid. 'Not really,' she said. 'He'd been at a meeting with his lawyer. I understood he'd received some bad news, but he didn't want to talk about it and couldn't stand the idea of me filming him. We sat talking about all sorts of other things instead.'

'About what, for instance?'

'About the plans he had for the house. About the future. Dreams and schemes. You see, it's on the cards that he's going to receive a large sum in compensation.'

Wisting posed a few more questions, jumping from one thing to another. He learned that she had arrived at about half past six and that they had sat outside in the evening sun behind the house. They had drunk a can of cola each, but not eaten anything.

'Did he mention anything about what he planned to do after you left?'

Ninni Skjevik looked down at the ground, seemingly gathering her thoughts. 'He was going for an evening swim,' was what she decided to say. 'He was working on building a terrace of slate slabs when I arrived. He continued with that while we talked. Have you been down at the lake to look for him?'

'A full search has been launched,' Wisting answered.

'I see,' she said, stealing a glance at the car boot, where her camera lay. 'In that case I'd better get myself up there. Are we done?'

Ulstrup's phone rang. She checked the display and walked away from them.

Wisting was not quite finished. 'Did you talk about Sten Kvammen?' he asked.

Ninni affected a smile. 'That name was a term of abuse as far as Danny was concerned,' she said. 'Like a swear word. Why do you ask?'

'He was found dead a few hours ago,' Wisting told her.

The smile abruptly disappeared. She looked startled, as if something had scared her. 'How did it happen?'

Wisting weighed up how much to tell her, but he was

keen to see her reaction. 'He was imprisoned in a dog cage in the back of his car,' he replied. 'Probably died of heatstroke.'

Ninni stood with her mouth open. 'Do you think Danny . . . ?'

Wisting backed away towards his car. 'I don't know,' he replied.

Ulstrup ended her call as Wisting opened the car door. 'We need to get moving,' he said, clambering in.

Ninni Skjevik stood watching them as they drove off.

'They've found him,' Kathe Ulstrup said, tucking the phone into her shirt pocket. 'At a depth of five metres.'

71

The stretcher with Danny Momrak's body was sliding smoothly into the vehicle when Wisting arrived back at the house in Oklungen.

That Ninni Skjevik was being cheated of her photographs was the first thought to cross his mind before the hatch was slammed shut.

'The lake bed slopes pretty steeply out there,' one of the local crime-scene technicians told him, the same man who had been in charge of the investigations at the garage on the old road.

'The body was almost seven metres from shore,' he continued. 'But that's consistent with him walking out from the edge. The underwater currents have dragged him a few metres in an easterly direction too, in relation to where his clothes lay.'

'Have you spoken to the forensics folk?' Wisting asked.

'They'll start the post-mortem tomorrow morning. We may have cause of death by lunchtime.'

'What do you think?'

'He had a cut on the back of his head,' the technician answered. 'Perhaps from a fall somewhere at the swimming location. But then we have this.'

He held up an oblong lump of slate. There was only just room for it in the thirty-centimetre-long evidence bag.

'The divers found this at seven metres, a couple of metres further out than the body,' he explained. 'It most likely comes from the back of the house and must have been thrown out into the water.'

They walked round to the terrace where Wisting had sat with Momrak several days earlier. The stacks of slates appeared untouched and the wheelbarrow still stood where Wisting remembered.

'I want you to concentrate on this area,' he said, studying the stone slabs around the table and chairs. 'When I was here on Thursday, it was all covered in bird shit. Cigarette ash and stubs. Now it looks as if someone has scrubbed it all down.'

The divers had packed up their equipment and were walking along the path from Farris lake. They were dragging oxygen cylinders behind them on a trolley and struggling to haul it past a cordoned-off area.

'What have you found there?' Wisting asked.

'Nothing at present,' the technician replied. 'Part of the path is a bit sodden, from a stream. Apart from that, the ground is dry and hard-packed. We've sealed it off to search for footprints.'

'Look for wheelbarrow tracks as well,' Wisting told them. 'If he was killed here, he must have been transported down to the lake.'

He moved across to the old barrow that had been full of rainwater. The birds had bathed in it. Now it was empty.

A vehicle with the necessary equipment was reversing across the long grass as far as it was possible to drive. Floodlights were being set up and the crime-scene tape stretched out. The technicians were wearing fresh sets of protective clothing.

Wisting stood watching them as moths fluttered in and out of the light from the work lamps. The cat appeared, slinking past his legs, but was soon scared off when Stiller arrived to stand beside him.

'When you reopen old cases, unexpected things always happen,' he said.

One of the crime-scene technicians crouched down, picking at something between two of the slate slabs, but it did not look as if he had found anything of interest.

Wisting repeated what Ninni Skjevik had told them.

'Do you think she knew about Sten Kvammen?' Stiller asked.

'I don't know,' Wisting replied.

He cast a glance at the door into the kitchen, where they had found Kvammen's car keys.

'Maybe he wanted to let Kvammen feel what it's like to be incarcerated,' Stiller suggested. 'Maybe there was no intention for him to die. Maybe he thought it would only last a few hours and then he would go back and let him out again.'

The same thought had crossed Wisting's mind. He thrust his hands into his pockets and shivered. It was going to be a long night.

72

An operations room was established at the police station in Skien. Formally, Oklungen was within their area of responsibility and the technicians had been called out from there. Wisting felt unfamiliar in these offices and stayed in the background of the activity.

Just after midnight, Maren Dokken phoned to say she had sent him a provisional analysis of the electricity consumption.

'The electric appliances in the house have to be control tested in order to make a comprehensive analysis,' she said. 'But there's a spike between 17.30 and 18.30 that corresponds with use of a hotplate, just as you suggested.'

Wisting was keen to have more detail and they reached the conclusion that the stove must have been switched on immediately after 18.00, subsequently turned down after about ten minutes and then switched off completely ten minutes later.

'About 20.00 there's another significant spike,' Maren went on. 'A thousand watts.'

'What could that be?'

'I don't know enough about the case or the circumstances in the house,' Maren replied. 'But in the case against Erik Roll, we saw a similar increase in consumption when the hot water was hooked up.'

'So someone was running hot water?' Wisting asked.

'It looks like it,' Maren answered.

Thanking her, Wisting jotted down the information on a timeline. He considered going home to catch a few hours' sleep before the post-mortem report was ready, but it was too soon. Kathe Ulstrup called him and asked him to come with Stiller down to the computer lab.

'They opened Momrak's phone and reset the password before he was carried away,' she said.

Wisting realized they must have used the body to do that, using a fingerprint or facial recognition.

'The contents have been transferred to hard disc,' Ulstrup continued. 'We can go through it all.'

The investigation room, where computer fans were whirring and LED lights blinking, was on the floor below. The dry air caught at the back of his throat.

The technician in charge had relinquished one of the largest screens to Kathe Ulstrup and she was already busy working through the call log.

In the past twenty-four hours, Danny Momrak had two unanswered calls from his mother, but apart from that there had been no activity since the previous day. In the afternoon he had had a conversation lasting almost three minutes with Ninni Skjevik.

In all other respects, the number of contacts was limited. They came across Maren Dokken's number from the time she had called him in for interview, and his lawyer's number. The remaining numbers were not linked to known relationships.

Kathe Ulstrup moved on to the messages. Several of these had been exchanged between Momrak and Ninni Skjevik, but they did not contain anything revealing. There were arrangements about meetings and brief messages, as well as replies to earlier conversations and discussions.

'Look at the pictures,' Wisting told her.

The images were organized in chronological order. Momrak had been an enthusiastic photographer but not so good at tidying and deleting. In total there were 1,722 pictures, often several of the same subject.

He seemed to have taken photos of various everyday situations. His cat was a recurring motif in many of them, as well as pictures of food he had eaten and places he had visited. Landscapes and townscapes, but not so many of other people. A series of photographs showed Ninni Skjevik setting up her camera and lights in his living room in preparation for an interview. These were taken the day before Wisting had travelled to the USA. Ninni must have taken one of them for him, as it showed Danny in front of the camera with him also visible in the small screen behind the camera.

'May I?' Wisting asked as he took over the computer mouse.

He scrolled to the night when Agnete Roll was murdered and Momrak had been in Stavern. Two photos had been taken, both of Wisting's house. In one he could make out his own silhouette at the kitchen window, where he was in the habit of standing, looking down at Line's house before turning in for the night.

He did not stop there and went on to scroll to the pictures taken three and four months ago. He found even more than he had hoped for.

One photo had obviously been taken from a passenger seat. The phone was held slightly askew so the subject was at an angle. It was a picture of Hanne Blom's delivery van, parked in the middle of a car park with a sheet of white paper attached to the front windscreen. Across the image there was a crack on the car windscreen through which the picture had been taken.

'That's from Ninni Skjevik's car,' Stiller said. 'She's been involved in everything from the very start.'

Wisting turned to the technician. 'Is it possible to take a look at his step counter?' he asked.

The technician trundled his chair across to them, took over the mouse and called up the data from the activity monitor. The figures could be broken down into days and hours. The last steps were recorded between 19.00 and 20.00 the previous evening. Only eleven steps.

'It's not certain that these are actual steps,' the technician said. 'They could be nudges from the phone being moved.'

In the hour before that, 174 steps had been registered.

'Can you find out when the phone ran out of charge?' Wisting asked.

The technician produced the answer with a few keystrokes. 'At 02.37 last night,' he replied.

Wisting had to ask to be entirely sure: 'So after 8 p.m. the phone hasn't moved? It's been lying in the same spot?'

The technician nodded.

'Ninni Skjevik didn't leave until nine o'clock,' Stiller reminded him.

Ulstrup became agitated. 'She told us he was thinking of going down for a swim after she left,' she said. 'That must have been a lie. We've got her.'

She returned to the call log and the last conversation between Ninni Skjevik and Danny Momrak from the previous day.

'This is right after he drove back from his lawyer's,' she said. 'Just after Momrak had learned that his plan was not going to work, that the semen found on Tone Vaterland's clothes could not have been from 1999.'

Wisting nodded. This made their suspicions against Ninni Skjevik more specific. It gave her a motive.

'They'd been rumbled,' Kathe Ulstrup went on. 'But the leads pointed only at Danny. He was the only one who could say that she was also involved.'

'She stood to lose everything,' Stiller said. 'Her whole journalistic integrity. If her colleagues had scoffed at her in 1999, she would certainly be a laughing stock now.'

He turned to face Wisting. 'When will we bring her in?' he asked.

'Tomorrow,' Wisting answered. 'When we know for sure that this wasn't a swimming accident.'

73

He had walked almost six thousand steps already, most of them back and forth across the conference-room floor.

They found themselves at the restless stage in the investigation, the point at which a case was about to close down.

Wisting pulled out a chair to sit at the conference table.

The Chief of Police sat opposite him. One of the slats on the venetian blinds was damaged, causing a ray of sunshine to strike her face. The section leaders and other members of senior management at the police station who had not received any kind of briefing prior to this were also present in order to bring them up to date. Several had worked with Sten Kvammen in the course of his career.

Wisting ran through the background to the entire case and all the recent developments before the Chief Crime Scene Investigator furnished an account of the findings in the post-mortem report.

The damage caused by the wound at the back of the head could have been fatal, but Danny Momrak had in fact drowned.

'Rust particles were found in the water taken from his lungs,' he said. 'Our hypothesis is that he was knocked unconscious with a lump of slate beside the house and his head was forced under the water in the wheelbarrow, hence the rust particles. Then the barrow was used to convey him down to Farris lake.'

'Have you found any evidence of that on the path?' Stiller asked.

The technician shook his head. 'We've eliminated prints from our own crew,' he replied. 'After that, there were no prints remaining. Not even from Momrak's own shoes, which had been left on the shore. It may well be that old prints had been brushed away. We're going to head out there again to search for branches from the vegetation there that might have been used to sweep the ground.'

The report was supplemented with photos of the area outside Danny Momrak's house on a large screen, showing how a perpetrator could have operated unobserved, without fear of neighbours or anyone else disturbing the activity.

'A gun was found in his car,' the technician added, calling up a picture of the Volkswagen Touran. 'There was a Colt under the driver's seat.'

The image showed the serial number engraved along the barrel of the pistol.

'It's registered to a Halvor Momrak,' the technician said. 'That's Danny Momrak's uncle, the previous owner of the house. The pistol was probably part of the effects when Danny took over.'

The Chief of Police and several of the local top brass were craning forward now. It was easy to envisage how Sten Kvammen had been forced into his own dog cage.

'The magazine is fully loaded but the gun bears no evidence of being fired, at least not recently,' the technician concluded as he passed the baton to one of his colleagues.

They discovered that blood had been detected on the terrace outside the house, despite it having obviously been scrubbed and cleaned.

'Momrak must have been undressed after he was killed,' he continued, airing a theory that his T-shirt must have been stained with blood and that the perpetrator had probably replaced it with a clean one from his drawer.

'What's become of that T-shirt?' someone asked.

'It hasn't been found,' the technician answered. 'The perpetrator has most likely taken it with him – or her – along with the rags used in the cleaning.'

He leafed through a notebook. 'We've gone through all the surveillance footage from the dash cam,' he went on, looking in Wisting's direction. 'There's been no traffic in or out of the place apart from Ninni Skjevik's car.'

The Police Chief now addressed Wisting. Although he did not have formal responsibility for the investigation, he had authority and knew the cases better than anyone.

'Where's Ninni Skjevik now?' he asked.

'She's on her way in,' Wisting replied as he pushed his chair back from the table.

74

Wisting stood in front of the screen where both sound and vision from the interview room was being directly transmitted. In his very first interviews, he had sat opposite the suspect and hammered down the statement on a typewriter. It hadn't even had a correction key. That had been in 1984, but he did not feel old. In the course of the past few days he had been faced with, and made use of, investigative methods he had never before heard of or even imagined. And he had understood it all.

Ninni Skjevik was speaking in soft tones. The volume was turned up. She gave short answers to the formal, introductory questions, but Wisting noticed the uncertainty in her voice. Uncertainty about how much the police actually knew.

He had grown up during the Cold War. While he attended Police College in the late seventies, he had been secretly critical of police surveillance and mapping of political interests, views and ideology. It had been invasive and, instead of increased security, it created uncertainty. In later years it had also been shown to contravene the law.

Since that time, surveillance had changed shape and character. It was no longer something the authorities imposed on the populace, but something most people themselves chose to click 'OK' on. Every single step taken by people was literally watched over.

Kathe Ulstrup pointed to an empty chair, but Wisting remained on his feet.

He heard the charges being read out over the loudspeakers. Onscreen, Ninni Skjevik shook her head. In a few decades, or perhaps even before that time, it was likely that new journalists would come along and request release of her film footage.

He wondered whether future investigators would employ new methods and even newer technologies in an effort to solve cases he had been forced to set aside, or to review cases he thought he had solved.

Ninni Skjevik began to give her statement. She chose the easiest way out. Denial.

What she said had no practical significance. The network of other information had already provided them with all the answers. When the case had started to shift, it had moved fast. Everything had happened at breakneck speed.

Wisting withdrew to the door. Opening it quietly, he slipped out. There was no need for him to be there. Other younger, more energetic officers could handle it, probably better than he could. They would drive the case forward and through the court system.

He pushed the door shut, in full knowledge that the question of guilt in case 1569 would remain unchanged.

75

Two weeks later

The picture on the screen flickered slightly, as if there was movement in a loose contact when Maren Dokken closed the interview-room door behind her.

Erik Roll and his lawyer looked up. Maren took a seat and introduced them to the new evidence. Erik Roll's fingerprints had been found in the shed in the herb garden from which a petrol can had been stolen.

Wisting had seen this happen many times. An accused person who clung to his statement and repeated the same story, but as soon as new elements entered the picture, the lies became increasingly difficult to sustain. Changes began to emerge. Times were revised and details adjusted. Fresh details were entered and others removed. Cracks began to appear, as well as inconsistencies and discrepancies in the story, and flaws, mistakes and huge holes in the statement that, in the end, grew too large to patch together. The atmosphere in the interview room changed and the conversation took a new direction.

In the end, that had happened with Ninni Skjevik. Now it was Erik Roll's turn.

'I knew she was in a relationship with Jarle Schup,' he said. 'When she wasn't at home, I guessed she had gone to him. I waited outside until they parted, then followed her for a while before I caught up with her.'

With small steps, Maren Dokken led him through the chain of events. A polished, well-honed version in which Agnete had started another argument, in which she had pushed him first, in which he had merely pushed her back, in which there had been no intention for things to go so wrong. A version of what had happened that could not be contradicted.

His memory let him down when the questions became too difficult to answer. The ones about concealment of the body, about returning and starting the fire.

Ninni Skjevik had also come up with a polished version. She had believed Danny Momrak innocent, but during the course of the production she had grown suspicious. In the end, when she had gone to his home and confronted him, he had reacted angrily. She had acted in self-defence. Afterwards she had panicked and tried to cover up what had taken place. But when the investigation of the case was over, everything would point to her being behind it all, right down to the comparative analysis of the ink used in the anonymous letters and the felt pens in her home. She would stand up in court, stripped of all credibility.

At one point, Erik Roll broke down and cried. Tears were not unusual in an interview room, but they seldom came in sympathy for others. They came when reality dawned for whoever sat there, about how what they had done would impact on them personally.

Turning his back to the screen, Wisting headed out of the control room and on to the roof terrace. He took a few deep breaths of cool air before going down to his office. The holidays were over.

76

One month later

After breakfast Wisting moved out to the garden to rake the lawn. The day was chilly and he worked slowly. There was no rush. He gathered all the golden autumn leaves in heaps to dispose of later.

Line and Amalie appeared. Amalie raced across the grass and launched herself at the largest pile. She lay there with legs sprawled, tossing leaves up in the air. Wisting laughed with her and used the rake to bury her completely. As soon as she was totally covered, she sprang back up again.

Line had brought a Thermos flask and three cups. 'Hot chocolate,' she said.

Supporting himself on the rake, Wisting coughed in the damp air, clearing his throat noisily.

'Aren't you well?' Line asked.

'Yes, of course I am,' Wisting said with a smile.

He was totally fit, in really good shape. He had seen his GP the day before.

They sat down on the garden furniture on the verandah. Line filled the cups. Wisting told them about a squirrel he had spotted that was probably still hiding somewhere up in one of the trees.

Amalie put down her cup and dashed off to search for it.

'Can you look after her on Friday?' Line asked.

Wisting took a sip from his cup, leaving a line of froth hanging from his upper lip.

He had taken some mandatory holiday leave and had no other plans.

'What are you going to do?' he asked.

'I'm going for a job interview,' she replied. '*September-film* are putting together an editorial team to work on an old missing-person case. They're planning a documentary series.'

Wisting took another gulp. 'Isn't that where Cederik Smith works?' he asked.

'Not any longer,' Line told him. 'He's out. I don't know anything more, but maybe they too sussed out what he was really like.'

'Look!'

Amalie pointed and shouted gleefully. The squirrel scurried along a branch and leapt across to another one, climbing up the trunk and disappearing into the treetops.

'There's more to come, you know,' Line said.

Wisting did not understand what she meant.

'Leaves,' she said, gesturing towards the trees in the garden.

Wisting got to his feet, grabbed the rake and gave her a smile. 'I know,' he said, stepping out into the garden again. 'New leaves will come next year too. This is a job you never finish. I just like to clear away what I can.'

He just wanted a decent book to read ...

Not too much to ask, is it? It was in 1935 when Allen Lane, Managing Director of Bodley Head Publishers, stood on a platform at Exeter railway station looking for something good to read on his journey back to London. His choice was limited to popular magazines and poor-quality paperbacks – the same choice faced every day by the vast majority of readers, few of whom could afford hardbacks. Lane's disappointment and subsequent anger at the range of books generally available led him to found a company – and change the world.

'We believed in the existence in this country of a vast reading public for intelligent books at a low price, and staked everything on it'
Sir Allen Lane, 1902–1970, founder of Penguin Books

The quality paperback had arrived – and not just in bookshops. Lane was adamant that his Penguins should appear in chain stores and tobacconists, and should cost no more than a packet of cigarettes.

Reading habits (and cigarette prices) have changed since 1935, but Penguin still believes in publishing the best books for everybody to enjoy. We still believe that good design costs no more than bad design, and we still believe that quality books published passionately and responsibly make the world a better place.

So wherever you see the little bird – whether it's on a piece of prize-winning literary fiction or a celebrity autobiography, political tour de force or historical masterpiece, a serial-killer thriller, reference book, world classic or a piece of pure escapism – you can bet that it represents the very best that the genre has to offer.

Whatever you like to read – trust Penguin.

read more
www.penguin.co.uk